WOLFSBANE

By
Bethany Shay Porteous

WOLFSBANE

Copyright © 2015 by Bethany Shay Porteous

All rights Reserved. No part of this book may be reproduced in ANY form without the direct permission of the author. Wolfsbane is the work of fiction, any similarities to real people or events is purely coincidental.

Book layout by www.ebooklaunch.com

No one can make you feel inferior without your consent.
- Eleanor Roosevelt

Acknowledgements

There are plenty of people I want to thank for Wolfsbane. So many people have helped me get this story to where it is now, so hopefully by listing I won't forget anyone and if I do I am sorry.

I thank first and foremost all of you who have been with me since the very start. You stuck with me through the first poorly written draft I wrote when I was fifteen/sixteen and guided me with ideas and inspiration. You have waited patiently since I took the story off the internet while I rewrote it, and have continued to support my dream of wanting to become a writer. Thank you guys so much, you have no idea how much you mean to me.

I thank my mum and dad for giving me my first computer and never once squashing my dreams of wanting to write. I thank you both for not pressuring me to be someone I'm not and allowing me to pursue this dream with your support and acceptance. My family was a big help in creating this book and making it what it is. So this book is also for you, mum, dad, Jessica, Luke and Faith.

I thank God for gifting me with the imagination I have, and giving me the gift of getting all my thoughts onto paper. Thank you for guiding me when I was lost and being a rock when I needed it.

Thank you.

Introduction

CHANGE.

It's a constant in a werewolf's life.

Well, you could say it's a constant for anybody really, but a werewolf would experience it more frequently. From the moment they're born they are evolving and growing, rapidly adjusting sharing their mind with a volatile creature.

A werewolf will share its mind with its shifter side from the moment he or she turns eleven. They feel their wolf's primal instincts and can eventually be trained into understanding them fully and being able to converse both in wolf and human form.

This takes a lot of time and training and if your wolf doesn't show up in your head when you reach eleven you aren't to partake in any training. Eleven is a milestone year, it's a year parents fear their children aren't like those around them, and a year when children wonder if they've been gifted a wolf by the Moon Goddess.

If all goes well at age eleven, then the age of fifteen is the next big one. The wolf in their mind now has the ability to shift, taking over your human side and taking on the physical form of a wolf.

The wolf is a volatile and jealous creature. The change for a young shifter is like puberty for humans only with more mood swings. The wolf that has been trapped inside their humans mind is now able to run free. A young wolf will anger easily and with the right amount of coaxing or bating can push any young wolf over the edge to shift.

A young wolf is a dangerous wolf.

It's at this stage the werewolf/human gains all the cool abilities such as healing super quickly, excellent hearing and brilliant sense of smell to say the least. They would also gain some massive amounts of strength and speed.

The third major change in a wolf's life is their biggest, because it changes the whole course of their future and the makeup of their personality. This change can either make you or break you as a being.

This next step is where they find their soulmate. This usually occurs around the age of eighteen but some wolves have been known to only find their mates much later on in life, simply because their wolf was stronger than their human side. The mate would help balance the other and create a stronger wolf in each of them.

A wolf is able to find its mate just by a scent. It's usually confirmed by looking into the others eyes but a scent is usually the first giveaway. It's enticing and it clouds your mind in such a way that it only really mellows out once the two mark each other.

Like humans wolves have their own God - Goddess correctly put.

The ultimate Luna.

According to the stories, the Moon Goddess was a witch - she created the first wolf. He was powerful and strong, the perfect Alpha, however his temper and lack of control over the beast within him drove him to the brink of madness.

The Moon Goddess knew that he would not survive without another by his side. Splitting his being in two she sent the other half of him into the universe, and the magnetic pull of the two souls would eventually drag them together. If a wolf wanted to feel whole, they had to control their beast, or live a half-life.

Each supernatural culture has their own story and name for the Moon Goddess. She was the same being - still the most famous witch who created different magical beings. For Vampires she was known as the Great Mother, for Merfolk she was the Siren. To witches, she was Morgana and I believe that was her actual name. For the Lycan's she was a symbol that was held so reverently you'd never blaspheme of her in their presence. A Lycan is the ultimate werewolf; they're stronger than your regular wolf - much stronger. They don't live in large packs, just usually in small close groups. They never shifted into a full wolf; they looked like every terrifying Halloween werewolf you'd ever seen. You'd never mess with a Lycan.

I'm not really a wolf but I'm not really a human, I'm somewhere in the middle which isn't fun, especially in one of the most blood purity conscious packs in the United States.

The only reason I'm talking about this is because I'm just a year off turning eighteen - and I have no wolf physically or in my mind, which further strengthens the pack view that I shouldn't be here. Half-breed mutt is what they called me.

An apt name considering that's technically what I am. I didn't get the wolf in my mind at eleven, or the physical wolf at fifteen so the chances of me getting the mate at age of eighteen were not high. I still had a year to prove myself. I doubted any miracles would occur.

My mother - who is mated and married to the pack Beta, Michael - had been buying me as much time as she possibly could. Maybe I was a late bloomer - heck it happened, but if by the time of eighteen you showed no signs…I knew what would be coming for me and she couldn't protect me forever.

My half siblings were fifteen now and were in the training group with their wolves. They didn't associate with me, not like they used to before they knew about pack prejudices.

Michael despised me, not because I was a half-breed, well I'm sure that was part of the reason, but he really hated me because of how I was conceived.

My mother had been raped when she was seventeen and I was the result.

The only thing that confused people was what had been strong enough to subdue her wolf for the attack to happen. Whatever it was had been classed as evil which of course in turn, made me evil. Werewolves are strong, almost up there with the same strength as a vampire - yet I showed no vampire traits.

But I could do things…only recently anyway. Maybe they had been flukes, like closing my eyes when I wanted the sensor light to turn off - it felt too early but maybe it hadn't. The dead plant I walked past in Miss Jones' garden the other day and I'd felt sad about it, when I came home it was alive again.

No one knew that I was doing - or wasn't doing - this stuff.

Aside from the weird things I could do - or couldn't do - I did get *some* werewolf traits. For instance, I was fast. I could run like the wind. My vision was slightly better than a humans but not by much and my hearing was alright but it was nothing to brag about.

But I was still strange.

No one understood what I was so I couldn't be accepted.

I didn't want to be, not here anyway.

This was fine because once the school year finished I would be exiled from the pack and all contact from my family would be off limits. I didn't mind being exiled so much, the only thing I minded was never seeing my mother again.

The whole course of my life she has protected me, or at least done her best. She couldn't shield me from every beating or abuse I suffered from these people. I stopped going out alone altogether just to survive and get out of here in one piece.

I have nothing but horrible memories of this place and to see the back of it would be the best thing to ever happen to me.

Chapter One

I FELT LIKE I WAS drowning, my hair was wrapping around my neck and going into my mouth, along with the water that was choking down the back of my throat and up my nose and into my eyes. I could feel the hands on my head and shoulders that pushed me further into the porcelain bowl and I wondered if death was a better alternative than receiving my weekly swirly.

Finally the flushing stopped and the pressure on my shoulders left as my attackers vacated the bathroom, letting the toilet lid smack onto my head. I ended up heaving my breakfast into the bowl, discoloring the water and I was glad they weren't here to shove my face in it.

It had happened before.

Getting up I stumbled toward the sinks, washing my face the best I could, but the smell of toilet water would be stuck on me all day. I can't believe people buy perfume that smells like this. I hovered under the hand dryer for the whole first period until all the remnants of the water vanished and I stumbled into the hallway as all the classes emptied, following the sound of the siren.

I watched as people either thudded or trotted through the halls, laughing and slamming lockers. The girls wore their nicest clothes and cute little bags as they flicked their hair and paraded about like some bad teenage sitcom.

I didn't dress like them - it would bring way too much attention to me from the wolves if I did. Seeing as they were very visual creatures if I dolled up it would be like painting a big bright red target on myself saying, 'come here guys and beat me up', no thanks. I made sure I didn't under dress either, that would still bring me attention from the humans and the last thing I needed was them on my back as well.

My clothes generally consisted of jeans, T-shirts and a pair of muddy worn sneakers that had once been white. I needed a new pair but I didn't dare ask mom in front of Michael, he'd throw a fit.

It was Tuesday morning so my next session was art, hopefully no one would call me out on the fact that I had missed the whole first period - the fewer questions I had to lie over the better. This class was relaxing for me, there was only one other werewolf in this class however she didn't even look in my direction so I was able to enjoy this one solid hour of peace.

"You are all aware that today is the final day you have on this assignment, and that I'll be marking them over the weekend so I expect that when you leave here today, your easel will hold a completed portrait. If it doesn't…" Miss Fields gave those who she knew wouldn't be finished a sour smile but didn't continue.

The assignment was supposed to be a painting of the vase in the center of the room and we could choose whatever we decided to be inside it.

I wasn't putting anything inside it; instead I was focusing on the vase instead, the intricate details. Everyone else was doing flowers - though Amy, the cliché looking emo girl was drawing thorn sticks coming out of hers.

As the class neared its finish I leant back on my stool to admire my work. I had done a plain white vase with light pink triangle patterns going across it. I did put one flower inside after changing my mind, but seeing as I had rushed it, it looked limp and wilted.

Jumping as the siren went I dropped my brush and hurriedly picked it up as people gathered their bags and left their pictures on their easels. Miss Fields was already circling the room like a vulture, murmuring to herself with her marking sheets.

I slung my bag over my shoulder and made to leave; tripping on my shoe as I haphazardly grazed my foot on the floor.

"Oh, Evelyn?" Miss Fields chirped.

I cringed and shut my eyes. "Miss Fields?"

"I hope to see you enter last semester's piece into the winter festival. I think you'd place well and if you wish to go on and study art it would be good for you to start building up a portfolio." Suddenly she was in front of me, smoothing her blonde bob and pressing her lips against her teeth, I watched in avid fascination as her lipstick got stuck on her front tooth. "Every year you say you will but I never see it."

"I'll try Miss Fields." The lie sounded overused and exhausted, even to my ears.

Michael never let me get involved in anything outside of school and as I mentioned earlier, no need to single myself out further.

Miss Fields looked at me with a firm gaze that had me dropping my eyes nervously to the floor. "I hope so," she said after what felt like centuries. "Have a good day."

I managed to slip into my English class unnoticed by Mr Maller who sharpened his row of pencils as the room bustled with chatter. People were planning their weekends, it was a typical Friday, and the school was less doom and gloom.

I'd never planned my weekend before. I didn't have any friends to plan anything with, plus it was safer to hide out in my room and not get beaten for two days.

Sitting down with a sigh I pulled out my copy of 'To Kill a Mockingbird', our assigned book for the month. We had to read it as a class, together. It was tiring because I had read the page seven times before it was my turn.

All my classes were remedial. Michael wouldn't let the school move me up and I was stuck doing work I did in eighth Grade. I spent so much time at home on the computer, teaching myself what students my age were learning now, that I could probably be a teacher.

"Alright!" Mr Maller barked, bits of apple spraying out of his teeth. "Pages open to fifty-six. Jenny, you start."

"I did the last reading, it was Ella's turn!"

"I have a sore throat today sir, my mother advised I shouldn't be doing any extra talking."

"We all know why she has a sore throat," coughed someone in the back of the class. Her face went red as people giggled.

Even humans were cruel.

In this class there were a couple of werewolves, most of the time they did harmless stuff like flick clips at me, or gum or something like that. Nothing violent like some of the others did.

"I hope that wasn't a derogatory comment being announced in my class Mr Jones."

"Absolutely not sir." Max Jones was always saying filthy things. He was crude and disgusting and spent more time on his iPhone watching porn than actually doing any work. He didn't even use earphones.

"Jenny read from where we left off," Mr Maller ordered looking flustered.

"Oh my God!" Her annoying pitchy voice cried out, "It's like you have a thing for me sir, you always pick me."

I crinkled my nose in disgust. He was forty years old.

I watched as the tip of his nose turned white and I sunk further into my chair as he began his verbal lashing about how he shouldn't be teaching a class of idiots. It happened every session. I focused on the book, continuing to read and by the time I had gotten through five pages, he had given up and was behind his desk. Jenny had been sent to the principal's office and the rest of the class did what they wanted to.

My palms began to sweat as the class was almost over. I had gym next and that class was - it is - Hell with a capital 'H'. Jonah, the Alpha's son, is in that class along with his friends and mate. They were the main instigators behind my attacks.

Jonah's mate, Heather, she was the giver of my weekly swirly's along with her friend Jackie. The boys wouldn't be seen dead going into the girl's bathroom after all.

Gym was one of the many places where he could get me.

I had copped a lot in this class and it was a miracle my bones still functioned properly.

I could never really grasp why Jonah hated me so much, above all the others. I get that I wasn't a purebred wolf but he took it further than shunning. The physical and mental abuse I received from him was astounding to me. It hurt my head to try and understand it, so I had given up and just accepted it.

Changing for gym was an awkward and awful event. Heather and all her cronies would be up near the mirror, squawking away while shooting looks down the back of the change room to me. Thankfully the room was always too full for them to do anything to me in here, and if I changed quickly enough, I wouldn't be alone with them and could follow the crowd outside.

"You know Evelyn," Heather called out. Some people lifted their heads in vague interest as they usually did when Heather was ready to insult me. "The point of wearing a bra is to keep your boobs in place. You don't have any."

How original.

They all found themselves hilariously funny though, giggling away as they finished getting ready.

Slipping out of the room and into the gym I slowly made my way over to my class; positioning myself as far away from Jonah as possible. As I looked around the room my heart slowly sunk into a puddle of depression.

The class was going to consist of rope climbing, archery and trust exercises.

"Everyone needs to pick a partner," ordered Miss Winde as she rubbed her forehead. Miss Winde was probably the best looking teacher at this school - according to the male population. She was a werewolf so no wonder she was beautiful. "We are doing group cycles today. I'll group each pair and you will either start with rope climbing, archery or the trust exercises until you get rotated out and move on. Questions?"

Met with silence she nodded and began moving people toward their first exercises.

Feeling a tight grip on my arm I jumped in shock, my skin crawling as I was turned to face Zac Keenan.

"Hey Evelyn," Zac smirked down at me, his platinum blonde buzz cut glinting under the lighting of the gym. "You look like you need a partner."

My palms felt slick and I rubbed them on my shorts as I tried to swallow the lump of fear in my throat as his hold tightened. Zac is Jonah's closest friend, if he was partnering with me, then they had something up their sleeves.

Sometimes I wish I was strong enough to be totally feisty and just punch him in the face or shove him off - I tried that once. Normally people learn from their mistakes and I make it a point to do so.

I wondered what injuries I was going to sustain in this class.

"Zachary and Evelyn," she wrinkled her nose as she said my name, and her eyes glanced at Zac as she tried to grasp why a wolf was pairing with me. Her eyes glazed over slightly and I realized she was using the pack link to speak to him. Coming back to awareness she shrugged and said, "You two over to archery."

"Alright!" Zac nodded and slung his arm over my shoulder. "Come on team mate."

Dragging me like a ragdoll I stumbled on my footing and tried to ignore the whispers and hisses in my direction. I considered feigning an illness, pretending I was having cramps or anything that would get me away from Zac and whatever he was planning on doing to me.

As the leader for this section listed the rules and demonstrated how to use the bows I found myself increasingly nervous that I was paired up with someone so sadistic and was going to be shooting flying objects into the air.

At least the ends were blunted, they'd still hurt if it hit you though.

"I think I'll go first," Zac said cockily as he prepared his arrow. I stood back and toyed with my bow, thinking up ways to get out of this mess. I watched as his arms flexed as he pulled back the string, aiming at the target.

It was just a formality for any watching humans; a werewolf didn't have to aim.

He hit the target perfectly.

"Alright, your turn."

My heart was beating too fast and I knew his senses would have picked it up. He wolfishly grinned at me, and not in a nice way, his canines poking out, glinting. My arms shook as I lifted the bow and aimed at the target and I jumped in fright when his hands went to my waist, his back pressed up behind me.

"Your posture is off," he purred into my ear.

My eyes shut in disgust at how his hold tightened briefly and he manoeuvred my body. The boys did this a lot. Jonah didn't get involved anymore, not when he found Heather as his mate - hell if he touched me like that she'd kill me and him.

Werewolves were crazy possessive over what was theirs.

Zac however hasn't found his mate yet, which left me susceptible to his… assaults.

Making to move out of his hold his hands tightened and held me in place, his lips at my ear. "It's almost not as fun anymore, having you all to myself. As weak and pathetic as you are, you still have a hot body." My skin crawled and I swallowed the bile that rose in my throat as his hand ghosted across my mid-section.

Where the hell were the teachers? This was practically foreplay.

"I think even Jonah misses it, wouldn't want Heather to know that would we?" He bit my ear and I ducked my head, clutching the bow. "You know if I didn't have a mate out there somewhere - boy, I'd have some fun with you. I don't know why you don't enjoy this," he murmured, his grasp tighter. His wolf was getting worked up; I could feel the evidence pressing into my back. "It's not like you'll ever have a soulmate."

Smack.

He jumped and stumbled backward as my arm came back and hit him in the chest, my arrow hitting the target dead on. I blinked back the stinging assault of tears and turned to face him, his evil smirk still in place.

"Your turn."

Chapter Two

I WASHED MYSELF UNDER SCALDING water, trying to see what I was doing through my vision that was blurred by an attack of tears. I was washing his scent off me completely; he'd been so close you could smell him for hours. Hot water and coconut soap, I found, did the trick.

Werewolves love to touch.

They didn't have to actually have sex with you for them to feel satisfied. Touch was mostly enough and for wolves with mates it had to be. A lot of wolves stayed pure for their mates - it's how it is done, in most packs its law. In most packs you could be exiled or even killed for losing your purity to one who wasn't your mate. This law saved me many times from Zac and Jonah getting too out of hand with me.

I shut off the shower and wrung out my hair before rubbing my face with my wash cloth and quickly wrapping myself up in a towel. The steam fogged up the bathroom and I knew I'd be hearing about it later from Michael that I either had to open or window or not shower at all.

I liked the steam - I could barely see myself. I avoided looking in mirrors. I didn't need to validate myself further that I looked nothing like my mother or my half siblings.

Pulling on some leggings and a gray cotton shirt I wrapped my hair and collected my things, sniffing slightly as I pulled open the door. Padding across the hall to my room I watched as my hot feet left marks on the hardwood floor.

I threw my dirty clothes in the hamper of my room and was relieved I no longer smelt like the toilet or Zac anymore.

"Dinner!" Mom called up the stairs.

Great, I thought with disappointment.

Dinner isn't fun. Not for me anyway. Jada and Laurance, my half siblings, were always questioned by Michael about their day and in turn they'd question him. Whenever mom asked me about mine I'd utter out a 'fine' as Michael glared over his food.

Seventeen years of dinners that I never felt comfortable enough to eat.

I heard Jada leave her room and another set of feet followed her and I closed my eyes in frustration as I realized the Alpha's daughter, Fiona, who is also Jada's best friend, would be here for dinner.

Sullenly I made my way downstairs and into the living room, admiring the finely dressed table that my mother would have worked on for a while, along with the roast she set in the middle of it.

"Evelyn sweetheart, I didn't see you come in," she exclaimed as she pulled me into a hug.

"I just needed a shower," I said quietly. She looked at me with a crease in between her brows and I thought up a lie. "I spilt paint on myself in art class, I smelt terrible all day."

She let out a laugh, "Oh dear. I'm afraid you get the clumsiness from me."

"I'm not clumsy," Jada said snootily - as does any fifteen year old bratty pre-wolf.

"Of course," mom said absently as she placed the last set of glasses on the table.

"Fiona," I murmured as I respectfully bowed my head. She lifted her nose up in the air, like I was a piece of mud on her shoe. I ignored the look; I was so used to being looked at like that, that I didn't even care anymore. Besides, conversation was off me and that's how I liked to keep it, I hated trying to lie to mom. A werewolf can smell a lie so if you're going to tell a cover story you're going to want to truly believe it yourself.

Taking a seat at the table, across from Laurance who was reading a medical book I awaited the impending arrival of Michael. The worst part of the day. The front door opened and shut and I held onto my seat as his footsteps thumped on the floor and came in our direction.

"Michael!" My mother cried happily as she wrapped her arms around him. I watched - as I always do - as the meanest person I had ever met acted so tenderly toward her, like she was a precious gem that could be snatched easily.

That's what mates were like. They were after all, designed for one another, and linked in body and soul. There was no higher level of devotion among our kind. Their kind. Vampires disputed however, saying their connections ran far deeper after centuries of learning what it meant to love.

Sometimes I was saddened by the fact I'd never have a mate. Then I remembered the last thing I wanted in life was to be trapped in this community.

"I have some interesting news, which I'm sure Fiona; you have already been informed of." Michael sat at the head of the table, nudging Laurance's arm as Fiona nodded knowingly. Laurance set down his book, irritation dancing across his face.

"What is it?" Mom asked curiously.

"How come you didn't tell me first?" Jada demanded looking betrayed.

"Strict orders not to," Fiona said smugly.

"Well what is it?" Laurance huffed; he looked at me briefly before turning his attention to Michael.

"The Alpha of Wolfsbane is hosting the Allied Gathering this year," he started but was interrupted by squeals from Jada. I didn't get what was so great about it. "Because we are only freshly allied it is a surprise we got an invite, we haven't even signed the treaty yet, but apparently, they want to do it in front of the other allied packs."

"Wow," Laurance muttered actually sounding surprised.

"This does wonders for our pack. We've never been up there with Oregon or Alaska or Michigan, but here we are. We're signing an alliance with Wolfsbane, Oregon!" Michael was beaming with pride as he took in the reactions around the table.

Everyone was clapping and I was unsure of what to do. I pat my hands together awkwardly as I looked around the table.

"Also," Fiona started. "The Alpha's son has just turned eighteen which means he is eligible to find his mate. Which means, we may be allied by - a mating!"

Jada began squealing again and I inwardly rolled my eyes. A party turns into a marriage preparation.

"Both the Alpha and Beta family has been requested to go. So Gamma Stevens will be running things while we are away." Michael literally looked like he won the lottery. I guess it was a big deal for them; I didn't quite get the excitement though.

"Well, wow," mom said breathlessly. "This is amazing. When is it?"

"This Saturday," he announced grandly. "I have never been a more proud Beta."

"We need to get new outfits for it! Wolfsbane throws the most amazing parties, did you get the last newsletter, all those photos, the gowns!" Jada was going crazy, along with Fiona who was bouncing in her seat and no doubt imaging herself as the Alpha's sons mate.

"I agree. School is off tomorrow, we are going shopping!" Mom declared. "Evelyn we need to get your measurements taken again, you seem to have dropped some weight I think."

At this the table silenced and turned to look at me and I was surprised.

"I'm going?" I questioned nervously, not sure I had heard correctly.

"Well you are a part of the Beta family sweetheart." Mom began serving plates and I could feel Jada's rage from across the table. Fiona was practically frothing at the mouth.

The only thing I could think of as a large serving of beans were put on my plate, was the fact I'd be in a room with four other Alpha and Beta families.

And I'd be the only half-blood there.

∞

"Okay, this is the one. Look how it flows down my back, and I like the open straps…" I could hear Jada outside the dressing room as she tried on her seventh dress that she also thought was the one. Shopping with her was a nightmare. Then again I'm sure having me here was her worst nightmare too.

"Evelyn darling, how is it going in there?" Mom called.

"F-fine!" I called out as I pulled up the zip on the side. It was a gorgeous dress, but it would need tailoring to fit my smaller frame.

It was a sleeveless lace that ran up over my collarbone before it fanned down my body in gentle red waves. The back was open as the dress stopped at my neck and dipped in an oval shape down my back.

Blinking I ran my hand through my chocolate brown hair and pulled away the shirt I had put over the mirror, opening the curtain and stepping out to face my blonde mother and half-sister.

"Oh Evelyn, you look beautiful. It needs some tightening, about here…and here…" she pinched at the bits of fabric as she pinned with the seamstress as I heard Jada in the dressing room, trying on another dress.

She pulled back her curtain roughly, and stepped out in a strapless blue gown that had sequins around the breast area. I watched as her green eyes raked over my form with a scowl, "Goddess, Evelyn, eat much?"

I bit the inside of my mouth as mom looked up from the dress and gave her a warning look.

I had lost weight lately and Jada knew why. Everyone knew why, they just couldn't say anything about it. Jonah had given me an Alpha command to starve myself for a week. An Alpha command was all mental, if you wore the pack mark you were forced to follow whatever order had been given to you. I didn't wear the mark and his command didn't technically force me, however I knew if he caught me eating I'd be beaten. My mother could never say anything, questioning an Alpha command could get you into a deep pile of trouble.

Coming back to reality I looked at the dress Jada wore, it looked too tight for her thicker form, she trained hard but she had caught the pudgy gene from mom. The dress almost looked too tight and I imagined her looking like the purple girl from Willy Wonka as she expanded. Maybe she would feel as awkward as she made me feel.

"What the hell!" She wheezed slightly as she clutched at the dress, screeching as the zipper dug into her back as the dress seemed to shrink on her.

My eyes widened in horror as I leapt to help her, only to have her claws extended as she swiped my hand away. She clawed the dress off her body savagely and I was relieved - for the sake of humankind - we were in a werewolf owned store.

"Jada!" Mom scolded. "What in the name of the Moon Goddess was that?"

"The dress - it was too tight, it got tighter and tighter…" Jada looked at mom with wide eyes, panting.

"You were shifting!" Mom snapped, "Your body expanded. Jada if you cannot learn to control your wolf you'll need to do more training."

I breathed a sigh of relief as she scolded her. I didn't do that. She was shifting out of anger of me being here. What I thought did not actually happen. It didn't, I assured myself.

"Oh Evelyn, your hand!" Mom exclaimed as she quickly pulled a rag from Jada's shredded dress over it.

"I'm fine, I can barely feel it," I lied as the stinging sensation got worse.

"That looks deep; we need to get back to the pack doctor. I'm so sorry Cynthia; we'll pay for the dress, and we'll buy the one Evelyn is wearing, but we'll have to come back for alterations."

"It's fine Maria; I remember what it's like to be a young wolf. I shifted over everything. I'll see you when you come back; hopefully we'll have better luck finding Jada a dress."

The ride home was silent, Jada was fuming and I was worried she'd shift in the car. I stayed quiet - as always - and eventually found myself at the pack clinic having my hand inspected by a training Doctor named Tom.

"It's kind of fun," he said smiling as mom filled out the paper work outside. I looked at him nervously, surprised he was even talking to me. "Everyone heals so quickly sometimes

I think it's useless us being here. I mean, I get to actually stitch you up - this doesn't happen for me."

I tried to smile but I think it looked like a grimace.

"I feel like I hear about you all the time," he said, "I mean people are constantly talking about you and when…well…"

"When the Alpha removes me?" I said quietly.

"Yeah. Everyone's so surprised it's taken this long."

"I'm surprised you're stitching me up."

"Contrary to popular belief, not everyone in this pack hates you. I mean okay, the majority does, but I just think you got given a life you didn't ask for. Make something of yourself okay? When you get booted out, it's probably going to be the best thing that ever happens to you."

I couldn't agree with him more.

∞

"Stop it!" I screamed as I pounded on the hardwood door in front of me, blinded by the blackness of the small storage closet. "Let me out! Let me out! P-Please let me out!" My breaths came out in frantic puffs as my heart catapulted in my chest.

Laughter was heard on the other side of the door before flame was sprayed under it via a lighter and aerosol can.

With a yelp I jumped into the air, stumbling into the shelving and hitting the back of my head on something sharp. I was completely trapped as they kept spraying the flame under the door and I could feel a stickiness coming out from the back of my head.

"Ooh! I smell blood," Heather taunted in a song-song tone.

"She hurts herself," someone else commented. "We don't even have to touch her."

"Maybe we should let her out." Was Jackie Morris actually feeling compassionate?

There was silence outside the door and I licked my dry lips as I tried to catch my breath. When I felt a crack of light over my eye I jumped at the door, only to be shoved back in and land in a heap on the floor as darkness once again surrounded me.

"Nah, not yet."

I couldn't stop the onslaught of tears as my jean leg got singed before I heard the door lock and they sauntered off. I didn't have the strength to bust down the door nor did I have the energy.

Small spaces and the dark equally made me freeze up. I was terrified of them, mainly because when I was younger; Jonah falsely led me to believe we were friends and ended up pushing me into a suitcase, padlocking it and dumping it in the woods. I was stuck in there all day until someone finally came and rescued me.

He didn't even get in trouble when I was found.

I couldn't make out anything around me, the room was pure darkness but I could feel the shelving, I could feel myself sitting in between two box like objects. Hearing shuffling within the shelves I cringed and shut my eyes tighter, sniffing loudly and clutching at my jeans like it was a lifeline.

I heard the sirens signalling the end of the day and I knew it would be around four in the afternoon before the janitor came in here.

When the door finally opened my eyes stung and I peeled them open. Looking up I saw the janitor he had a confused expression on his face as he held out his hand, lifting me up and pulling me into the hallway.

On shaking limbs I thanked him and slowly left the school building, surprised to see mom's car pulling into the parking lot. I limped toward it, my legs having been cramped for three hours, and pulled open the door sliding in.

"Evelyn! What happened? Why do I smell blood?" Her fingers touched the tender spot on the back of my head and I winced.

"It doesn't matter," I said, defeated. It would never matter because every day until I get out of this place would be the same.

"It does matter Evelyn!"

"No it doesn't, because nothing can be done about it. So, let's make our weekly trip to the pack clinic, stitch me up and count the new scar I've obtained while I prepare for a life as far away from here as p-possible," my voice cracked and I gained a hold of my emotions.

My mother stared at me for a moment, her mouth gaping before putting the car into gear, squealing the tyres on the road and flooring it out of the school.

∞

Lying in bed that night and feeling the safest I felt all day my thoughts drifted to the trip to Oregon tomorrow. The house had been buzzing with so much excitement that the extra abuse I had received at school throughout the week had gone unnoticed by mom, until when I hadn't arrived home on time today.

Sometimes I blamed her.

She could have gotten rid of me - heck enough people encouraged her to do so, she would have known the life I was going to have if she brought me up in this pack, a pure-blood loving pack. I thought she was selfish.

But she was also just a young teenager when she'd had me, and she had gone through so much maybe she wanted to have the control back in her hands and decide what happened to her body.

I guess I'll never fully comprehend what she went through but I knew what it was like to have your choices torn from you, to have things happen to you beyond your control.

I was never going to understand anything here, I knew that. I just longed for the day when I'd finally be free..

Chapter Three

Our pack was located in Idaho Falls, Idaho.

We were taking a four hour flight from Idaho Falls to Portland, Oregon and then a four hour car ride to Baker City where the Wolfsbane pack was located. Four hours stuck in a car with the Alpha family and my family.

I felt sick just thinking about it.

The Oregon pack were more commonly referred to as the Wolfsbane pack, as their first Alpha had invented the only alcoholic drink a shifter could get drunk off before their blood temperature could burn it off. This was great for all the wolves who wanted to party so of course it took off like wildfire and made them the richest pack in the US.

I was kind of excited to go. Not for the party or anything, but for the fact that for two days I wouldn't get smacked around so any lingering bruises had time to heal before the new ones arrived.

It was three in the morning when my alarm went off and I stumbled out of my bed, dressing in my comfiest travel clothes I had laid out the night before. I was a little excited to be leaving the pack territory for the first time in my life - to see something other than Idaho Falls.

Bunning my hair I grabbed my suitcase and made my way to the landing where I could hear mom rattling on to Michael about the tickets and everything else she had going on. Pausing at the top of the stairs I adjusted my handle so I could carry it down, only to be shoved into the wall as Jada stomped past.

"Move," she snarled as she bared her sharp extended canines at me.

My eyes widened in surprise as I fell into the wall and I quickly gathered myself as I stumbled down the first two steps.

She was not a wolf I wanted to be stuck in an enclosed space with for eight hours.

After mom did a triple check over the house and made sure it was locked we were all ushered outside toward the car, loading up our bags in the back before climbing in, driving to the Alpha House.

Jada's mood increased significantly as she chose to ride with the Alpha family instead. Heather was draped all over Jonah as they did an over the top farewell and my mouth dried at the thought that even though we were leaving the State, I was still going to be stuck with him.

Five minutes later we were driving to the airport; I had the backseat to myself and Laurance who was in the row ahead of me seemed happy he didn't have to share with Jada and her bad mood.

It was exciting to leave the pack district, I wouldn't feel it seeing as I never had the pack link made with me - a connection made through a bite of an Alpha - but I could tell when it happened because the wolves in the car shivered the moment we crossed it.

For the first time in a long time, the tiniest smile broke out on my face.

∞

My seat was nowhere near anyone's from the pack - I'm fairly sure that was deliberate but I was happy for it. They were further up, closer toward the first class section, of course.

I was sat next to the window and a small girl with hair crazier than a birds nest sat beside me. Her mother sat beside her, her eyes shut as she tried to get some last minute shut eye. I watched with interest at the math game the young girl played on her iPad.

Suddenly she looked up, her large brown eyes catching me off guard.

"Do you want to have a go?" She asked.

"Uh," I managed to say, surprised.

The children in the pack avoided me like the plague - probably because their parents told them to.

"It's easy. I have other games, not just this one. My mom gets me heaps to play, I have spelling games. I'm good at those. I have games that aren't for learning, but I don't play those ones a lot. I'm not good at them. I have games that-"

"Sure, I'll have a go," I said quickly, before she could go through the list of games she had.

Taking the iPad I went through the game, pretending I was bad at it so she could help correct me.

As the stewardess came out to direct us through the safety precautions, I listened with interest, I'd never been on a plane before, this information may come in handy. The girl put her iPad under her backside, nudging her mom who woke with wide eyes.

She fastened her daughter's seatbelt and gave me a tired smile before adjusting her own.

Sighing I made sure mine was adjusted, eyeing my family and the Alpha family further up who were chatting in excitement.

I was excited for this trip, only that I was leaving the State for the first time. Not for the fact that in twelve or so hours I'd be surrounded by wolves and three Alpha families.

The take-off was the worst thing I had ever experienced in my life, and that was saying something.

My interactions with the girl beside me, whose name I found to be Gina, continued throughout the flight as her mother slept soundly, barely even waking at the squeals from her daughter as she laughed at anything.

At some point Gina fell asleep and I was able to go through the profiles of the Alpha and Beta family of Oregon, who I'd be acknowledging at the pack meeting, by name and rank. I felt nervous that I had to directly interact with them - what would they say when a half-breed bowed to them? Would they even let me into the compound?

As we began the descent into Portland I held on tightly to the arm rest, feeling sick to my stomach as I waited for the wheels to touch down on the tarmac and I could get off this flying death machine.

I said goodbye to Gina and her exhausted mother before finding my way toward my family, sighing as conversation was on Fiona mating with the eligible Alpha's son. Sometimes I wondered if they understood their own mating process.

After a slight mess up over someone taking Jada's bag that looked similar to the stranger and Jada nearly tearing their face off we received our supplied vehicles from Wolfsbane and began the drive toward Baker City, eating a takeaway breakfast.

I hated egg so I ended up eating only the bacon and the bun in my McMuffin.

"I wonder how many she-wolves hearts will break tonight with my daughter being mated to the Alpha's son," Luna Larissa said with a laugh.

"We shouldn't get ahead of ourselves," Jonah commented, actually sounding smart for once. The whole trip he'd barely even glanced in my direction as he stayed close by his father and absorbed as much knowledge as he could. After all, he was set to be the next Alpha.

"We should be ready for anything. Not all wolves - especially Alpha's - wait around for their real mates. A lot of packs still are very political." Larissa was strange to me. Sometimes I thought she was a bit of a ditzy airhead. Then she said things that made her look like an adult and she'd completely change my opinion.

She never looked in my direction, like ever.

After a while I knew I was getting motion sickness, being trapped in the car all this time had me feeling cramped and dizzy. Holding it in I didn't say anything, I'd get the lecture on what it's like to be a real wolf and how hard it is to be cramped up like this.

I was too tired to bother with pretending to listen.

Even though it was never going to happen, I had allowed myself to dream of what it would be like to have a mate. From what I witnessed it was a pure bond that was looked after carefully by the wolves. Besides their ability to shift it's what made them different from humans.

One time, Jonah had tricked me into believing I had a mate. He ordered one of the freshly turned eighteen year old wolves to claim that I was his mate and when I finally believed it was true, I got the harsh and humiliating shock that it was all just a lie.

That story hurt and I wasn't going to share it with anyone, ever. Not like anyone would stay around long enough to hear it anyway.

It was always strange to me how a wolf could switch from being so caring and tender to their mate to so violent to anyone they didn't like. It was like a switch was instantly flipped in their brains, probably because of the wolf. I couldn't imagine it being easy to share your head with another mind.

"We're approaching the gates," Alpha Hess told us, his voice giddy.

I looked up in mild interest and wasn't surprised with what I saw.

It was basically like a home, a massive secluded estate backing onto an expanse of forest. The only thing that made it different was the large gate that wrapped around the land for miles.

Pulling up to the entry booth a young man stood out, dressed in a white button up and black pants, pulling out a booklet. "The Idaho Pack?" He asked stiffly as he looked through the car.

"Yes," Alpha Hess snapped, obviously annoyed he was being treated so casually.

"Both Alpha and Beta family in attendance?"

"Yes."

"Please, follow the silver 4WD when you enter, it will guide you to your lodgings and then both Alpha and Beta have been requested at the Pack Hall to meet with Alpha James and the other attending Alpha's."

Pressing a button on a keypad the gates slowly opened and the car rolled through them. Looking at the gatekeeper I saw that his eyes were glazed over - like all wolves eyes did when they were talking through the pack link.

He frowned briefly at me, his pupils widening before I quickly looked forward, the car going a bit faster to keep up with the 4WD.

Driving through the streets of the Wolfsbane pack I was taken aback by the richness of my surroundings. They did well for themselves financially; the houses were all grand, manicured to perfection. Anyone who was in the streets stopped what they were doing to watch the car drive by, nudging whoever they were with.

As the houses became less close to each other, we turned onto a lonely street where only five buildings stood. Cars were already in the driveways and baggage was being taken into the houses.

"Is - is that the Alaskan Alpha?" Laurance asked in awe as he pressed his face up against the window.

I looked in his direction, nearly cowering into my seat at the massive man who carried all the bags from his car, his face wearing a permanent scowl that looked like he wore it often.

"I still don't get why he allied with Oregon. Alaska is so far away it serves no purpose."

"Probably signed up so he'd get free Wolfsbane for life," Michael commented.

"He still hasn't found his mate yet. Surprising for an Alpha of his age," Larissa commented.

"Goddess help the poor woman she paired with him," mom sighed. "He killed his own father for the title."

The Alaskan Pack was probably one of the most controversial packs of this age. The pack had been created by a rogue wolf, running wild from the age of eleven before gaining a following of other werewolves and setting up in Alaska. Looking back at the huge hulking man I shivered, he killed his own father?

Pulling into the only empty drive everyone rushed out of the car, eager to stretch their legs. Once the car was empty I scrambled out, stretching my back and closing my eyes as I breathed in the fresh air.

"Move," Fiona hissed as she shoved past me with her massive suitcase, effectively making me topple to the floor. Smacking my chin on the grass beneath me I felt my teeth click together and I cringed at the feeling.

Getting up quickly I brushed off my clothes, not surprised to see myself as the only one waiting by the car with my bag still in the back. Rubbing my mouth and chin I quickly pulled my case out of the back, wheeling it toward the house.

It was nice accommodation; even our guest houses didn't look this nice.

The entry was overwhelmed by a large staircase that led upstairs and there was a theme of warm coffee and chocolate colors either on the walls or floors.

As I made it upstairs there were two halls which were to my left and right with various doors.

Following the feminine squeals I ended up outside the room Jada and Fiona occupied and I looked at the third bed with a heavy heart. I had to share with them?

They didn't look too pleased about the arrangement either and I tried my hardest to ignore their hostile glares that pierced the back of my head as I lifted my suitcase onto the unoccupied bed.

"If you touch anything of mine and get your hideous smell on it, I will kill you," Fiona threatened as she guarded her bed.

"Girls, here are your dresses!" Luna Larissa and mom stormed into the room and Fiona and Jada forgot about me, pouncing on their bagged gowns in excitement. Taking mine from mom I laid the bag on my bed, eager to shower and wash the trip off me.

"The Alpha and Michael have gone to meet up with Alpha James, so we have five hours to be completely dressed and ready for the gathering tonight," Luna Larissa clapped her hands in excitement.

"In five hours I'm going to meet my mate," Fiona said breathlessly as she swooned onto her bed. I put my lips together to hide my amused smile as I turned to face my dress on the bed. These girls were beyond deluded.

"It would be like a fairy tale," Jada whispered.

"Okay," mom clapped her hands together. "Showers first please, we all smell terrible. No more than five minutes each," she looked at Jada knowingly who usually took a good half hour. "There's too much to get done."

By the time I got into the shower the hot water had run out, which was probably to be expected given my luck in life. I quickly showered before getting out and wrapping the towel around me, shivering before hurriedly drying off.

Exiting the bathroom, my towel wrapped tightly around me, Jonah suddenly appeared in my path, his brow cocked. "Enjoying the trip Evelyn?" He asked smoothly as he blocked the walk way.

I looked at the floor immediately, holding my breath, my heart racing in my chest.

"Just because we aren't in Idaho, doesn't make me any less your superior. Are you enjoying the trip?" His voice was venomous and for once I wished Heather was around to distract him like she had been.

"Y-yes," I stuttered.

I jumped in shock as he pulled the towel open, raking his eyes over my body before he laughed. "Amazing, absolutely amazing. What once appealed to me no longer does. The Moon Goddess does her job well."

"Evelyn? Are you out yet? We need to start your hair."

Pulling the towel around myself I pushed past him, flinching at the snarl as I quickly rushed into the room.

∞

As mom finished off my makeup - seeing as I had never applied it before in my life, I heard the Alpha and Michael arrive home, cooing loudly at Jada and Fiona who were squawking with excitement and clomping around in their heels.

I kept my eyes closed as nerves settled deeper and deeper into my stomach as the evening approached.

"Finished," mom murmured as she put down whatever she had been using. "Will you look in the mirror Evelyn?"

I opened my eyes slowly but kept facing away from the mirror. "I don't need to," I said quietly.

"You're not going to see all my hard work?" She said with a playful pout. "If I was as beautiful as you I'd look in a mirror every chance I got."

"Mom," I felt my face heat up and I reached up to cover it with my hands.

"Don't touch your face," she said quickly, taking my hands and giving them a squeeze. "Don't want to smudge."

"Sorry."

She smiled softly at me before kissing my head. "Okay. Put your dress on, I need to finish getting ready and speak to Michael, make sure you're downstairs in twenty minutes."

As the door closed slightly I closed my eyes and took a breath in.

Mom had pinned my hair into a loose bun, I could feel what she had done. I wasn't sure about my makeup though but I knew she wouldn't intentionally make me look terrible. She didn't hate me.

Walking over to the bed I unzipped the bag where my dress was kept and dropped the robe, taking the dress out of the bag.

It was as beautiful as it was in the store.

Slowly I stepped into the side zipper and shimmied it up, enjoying the feel of the soft material on my bare legs as it glided up and over my thighs, over my backside and up my chest. I found myself smiling as I slowly pulled up the zipper; the dress having been tailored and now fit me comfortably.

For a fleeting moment I felt what it was to be included.

I felt beautiful.

I slipped on the matching shoes I had chosen, the heel low so I wouldn't be stumbling about. Jada's were huge and watching her walk in them was like watching a foal take her first steps.

I had a clutch to match the dress which was filled with female essentials for a through-the-night touch up, as mom called it. I knew I wouldn't use it, I didn't know how to touch up whatever she had created.

Taking a calming breath I left the room, beginning my descent of the stairs as I made my way to the voices in the living room. Everyone stopped talking as I entered - people always stopped talking as I entered a room - but this silence felt too long.

I grew even more uncomfortable in their presence than I already had been. I held my arm awkwardly and looked over at mom, biting my lip.

"Oh Evelyn!" Mom gasped, "You look breath taking."

Toying with the clutch I uttered a thank you before moving to stand in the corner, conversation slowly picking up. I sighed in relief and let my eyes wander around the room, taking in how nicely dressed everyone was.

"So tell us, what was the Alpha's son like?" Fiona demanded.

"He wasn't present," Michael commented as he drank a glass of Wolfsbane. "Apparently he was doing pack duties. In my opinion I think it's foolish to entrust his son with such important things, at this age at least."

"Or smart," Luna Larissa commented as she eyed Jonah who did not look impressed. "As he learns the basics now he'll be more than ready to take over as Alpha when the time comes."

"Wolfsbane is a successful pack. Maybe it's a good idea to start training you Jonah," Alpha Hess murmured.

"Either way, the Alpha's son won't be joining the party until later. He's patrolling tonight."

"He patrols?" Jonah asked, his voice holding a tone of awe and disbelief.

"Yes, has been since he was sixteen."

I could tell Jonah was getting angry; his father barely let him sit on conversations with his *mother* let alone pack duties. Sometimes I felt that Alpha Hess didn't trust his own son to take over.

I'd never say that out loud, I like my head where it is.

"Well we better move off," Alpha Hess said as he looked at his watch. "Don't want to be the first to arrive but you don't want to be the last either."

My blood seemed to be fizzing, my stomach kept churning and the minute long drive to the party felt like a lifetime. I could barely take in the grand splendor of the hall, which was lit up by twinkle lights and set up backing into the mountain, a large balcony to the side that overlooked most of the pack estate.

As everyone cleared out of the car I watched as other cars showed up, four in total either small or large company. The party seemed to be starting inside, the Wolfsbane members would be in attendance as well and I suddenly felt like my dress was constricting any kind of breathing.

My legs felt shaky as we walked toward the entrance doors and as I stepped over the threshold and into the main foyer, I spied people laughing and dancing just beyond two white double doors my breathing stopped altogether.

Wolfsbane is a very large pack and as I watched people dancing and chatting I knew that this was a half-breed nightmare.

I could see up ahead the Alpha and Beta family by the door, greeting our Alpha family and I realized I would have to shake hands with these people.

Would they even shake my hand? Would they take in my scent and demand to know why I had been brought along?

By the time I reached the Alpha I was encased in his large shadow and I could feel my body trembling as I looked at the floor.

"Alpha J-James," I practically whispered as I bowed on unsteady feet. Rising up I extended my hand, holding my breath until I felt myself feeling dizzy.

When it was grasped and pumped firmly I lifted my head in surprise, shocked as he nodded his head at me and then I was nudged along to his mate - his Luna. She was what defined beauty. She had amazing blonde waves that cascaded down her back, an amazingly full smile and deep brown eyes that reflected the light of the party

"Luna James," I said thickly as I tried to swallow the nervous saliva that gathered in my mouth.

"Lovely to meet you sweetheart, I hope you enjoy the party."

My mind was going in a billion different directions as I moved down the line to the Beta family, still receiving a hand shake and acknowledgement.

After paying my respects to the Beta female and male, I reached a girl who looked about my age, her jet black hair slicked over to one side of her face as her tight red dress barely concealed her chest she glowered at me.

"Beta Katherine," I said softly as I once again bowed.

She lifted her nose and sneered down at me. If she thought a haughty nose lift would hurt me it wouldn't - I got worse from my own pack. Her cat-like green eyes regarded me with disdain, like I was mud on her expensive looking heels.

As I moved to the Alpha's daughter I stopped, my eyes widening. I forgot her name. Oh, please no. My palms sweat as my mind raced to remember her face and match it to a name.

"I'm sorry…"

"It's fine, you can't be expected to remember everyone's name can you?" Her brown eyes held a twinkle in them as she smiled widely at me, her brown hair loosely curled around her face, "I'm Grace, maybe we will see each other sometime throughout this evening."

"O-oh sure…maybe," I was stunned as I moved onto the boy beside her, the Beta's son and next in line to be the Beta of Wolfsbane after his father. He was as cool and calm as his father was.

As the line finally ended and people moved behind me to greet their hosts I let out a sigh, walking toward my mother. Fiona and Jada were already out dancing and Laurance stood against the wall on the other side of the room with a drink in his hand, staring at people.

I got some stares as people who walked by me caught my scent; however they kept on walking like it didn't matter.

Mom looked at me with a smile as she grabbed my arm and said, "Make sure you have fun tonight."

I gave a small nod as I looked around at all the people, dancing, laughing and enjoying themselves.

I hoped I would.

Chapter Four

"...AT LAST, MY love has come along...my lonely days are over..." As the beautiful tone of Etta James played inside the hall, I stood outside on the balcony, sighing with content as I looked over the dense forest, finally feeling free for the first time in a long time.

Jonah had disappeared somewhere and wasn't around to bother me, Fiona and Jada had found some single wolves to dance with and my parents mingled with the other Alpha families, strengthening bonds and all that other important pack stuff that didn't concern me.

As I stood in a place of pure serenity I wondered if this is what life was really like - not having to look over my shoulder, not having to nurse a bruise or fear when my next attack would come. I could just stand here and *exist* and enjoy *existing*. I didn't have to hide away tonight and I felt a little lucky to be here.

I let out a small squeal of surprise as a pair of arms crossed over on the balcony. Stumbling backward from the railing I eyed the strange male whose outfit was surprisingly unkempt for the event. His crisp white shirt was crinkled and rolled up his arms, roughly tucked into his black dress pants, his bow tie not even tied up.

"I wanted to see what was so interesting out here," his voice broke the awkward silence of me just staring at him. He rotated and leant back on the railing, staring at me with an odd expression. I became so lost in his face that I barely cared how he looked at me.

That face.

He was handsome to say the least. His jaw was strong and it looked as if it had been chiselled to perfection. His lips were full, only his lower lip seemed to be slightly fuller than the top. His nose was sharp and shaped to his face nicely, and his eyes…a girl could get lost in those shining brown orbs, heck I *was* lost.

"I also wanted to see if you were who I thought you were." His words snapped me out of my haze and I blinked at him. He let out a laugh, "I'm glad to say you are."

"Um…"

My eyes widened as he took my hand in his, and I secretly marveled at the feeling of his rough palm encased around my own. I nearly shut my eyes. What was happening?

"I can't believe it's you," his voice was wondrous as he got off his position on the balcony and I watched as he seemed to get taller. Suddenly I felt awkward, coming up to his chin and having him still holding my hand.

This was strange and frankly shouldn't be happening.

He was a wolf, I knew that. I could identify one quite easily - their teeth gave it away.

"I'm not sure - You seem to think you know me, I've never actually been h-here before…" as I slid my hand out of his I crossed my arms behind me and took a couple of steps backward so I could clear the cloud forming in my head.

He frowned a little, looking surprised. "You don't know what we are do you?" I cocked my head in slight confusion, not following. "I know you're half-breed, I can smell it…I didn't realize your wolf was so dormant."

I felt my cheeks heat up in embarrassment and I looked away.

"Sorry, that was rude. That isn't a bad thing or anything. I just thought you'd still have wolf qualities."

"I have some," I quipped, suddenly feeling the need to defend myself.

He smiled again and the air nearly left me.

Don't faint.

"What's your name?" He asked as he took a step closer to me.

I bit my lip and took a shaky step backward, "Evelyn."

"You came with the Idaho?"

I could only nod as I felt dazzled by - just by his presence.

"Well, *Evelyn,* seeing as you don't know," he took my hand again and my mouth dropped open in surprise. "I knew it was you just by your scent, but now I know for sure. Evelyn…we're mates."

No, not this again.

Did they really think I'd fall for it a second time? Now I knew why Jonah had disappeared, he'd found another wolf to concoct this plan with. I could feel my mouth turn down and I pushed the urge to cry away.

This was the cruellest thing they could do, or had done. I had believed it the first time, even though I hadn't felt the amazing connection they all spoke about. I had been told it was because my wolf was so dormant, until they had me really believing them, did they pull the rug out from under my feet.

I wouldn't fall into that trap twice.

"I'm not doing this again," I whispered, mainly to myself. Taking my hand from his roughly I went to walk away, only he grabbed my arm and stopped me from doing so.

"Pardon me?" His tone was disbelieving. "Again? Do you already have a mate?"

"Stop, I'm not falling for it. I don't have a mate, I'm not supposed to have one," I felt smarter this time, an attack I could finally deflect. Maybe they'd hurt me later for not playing along, but it hurt more when I did.

"Evelyn, we are mates, I can tell just by your scent." He took my hand again and I felt electric shocks run up my arm, my skin breaking out in goose bumps. "Do you feel that?" His tone sounded breathless, "I'm not lying to you."

"Stop," I put a hand on my forehead, feeling my head spinning as I tried to decipher my thoughts.

"I could mark you if you need proof."

"No!" I gasped as I snatched my hand out of his. "T-this is too much." I don't have a mate, I repeated over and over in my head. I had accepted that. I was going to move on with my life, I was going to get away from the wolf pack drama and hierarchy. If this was real then I'd be stuck in it for the rest of my life - did I want that?

Breath was coming short and my stomach felt like it was heaving and a few voices called out in our direction before darkness fluttered over my eyes and I was falling into oblivion.

∞

"...She thought I was lying to her, why would she think that?"

"I - uh I - I'm not sure...Evelyn has always been a strange girl...her blood status led us to believe that she wouldn't h-have the qualities to find mate." The voice sounded like it belonged to Jonah, but my mind felt so disconnected it could have been anyone saying it.

Someone snarled and I could feel myself coming into awareness as I heard the conversation.

"She said *not again*, has she - has she had a mate before?" the familiar male voice choked the words out.

"N-no. Evelyn believed a f-few years ago this boy was her mate...practically stalked him to be honest. It took a lot to convince her she wasn't his mate." Jonah's voice was earnest, and even I nearly believed it.

"No," I croaked out at the lie, dragging my eyes open.

"Evelyn?" The man from the balcony was by my side again and I looked at all the faces crowded around me, most staring in contempt, minus my mother who looked at me with pure elation.

"Where am I?"

"You fainted sweetheart; you're at the pack clinic." I looked at the doctor beside the bed who was taking my blood pressure. "Gave your mate quite the fright."

My eyes immediately flashed to the man beside my bed who was holding onto my hand with both of his, a relieved smile on his face. "My mate..." I slowly drew out.

"Can we have a minute?" He asked the room, who looked like they wanted to do anything but leave me in a room alone with him. Grudgingly they left and I was once again alone with the liar.

"Gosh," I rubbed my temples as I calmed myself.

"I wasn't lying. I'm not lying," he whispered earnestly. "I promise you, I swear on my life and my pack - my status- I'm not lying to you. We're made for each other; my soul job in life is your happiness and protection Evelyn."

I wanted to believe him. I really did. I wasn't sure I could take two rounds of this kind of humiliation though.

"Did you really stalk another wolf?" He asked.

Anger rose up in my body, as it always did when those *people* twisted a story of abuse on me. "No I did not." I snapped, surprising myself. "They all convinced me he was my mate; they told me I wasn't feeling the sensations because my wolf is dormant. So I believed them. He was going to mark me, until they all came clean right before it was all planned." It was nothing but a cruel joke.

I heard his growl and I quickly backtracked as I realized how I had just talked back. Jonah beat me for less. "I'm sorry," I said quickly. "I'm sorry."

"Why are *you* apologizing? I know Idaho had a blood purity thing going on but I didn't know they messed with half-bloods this badly." He looked supremely pissed; his fists were clenching and unclenching.

If he was reacting like this, just to this story, then there was no way I'd tell him the rest of my treatment. A knock sounded on the door and the doctor popped her head in. "Alpha Aiden, your parents and sister are here."

I felt like I just swallowed a lemon.

Alpha Aiden?! What? Oh no, this was a whole other ball game. I quickly climbed off the other side of the bed, straightening my dress.

"What are you doing? You need to lie down, you just fainted."

"You're - you're," I quickly lowered my head. I had been staring him in the eyes constantly, somebody knocked at the door and I nearly fell over when I saw who walked in.

Alpha James came in, followed by his Luna and then his daughter Alpha Grace who was wearing a small grin on her face, I quickly averted my eyes to the floor.

"Dad," Aiden said, relief coloring his tone. "I found my mate."

"Yes I believe we heard your jubilation son," Alpha James' voice held a hint of humor.

"And then you fainted, poor thing, he wasn't boisterous with you was he?" The Luna slid her arm around my shoulders and I looked at her in shock as she sat me back on the bed. "Aiden better not have gone caveman on you. I've taught him better than that."

"I didn't," he protested.

"He d-didn't," I said quietly.

"She won't believe that I'm her mate."

The room was silent and I continued looking at my hands, too afraid to look up at all this Alpha blood in the room.

"Evelyn, why don't you believe my son is your mate?" Luna James asked gently as she sat beside me.

That surprised me even more. The Luna of my pack had barely acknowledged my existence. I had to answer - an Alpha was asking me a question after all, but how was I to explain it? In as few words as possible.

"I'm not supposed to have one," I murmured as I played with my dress material. "I'm half-blood, my wolf doesn't - doesn't exist. So I don't have one."

"Who told you that?"

"My pack."

The room was quiet for a moment before a new voice jumped in. "Well that's ridiculous. How do you explain wolves that are mated to humans and have half-human pups? You are definitely not the only half-blood in this world," it was Alpha Grace, who looked at me shaking her head.

"My pack doesn't have any half-bloods beside me...and none of them are mated to humans. All wolves."

"Yes, we know about Idaho's purity ideals," Alpha James said, disapproving. "We've heard stories, unable to prove them of course, that they've kicked out members who found themselves mated to humans - or any kind that isn't werewolf."

"Her pack also led her to believe she did have a mate, and then told her at the last minute he wasn't. They ought to be taken to the council dad, they break so many laws it's a joke. Misleading a wolf, that doesn't know any better, that her mate isn't what the Moon Goddess destined? It's blasphemy."

"Calm down Aiden," Alpha James ordered.

"We can say for sure, sweetheart, that Aiden is indeed your mate. We saw the bond through his mind-link. We know for sure it's real." The Luna smiled at me and stroked my arm, looking into my eyes; I couldn't hold her gaze and I dropped mine. "As Alpha's it would be improper to mislead you on this, as you would be the future Luna of Oregon."

I don't know how that news made me feel. Nauseous maybe?

On one hand I felt good I wasn't being lied to, but on the other, I realized this meant I was going to be stuck in pack life for the rest of my life. I didn't want that. Then a new thought occurred to me…if Aiden was indeed my mate I'd be given the option to stay here…I'd never have to go back to Idaho again.

What was to say all this niceness wasn't just an act though? Would I be treated the same here as I was in Idaho? At least in Idaho I had my mother, who would I have here?

"Do you believe me now, Evelyn?" Aiden was crouched in front of me, his hands on my knees, sending those little jolts of electricity once again through my body. He seemed genuine…I felt my face heating up as I was once again ensnared in his warm gaze and all I could do was nod like a mute.

"Good," he sighed out, like I had just taken the weight of the world off his shoulders.

"I think we are going to need to have a meeting about this whole situation…I believe Alpha Hess was under the ludicrous impression that his daughter would be your mate Aiden."

Aiden's nose curled as he stared at his father and I held back the smile that so desperately wanted to creep onto my face. Then the urge left as I realized Fiona would quite possibly want to tear me limb from limb right now.

"The party is starting to wind down," Luna James said. "If you want to sort out the meeting I'll see our guests off."

As the Alpha and Luna left the room along with Grace, I could hear my family on the other side, demanding to come in.

I hoped they didn't.

"So you believe me then?" Aiden asked, still in front of me.

Blinking back into awareness I looked down at him, not sure how I was to gauge him. I had stopped trusting people who were nice to me a long time ago, usually it was just to lead me into a false sense of security and then to toss me to the side once they had their laugh at my expense.

His family had confirmed that he was my mate, okay, I could take that. I knew by Moon Goddess law he could never physically hurt me, it went against the grain of any mated couple, but deep down there was this nervous twinge in my stomach, that all of this would fall apart.

"Evelyn, you in there?"

"Sorry...I..." I simply stopped talking, not really sure what to say.

He smiled and I looked away again. This felt awkward, what was I supposed to say? Do?

"So your pack mate thought I was going to be her mate?" He asked as he stood up, going to the sink and getting a cup of water.

"Yeah...she was planning the wedding on the way here."

He let out a snort as he turned to face me. "You didn't think we'd be mates? When you found out we were coming?"

"No. I w-was under the impression I'd never have one. Saves getting your hopes up."

The room was silent as I toyed with my fingers. I tried thinking of things to say, often opening my mouth and then shutting it again.

"It's a little awkward isn't it?" Aiden asked with a nervous sounding laugh. "So many different feelings all at once? I feel like my head is exploding."

"I only feel the feelings when you touch me," I admitted.

"How many wolf traits do you have?" He asked as he sat down in a chair.

"Not a lot...I have good vision and I can run as fast as a wolf in human form but really beside that...nothing. No super-fast healing, no sickness immunities."

His face paled at that, like he feared I would die from a cold, before a resolved look graced his features. "I'll just have to take extra care of you then."

My face went red and I looked down at my hands, trying to control my breathing.

No one beside my mother took care of me. No one offered or stated so simply they would - is this what the mate bond is? Overlooking all flaws and aspects of someone's character and accepting them straight away? Not needing to change anything about them?

He seemed so easy with it, so comfortable; I was still coming down from the shock that I actually had a mate.

"You have strange eyes."

I looked at him in surprise, "I do?"

"Yeah, almost wolf-like really. But not. They're brown, but you have a really pale ring of amber around them, strange for someone with a dormant wolf is all."

"I've never noticed it…" I thought my eyes were brown…I would have noticed an amber ring surely. Then again I avoided mirrors like the plague.

The room was silent - in a partially awkward way, before someone knocked on the door and a familiar face popped in.

Grace smiled. "It's time for 'the meeting', what do we even have to discuss?"

I thought the same, but I wouldn't be surprised if my pack tried to stop this. Alpha Hess would already be furious that it wasn't Fiona in the mating.

I widened my eyes in surprise as Aiden outstretched his hand and I hesitated nervously, before the look of nerves on his face had me sliding my hand into his and following him from the room, with a looming feeling in my stomach.

Chapter Five

Fiona's tight green eyes went straight to mine and Aiden's interlocked hands before her dark glower ended up on my face. Jada's stare was almost as withering, if not more. My eyes immediately dropped to the table, too afraid to look at anyone else.

Taking the seat Aiden offered I crossed my hands in my lap, my palms starting to sweat.

"Well, may I say that this gathering was one of our best? I couldn't be happier for my son that the Moon Goddess chose this young lady to be his mate - and our future packs Luna," Alpha James' tone was warm and I glanced up at him nervously.

"We believe that a mistake has been made," Alpha Hess cut in as Alpha James opened his mouth to speak again. "Evelyn isn't a strong wolf. She isn't even a full wolf, so the fact she is paired with an Alpha wolf doesn't make any sense."

"Are you questioning the Moon Goddess, Alpha Hess? Her decision?" Luna James' voice held a tone of shock and disbelief. "I won't tolerate that kind of blasphemy in my presence. The Moon Goddess," she touched her forehead in solidification to her statement and those around the table who disagreed grudgingly touched theirs. "The Moon Goddess does not make mistakes."

"Evelyn was due to be - *turned out* of the pack following her graduation, as her wolf has made no appearance."

"She could be a late bloomer," Luna James said tersely. "If we turned out every wolf that didn't follow normal protocol we'd hardly have a pack left."

"We know how you run your pack, Alpha Hess. It is not our right to question it, or question your protocol on wolves that haven't matured, but it is our right to question our alliances, given that you don't seem agreeable to this alliance. Evelyn will in some short time become Luna of this pack - will you still be allied with us? Or should we not waste any time and discontinue our relationship?"

"I was under the impression that Fiona would be joined in this pack with an allied mating, that was briefly stated." Alpha Hess looked like a petulant child as he folded his arms.

"We said if our two had not found their mates by the time they were twenty that it *possibly* would go ahead," Alpha James said, irritation in his voice.

"What?" Aiden asked in disgust. "What if I had never come across Evelyn until I was twenty-one?"

"Allied mating's are not legal," Grace piped up, only to quickly shut her mouth when her father glowered in her direction.

"It was never set in stone."

"We come from two very different packs, Alpha James," Alpha Hess said. "Evelyn is not a pure wolf; she's the only impure wolf in our pack."

"Well you won't have to worry about that anymore," Aiden practically snarled as he clenched his fists under the table. "She's no longer part of your pack."

"That is Evelyn's decision sweetheart," Luna James smiled down at me. "She's still seventeen and studying. A lot of wolves stay with their pack family until they've graduated and are ready to leave."

Suddenly all eyes were on me and my eyes quickly darted around the table as I took in all the faces staring back at me.

My mother looked elated, wearing a proud smile on her face. Michael looked as angry as Alpha Hess - maybe because my station was higher than his now. The thought made me feel somewhat happy as he actually dropped his eyes.

Interesting.

Jonah looked too calm - I knew that look and it gave me nightmares a lot. That was the look he had on before he did something awful to me. It was too neutral. Fiona was still glaring at me and Jada had her front canines partially extended.

"Where's Laurance?" I wondered aloud, realizing he wasn't at the table.

"He went to bed, he wasn't feeling too well darling," mom said softly. I nodded and played with the material on my dress, avoiding answering the question.

"Evelyn?" Luna James asked gently. "Do you want to go back to Idaho or do you want to stay here in Oregon?"

I felt Aiden tense beside me and I looked up at him, admiring his profile from the side. He had nice ears, I mused. Not too big, not too small. His hair was short…I wouldn't' be able to run my fingers through it. I stopped myself after that thought; I shouldn't be having thoughts like that, not until I knew where I sat with all this. When he turned his head and his brown eyes locked with mine my brain turned into a giant puddle.

I wondered if his did that too.

"Evelyn?" Alpha James brought me back to the real world.

Quickly I looked back down at my hands on the table, splaying out my fingers as the cold wood soothed the heat in my palms. It was as if I had no voice.

"You can be honest Evelyn," Aiden murmured as he took my hand in his.

My stomach flipped, how was I supposed to think with skin to skin contact?

"Can you please use your words, you already have enough attention!" Jada snapped.

Aiden growled next to me and stood up, slamming his palm hard on the table. I jumped in surprise as some of the wood chipped away on impact. "You will address your superior with respect. She now holds a higher rank than you do."

Jada's face paled. She looked like she was about to be sick as she shakily bowed her head, uttering, "*Alpha.*" I watched mom quietly scolding Jada as Aiden resumed holding my hand, gesturing for me to go ahead.

I felt sick. Like I was in some sort of school presentation - those were the worst. Only this time…maybe I wasn't on the lower rung of the ladder as I always had been. Could I tell the complete truth? Would it hurt Aiden's feelings?

Taking a breath and tucking a loose brown bang behind my ear I closed my eyes to keep control of what I had to say.

"I-I was supposed to be turned out…I had accepted that." My voice sounded weak and I cleared my throat. "I was - I was th-thrilled for a life outside of p-pack hierarchy and rules and-" I stopped myself from that last part. If Aiden knew my treatment, the Idaho Pack would not be leaving this room. "I was going to go to college and live a human life…away…far away." I peeked up at Aiden who watched me intently, giving me a small smile.

"May I ask, Evelyn, why do you want to be so far away from pack life?" Alpha James asked.

My heart rate increased as I tried to think up a reasonable excuse that would allow the people in this room to leave in one piece. If I said, 'Oh you know, there's only so many times a girl can get her head shoved down the toilet,' who knows what would happen, and that was mild compared to some of the stuff I had gone through.

So I told a half-truth.

"I don't fit in…I never have. I never will. I'll never shift, or have a wolf in my head…I'm more human than I am wolf."

"Yes…that's another thing I wanted to know…how Evelyn actually came to be…we know she is not Beta Michael's offspring, but she is yours, Beta Maria." Alpha James looked intently at my mother whose features darkened slightly.

"This is a sensitive topic for my mate," Michael snapped angrily. "She does not have to answer."

"Michael its fine," Mom murmured. She bowed her head at Alpha James, her cheeks slightly flushed before opening her mouth to speak. "I was raped when I was seventeen. I fell pregnant with Evelyn and met Michael shortly afterward."

"Seventeen?" Luna James asked with a frown. "How could a human be strong enough to hold down a mature wolf?"

Mom looked a little flustered and I felt my brow crease as she couldn't get out a decent answer. Sure, I had thought about that question before as well, but I'd never ask her. How did you ask someone a question like that?

"She's said enough," Michael snapped.

"So there's no way of tracing back her father?" Aiden asked, squeezing my hand.

"I'm not sure women keep in touch with their rapist," Jonah said mockingly as he leant back in his chair.

I was surprised, by Jonah's blatant lack of respect and blunt wording as my mother rubbed her face. I had to get the subject changed.

"How I came to be doesn't matter," I said quietly. "But I'm not sure if I- if I can stay here."

Aiden's hold on my hand fell slack and I felt him turn to face me. "Why?"

My hair being up for so long was giving me a headache, I wanted to just get out of this dress and take the powder off my face and go back to hiding under my blankets - my safe place. I was too in the spotlight here, my blood, me as an individual, and if I stayed here, I was always going to be in the spotlight.

"If I join the human world I can d-disappear," I whispered to myself. Shaking my head I continued, "I'm not a full wolf…I - how can I be a Luna when I'm not even a wolf?"

"Exactly," Fiona said across the table. "Finally some sense."

"Shut up," Grace snapped at her. "Thank the Goddess it wasn't you who was chosen for my brother. I may have committed my first homicide before I was eighteen."

"Grace," Luna James growled. "Enough."

"Why is everyone ignoring the fact there is obviously something else going on here? This pack has some seriously disturbing purity issues. Evelyn, did they hurt you?" Grace demanded as she stood up.

I could feel my breath catch in my throat as I locked eyes with Jonah who ever so slightly tilted his head. A cold chill ran down my spine as I tried to block the images of torment and abuse from my mind.

"No," I lied. I prayed I had lied well enough for them not to scent it.

"Grace, you need to go. You are dismissed," Alpha James ordered.

Her blue eyes widened in annoyance, her round cheeks bright red from her outburst before she turned and left the room growling, slamming the door shut.

"My apologies," Alpha James murmured respectfully.

"Evelyn, you are not the only half-blood out there. Alpha Kane in Ireland, his mate is fully human." I was surprised at mom's admission, and I think everyone else at the table was, as Idaho looked at her with a look of betrayal. "The minority always end up doing big things sweetheart…you need to give it a chance."

"We aren't concerned with blood purity," Aiden waved his hand. "Blood means nothing. The Moon Goddess has decided and planned this. To question it is blasphemy in itself. Evelyn," he said my name with a tone of urgency that surprised me as he turned my chair to face me. "I will do anything, give anything, if you'd just let me try. Please give me a chance - this pack a chance."

"A lot of our pack members go to college after high school Evelyn. That opportunity is available to you as well," Luna James said. "That also gives you some time to try living outside of pack life. It's good experience for everyone."

College? I'd get to try College?

As I looked at Aiden and took in his face - noting the light colored freckles over his nose, and the way his brown eyes darted across my face. I suddenly felt the urge to draw him and the urge to give it a go…and if it was horrendous I could do a runner once I got to the college stage of this arrangement.

"Okay," I breathed out as my hands shook in his. "Okay I'll give it a try."

I jumped in shock when he cupped my cheek, a bright smile on his face. Thankfully he didn't try and kiss me or anything, because who knows how that would have turned out, but his smile was contagious and I found myself smiling back.

"Okay, now that's settled," Luna James said excitedly. "Are you staying with your pack for the remainder of the evening or will you be moving in tonight?"

"May I speak with Evelyn, alone for a moment?" Mom asked quickly before I could respond. Slowly I got up and followed her outside of the room where she took me by the upper arms. "Evelyn leave tonight. If you come back with us, who knows what will happen. There are two furious young wolves in that room...don't come back tonight...your chance for a better life starts here. Take it and don't look back."

"Mom-"

"My choice to keep you was my choice, but it wasn't yours," her voice cracked as she brushed my forehead with her fingers. Her fingers hesitated over the spot near my hairline where I knew a white scar sat wickedly. "You have the choice now, for a better life. Mates are amazing Evelyn, you'll never have to live looking over your shoulder again. You'll always have a companion, a protector. He will protect you a lot better than I ever could."

I nodded, feeling my eyes welling up. "Alright."

Offering a shaky smile mom took my hand and guided me back into the room, going around the table and taking her seat.

I sat down beside Aiden once more and tried not to feel sick from the tension in the room. What had been said while we were away?

"So Evelyn, will you be moving in with us today?" Alpha James asked tiredly.

"Y-yes," I murmured, trying not to smile at the grin that broke out on Aiden's face. "My bag- my bag is a-at the guest house..."

"That's fine; we'll send someone over to get it."

"What time is your flight?" Alpha James asked Alpha Hess conversationally, like we hadn't just been having serious conversation moments before.

"Eight thirty," Alpha Hess grumbled.

Alpha James held out his hand and said, "We'll see you off in the morning then."

As Alpha James shook hands with the retreating Idaho members I received a happy smile from mom before she disappeared from the room and then it was just me and Oregon left.

"Well I'm exhausted. It's past four," Luna James sighed.

I felt bad for causing so much trouble; I had ended their party early and kept them all awake. "I'm sorry."

"Don't be sweetheart, we couldn't be happier with how tonight ended. My son found his mate and I received another daughter and Oregon has gained another pack member. We ought to have another party to celebrate tonight."

"No more parties Claudia," Alpha James groaned as he led us from the room.

As Alpha James and his Luna walked out of the room, Aiden's hand on my arm stopped me from following, and I looked at him nervously.

"Thank you," he said quickly. "For giving me a chance…Idaho isn't one of the best packs…I'm not even sure why my dad allied with them…but whatever experience you had there, I promise you - you will be happy here. I'll make sure of it."

I plastered a small smile on my face as I nodded; taking his offered hand and following him from the room and toward the hall the party had been in.

"So what's your full name?" He asked as he stepped outside and led me in the direction his parents had gone.

I lifted the dress off the floor, feeling the chill on my legs before I answered his question. "Evelyn Lilith Wright."

"I like it."

"Thank you."

The tone between us was light as he continuously wore that small smile that I was finding to become a permanent fixture on him. I had to stop myself from getting all dreamy eyed and just staring at him.

"You look beautiful tonight."

It was impossible to stop the blush and the nervous breathy laugh, "I'm sure it's just a lot of makeup." Taking the conversation off my appearance I looked around the well built up pack. "How far off is your house?"

"Just there," he smiled as he leant into my line of vision and pointed at the grand white house that stood proudly amongst all the others. As I briefly shut my eyes I shook my head. I hadn't thought of this trip ending like it had…it would have been laughable if someone had said all this was going to happen to me.

It had though, and I was surprised to find myself interested in what life in this pack would be like. I only hoped that it wasn't some façade and that this was an elaborate set up, because if it was…I didn't have the energy left in me to recover from that.

It would finish me.

Chapter Six

"You can have this room darling," the Luna said gently as she pushed the door open.

It was a warm looking room. The walls were a soft cream color; the double bed was adorned with chocolate and cream colors. A chest of drawers sat off to the right side of the room, under the large square window that was blanketed in a lace white curtain and then a brown drape over the top.

It was a comfortable space.

Until I saw the giant mirror on the sliding doors that obviously led into a wardrobe.

Still wearing the dress from the party I got my first look at what my mother had created...I looked different. My makeup was soft, I was thankful she hadn't gone over the top. I ached to take my hair out and let it fall free, but I had to admire the pins and delicate styling my mother had made.

"Is this okay for you?"

Blinking back and quickly looking toward the Luna I nodded, wondering if I could find a sheet to cover the mirror. "It's lovely...t-thank you Luna James."

She scoffed and put her hand on my shoulder. "No need for the formalities, we're going to be in each other's lives for a very long time, call me Claudia." I was taken aback. Call the Luna by her first name? I'd never done that in my life, and I wasn't sure if I had it in me to change that conditioning. "Okay well the bathroom is just across from your door." Not sure what else to say and desperately trying to keep my eyes off the mirror I tried my best to give a small smile as she turned and left the room.

"Oh Evelyn," she popped her head back in. "Welcome to the family."

As the door clicked closed I shut my eyes and tried to get a hold of my emotions. This was in no way how I had expected this trip to go at all. Twenty-four hours ago I was in my small room back in Idaho dreading it. Now I was in a new pack, I had met my soulmate and left Idaho for good…part of me wondered if this would have felt just as great as being kicked out on my own.

As I slid out of the heels I had been wearing all night and threw the clutch onto the floor, I pulled open the wooden chest at the base of the bed, hoping to find a sheet to put over the mirror. There was a nice amount of linen in here, mostly towels. Finding a creamy colored sheet at the bottom I pulled it out and went over to the offending object.

It was impossible not to look at myself, the mirror was huge and I was going to catch glances. It was natural for anyone to stare at their reflection, and seeing as mine was so different tonight - I was curious.

The dress fell elegantly in soft ripples down my body, the dark red material setting a cool glow to my tanned skin. Trailing my eyes over my thin arms and up to my collarbone I knew that I had to put on some more weight.

Maybe here they wouldn't starve me.

As my eyes met my reflections I tried to find the amber glow Aiden had said he saw. All I could catch were dark brown eyes that looked puzzled. I was puzzled. What had he seen that I couldn't? Catching the faded scar that ran from the edge of my hairline up inside my hair I looked away immediately.

No more looking.

"Oh, uh, hey…"

Spotting Aiden in the background, I noticed he had changed out his evening wear and into a white shirt and some loose gray sweats. I spun around quickly, clutching the sheet.

"H-hey," I managed, trying to ignore the party of nerves in my stomach.

"I was just going to say goodnight or good morning." He rubbed the back of his neck and smiled in a way that hit me right in the stomach. "Thought you'd already be asleep…do you need help with that?" He pointed at the sheet and came closer.

I felt my face heat up. Did I tell him what I actually wanted for? I mean, looking at the mirror now I don't think I'd be able to get it all covered by myself. Running my fingers nervously over my collarbone I tried to calm myself and make my voice sound a little stronger.

"I'm just covering the mirror."

"Why?" He asked, looking confused. "Don't girls love mirrors?"

Laughing nervously I wrung the sheet tighter in my hands. "I uh, had a nightmare about mirrors when I was younger…haven't been able to sleep in t-the same room with one for years." Lying had become so easy for me, and no one could smell otherwise. My heart rate never increased so no scent would be given off.

Aiden shrugged and took the sheet from my hand. "This will do for now. We can get one of those proper stick-on covers tomorrow if you want."

My mouth hung open as he effortlessly got the sheet up over the mirror, which would have taken me a lot longer to do. "Thanks…I wouldn't have been able to put it up so quickly."

He smiled and said, "Kind of wishing I took my time with it. Now I have no real reason to be in here."

I could feel the blush rising in my cheeks and I scolded myself, keep it together!

"Well…goodnight…good morning uh," he did that thing again - where he ran his hand over the back of his neck. I was beginning to find it was something he did when he was nervous. At least he was nervous as well. I murmured out a goodnight and he left the room, leaving me to deal with the cluster of feelings going on inside of me.

∞

I'd felt like I'd only been asleep for a second before a knock at the door woke me up. I squinted up over my blankets, spotting Luna Claudia.

"Sorry to wake you so early, but I thought maybe you'd like to see off your family."

She stood dressed for the day and not looking like she'd only had about four hours sleep. I could already feel the heavy bags under my eyes and I knew they'd be bloodshot. However, I was not going to miss saying goodbye to my mom.

"Thank you," I yawned out as I slid my legs over the side of the bed and bent down halfway to my open suitcase.

The beautiful dress I had worn last night was on the floor beside it and my travel clothes sat folded, neatly, at the top of the small case. Hearing my door shut I slipped on jeans over the leggings I had worn to bed and pulled a black sweater over the white stretch shirt I was already wearing. Pulling on my black boot slippers I forewent putting up my hair - I was already running late according to the clock on the nightstand.

As I made it to the hallway upstairs I followed the warmly decorated hallway, eyeing the beautiful yellow flowers that sat on a table against a wall. Finding the landing to the stairs I quietly walked down them, taking in the elegance and warmth of the home.

The Luna definitely decorated it.

"Morning!"

I jumped at the excited voice in my ear - normally Jada was growling her way downstairs. Aiden's sister Grace was walking a step behind me; her face smudged slightly from sleeping with last night's make up on. It made me wonder what mine looked like.

Realizing I hadn't answered I quickly uttered a good morning, keeping an eye on the stairs and wondering why she was talking to me so casually.

"I haven't been able to sleep all night. I have literally been tossing and turning, waiting for today to start so I could meet you properly. I can't believe you agreed to stay - I mean why wouldn't you? This pack is amazing, but wow. That's such a huge decision. I don't know if I'd have the guts to do that right now." She stopped and took a breath and I was able to try and collect my thoughts as we reached the landing. "I'm Grace by the way."

"She knows who you are." The Luna came around the corner her hand outstretched as she handed me a muffin. "Greg and Aiden are already meeting with your family. Have a muffin, no time for a real breakfast I'm afraid." Greg must Alpha James.

As both Grace and I were ushered out of the house and to a sleek looking 4WD I nearly choked on the muffin in shock as Grace offered the front seat to me.

"You can have shotgun, I don't even think I'll be getting out."

"You will send off our guests politely Grace, so you will be getting out." The Luna shook her head at Grace before pushing me toward the seat which I hesitantly sat in, eyeing Grace in the back.

What was this?

She was still Alpha by birth. I was Alpha by mating - a mating that technically wasn't even effective yet. It felt wrong and I felt years of lessons in pack hierarchy working their terrible magic on me.

The drive from the Alpha House to the guest houses was short, but I was surprised to see so many people up and already on the streets. Some were dressed in exercise gear and I knew that they would most likely be heading off to the training grounds.

"Oh, that's Lucy!" Grace squealed from her seat, "She's brilliant you'll love her."

My stomach knotted up further as people began looking at the car and I was happy for the dark tinted windows, even though their brilliant eyesight could probably still see me. Pulling up at the guest houses I saw the visiting packs, all ready to leave waiting by their cars for the formalities of a goodbye.

I spotted Idaho straight away - a scowling Jada and a pouting Fiona wasn't hard to miss, but my eyes went from them straight to Aiden, who stood off to the side in faded jeans, old sneakers and a black hooded jumper.

The moment he looked over I looked down at my hands, my breath quickening.

The day was fresh now; would I find it was all an act? Was I going to get laughed at and then stuffed into the car with Idaho and go back with them? Suddenly I wasn't feeling so good.

Stepping out of the car I jumped in shock as Grace took hold of my hand, giving it a squeeze - not a painful one like I'd had before. Like when Jonah had cracked all my knuckles and then proceeded to break my hand.

This felt like a comforting squeeze my mom would give me…except it wasn't from my mother. Someone besides my mother was being kind with me, it was so weird.

As we walked over to Idaho, Grace let go of my hand and instantly it was replaced by a much larger, warmer one and the way my body did those dancing tickles on my skin I knew who it was. Peeking up at him I tried to ignore the sucker punch feeling to my stomach when he smiled at me.

"Morning."

"Uh, morning." I cleared my throat and looked toward my mother who was smiling sadly at me.

"Well, Idaho…thank you for coming," Alpha James said politely as he shook hands with Alpha Hess. "Also, thank you for bringing my sons mate to him. Saves him a lot of search time. I only hope your daughter - and yours as well Beta Michael - have the same easy luck finding their soulmate."

"We're sure they will," Alpha Hess bit out.

Practically feeling my skull being laser beamed by Jada and Fiona I kept my eyes on mom who stepped out from the group and opened her arms. Releasing Aiden's hand I walked into them, sighing as I took in her familiar smell, planting it in my mind so I could try have it there when I needed it.

"I'm so happy for you sweetheart," she pulled back and held my cheeks in her hands. "This is a blessing from the Moon Goddess like no other. You can live now. Please, try and live, you have a great shot at life now…don't let what happened in your past dictate your future."

I wasn't able to stop the sting of tears in my eyes as I quickly went back to hugging her, urging myself to keep it together. "I'll call and email," I murmured quietly, trying to clear the thick emotion from my throat.

"Send pictures as well."

"I will."

"We have to get going," Alpha Hess said enthusiastically. "Our flight leaves in five hours, we have a long drive."

Pulling away from my mother I was surprised to see Laurance standing beside her. My surprise grew however when he gave me a pat on the back and a nod of his head before he went to join the rest of the pack.

That was the most I'd gotten from him my whole life.

"Contrary to popular belief, not everyone hates you." I recalled the doctor's words and for a brief second I felt myself warm…until I faced the others.

Swallowing the bile in my throat I lowered my head at Alpha Hess whose eyes burnt with hatred as he looked down at me. "Thank you for h-having m-me in y-your pack."

"Yes. Hopefully you will visit."

That sounded the farthest from an invitation and there was no way I'd ever go back there. Stumbling backward toward Aiden and his family I was silently comforted by the arm that went around my shoulder.

As Idaho and the other packs began pulling from the driveway I felt a sense of relief wash over me, followed by a sense of foreboding. This could become my future, if this wasn't all an elaborate act then these people, this pack, could become my life.

I hoped for the latter because I wasn't sure if I had the energy for any more emotional trauma.

∞

"So Evelyn, we'd best start organizing your school admission tomorrow. At least it's only the start of the school year; the kids went back a week ago." The Luna handed a bowl of roasted potatoes to Alpha James as she sat down at the dinner table.

Blinking into awareness, seeing as I usually zone out during dinner I tried to not look like a mute idiot and answer her. "Oh uh, we went back the week before."

"Unlucky," Grace giggled. "But at least you won't have any dramas getting in."

"They'll probably have you sit their entry test, to see where you're at and what classes to put you in. What was your favorite back in Idaho?" The Luna looked at me genuinely, smiling in open invitation to enter into the conversation.

I clenched my hands on my chair as I tried to ignore the heat in my cheeks. "Art."

"I was never very good at art. Greg was though, still can draw quite wonderfully."

I looked over the imposing Alpha who sat at the head of the table, eating and looking directly at me. I dropped my gaze quickly and slowly picked up my fork as I looked at the huge plate Aiden had loaded for me.

"You know we're having a party next weekend," Grace said as she pointed her fork at me across the table. "We have one at the start of the school year, kind of a goodbye to Summer, everyone goes to the falls and we eat and dri- we dance a lot." She looked at her parents and then at Aiden, who from the corner of my eye was slowly eating. "You're going to love it."

Internally I balked. Me at a party? A high school party? Sure they went on in Idaho but I never got an invite, in fact if I showed up there they'd probably take the grand opportunity and drown me.

"Oh Evelyn, I also spoke to your mother, she's going to be sending your things over as soon as possible, she'll just have to pack it all up."

Wouldn't be much packing then, I thought as the image of my sparsely filled bedroom entered my mind. I nodded so she knew I'd heard her and went back to the mountain of food in front of me, feeling my stomach expanding.

As dinner came to a close Grace was tapping away furiously on her phone and I felt Aiden's hand on my shoulder. I looked up at him wearily.

"Want to watch a movie?" He asked.

"Oh…yeah sure."

Hesitantly I got out of my chair, getting ready to clear my plate.

"That's fine Evelyn, Greg and I will clear up. You kids go watch a movie, but don't have a late night guys. You have school tomorrow morning and you pulled an all-nighter last night." She gave Aiden and Grace a stern look before I was pulled from the dining room, across the hall and into the huge theatre room.

Wow.

I'd only ever been into a movie theatre once and this could be one, if on a slightly smaller but grand scale.

Slowly I sat down on the plush suede theatre chair that sat in front of the huge white screen. Trailing my eyes up to the roof I spotted the projector. The wall where Aiden stood, was lined with movies that would put any kind of video store to shame.

Taking my eyes off the impressive collection I moved them to Aiden's back. He had a good back. That back trailed down to a nice looking butt and firm looking legs.

"What do you want to watch?" He turned suddenly and I quickly made it look like I hadn't just been staring at him.

"Anything…I'm not picky," I said quietly. Mainly because I just never watched movies, that would mean sitting in the same room as Jada. When he turned back around I ran my hand down my face.

Do not check him out.

Feeling a thump beside me I gasped in surprise as Grace sat down, once again on her phone.

"Grace could you not climb all over the furniture. Mom will get pissed if you break *another* chair." Aiden walked over to the DVD player with a movie and Grace flipped him off behind his back.

I nearly, very nearly, laughed.

I wouldn't take that risk however. The risk of feeling comfortable…getting too comfortable. I needed to stay on guard and in control.

"What's the movie?" Grace asked as she lowered her hand back to her phone and winked at me.

"Transformers."

"Ugh!" She grunted and got up, leaving the room.

Aiden sniggered as he came over to the couch, sitting next to me. Pulling open a built in cupboard under the cushion beside him he took out a bag of crisps. How could he still want to eat? His arm was grazing my arm and I wasn't sure if I moved over slightly, he'd get offended. Heck, I wasn't even sure if I wanted to move away. This wasn't good. As weak as my wolf side was, I could feel the bond. The more skin contact he made with me, the more I felt.

Gluing my eyes to the screen I frowned as the opening credits rolled in and then the movie title. "This isn't Transformers…" I murmured as *The Amazing Spider Man* popped up.

"I know. I wanted to get rid of her. She hates Transformers." He gave me a grin I hadn't got from him yet. It was cheeky…his eyes mirrored the smile and he offered me some crisps from the bag.

To distract my mind I took some and quickly looked back at the screen.

I don't think I've ever watched a movie so intently in my life. The other option was to let my eyes wander and just hugely embarrass myself which was not an option.

"We didn't get those mirror stickers for your room," he said suddenly and I jumped.

"It's alright…I can use the sheet for now."

"I'll get them tomorrow after school."

I found myself looking at him, which was a bad idea because he looked at me and I found myself falling into la-la land. "It's okay…the sheet is fine."

He smiled again, he must smile a lot…it came so naturally on his face. When I smiled it took a lot of effort. "You're going to want to use the wardrobe behind it soon, and the sheet will fall…its fine I can get them."

When I saw his eyes drop to my lips I quickly gathered myself, taking a breath and turning to look back at the screen. "Thanks," I practically whispered.

"No worries," he sighed as he took my hand.

The hand was fine.

I didn't know if I had anything more to give beyond that. I wasn't sure if I could…and I suddenly found myself doing something I never thought I would do…I was thinking about a relationship.

As I slipped into bed that night and lay facing away from the mirror I was completely lost in thought and fear.

Mostly fear.

What if I couldn't do this? The mate thing? I had been so thoroughly convinced it would never happen for me, and I had accepted that for so long that I shut myself off to the idea. I didn't flirt with guys like the girls in pack did, or make out with them in the library during a free period. The only time a guy had touched me was when Jonah or Zac - I squinted my eyes. My mind was not going down that path.

What would it feel like to have Aiden hold me the way Zac had done in that archery class? Would I find it repulsive? Would my skin crawl the way it had when Zac had grazed his fingers up and down my sides? Or would I enjoy Aiden doing that? Would it feel right?

Too many questions.

I sat up in frustration, running my hands through my hair. I didn't know how to do this…how did it all work? After watching so many different couples my whole life - each one was different - what was my relationship going to be like?

Was I even ready to have one?

With my mind spiraling out of control I closed my eyes tightly and willed sleep to come and not long after a thick heaviness fell over me and my worries and fears drifted into nothing as my mind became a blank dark canvas of peace.

Chapter Seven

"Well we've received Evelyn's past records from Idaho; however she will still have to sit an entrance test." The principal of Baker City High School was a large man, and definitely human considering the way he addressed the Luna.

"That's no worries, when can we do that?"

"She can come back tomorrow and sit it," he said as he slicked back his greasy dark hair. "Nine o'clock should be fine."

The Luna stood up and smiled brightly, extending her hand. "Thank you very much Principal Hill, we'll see you tomorrow." After a stiff handshake we both left the office, smiling politely at the receptionist before entering the parking lot.

Classes were in session and I was glad there was no one around to gawk.

"I was thinking we should go to the shops and get you a couple of outfits," Luna Claudia said as she adjusted herself in driver's side.

I looked at her in surprise. "My mom's sending my stuff over…"

"Yes but that won't be here for at least a week. You need some new outfits for school. Grace doesn't mind lending you clothes, however I'm sure you'd feel better in clothing that was more your taste, am I right?" She eyed the way I sat in the uncomfortably short shorts that Grace had leant me and I tried not to fidget.

"I can't pay for them…I don't have any money." Great job Evelyn, that was barely audible. Unfortunately her super hearing picked up on it.

"Sweetheart it's fine, you're practically another daughter now and Grace never shops with me anymore." She pat my knee as a way to end the back and forth and I stopped myself from commenting. I wasn't going to talk back to the Luna.

As we drove along I was amazed at the fact that I was in the Luna's car, trying not to get her to buy me new clothes. This would have been something to laugh about if I wasn't so nervous. This never would have happened in Idaho.

We pulled into the mall parking lot and I looked at it darkly. Shopping was never fun. I'd always gone the odd few times with mom and Jada and she spent the majority of the time making me feel so uncomfortable I didn't want to buy anything.

As the Luna smiled at me and ushered me out of the car, flicking her gorgeous blonde hair I felt a little hopeful, that maybe it would be fun this time. I could be a real girl and enjoy shopping.

An hour and too many shopping bags later the Luna was pushing me into another changing room, excitedly babbling about how much shopping she used to do when she was my age.

"These jeans are lovely on you; they show off your legs. And it goes brilliantly with that loose singlet and the gray cardigan we got. I think we should get them, but we'll need to get some extra shoes that go with this outfit." The Luna was on a rampage, we already had four different outfits and I was under the impression there'd be more on the horizon.

"It's really okay; we have the same jeans in blue-"

"Yes but you need a pair in black as well. We'll get them." She smiled brightly at the sales assistant before pushing me back inside the changing room to get changed.

I shimmied off the jeans, not looking at the price tag otherwise I'd probably faint. I folded them and reached for the dreaded shorts Grace had lent me. She had a great body, she deserved to show it off but they were not me at all.

From the corner of my eye in the wall full of mirrors this changing booth had been cursed with, I caught the faded scar on my right hip, that had been carved in viciously and deliberately by Jonah and his posse and I had to resist the urge to yelp out each time I looked at it. I felt like I had been punched in the stomach as I breathed like I was winded. Hurriedly I changed; holding in the sting of tears as I quickly exited the room, trying to find the Luna.

"Oh perfect, Evelyn darling!" She called over from the counter where there seemed to be more clothing. "I got a few other things for you, no need to try them on I know they'll look great."

My face fell at the amount she had already bought me and what she intended on buying as well. "Really C-Claudia I think I h-have enough."

"Nonsense, there's no such thing as enough clothes. Am I right Annabel?" The sales assistant nodded enthusiastically - of course she would, she's on commission.

As we left the store the Luna smiled at me, looking accomplished. "Time to go home and have some lunch. Grace and Aiden will be home soon. They'll have training tonight, you could go with them, use those new workout clothes."

"Go to training?" What pack had I walked into? Idaho never let me near the training grounds.

"Of course, all the wolves train together."

"I'm not a wolf…"

"Yes," she said slowly, "but you have some traits yes? Speed was one of them wasn't it? Trust me, you'll be fine. Plus you'll get to mingle with other kids your age which would be good. Make some new friends and really settle in."

I just nodded mutely as we packed away the bags into the car. I'd never made a friend in my life; I didn't even know what it was like to have a friend. My ideas of friendship were pulled from the stuff I had seen in the movies.

"Are there any special kinds of food you like Evelyn?" The Luna asked.

I had never been asked anything like that in my life. No one cared what I liked, mom had never asked and I just ate what she gave me, heck I was thankful when I was given the privilege to eat.

"Evelyn?" The Luna asked gently. "You in there?"

"Oh, yeah," I said. Taking myself out of my head I tried to form a response, thinking back to the first meal I had eaten after Jonah had taken the eating ban off me. Mom had made a roast that night, perfectly golden crispy potatoes and supremely crunchy and well cooked vegetables. It had been heaven.

"Roast chicken."

"That's Aiden's favorite," she said with a smile, seemingly pleased that I liked the same meal Aiden did.

I was surprised to find myself feeling warmth in my chest as I realized I was pleased as well.

As we pulled up to the house a woman decked out in a bright pink shirt and lime green jeans bounced up in excitement, flicking her long black hair over her shoulders like it was a sari.

"Oh, that's Beta Sandra, she's Katherine and Josh's mother, and they'll be in your year. Josh and Aiden hang out a lot, but Grace doesn't get on very well with Katherine." As the Luna got out of the car and embraced the bubbly woman who I barely recognized from the party, I noted she was the spitting image of her scary looking daughter.

I could still remember the tanned beauty with her slicked black hair and piercing green eyes that had regarded me like mud.

Hesitantly, I pushed open the car door, closing it as quietly as possible to keep the Beta Female's attention on the Luna. No such luck.

"Oh, and this must be the darling Evelyn!" She pulled me into a tight embrace, but not before planting two air kisses on my cheeks. "I'm so happy Aiden found his mate, and so young too!"

"Well he found his mate before Alpha Hudson, which does put us a leg in front."

"Goddess help the poor woman who is fated to that terrifying man. It still astounds me that he allied with us."

"He wanted free booze and we wanted that extra bit of security. Win win." The Luna winked at me and opened the trunk and the two back seat doors.

"Someone's been shopping, where was my invite?" The Beta immediately took out some bags as the Luna did so I slowly followed suit, taking the last few before closing the doors.

"Evelyn needed some clothes for school."

"Girl, these clothes will get her through college as well, you need to be cut off from your card."

The two laughed their way up to the house and I found myself softly smiling at the friendship, the two had clearly been friends for a very long time, it showed in the lax way Sandra addressed her Luna.

As we got inside I was once again taken aback by the lavish interior (I don't think I'll ever get over it) the Luna turned to face me. "You'll be okay to get these up to your room won't you Evelyn? I'll put some lunch on."

Nodding quickly, happy to take the chance to be alone I was left at the bottom of the stairs as the two women walked off toward the kitchen.

After managing to bunch the bags up in hands - barely, I shuffled my way upstairs, nearly tripping twice across the landing before making my way into my room, releasing the bags immediately and taking the opportunity to flop myself down onto the bed, my body relaxing instantly after having been so tightly wound for the past few hours.

I closed my eyes at the peace and quiet, the ache in my head now decreasing as I let myself fall into twilight zone, my mind swirling with different thoughts, mainly focusing on the scar that I usually let myself forget about.

This is why I hated mirrors, it showed me things I never wanted to see and then it would plague my mind for as long as it possibly could. I still remember the day I got that scar. The one that had been created with purpose - intent to be there forever to remind me of my station, who I was, what I would always be. A half-blood.

"Will silver even work on her?" Heather asked, genuine curiosity covering her voice as she tightly held my left arm out, Zac holding my other.

"She still has some wolf blood. Silver will never leave. Which is what we want," he said, the smirk evident in his voice. "Don't be so upset Evelyn, think of it as a tattoo, Jada said you were talking to your mom about getting one, this one is for free."

"Please," I cried out, anticipating the pain this would inevitably bring. "Please d-don't do this. Ah!" My legs buckled as Jonah kicked behind my knees and my head made contact with the bathroom wall as the other two continued holding my arms.

"What did I say about shouting?" He snarled as he grabbed the back of my neck, yanking my head back. My chest heaved up and down as I tried to catch my breath, a trickle of blood coming down from my forehead, going over my eye. "Make one more sound and I swear to the Goddess this knife might do more than just give you a tattoo."

I could feel my chin quiver as he shoved my neck forward and I once again smacked my head into the wall, already aggravating the pain from the first blow. I was seeing spots now; I could barely hold myself up.

"Okay, Zac give me Evelyn's hand please." As my arm was released Jonah snatched it into his and I felt something cool placed into it. "Evelyn I think you're going to help me do this." I stilled in fear as the waistband of my pants was yanked down over my hips slightly, exposing the side of my hip.

"Evelyn, what are you?" Heather hissed into my ear.

My body trembled and I tasted blood on my lips as my tongue darted out, trying to clear my dry throat. "A half-breed," I uttered into the cold bathroom.

"What does half-breed start with?" Zac asked, like an over enthusiastic grade two teacher.

"H."

"Evelyn that is what we are going to make, a nice little H. If you stop your hand just once, I'll put it in a more visible place." I felt the blade press against my flesh and I choked back the sob as I squeezed my eyes shut.

As I felt it slice through my skin the pain was unbearable, it was after all a silver knife and because I got the crappier traits of being half-wolf, this would definitely hurt and scar.

My hand on the knife tightened only serving it to dig in further and I could feel the bile rising in my throat as I screamed, my leg jerking, causing the knife to once again shift in my skin.

"Evelyn, I'm trying to get a clean line!" Jonah shouted. "Shut up!"

My sobs drowned out their sniggers and shouts as the letter was carved roughly into my skin, and I felt consciousness slipping from me. I *was suddenly alone on the bathroom floor, and I dropped my tear filled eyes to my hand that covered my wound. It was stained red with blood.*

"Knock, knock!" A voice chirped outside my bedroom door. I sat up hurriedly and wiped my eyes, unaware that I had been crying. Grace's face dropped as she came over to me touching my arm in concern. "Are you okay Evelyn?"

Nodding quickly I gave her a shaky smile. "Y-yeah j-just h-homesick."

"Understandable, you looked very close with your mom." She looked around my room and zeroed in on the bags. "Mom said you guys went shopping, can I check out what you got? Better yet, try it all on."

I grimaced slightly at the thought of doing a repeat of the morning.

She laughed, "That is why I stopped shopping with her."

As she leafed through the bags pulling out all the clothes and just making a mess in general as she nodded in approval, I sat in the center of the bed, wondering where Aiden was.

"Grace?" An unfamiliar voice called out. Suddenly my door pushed open and in walked a pure blonde knock out. She had the gift of the body, perfect hips, legs, breasts - she looked like a model. Her hazel eyes flickered over me in interest and the way they sparkled led me to believe she had been filled in on me already. "So, this is Evie."

Evie? No one had called me that before.

"The one and only," Grace said as she gestured grandly at me.

"Well, Evie, I'm Lucy." The beautiful blonde sat on the bed beside me, looking at the sheet on the mirror. "What's up with that?"

I didn't miss the look Grace shot her, but she pretended not to see.

My face felt hot as I tried to think up my lie and her eyes narrowed marginally as she waited for my answer.

"I-I hate mirrors."

She nodded slowly, her face thoughtful. "I hate clowns. And this," she pointed at the small beauty spot on her upper lip, making a face. "It ruins my overall look."

I thought it looked great, but I wasn't going to tell her that. Heck she was so close in my personal space right now - the only time a girl had been this close to me and wasn't threatening me.

"We need to take the sheet down to put the clothes away though," Grace pointed out as she eyed the mess she had made.

"The sheet stays up until I get stick on covers," a voice said from the doorway. My head immediately whipped around to see Aiden, dressed in jeans and a white tee, staring at the scene before him, his arms folded. I tried to control the sharp intake of breath as he smiled at me. "I was actually here to see if you wanted to get them Evelyn."

"Aren't you going to training tonight?" Grace asked as she dropped one of the bags on the floor.

"No, I'm skipping. But you're still going, both of you, and you're running late." His voice held a tone of authority and I watched as the two girls moved a lot quicker, waving at me before hurriedly leaving the room. As he leant against the doorway I found myself nervously getting off the bed, not sure what to do with my hands.

Thankfully, he saved me. "So…want to go get that cover?"

∞

Aiden's truck was nice, not over the top like Jonah's; his was some overpriced European model that I couldn't even remember the name of.

It felt comfortable, like you could spill a drink in it and not be charged an arm and a leg to upholster it.

"How was the meeting with Principal Hill?" Aiden asked as he reversed out of the drive, waving to a couple of guys who whistled at the car.

"It was okay, um, he said I'll sit the test tomorrow morning so…" I sunk lower in my seat as people watched the car drive by, most all dressed in workout gear - probably heading to the training field.

"You'll be fine. You're the talk of the school already and you're not even there yet."

I cringed; I didn't want to be hot topic. I wanted to fade into the background and be non-existent.

We pulled into a parking spot outside an art and craft store and I slid out, cursing myself for not changing into some of the better stuff the Luna had bought me today.

"We should be able to get something here." My stomach was left doing somersaults as he took my hand and led me toward the shop and I had to keep my eyes on my feet so I wouldn't trip over.

The bell above the door tinkled as we walked into the small art store and I had to resist the urge to pick up all the items I saw.

I enjoyed art back home, though I only ever sketched because Michael wouldn't let me have any decent supplies. He said I could do it at school and that was it. Miss Fields did give me some decent sketching pencils though.

As Aiden went off to find the assistant I began looking at all the brushes and the paint, feeling truly peaceful as I imagined the things I could create with all this stuff.

"…we have this; it might do for what you want." The sales assistant walked past the aisle I was in with Aiden behind her looking serious. I quickly left the brushes and followed them, coming to a sticker section. "It rolls on like wallpaper, do you see?"

"Is that okay?" Aiden asked me.

I blinked in surprise. "Oh - yeah that's fine. Probably b-better than a sheet."

He laughed and I found myself smiling - mainly trying to mask my surprise that I even tried cracking a joke. What's happening to me?

"Okay just choose how much you need and then come to the counter and I'll ring it up."

As Aiden began rolling it off the spool he was humming under his breath, smiling at me every so often before he stopped, a huge wad of sticker around his arm. "This should be enough hey? Maybe we should get extra in case it isn't."

"I think that'll be enough…"

"Okay," he tore it at the tear line and gestured for me to walk in front. When we made it to the counter the assistant measured it out before ringing it up. I offered to hold it while he fished out his wallet however he said he was fine.

I sat with it on the way home, looking out the window at the training field as we drove by, watching the girls running laps. One of them looked like Grace and I spotted the lethal looking daughter of the Beta, who watched our car drive by.

Looking ahead I caught Aiden staring at me from the corner of my eye, looking away when he realized I had caught him.

"So, did you have fun with my mom today?"

"She's…"

"Enthusiastic?" He offered.

"Yeah," I said with a laugh, looking back out the window.

"You laughed."

I looked back at him in surprise, I guess I did.

"From the look on your face right now, I'd say it's not something you do a lot." We were reaching the house now and his statement was coming close to becoming a question of why I didn't smile a lot.

He was waiting for an answer though. With a sigh I ran a hand through my hair that felt like it needed a wash. "It isn't."

Once again we were wrapped in silence and I stared out the window as we pulled into the driveway. Feeling a slight flick on my arm I looked over at Aiden to see him grinning. "Well, we're just going to have to change that." With a quick wink he got out of the car and came around to my side, taking the mirror stickers off me. "At least you smile."

I hadn't even known I was doing it, but suddenly I became conscious of the smile on my face.

"I have got to stop telling you when you're doing it," he groaned as the smile fell from my face. "Come on; let's go wallpaper your mirror."

As he tugged me into the house after him, that small smile crept its way back onto my face and I thought maybe, just maybe, it could stay there.

Chapter Eight

"I SENT THEM OFF today, there were only three boxes. Your room was surprisingly easy to pack up," mom laughed down the line but she sounded tense.

"How's everything there?" Really I wasn't interested in the answer, and I knew how it would be. Everything would be running as it always had, my presence wouldn't change anything.

"Very interesting actually, Jonah has been really getting involved since visiting Oregon - I think he was jealous of how competent young Aiden was. How is he going? Kissed yet?"

"Mom!" I groaned down the phone as my cheeks went red.

"What? Come on sweetheart you're my first child with a mate, I want details."

"I start my new school tomorrow," I said quickly, changing the subject. "I'm nervous." She was quiet and I could hear her chopping, obviously starting on dinner. I wondered what I'd be doing right now if I was back there instead of here. Probably hiding in my room.

"You'll be fine," she said finally. *"This time your school experience is - it will be so much better for you darling. In Oregon, you're going to be seen as the future leader of their pack. You're never going to be hurt again. Your mate and his status can protect you in ways I never could."*

"Mom-"

"Sweetheart, I know we don't talk about it. It's against the rules. I'm just saying embrace what you can have there. Don't cling to the past." There was talking in the background and I recognized it was Michael. *"I have to go darling, but make sure you call me tomorrow, I want to hear all about your big day. I love you."*

"I love you too," I whispered.

I placed the phone on my bed, knowing I needed to gather myself to return it to the Luna. I remembered Grace's horror when she heard I didn't have a cell phone. Her phone was a part of her hand, she was never without it.

Looking over at the covered wardrobe door I rested my head on my hands, trying to relax myself after that conversation. I didn't like talking to mom about what happened to me, it made her feel awful and it was easier for me to pretend it didn't happen if we ignored it.

I wasn't too sure on how to move on and not take the past with me, but I think I could try.

"Hey," Aiden poked his head through the door, smiling. "Dinners ready."

"Oh, okay," getting up I picked up the phone with me and shut the light off, walking alongside Aiden.

"How are you feeling about tomorrow?"

"Fine," I said quickly, noticing how my voice went up a few octaves.

He stopped and took my hand, turning me to face him. "No one's going to hassle you, I won't let them." Briefly I panicked, wondering what he knew, but pushed it away knowing he couldn't possibly know anything about my past, I'd said nothing.

Growing nervous and feeling my neck warming up I smiled. "Thank you."

I was surprised when his hand cupped my cheek and I noticed a faded brown birthmark on his extended arm. My eyes quickly flickered back to his as my skin warmed from the contact of his palm.

Just as he opened his mouth to say something, Grace leapt to the top of the landing from the stairs.

"Oh! If I knew I was going to interrupt something I would have been patient. But dinner is getting cold," her eyes sparkled as she stared between Aiden and me and I quickly pulled backward, watching as Aiden's hand fell to his side.

Quickly I walked over to Grace who linked her arm through mine and shot a wink over her shoulder at Aiden before bounding us down the stairs.

"Ah, here we all are. I hope you like lasagna Evelyn." Luna Claudia sat at the other end of the table, smiling over at Alpha James who was looking at Aiden with a knowing expression.

I still felt like there was electricity running through my veins so I just stared at my plate. If I didn't have to make eye contact with anyone then I could try and calm down my bodies reaction to my previous encounter.

"How was your phone call Evelyn? I trust everything in Idaho is well?" Alpha James was pouring himself a glass of Wolfsbane while looking over at me and I had to resist the urge not to jump under the table in fear and shock.

Alpha James was speaking directly to me. I knew I had to answer him, but years of abuse and beatings made me want to keep my mouth shut and stay as far away from the Alpha as possible.

Taking an inaudible breath I looked over at his patient expression before lowering my gaze to the top button of his shirt. "Mom says they're fine. Um - A-Alpha Jonah is, uh, taking more responsibility." My voice shook like a leaf and I went back to trying to eat my dinner, which, due to the knots in my stomach, did not seem like a possibility.

"As he should. That boy is a disgrace to that pack. Aiden has been doing pack duties since his wolf first showed signs of appearance." The Alpha sounded proud of Aiden and the stirring in my chest enlightened me that I was proud as well.

This whole mate thing was bringing out a new side in me; I didn't know him well enough to be proud of him.

"Evelyn I hope when you and mom went shopping you guys got swimsuits."

I looked over to Grace and then at Luna Claudia who had an irritated expression on her face. "I completely forgot to pick one up for her; you girls will have to go sometime during this week. Is the party this Saturday?"

I felt my face lose its color at the thought of the party at the falls that Grace had mentioned earlier this week. I'd never been to a party in my life and the idea of walking around in a swimsuit and trying to fit in was not my idea of fun. Not to mention the fact I didn't swim, heck, I'd never owned a swimsuit before.

"It's okay; we can go after school tomorrow. Lucy needed to pick up a new pair of sneakers anyway oh and get this…" Grace trailed on about something that had happened at school while I watched my appetite disappear completely.

As everyone finished up eating, Grace, after being volunteered by the Luna, started clearing the tables and I found Aiden standing beside my chair with his hand extended. "Let's go for a walk."

I hesitantly put my hand in his and tried to ignore the watching eyes of his family as we slipped from the dining room and into the foyer.

As we walked out the front of the house I looked at how alive the pack was. All the houses were lit up, indicating people were home. Children played in the streets even though it was now after dinner and dark.

Some wolves watered their lawns; others spoke over the fence to their neighbors…the whole place just felt homely.

In Idaho anyone below the age of seventeen wasn't allowed out after seven. I'd been caught out after curfew once before, and I found myself shivering at the memory.

"Are you cold?" Aiden asked as he took in my shiver, already starting to slide his black and white jacket off. Before I could say no he was already putting it over my shoulders before taking my hand again and continuing our walk.

Some people called out to him, and he waved in return, I didn't fail to see the curious stares thrown in my direction.

"Alpha Aiden! Alpha Aiden! Come play street soccer with us!" A young boy who looked between the awkward stages of still being a pup, but almost reaching the stage of his wolf, bounded up to Aiden. He grinned at me. "Hello."

"Oh… h-hi," I murmured.

"I can't today Reece, maybe next time." A chorus of disappointed groans came from the group of boys waiting for their friend to return, who just shrugged.

"Okay." He made to walk off before stopping and turning around. "That's your mate isn't it?"

Aiden nodded and he squeezed my hand as many people stopped what they were doing to watch the exchange. "Her name is Evelyn."

Reece, the smile having never left his face, nodded and turned back to his friends to continue their game. Aiden continued walking and I followed beside him, watching as everyone went back to what they were doing.

"I train his age group on Mondays and Wednesdays. He's really talented."

"He seemed enamored with you," I mumbled.

Aiden let out a quiet laugh. "He follows me everywhere. He's incredibly hard to dodge."

At least he was a good role model. I remember the nasty twelve year olds that used to follow Jonah around, copying every cruel thing he did because they thought that's what they had to do.

I always wondered about the future of Idaho with Jonah in charge.

"You're happy here, right Evelyn?" Aiden asked out of the blue as he slowed our walk until we were stopped in the emptiest part of the street. I wasn't entirely sure what to say, I hadn't been expecting the question.

Was I happy here? I had gone a few days without being beaten up; it was a vast improvement from Idaho. I guess yes, I was happier here than I was in Idaho. I offered a nod before sitting down on the curb, resting my feet on the road beneath me.

"I'm just making sure. I - I don't want you to feel like you were forced to move here. If you want to be back in Idaho then that's okay, we can make all the arrangements and I can wait until you're ready for all this."

I felt fear run rampant through my body of his idea of letting me go back. That was the last thing I wanted. I wanted to stay here. I wanted to be here. The conviction in my own thoughts sent a thrill through me, and I felt tears stinging in my eyes.

"I don't want to go back," I whispered.

Aiden was suddenly in front of me, kneeling down, his eyes searching mine with concern. "You don't have to, I was just suggesting it. You just haven't seemed happy."

"I am," I said quickly. "I-I'm just trying to take a-all this in. My life has changed a lot in the past few days. Thoughts, ideas on h-how my future w-was going to be." I was surprised to find my hand shaking as I pulled the brown tresses out of my face. "I am happy here. Really. I'm getting used to the routine."

His eyes were calculative and I felt I had given too much away by my sudden outburst. Please, oh please don't press on this Aiden.

I wasn't sure if maybe he got my mental message or it was just his own common sense because he smiled, taking my hand in his and helping me up. "So I'm not annoying you or anything then?"

His light hearted question changed the mood completely and a shaky smile graced my face. Annoying me? No. Intimidating? Yes. How I felt around him changed with each encounter and these were feelings I wasn't used to at all.

"No, you're not annoying." Did I annoy him? It felt like a silly question but I was sure I was frustrating. He felt the bond one hundred percent - after all; he's a full blooded wolf. My reaction to this bond would take time and work, did that bother him at all?

"You hesitated," he laughed. "I have it on good authority that I can be a real pain in the ass."

"I assume it was Grace who told you that," I said quietly as I remembered the endless amount of insults I heard her hurl at her brother over the last few days.

"She loves me deep down," he claimed. "She just doesn't like the fact that she's younger than me."

"By two minutes?" A lot of littermates joked about this kind of thing. Generally a female wolf could have up to four babies at a time however many have had just one or two before, but birth order and time were the cause of constant bickering among some siblings.

"No, by a year. Grace wasn't born at the same time as me. I had another brother…he was stillborn though. Kind of rattled my mom for a while, Grace kind of brought her back to life." Aiden smiled, obviously reliving some memories in his head.

"Grace didn't have any littermates?" I asked, wondering if I was asking too much.

"We were surprised when it was just her. Alpha females usually have more than just one. They call her the miracle baby, probably why she thinks she's so great." We continued to walk in silence as I thought over what he had just revealed to me. Deep down I knew it would be easier on their family if they had only one son. Two boys fighting over their dads title? It didn't end well ever.

"What about your siblings? They seemed…" his eyes tightened a little as he searched for the right word.

"Interesting?" I offered.

"I was thinking bratty, but we can go with interesting."

The hand that wasn't in Aiden's tugged at the sleeve of his jacket as I searched for the words to describe my relationship with my half-siblings. "Laurance didn't really talk…he read a lot. Jada and I," I squinted my face, "hm."

"I kind of picked up on that," he commented and as I looked up I noticed we were back at his house. We must have walked a loop. The street was quiet this time, lights were still on but it showed now that everyone was in their houses.

"I know you have things you aren't ready to tell me, Evelyn. I'm not blind. But I'm not going to push you," I held my breath as he pushed a strand of hair from my face and tucked it behind my ear. "I'll always be ready to listen. Don't feel like you can't talk to me."

I found myself nodding and I knew deep down I wasn't going to be able to keep my past from him forever. However I wasn't ready yet and I knew I wouldn't be for a while, I just wanted to ignore it and try and embrace this new life.

My eyes widened when I saw him leaning in and I scared myself when the thought crossed my mind that he was going to kiss me. Did I want him to kiss me? I'd never kissed a guy in my life.

Sure Jonah and Zac had made their sloppy advances but I had never reciprocated and the thought sent my mind into frenzy, only for it to be cut short when his lips met my cheek before he pulled away.

He kissed my cheek.

Relief washed over me like ice cold water.

"Come on, let's go inside."

Following him into the house I couldn't ignore his smile and I felt it replicating itself on my face as my skin tingled where his lips had just been.

It felt right, and at the end of the day that's what truly mattered to me.

Chapter Nine

"WE DON'T WANT YOU here!" Grace snarled as she shoved me into a set of lockers, the impact was familiar but hurt all the same, as it always would. You can't grow immune to pain, just tolerant. She grabbed me by the hair and jerked me up, and suddenly her face morphed into Heather's.

"No one will ever want you, Evelyn!" she spat throwing me sprawling to the floor.

The dream shifted and I was standing in front of a classroom with a mixture of faces from Idaho and Oregon. My hand went to my mouth and I found my teeth wobbling, they all felt out of place and wonky and as I removed my hand a tooth fell out to the floor.

"No one wants you Evelyn!" A voice shouted, but none of their mouths moved.

I felt a tingling in my palms and I watched as they lit up and glowed gold, before a liquid like substance shot out and the room went completely white, a blinding flash. It disappeared as instantly as it came and the figures that had been sitting alive were all dead.

I screamed in horror at Aiden's corpse before a woman with long gray hair entered the room.

"Evelyn," she said calmly as she outstretched her arms. "Evelyn!"

"Evelyn, come on wake up!" A high pitched voice called out into my ear. I jumped up harshly as I was torn from the dream and I saw Grace standing over me, dressed and ready for the day. "You sleep like a log. Come on, you're going to be late and judging by the sweat you've been sleeping in, looks like you'll want a shower."

She pranced out of the room and I fell backward into the pillow as my heart still raced from the horrific dream. I immediately felt to make sure all my teeth were there before staring in wonder at my hands.

It made no sense.

As if I wasn't already feeling anxious enough, today was my first day at school. The thought sent a heavy feeling in my stomach as I grudgingly picked up the outfit I had laid out the night before and headed for the bathroom.

I showered quickly, as always. Not to mention I didn't want to make everyone late.

Luna Claudia hadn't bought me anything baggy like I had at home. Everything fit perfectly and as I slid on the black skinny jeans I briefly considered checking myself out in the mirror. Quickly I pulled on the peach colored top and pulled my hair up into a pony tail before leaving the bathroom in search of my shoes and jacket.

Colliding with Aiden I stumbled backward, only to have him steady me. Tingles shot up and down my arm from the contact. "Whoa, you okay?"

"Yeah," I rubbed my forehead. "I think I'm running late."

"You're fine; Grace can walk if she wants to leave earlier." As I took him in, noting the pair of faded jeans he wore and his well-fit black shirt I realized I was gawking like an idiot and quickly looked away.

"I - I was just getting my jacket," my voice seemed a bit too high pitched and I knew he could hear my heart beating that little bit faster.

He grinned at me, "I'll meet you downstairs."

"O-okay," I said weakly as he turned and left and I found myself staring after him. Shaking out of it I quickly went into my room and scooped up my jacket and bag, sliding on my flats and following in the direction Aiden had walked, hearing noise from the kitchen.

"Ooh, Evelyn those jeans look great on you!" Grace exclaimed as she handed me a plate of toast. I ran my hands over the jeans, feeling nervous. "Seriously, they look awesome!"

"T-thanks," I murmured, eyeing the toast with a lack of appetite. I had to try and eat something though.

"We'll go to the office and get your schedule first. I hope we have some classes together!"

I frowned in confusion. "Aren't you a year below?"

"I skipped a year," she said with a laugh. "I'm not just a pretty face."

"You kids better get a move on," the Luna walked in sipping her morning coffee. "Here Evelyn," she handed me a twenty and I looked at her in surprise. "Lunch money for the week."

"Oh I don't-"

"Evelyn you have to eat," Grace reminded me. "Come on, Aiden was getting the truck ready. Let's go." Taking the plate from me she took my arm and led me from the house as I hesitantly pocketed the money.

Grace slid in first, elbowing Aiden roughly and I saw the dirty look he shot her before beaming over at me as I closed the door behind us.

"Did you have a car back home Evelyn?" Grace asked as we pulled into the street.

"Oh, uh, nope." I left out the detail that I couldn't *actually* drive, Michael wouldn't let me learn.

Jonah also forbade me but I wasn't going to tell them that.

"Aiden took out the front of the garage at Trey's house when he first started," Grace recalled. "Then again neither of those two knew how to drive then. You'll meet Trey today. He's a total shit, you'll hate him."

"Grace." Aiden had a frown on his face and she rolled her eyes.

"It's not my fault he's disgusting."

"You know, no one is sure exactly why the two of you started hating on each other, but it's seriously got to stop."

I felt out of the conversation so I let them talk, happy to just stare out the window and watch as people began their day. We left the compound with a couple of other cars and started driving toward the main part of town and as we drew closer to the school I could feel my heart rate picking up.

With dread, we pulled into the school and already noticing the swarm of students had me sinking further into my seat. Regrettably, Grace was on my other side and practically pushed me out of the car.

As I slung my bag on my back Aiden came around and took my hand and I felt a little more relaxed. I felt like with him here I could get through the day.

Leaving the parking lot I followed the two of them to a large tree in front of the school where two other guys and two girls sat, one I noticed to be the blonde knock out from the day before, Lucy. The other girl however was her opposite. Still blonde she was quite thin, her shape resembled mine actually. Long arms and long legs, looked like a strong wind could blow her over. Her blonde hair was dead straight and her blue eyes flickered in interest when we approached.

Taking my attention off her as we stopped at the group I spotted the tall boy beside her who wore a blank expression immediately started sizing me up. Not in a perverted way like I had been in Idaho, but in a way he'd been told about me and wanted to see if everything was true.

His gray eyes went up and down, searching for something, for what I have no idea but it made me nervous. His black hair curled a little on his head and I noted a white scar that ran over his nose. The only way that scar could be on his skin was if he had been cut with a silver blade. I suddenly remembered he was the Beta's son.

The other boy had skin the color of milk chocolate. His hazel brown eyes glinted with mischief and his buzz cut black hair resembled Aiden's in style. He was built with muscle; he looked like he could snap me with one hand.

"Well, this is little Evie," he said with a grin. "Lucy you weren't lying, she's tiny." I jumped in shock when I heard Aiden growl and I watched as his friend put up his hands in surrender. "I'm just being friendly Aiden. Please don't turn into Josh and think everyone is hitting on his mate."

"Shut up Trey."

Trey laughed and extended his hand to me. "I'm Trey; it's nice to finally meet our future Luna." He pointed at the Beta's son. "That's Josh and his mate Hannah." Hannah waved at me with a small smile, closing the book on her lap.

"You've already met me." Lucy was in front of me in a nanosecond, pulling me in for a hug. "Pumped for your first day?"

I found myself tightening my hold on Aiden's hand as I nodded at her.

"I was actually about to take her to get her schedule and stuff, you girls coming?" Grace asked Lucy and Hannah as she all but pulled me from Aiden. Both girls got up immediately and I watched as Hannah whispered something to Josh before coming with us.

I was nervous now. I was with a bunch of girls, in a new place. Was this the part where everything would come falling down around me and they revealed their true intentions? Was I about to get a toilet swirl to welcome me to the school?

"Your outfit looks great Evelyn - oh speaking of, we have to go shopping this afternoon to get some new bikinis for the party this weekend."

"Yes! I saw this gorgeous white one the other day but I didn't get it. It really made my boobs look great-"

The door to the office flung open in front of us and three girls came out, the one in the middle looking painfully familiar. Her shiny black hair was flowing down her back and her eyes went cold as they landed on me.

"Oh I'm sorry," she smiled angelically. "I didn't see you guys."

"Real cute Katie," Lucy said with a smirk.

Katherine's lips thinned as she glowered at Lucy. "Don't call me Katie, *Lucinda*. My rank is higher than yours."

"Mmm, I love it when you get mad." Lucy shot her a wink and Grace snorted a little. I watched the exchange in surprise before her cat like eyes zoned in on me, once again.

"So, this is the little mate the Moon Goddess chose for our future Alpha. I have to say I'm shocked, and I'm not the only one. You have no wolf right?" A face I had once thought beautiful was now twisted in an ugly smile. I didn't know how to respond to her, it felt like Heather was standing in front of me. "Didn't mommy ever tell you it's rude not to answer a question?"

I felt my ears grow hot as embarrassment flooded me, but I was still unable to open my mouth, my tongue paralyzed.

"Hey Katherine, how many bitch pills have you taken this morning?" Grace asked.

"Oh come on Grace, she doesn't need a guard dog. She's the future Luna; she can stick up for herself."

"You should remember who you're talking to *Katie*," Grace hissed. "I'm your Alpha by birth. Leave Evie alone or I won't hesitate to tear a strip from you."

The area around us grew quiet and I noticed some humans watching in confusion. Katherine looked genuinely startled as she tried to play it off with a roll of her eyes and a click of her fingers to her friends as the sauntered off.

"Don't worry about Katherine, Evelyn, she's a real piece of work, no one actually likes her." Lucy took my arm and led me up into the front office toward the reception desk, tapping the bell rapidly as the lady wasn't there.

A plump red haired woman came out from the other room with a scowl on her face, snatching the bell from under Lucy's hand. "Yes?" She snapped.

"Good morning Mrs Chapel, we need Evelyn's timetable. She's starting today."

Mrs Chapel looked over her glasses at me before going through some papers on her desk, handing me a planner, my schedule and list of the school rules.

"Welcome to Baker City High," she grumbled. "Have a nice first day."

"Thanks," I said quietly, taking the items from her and glancing down at the timetable.

"Ooh, we have gym together, that's good. All of us are in that class it's so fun." Lucy pulled out her highlighter and began lighting up the classes we had together which was English, Math and Gym. Grace circled our class which was only Spanish; apparently Aiden was in that class as well. Hannah had Art with me as well as Chemistry and English.

"So there's always one of us in your class that's good!" Hannah said with a smile as we left the room. Her voice was gentle; she was calming, a lot calmer than the other two girls. Part of me felt better that I wasn't alone.

I didn't want to face Katherine alone.

Lucy noted with delight she had Math with me first and as we went outside back to the boys we spotted Katherine and her friends standing with them. My mouth felt dry as we approached, Grace muttering a numerous amount of death threats under her breath.

"We're back," Grace announced as she pushed past Katherine who glowered at her. "Sorry, I didn't see you," she mimicked Katherine's earlier words.

"Can I see your timetable?" Aiden asked me. Nodding I gave it to him and he frowned. "We only have Spanish and Gym." I felt myself feeling disappointed at the thought, and I had to make sure that it didn't show on my face.

"Aw, that's okay Aiden. *We* have every other class together." I watched as Katherine placed her beautifully manicured hand on Aiden's arm - the one with the birth mark and I was surprised to feel a bubble of jealousy rise in my body.

Aiden stepped back and her hand fell to her side and I watched as she narrowed her eyes on me before fixing a sweet smile on her face as she sat next to Trey. "How are you Trey-Bey?"

"Breaking hearts and keeping it real hot stuff." He winked at her and I watched as Grace shoved a finger down her throat behind them and cross her eyes together.

Hannah let out a giggle and all eyes turned to face her and she hurriedly looked back at her book.

The sound of the school bell rung through the yard and Lucy strutted over to me, smiling. "Come on Evie, we're going to do some Mathematics."

I hated Math; I was never good with numbers. Plus the teacher at my old school had been a wolf and she took great pleasure in singling me out and lording herself over me if I was incorrect. One time she had me stand in the corner of the room, facing the wall for a term.

I felt Aiden take my hand and Lucy let go of me with a huff, waiting. Facing Aiden I noticed a dusting of sun spots across his nose before my eyes connected with his. "I'll see you at lunch."

"Okay," I said quietly.

Like a repeat of last night he kissed my cheek and I was left to handle the tingles on that spot and a thudding heart as Lucy tugged us away in the direction of the large building.

"You know, my mate's in this class," she began in excitement. "He's so friendly. I'll point him out once we get in."

I was surprised; no one had mentioned Lucy having a mate.

As we walked through the corridors, Lucy promised to help me find my locker after the first session. Clearly she was eager to see her mate and I didn't hold that against her, I could wait to find my locker.

Finally we walked into a room which was half full and she took me to the middle of the class, sitting us down at the bench like table. It almost looked like a Physics room. There was a large board up the front and students mulled around at other desk, laughing and talking or throwing curious glances in our direction.

An ordinary classroom.

With wolves.

The wolves looked at me with much more interest than the humans did, but didn't approach. I wasn't sure if they were under some order not to but I was glad they didn't. Today was overwhelming enough as it was.

"So who's your mate?" I asked her as she pulled out her book.

"You'll see." She winked at me and fished out her phone, rapidly texting away.

"Everyone, please take your seats." I watched as the teacher walked in, definitely in his early twenties. His black hair was slicked back neatly and he was dressed in a faded white dress shirt and black slacks. He looked like a teacher to me, but as I watched Lucy stare at him and then watch his eyes flicker to her in and glaze over in that warm way mates do, my heart stopped.

He was her mate?

"I'm assuming you've worked it out," she whispered to me as she adjusted her cleavage in her shirt.

"Y-yeah. How old is he?"

"He's not that old Evie. He's twenty-two."

My cheeks flushed. "Sorry I didn't mean-"

"Its fine," she chuckled. "A lot of people are surprised when they first find out."

"Here's your copy of the book we're following Miss Wright." I jumped in shock as Lucy's mate placed the purple colored math book on my table. "Please pay attention girls." He walked back up to the front of the class and I stared down at the glossy purple book with a scowl before back up to the board.

Mr Collins was scribbled up on the top right hand corner of the board and I watched as Lucy straightened immediately, always putting her hand up when he asked a question. To humans she would have looked like the desperate blonde mooning over the hot teacher.

To the wolves it would have been two mates trying to interact, as under the radar as possible.

How did they manage to keep it a secret?

As the class finished up Lucy sighed sadly. "That's it now until the end of the day. It kind of sucks really. Can't wait until I graduate, I'm so over trying to keep this private all the time."

"So, when he turned eighteen you were-"

"Way too young for a mate," she laughed. "He never said anything. He went off to college and when he came back I was old enough and he told me. He's perfection really. I mean sure, he does annoying stuff like teach the worst subject ever, but he's still perfect."

"That's nice," I murmured. She was really happy, it showed. It showed on every wolf really. Mates were the best thing to happen to them, I found myself wondering if I would ever feel the bond the way they all did.

We found my locker and I put the math book inside it along with the five other blank text books and spare stationary before Hannah met us with a smile.

"We have art together," she reminded me. As Lucy went off to her next class I walked alongside Hannah who watched everyone either on their way to their class or taking the brief few minutes between classes to talk. "Are you enjoying your first day?"

"It's a little overwhelming but…it's okay."

"Sorry about this morning with Katherine. She's a real nightmare." She let out a sigh, "and I'm going to be stuck with her forever. I'm praying to the Moon Goddess she finds her mate outside this pack."

"Why will you be stuck with her?" I asked curiously

"My mate Joshua - he's her brother. She's frequently aired how she doesn't think I'm right for him…my family are really low in rank. He's a Beta so it was a bit of a shock for everyone when we found out we were mated…Lucy and Grace have been in my classes my whole life, but we've only started talking this year because of…well the mating."

Her voice seemed sad and I felt bad for her. It made me think as well. Had I not been mated to Aiden they wouldn't have spoken to me either. Well, I wouldn't even be here really.

"I find the mate bond strange," I admitted as we entered the art class. "People can go their whole lives without noticing each other and then suddenly they're joined at the hip."

"You don't feel the entire bond like Aiden does do you?" We both sat down at easels beside each other and I bit my lip as I thought about how to answer her.

"Only when he touches me, although the past few days I guess I've felt it more." She was so easy to talk to; it worried me at how easily I could divulge information to her. I looked her over, taking in her small frame, her blunted nails and her perfectly flat teeth I realized it. She had wolf-like qualities but her teeth…

"You aren't a full wolf," I said flatly

"No," she laughed. "I'm a witch. Well technically I'm part witch part wolf. More witch than wolf. I can still shift though. My mom's a witch. Dad was a fighter in the pack. He died two years ago…ever since, our family was kind of just forgotten…well until Joshua found me."

"I'm sorry," I murmured.

"I'm sorry I had to use some magic on you to get you talking."

I made a face, not sure if I was comfortable being around someone who could do that. I had too many secrets for that to happen.

"I won't do it again, promise." Her expression was sheepish as she started rifling through her bag.

"Okay everybody. We have a new student today." Please no, I moaned internally. "Her name is Evelyn Wright, she just moved here from Idaho. Evelyn, would you like to stand up and say a few words about yourself?"

Not really, I thought as I stared at the tanned woman, her sandy blonde hair littered with grays. Her green eyes were warm and I knew she wasn't doing this to me to be cruel.

Shuffling from my seat I knocked my easel and the drawing pencils over and they fell with a clutter. A few people sniggered and I felt my palms began to sweat as my heart rate increased, feeling like the sound could be heard throughout the room.

The few wolves in this class would be able to hear it.

As Hannah hurriedly gathered my pencils I held my sweating hands together. "I'm Evelyn," I started before realizing I didn't really know what to say. There wasn't anything great to know about me. I practically stood their gaping like a fish before I just sat down, hiding behind the easel.

"Thank you Evelyn," the teacher said kindly. "I am Mrs Fitz; if you have any questions see me after class." I could see from the corner of my eye Hannah staring at me with sympathy and all I wanted to do was have the ground open up and swallow me. "Today we're watching a movie, not much else planned I'm afraid so everyone get in a position where you can see. Good okay."

Throughout the movie I watched as Hannah read her book, I'm sure it was more interesting than watching *The History of Art*. By the end of it, I'm fairly sure everyone had forgotten about me and my lame 'about me' speech.

I was glad I could be forgettable.

The final class for the morning was English with Lucy and Hannah and no surprises they were reading 'To Kill a Mockingbird'. Thankfully Hannah wasn't questioning me anymore and was instead reading the prescribed book while Lucy texted under her desk.

I found myself pondering over the fact that nearly a week ago I was in my English class, sitting alone, reading this same chapter, and now I was here on the same chapter but in an entirely different situation.

I had gotten through the entire morning without being thrown into a locker or trapped in the janitor's closet. My head hadn't been shoved down a toilet and I'd had actual conversations with people my age.

Sure I knew I was going to have problems with Katherine, it didn't take a genius to figure out she had it in for me, but even with her blatant disregard this morning, I now knew for sure it was going to be different here.

The possibility of enjoying my life here grew as hope blossomed in my chest. If anything today was a confirmation for me, to embrace it. I knew it was going to be difficult. I've had years of mental and physical abuse I had to work through, but I knew it could be done.

Don't live in the past, were my mother's words.

I was going to try my hardest not to.

Chapter Ten

"How's your first day going?" It was finally lunch and Grace was waiting for an answer as she stared down at her dismal lunch. Cafeteria food was disgusting; I decided I'd try and pack lunch like I did when I was at home.

"Not too bad," I murmured as I swirled around the meaty substance on my plate, wondering how I could get out of eating it.

Grace jumped in fright when Trey bounced down beside her. She looked at him in annoyance and growled, "You know Trey, you don't always have to behave like an animal!"

"We are in a mood today aren't we? I hope her attitude doesn't rub off on you Evelyn." Trey winked at me and I heard a thump under the table as a look of pain flickered across his face, Grace smiling smugly at him.

Lucy and Hannah joined the table together laughing about something they had just witnessed in line before I felt Aiden's presence beside me as he dropped his tray piled with food next to me. As he slid into the chair next to me I looked up at him and he smiled. "Hey."

"H-hey," I whispered as my stomach did somersaults.

"How are you?"

"I'm okay…how are-"

"Hey Aiden which patrol are you on tonight? Your dad put me on for after training." Josh sat down beside Hannah, his tray also piled high with food. How could they eat this stuff?

Aiden sighed next to me and I looked up and he was glowering at Josh, but they looked as if they were having a conversation, especially when Josh's eyes flickered to me and then back to Aiden. While everyone kept talking around them I made eye contact with Hannah who was looking at me funny.

Immediately she turned her head and began talking to Lucy about shopping this afternoon.

"Ooh! Yes!" Grace chirped. "I'm so excited for this weekend. This will be the last party before the good weather leaves."

Part of me hoped it would start raining and it would have to be cancelled.

"I was talking to dad," Aiden said next to me and I turned to look at him. "He thinks you could join the human side of pack training. You still have werewolf speed after all, so he thinks it would be good to enhance those abilities."

"Oh," I said in surprise. I hadn't been allowed near the training grounds in Idaho, let alone allowed to partake in it. I wasn't too sure…they'd all been training since they were eleven; I'd barely done anything that consisted of exercise unless it was running from Jonah and anyone else trying to hurt me.

"Yeah he thinks it will be good, you'll meet more of the pack members and stuff. We do a lot - we uh, we do fighting technique, muscle and endurance building…stuff like that." Aiden sounded nervous, like he was trying to sell it to me.

It was then I realized I wasn't being given a direct order.

I was being given an option.

This pack amazed me beyond belief.

"I love training, you'll be great Evelyn. You should come with us, most of the time it's separated, the boys train in the other room, but sometimes they mix it up for a more realist approach, especially for the fighting technique and all that kind of stuff." Hannah smiled encouragingly at me.

"Hannah loves it because she just jinxes people all the time," Grace muttered, clearly remembering something nasty.

"You use whatever is at your disposal," Hannah defended.

The bell rang to signal the end of lunch and I noted that Aiden's tray was empty; mine however was still a mushed pile of goo. As everyone got up to empty their trays Aiden took a gentle hold of my arm, stopping me.

"You don't have to if you don't want to, it's just an idea. Dad - he wants you to feel included, but he likes to know everyone in the pack can defend themselves. It's not an order…but he doesn't want you to say no."

"I don't think I'd be able to keep up," I bit my lip with a sigh. "You've all been training for years."

He nodded and took my tray and I followed him over to the bins. "It's okay; I can teach you as well outside of training time. You'll be up there with everyone else before you know it. Think about it."

"Okay," I murmured as I toyed with a loose strand of hair.

"Good," he breathed out, sounding relieved. "What do you have now?"

"Chemistry…I have it with Hannah…" looking around the near empty cafeteria I noticed she was missing.

He smiled and took my hand and said, "I'll take you."

As my hand lit up with tingles and ran all the way up my arm Aiden led me out of the cafeteria, and I spotted a pair of angry green eyes death staring me as we walked past her, her black hair held back so tightly in her ponytail it looked like the roots of her hair were being pulled out.

At that moment I did something I had never done in my life. I smiled in her direction, smugly.

∞

"I think you'd look really *hot* in a bright red two piece Evie," Lucy declared as she held up a stringy little piece of material that would hardly cover anything. It was more her style than mine, as I glanced at the amount of bikinis she had draped over her arm.

"No way, this one's way better. It's sheer down the sides here." Grace's looked almost as bad and I was beyond this trip.

As the two argued about bikinis I let myself drift into the background and toward the other racks where Hannah stood, leafing through one-piece suits.

"Having fun?" She asked me with a half-smile as she looked at the price of a suit, widening her eyes and slowly putting it back. I crinkled my nose and she laughed. "Try this, I promise it's not overly revealing."

She handed me a plain black one piece and I looked straight away at the side where my hips would sit, happy to find the material would cover that awful scar on my upper hip. Disappearing into the change room I tried it on, knowing I'd have to look in the mirror to make sure my scars were covered.

That's why the bikinis wouldn't work; I had too many marks on my skin for it.

As I grudgingly looked in the mirror I noted the skinniness of my legs, my knees looked knobbly. My arms looked like a young child could snap them and you could slightly see the bones in my chest. Why did Aiden want to be with this?

Due to my size you could almost say my head wasn't the right size to fit my small body. My hair, long and brown sat in permanent waves, the only thing about myself that I could enjoy looking at. The bathing suit was the best of the day and to be honest, I was tired of having to look at myself all afternoon.

"How is it?" Hannah asked from outside.

After making sure no marks or scars were visible I said, "It's fine. I'll get it." I cringed at the wobble in my tone as tears peeked at the corners of my eyes. Hurriedly I changed back into my clothes and gathered myself before stepping outside the curtain.

All the girls were waiting for me, all sharing the same look. However they said nothing and I plastered my best smile on my face hoping it didn't look as fake as it felt.

"You didn't show us what it looked like," Grace pouted.

"I'm sure it looked great." Hannah smiled at me before looking at the other girls. "Are we all done? Lucy seems to have enough swimwear to last her the remainder of her life."

"It's all on sale. This stuff will get me through like three summers."

"Yet next summer you'll be buying more and saying the same thing," Grace laughed. "I think we're finished, we have to get back anyway. We can't be late for training."

All our shopping was loaded up into Lucy's bright red Jeep - I was beginning to find she had a particular color theme - and we drove back to the pack compound. Nerves were starting to eat away at me at the thought of joining the training today.

Everyone would be faster and stronger. I wasn't going to be able to keep up at all and I knew I was going to embarrass myself somehow. Would anyone else even want me there? A half-blood slowing them down?

"Today we're doing cardio, I think that's it. We did weights yesterday didn't we?" Lucy looked at Grace for an answer.

"I don't even know to be honest; she keeps mixing it up lately."

"Today is cardio," Hannah informed them.

Well my stamina was alright, I guess. It was nothing to brag about, but when you've spent the majority of your life running away from people you gain some staying power.

We pulled into Grace's driveway and I spotted Aiden on the front lawn with Trey and Josh all dressed in workout gear. My breath caught in my throat as I took in Aiden in his black gym shorts and gray tank top. His strong, sculpted looking arms were on full display and I spotted that birthmark I had seen a few days ago.

"Evelyn, are you staying in the car or coming with us?"

Looking over at Lucy I realized Grace and Hannah had already got out and were collecting the bags. Glancing back at Lucy she was giving me a knowing grin and I quickly looked away, getting out of the car, near stumbling into Aiden who had made his way over.

"Hey, have fun?" He asked as he folded his arms across his chest. I watched as they seemed to get bigger from that action and I had to move my eyes to his to try and keep my head clear.

"Yeah, we got some suits," I mumbled as I felt my ears growing hot. Why was I blushing?

"Cool," he said with a smile. "So, are you coming to training?"

I chewed the inside of my mouth, deliberating. If I went I could probably stare at him more, plus he'd be happy that I came right? Suddenly it occurred to me that I was starting to feel more of the bond. It was strange. I got feelings that I wanted to make him happy, to see him smile. It was also getting more difficult to not look at him.

Making up my mind I said, "Yeah…yeah I'll come."

"Great!" He beamed. "I'll wait here for you to get changed, we can go together then."

His enthusiasm was nearly contagious as I quickly nodded at him and hurriedly walked inside, nodding nervously at Trey and Josh when they said greeted me. I met Lucy and Hannah halfway down the stairs and they told me to meet them outside.

I walked past Grace's room and heard her changing so I quickly went to mine, trying to find the exercise clothes the Luna had bought me. Grace had packed my wardrobe away, not me, so when I finally found the black knee length pants and a white tank top I was relieved.

I added a black jacket to hide the skinniness of my arms and slipped into some black joggers before wandering back downstairs, seeing the tail end of Grace's ponytail as she stepped outside.

Closing the front door behind me I heard a wolf whistle and I spun around to see Lucy next to me. "Evie, you look great in work out gear."

Once again my face was hot and I sighed internally.

As everyone got up from where they had been lounging on the grass I noticed Hannah looked upset. What had happened while I'd been upstairs? As Aiden came over to walk next to me I was shaken from my thoughts.

"I'm glad you're doing this. Dad will be too, it will give him some peace of mind." I wasn't entirely sure why it was so important to the Alpha that I join training - I'd be the last person in the pack that would be asked to fight when push came to shove, however, if he wanted me to learn I would.

You don't disobey your Alpha even if it isn't a direct order.

"I'm a little nervous," I admitted as I eyed his hand that was hanging by his side as we walked. Usually he grabbed mine by now, why wasn't he?

"You'll be fine. Training is great, for social aspects and physical." Still no hand holding. Just as I summed up the courage to maybe try and hold it myself, he started to say something. "Hey Evelyn, I've been meaning to ask you...d-did you maybe want to go-"

"Hello!" A voice chirped in between us and I was roughly pushed away from Aiden's side, tripping over the curb and falling into the road between two parked cars. I grunted as I smacked my knee on the bumper and grimaced at the sting in my hands from making contact with the pavement.

"Evelyn!"

"Oh I'm so sorry! I forget you aren't as strong as we are." Katherine stared down at me, her long black hair in a high pony tail and her workout gear looked basically like underwear. Did her shorts have to be *that* short?

Aiden was in front of me, lifting me up by my shoulders and setting me on my feet. I winced at the dull pain in my knee and dusted my hands off on my pants.

"You need to be more careful Katherine," Aiden snapped as he looked at my knee.

"I'm so sorry." The way her eyes narrowed marginally indicated that she wasn't, but I wasn't going to play this game. No.

"I'm fine," I murmured as I braced my hands on Aiden's shoulder while he inspected my knee. He felt nice beneath my hands.

"It's just so weird; you went down like a human!"

"Well she is part human *Katie*," Grace snapped. "Are you stupid?"

"Grace," Aiden sighed as he got up. He took my hands in his and inspected my palms for any cuts or abrasions. Maybe I should fall over more often. "Does it hurt?" He asked as he crinkled his forehead at the grazes on my hands.

I nodded and sighed. "They won't heal as quickly as you guys will. Probably by tonight it will be like it never happened, not in a few minutes though."

"Do you still want to go to training? I completely understand if you're not up for it now." Aiden really looked genuinely concerned, heck I had only tripped. I'd had worse falls. I spotted Katherine over Aiden's shoulder who looked genuinely interested in whether or not I'd be at training.

Did I go and risk her trying to hurt me? I knew what she was doing. Fear that I hadn't felt since leaving the Idaho pack was starting to creep in. She had been here longer than me; she could turn everyone on me.

Grace was nodding frantically at me and Lucy was staring at Katherine with coldness like no other.

Looking back at Aiden I tried to smile and nod. "I'll be fine, I can still train."

Aiden looked pleased and then did something that shut everyone up. I watched in curiosity as he picked up one of my injured hands, bringing it toward his lips and kissing it, which sent bolts of electricity through my body, before he did the same to the other. "Does that help a bit?"

I wasn't sure of my ability to form a sentence so I just mutely nodded, my eyes felt wide and I knew I had to get a hold of my expression. I probably looked stunned.

Katherine did. In fact she looked as if she had just smelt something really sour - or she was plotting another way to injure me.

It made me feel better.

Rather than hold my hand, seeing as he was minding the abrasions he slipped his arm around my shoulders instead. This was new, I liked it better than hand holding I found. Everyone started walking again and Katherine walked behind, tapping on her phone.

She didn't get what she wanted clearly…but her little stunt got me a bit more contact with Aiden. Never thought I'd say this, but thank you Katherine.

∞

"Alright! Line up!" The terrifying woman who was obviously our trainer had her blonde hair bunned tightly, she already had a sheen of sweat covering her forehead and she looked like she was made of steel, but still somehow managed to come off feminine.

Scrambling to get in line I was between Hannah and Lucy who stared straight ahead at the wall in front of us. I was glad we weren't facing the mirror wall. Aiden could have warned me. Looking slightly to the left at the other room I noticed the boys already going through their paces.

"I want four laps of the room, don't stop until I say stop! When I say stop I want as many pushups you can do before I say up and you keep running." She tucked a strand of hair behind her ear before continuing. "Listen to me for your cues. Anyone holding up the line will come out here and do fifty burpees, am I clear?"

"Yes Sharon!" The room chorused loudly, so loudly I near jumped out of my skin as I looked at all these well-built females in wonder.

"Well go!" She shouted violently.

As the line began moving my nerves started to fall away as I realized I had to concentrate to keep up. The last thing I wanted was to be singled out and do burpees. What were those anyway? Did you have to belch in the middle of the class while everyone watched?

"High knees!" Sharon shouted as she ran on the spot.

The class all stopped and I skidded to avoid running into Hannah who was moving her knees up and down so fast I'm surprised she didn't knee herself in the face. I followed suit, already feeling myself growing tired.

"Let's go!" The trainer shouted, circling her hand in the air, signaling us to keep running the room. We got through half a lap before we were told to drop and push. All the girls were doing it on their hands and feet. I could barely do one. Suddenly Sharon was next to me. "Just rest on your feet and knees, you'll get the upper body strength eventually."

Copying her pose I began doing the pushups, glad I could at least do something. I was also glad she didn't shout at me.

"Up! Up! Up!" She yelled.

Everyone scrambled to their feet immediately and began running. My throat and mouth felt dry. I wanted to stop. We finally finished the nightmare event and I was relieved to see some of the girls looked tired as well.

"That was a good warm up girls, grab a drink and meet back here in four minutes. Stacey, Zoe help me set up the rowing machines." As the girls walked off to their bags I sidled over to Grace who grinned at me, her face red.

She chucked me bottled water from her bag and I had never been happier to see anything in my life. "Thank you!"

"No worries Evie, how you feeling?"

"Dead."

She laughed and quickly put her water down, taking mine. "Wait until you start rowing, she makes us race!" Four minutes seemed to fly by and we were being called back way too soon for my liking. I personally didn't want to leave the safety of the rest period but clearly this was a fast paced session and I didn't want to be left behind.

As Sharon went through her iPod to find the track she wanted I watched as Katherine who was positioned at the front of the class - and closest to the adjoining window to Aiden's class - looking in, directly at him. He was lifting god knows how many pounds while the trainer shouted in his face.

Gutsy man.

"Alright let's do this!"

∞

My entire body was aching. I felt like someone had attached weights to each limb and were waiting for me to collapse in a heap on the floor.

"Good job today Evelyn." I blinked my eyes open in surprise as Sharon was in front of me, her hair sticking to her forehead. "You kept up well."

"You did really great Evelyn," Hannah exclaimed as she put her towel in her bag. "I'm surprised you didn't fall to the floor."

"So am I." Really I was surprised; I'd never worked out a day in my life before this.

"I may have given you a bit more energy," she whispered in my ear with a grin.

I felt hysterical laughter bubble up in my throat as I shook my head, "I knew I wasn't that fit."

"Yeah well, don't get used to it. I only helped you today because I didn't want Katherine to think she was better than you. If you piked out she would have loved it."

"She hates me right?"

Hannah made a face looking sour. "Katherine doesn't get along with a lot of people. But yes, you are a huge problem in all her grand plans."

"Grand plans?" I asked with a frown as I watched Aiden coming over to us, with no shirt. It was very hard to concentrate on Hannah now.

"She wanted to mate with Aiden. Badly. She always thought it would happen, for some crazy reason. I don't think she understands that the Moon Goddess decides not her," she scoffed.

Aiden reached us by this point, coated in sweat and I took in the expanse of his sweaty chest, the dusting of freckles across it and the way he basically just looked like someone carved him out of stone.

Don't be caught staring!

"You look like you've been to hell and back!" Hannah laughed. "How did Josh go? He said he wasn't looking forward to Yale coaching today."

"Because he doesn't like Delta's yelling in his face." He smirked and dank some water. "He is so rank occupied."

"I better go and find him." Hannah shook her head, rolling her eyes. "See you later Evelyn."

"Bye," I called out after her, before I was alone with Aiden who was using his shirt as a sweat towel.

"Let's go home," he groaned. "I need a shower." I agreed wholeheartedly and followed him from the room, happy to be outside in the cool air. "How was training? Sharon's great, one of our best female fighters."

"It was good…Hannah was working some magic on me though, I think she kept me going from the halfway mark."

He laughed and slung his shirt over his shoulder, "Hannah and her magic. Have you seen what she can do with it? It's actually pretty cool. Especially what she does with fire. I think it would be so cool to be able to do magic."

"She hasn't shown me anything yet, I'm sure she will. I know she likes using it on me though." I folded my arms and continued walking with him, enjoying how things flowed when it was just us, no one else watching.

"What about this, if you could have one kind of super-power what could it be?" He asked with an eager expression.

The question kind of threw me to be honest. I had thought about it - it was a normal thought to have really, but I could never decide. I bit my lip with a thoughtful frown. "It's a toss-up between being able to fly or turn invisible."

If I flew no one could catch me, if I was invisible…no one could see me.

"Interesting," he rubbed his chin all wise-like and I sniggered. "I'd want to control the elements. Rain, wind, earth and fire. Let me play with it, it'd be amazing."

"Yeah?" I asked with curiosity. "I don't know, I pegged you as a 'be able to read minds' kind of guy."

He grinned at me, taking my hand. "That would be advantageous when it came to you. But, you're the only person whose thoughts I'd want to read." We slowed to stop and he brought my hand to his bare chest. His skin felt cool now from the wind, but it was still a little warm from his workout.

I didn't know what to say, I felt like there was a lump in my throat. I looked down at the ground, toying with a loose strand of hair as I grazed the toe of my shoe over some gravel before looking up at him.

"Maybe I don't want you to read my mind."

"I'd still like to. I know there's a lot going on up there, you get lost so quickly." I know he wanted some answers, some insight into why I was the way I was. He deserved some truth, not all of it, but something. I knew that. I sighed and looked down only to have him tilt my chin back up. "I wish you wouldn't always look away."

"It's habit," I breathed out.

"Strange habit for a Beta wolf, to feel as if she can't look at her Alpha's."

He was encroaching on dangerous territory now, this conversation had to stop. I needed to get it going somewhere else.

My thoughts went back to Katherine interrupting us earlier; he had wanted to ask me something.

"What did you want to ask me earlier? Before I fell?"

It was his turn to look uncomfortable. "Oh uh…yeah." He let go of my hand and I was somewhat relieved to have a bit of distance between us. "I was going to ask," he took a deep breath like he was willing himself to hold it together and did that nervous thing he did, when he rubbed the back of his neck. "I wanted to ask, if maybe you wanted to go out this Friday night. On a date."

A date?

With Aiden?

I was being asked on a date by my mate. If you had told me two weeks ago my mate would be asking me out on a date - well I would have hid in my room and just added you to the list of tormenting people in my life.

This was happening though; this was real *right now* in front of me.

It's a strange feeling, happiness. I didn't experience it too often so when it bubbled its way up my body I was surprised, giddy even as a beaming smile graced my face. "Yes. I'd like to go on a date with you." Despite my elation my voice sounded quiet, nervous even.

Aiden, whether or not he picked up on it didn't seem to care. He grinned in relief and then wrapped his arms around me, pulling me into a hug.

A hug.

From someone other than my mother.

A hug from someone who wasn't trying to hurt me.

A hug that wouldn't turn into my ribs being broken.

I wanted this feeling to last for the rest of my life. I wanted to be hugged by Aiden constantly if this is how it made me feel. I suddenly felt more stability in this. That it wasn't some prank and that I wasn't going to be abused here.

I was ready to really give this a go.

Chapter Eleven

"So, this date, do you know what's going to happen? A movie? Dinner? Both?" Mom's voice was practically giddy down the other end of the line while I tried to hold it together myself. Her enthusiasm was a little contagious.

"I'm not sure."

"Oh sweetheart, I'm so happy for you. You sound happy as well."

"I guess I am," I said with a smile.

"I can hear it in your voice. Oh darling. Have your things arrived yet?"

"Probably tomorrow, I've just got back from training so I haven't spoken to the Luna yet." I was so caught up in my excitement that I realized I'd just told her about training with the other wolves, and with the short silence on the opposite end of the line I'd say she was surprised.

"You're…training with them?" She asked, her tone a little high pitched.

"Y-yeah," I stuttered as I felt my palms become sweaty. "It's n-not that bad…I actually kept up." With a little help from the neighborhood witch, I added as an afterthought.

"She's training with them?" Jada's snippy voice could be heard in the background and I felt my heart rate increasing as my mouth became dry. *"Why? She can't even shift."*

"Jada!" Mom snapped. *"I - I just want you to be careful Evelyn. Y-you shouldn't over exert yourself too much. You could - you could hurt yourself. You don't have to try being like them to fit in, that's all I'm saying sweetheart."*

Try being like them, to fit in.

I wasn't feeling too good about this phone call anymore. "Hey mom, um, d-dinners ready so I'm going to go. I'll…I'll call you soon." I hung up, cutting off whatever she was going to say and set the phone down on the bed, running my hand over my face as my eyes began to sting.

She was right, I mean, Hannah had to keep me going for the second half of it. What was I even doing? Was I trying to prove something? That I was worth being Aiden's mate? Did I have to prove that?

Was I supposed to compete with Kate? It was like suddenly a veil had been lifted from my eyes and I felt like I was right back in Idaho, realizing that this pack was no different than all the others, that I still wasn't anything or anyone here. I was still stuck in amongst pack politics and hierarchy; I just wasn't being beaten anymore.

I felt overwhelmed with a build-up of frustration as I let out an angry yell before I heard a loud pop, like something had burst and the room went dark.

"Hey!" Grace shouted from the bathroom. "I'm trying to pluck my eyebrows!"

I sat still in the dark, paralyzed. What the heck was that?

It was my light that broke though, and the whole house had shorted out. I was too afraid to step off my bed in case I stood on any broken glass.

"Evelyn, you okay?" Aiden's voice could be heard in the room and I could faintly make out his shape in the dark. "Dad's checking out the fuse box."

"Are you barefoot?" I asked quickly. "My light shattered."

"Oh yep, I see that," he suddenly filled the room with light from the torch on his phone. "I forget you can't see. Come on, I'll take you downstairs." Surprising me, he scooped me up in his arms off the bed and began walking out of the room. "I wonder how it happened."

"I'm not sure…I just finished talking to mom."

"It's alright; dad will have it sorted in no time."

He smelt nice, he'd showered before Grace had, and his hair was still slightly damp. I'd only ever been carried like this once before in my life, when my leg had been broken by Heather and her friends, a human had found me and taken me to the nurse's office.

What different circumstances these were.

"You gotta stop staring," he said with a laugh. "You're making me self-conscious."

I quickly looked away, feeling my face grow hot. Thankfully we were nearing the kitchen where there was a small amount of light coming from it, as we entered the Luna sat by a lantern with Grace.

I placed the borrowed phone back on its stand and the Luna smiled at me. "How was shopping today darling? And training? Grace said you did really well."

"Oh yeah it was good…" I watched as Aiden left the room and walked into the laundry, clearly going to help the Alpha who I heard flicking switches. I quickly looked back at the Luna who was smiling. "I got a swimsuit for the party on the weekend."

"It took us ages to find one she actually liked though. I thought I took a while on deciding, Evie took it to a whole new level."

The lights flickered on as my fingernails dug into my palm. At least the power was back, I hated the dark. Aiden and the Alpha walked back in, both smiling which surprised me because I thought the Alpha never smiled.

"Well, not sure what that was. Evelyn, Aiden said the light in your room shattered? The main part may still be in the actual fitting. Don't touch anything; I'll call Bob over to fix it up for you."

"Bob's the handy man," Grace informed me with a wink. "How did the light shatter?"

"Honestly this house is due for a bit of a fix up; things have been falling apart lately. The doorknob to the office keeps falling off as well. Okay, who's ready for dinner?" The Luna got up and switched off the lantern, putting it back under the sink.

Grace and I ended up setting the table while Aiden and the Alpha chatted in the other room. I wasn't sure why but in my already emotional state I felt it was about me. It probably was.

When dinner was served I was surprised to find how hungry I felt. Must have been from the amount of physical exertion I had put myself through earlier on, because I actually felt like for the first time in a long time, I could eat.

"How are the Melrose boys, did they settle in with Jack and Olivia?" The Alpha asked the Luna.

"They're much better today. I think this will work for them, and it gives Olivia some renewed purpose now. It's good for all of them." I listened with interest, wondering what they were talking about.

Aiden must have read my mind, because he answered my unspoken question. "Mom finds homes for the pack children whose parents have died in combat," he explained. "Usually they go to families but the Melrose boys…they were a little difficult to place. Olivia was recently pregnant with triplets but they were all stillborn. She didn't want to try again."

"I placed them with Olivia because they're as broken as she is," the Luna said softly. "I'm hoping they can heal each other."

I looked at her in wonder. Larissa - the Luna from Idaho - she never got involved in anything like that. Her idea of working in the pack was gossiping about everyone and reminding them of where they belonged.

"They didn't do that in Idaho?" Grace asked she took in my reaction.

"No," I said quietly. "They didn't." My stomach tied up in knots as I set down my fork, unable to get rid of the image of countless orphaned children being turned out from the pack.

"What did they do then?" She asked with a frown, watching me closely.

I had to answer her, Grace was an Alpha asking me a question, and I didn't even have enough time to think of a good lie. I toyed with the edge of my fork nervously. "They - they turned them loose."

"Turned them loose?" The Luna asked her hand on her chest. "As in - they kicked them out of the pack? How old were these children?"

I felt my throat constricting, my skin tingled and not in a good way like when Aiden touched me. "They - s-sometimes…sometimes they were as young as…six," I uttered.

"Six?" She exclaimed. "What the heck is Idaho doing?" This question was directed at the Alpha who shook his head with a tired expression. "Why did we even ally with them?"

"It's political Claudia."

"They're disgusting," she spat, looking furious. I'd never seen her angry before, but the normal sweet look had vanished from her features and was instead replaced by the most terrifying look I'd ever seen.

As I finished the last chip off my plate I reveled in the fact I had eaten everything in front of me. That hadn't happened in a very long time. The table was still quiet and I could see the Luna was visibly upset, but there was nothing I could say that would fix it.

It happened.

I questioned it once and received one of the worst beatings I'd ever had, from the Alpha himself. After that I kept my mouth shut and looked away.

Slowly I looked at Aiden who mouthed 'don't worry' at me. He set down his cutlery and stretched his arms out. "Evelyn and I are going to go for a walk. Thanks for dinner mom, it was great."

"Thanks, C-Claudia," I said quietly as I got up, eager to escape before they forced me to divulge more information. Part of me felt like Jonah or someone would find out and they'd get me somehow and punish me for telling them.

I was a lot calmer when we got outside; the tension in that living room was intense. It felt like an Idaho dinner.

"You okay?" Aiden asked. I nodded quickly and put my shaking hands behind my back. "Mom's a little passionate about kids. That would have been crappy for her to hear."

"It was crappy to witness," I muttered.

"Let's talk about something else," he said suddenly. He sat down on the front lawn and pat the ground beside him. I sighed and sat beside him, looking up at the sky. A thin layer of clouds blocked the stars and the moon, giving it a ghostly pattern.

"I like the stars," I said quietly as I ripped up bits of grass. "I watched them a lot back home. I hate the moon."

"Why?" he asked, sounding surprised.

I shrugged and looked at him. "It symbolized everything I wouldn't have. Can't have. At least with the stars…each one is a little different really. And there's so many. The same with people."

"I understand that," he said quietly. It was silent between us for a while before I felt him look at me. "Hey Evelyn?"

"Yes?"

"You know earlier…how you said you'd want to be invisible, if you had a super power?" I nodded at him, wondering where this was going. "I didn't get to say what I wanted to say to you. If you ever get that option…don't choose to be invisible."

I laughed quietly. "Why not?"

He hesitated a little as he rubbed the back of his neck. "Well - you know, you are like those stars. You're unique…different. You should never want to hide who you are Evelyn. It's our differences that make us who we really are."

I felt my heart give a sharp tug; something ran through my body as I warmed from his words, only to feel a little sad. "My differences are condemned in nearly every pack in the US."

"Not here they're not. They never will be either. I'm always going to be here for you Evelyn, so you can't choose invisibility. I won't let you be invisible." His face was dangerously close to mine. I felt like I could hear my heart beating in my ears. He was saying such nice things, things I'd never had directed at me before.

To be honest, I felt like crying a little.

As I refocused on our current predicament I saw him leaning in and on their own accord my eyelids fluttered closed. His lips had barely brushed my own when the front door was thrown open.

"Hey lovebirds, desserts ready!" Grace shouted, and I jumped violently, pulling away as she slammed the door shut.

Aiden sighed and cupped my cheek, leaning his forehead on mine. "One day, I swear, I'm going to kiss you and we won't be interrupted."

With a shaky laugh I got up, extending my hand down to help him up. Secretly, I hoped he made good on that promise.

∞

"Here try on this outfit, it's so cute." Grace threw me a baby blue skirt that went to my knees and a white top that was sheer and had pale gray buttons down the front of it. "I think that's the outfit."

"You said that about the last one," I complained as I went behind the white dress screen in her room.

"No, I know for sure this is the one. Hurry, change into it, I want to see!" Grace ordered, impatience coloring her voice. Thankfully Grace only had one mirror in her room and that was at her dressing table on the other side of the screen.

I shimmied into the clothes and decided that the outfit was in fact perfect for mine and Aiden's date tonight. The skirt was flowy, and I felt like I could do the Marilyn Monroe dance over a grate - not that I'd ever do that.

Stepping out from behind the screen I gestured at the outfit and Grace nodded enthusiastically, turning her music up louder. "Brilliant! Amazing, my mom has good taste. Come on give us a spin!" She laughed.

Feeling her enthusiasm rubbing off on me I let go of my inhibitions and began spinning, laughing in surprise as Grace used her hands to fling the skirt up. Her own laughter died when she seemed to notice something, holding the skirt up higher.

"Grace!" I protested, realizing she was too close to where my scar was, her head now under the skirt.

"Evelyn, what the hell is that? And that one? Evelyn why do you have scars I thought you said you could heal!" Grace came out from under the skirt and kept the music on loud, and I was glad for it as I felt the color draining from my cheeks. At least no one else could hear us. "Evelyn, you better tell me or dammit I'll go get Aiden!"

"No!" I cried frantically. "Grace please, leave it alone it doesn't matter."

"Yes it does, because you have scars on your skin and that one specifically is way too artistically done!" She pointed at my hip and my mouth went dry.

"Please Grace," I pleaded weakly, folding my arms over my stomach "Please drop it."

"Evelyn come on. I can't and you know it," she sighed. "I know your pack wasn't flowers and sunshine, anyone could see that from your own body language around them and the way they behaved around you, but they caused you physical pain and I know it. You're affected by silver aren't you?"

I nodded mutely, feeling my stomach churning.

"So, they cut you up?"

"N-no!" I winced at my own loudness and tried to control myself. "I mean - yes, sometimes. Not all the time." I put my face in my hands, sighing. "O-only...only when I didn't do what they wanted."

"What who wanted, Evelyn?" Grace demanded in frustration.

"I can't tell you," I whispered shaking my head.

I felt her hands on my shoulders, and I peeked at her slightly to see her concerned look. "Evelyn, I know that you have some sort of weird loyalty connection to them, I get it, you still have wolf traits and you lived with them your whole life, but they hurt you Evelyn and you need to tell me what they did to you."

I swallowed the rising lump in my throat as I sat down on her bed, trying to think of a way out of this. I knew there wasn't one but it helped me stall for time. "J-Jonah," I croaked. "His friends...it was always them. Grace if I tell you, you have to swear to me you won't tell Aiden, ever."

"Evelyn!" She protested.

"I can't tell him any of this yet. I'm not ready. I'm not even ready to tell you. Please let me just have this and I'll tell you everything." I gave her a look of utter pleading as I waited for her to make up her mind. She looked torn but as defeat washed over her eyes I sighed a little in relief.

"Fine, but you have to tell me everything, starting with that scar on your hip."

I wasn't going to tell her everything, she was going to get the mildest version I could create, however the scar...she'd have to know all about that one. I couldn't cover that up properly on the spur of the moment.

"When they found out I could still heal, even though it was a lot slower than them...they used silver blades, seeing as even wolves get scarred from those. It hurt. God, it hurt so much. They were reminding me of who I was and where I stood within the pack. I can't remember what I did to annoy them..."

Throughout telling Grace I watched all the different emotions on her face. Horror, anger, disgust and more horror. When I was done she had tears glistening in her eyes as she pulled me in for a hug. "Goddess, Evelyn," she whispered. "It explains so much."

"You can't tell Aiden, Grace. He hasn't even marked me yet...I-I...this could change h-how he feels about me...or what he feels for me."

"Evelyn, Aiden isn't going to stop feeling the way he does about you because you have a past. He's your mate; you guys were created for each other by the Moon Goddess herself. If that's all that's stopping you from telling him then don't let it. Aiden won't mark you because he wants you to ask him to. It's a big thing and a lot of male wolves wait for permission." Grace wiped some stray tears off her face as she leant back.

I shook my head, trying to hold back my own. "Please Grace...just don't say anything."

"I won't," she sighed as she shook her head. "You know you will have to tell him though right? I mean...one day he's going to see you...you know, you can't hide them forever."

"Grace!"

She laughed a little, shaking her head. "Come on, we have to get you finished. We still have to do your hair and makeup. What time did he say he was coming to get you?"

"Six," I murmured as she began pulling the brush through my hair.

"I get one hour to create this? Evelyn!"

As she worked our conversation and my past drifted into the background and I was thankful for it. I knew though, that I had given her a lot to think about now. Part of me wondered if she really could keep it to herself like she promised.

∞

"Whew," she whispered as I got up from the chair. "Evelyn you have got to see yourself!"

"Nope," I said quickly as I dug in my heels before she could take me over to the mirror. "I'm good, I'm sure you've done a great job."

She was silent for a second before she toyed with the white ribbon at the base of my loose plait. "The mirror thing…is that because of them or did you really have a nightmare when you were younger?"

I sighed and looked down. "There was no nightmare."

She nodded and popped her lips, "Okay then. No mirror." Taking my hand she led me from her room and I suddenly felt like I had a million butterflies in my stomach as we went downstairs toward the kitchen where I could smell the Luna cooking.

"Oh wow, Evelyn you look breathtaking," the Luna gushed as I walked in. She got up from her seat, clutching her phone. "I have to get a photo of you to send to your mother." Before I could protest Grace put me up against the blank part of the kitchen wall and ordered me to smile, to which I complied, wanting for it to be over. "Okay Grace you get in as well."

After what felt like a million photos Aiden finally arrived in the kitchen doorway and I lost my breath when I took in his appearance. Black dress pants, shiny black shoes…dark blue shirt, he was as casual as I was, but it was still dressy.

Out of the corner of my eye I saw the Luna and Grace slip out of the room and I was glad for the privacy as Aiden pulled his concealed arm out from behind his back holding a bright looking sunflower.

"You look beautiful," he said with sincerity as I took the flower off him, admiring its deep, warm colors. It surprised me though; usually in the movies the guy would give the girl a rose. A sunflower was very unique, I loved it.

"Thank you," I whispered as he put his hands on my upper arms, kissing my forehead. I had to remind myself to breathe. "You look nice too."

"Thanks," he chuckled. "Are you ready to go?"

I nodded quickly and placed the flower behind me on the counter. The Luna would no doubt put it in water. Taking his extended hand I followed him from the house.

He had definitely cleaned his car; as he opened the door a gust of air freshener hit me. It definitely didn't smell like that on the way back from school today. Once I was comfortably seated he shut the door and made his way over to his side, smiling at me through the front window.

I could hardly contain the smile on my face.

"So, where are we going?" I asked as I strapped myself in.

"It's a surprise," he said mysteriously, pulling out into the street. "You'll like it though…at least I hope you will."

"Okay," I laughed.

We left the pack compound so we definitely wouldn't be having our date within the confines of the pack, which kind of made me feel a little relieved. I didn't want all their sensitive hearing to pick up on our conversation.

Aiden held my hand as he drove, still smiling and I was sure I was as well. My cheeks nearly ached, clearly not used to it.

Not long after leaving the compound we pulled into an empty parking lot out the front of an old looking building. It was dark red with deep green windows and white curtains that shielded the interior.

Bella's hung off the antique looking sign.

"I hope you like pizza," he said nervously as he parked the car.

"Love it."

"Let me get your door," he said quickly as he got out. I had to hold in my laugh as he opened the door for me and helped me out. He seemed a little nervous and I was glad I wasn't the only one.

Leading me to the building he pushed open the wooden door and we entered an empty restaurant. It was all quite dark minus the one table in the center with candles on it and the few around it lit up as well.

It looked amazing.

The tablecloths were a dark creamy color, the napkins a deep red. Two tall candlesticks stood proudly in the middle of the table along with a lone rose in a thin vase and a jug of cold water.

"I booked out the whole restaurant," he admitted, rubbing his neck like always.

"This…this is amazing Aiden," I said breathlessly. "You didn't have to…"

"Yes I did. I want this evening to be as perfect as you are." If I spent any more time with him my ego was going to go through the roof.

I settled on a small smile, not totally sure how to answer him without sounding like a giddy thirteen year old girl. He moved quickly and pulled out my seat which I took before he sat down himself.

"Welcome to Bella's!" A happy voice chirped. I looked up at the young looking girl, she looked no older than fifteen. "Are you ready to order?"

"I'll come back there and order directly from Bella, Kylie. Thank you though."

She made a small squeal in the back of her throat and ran off with red cheeks.

"I think someone has a crush," I whispered quietly, trying not to laugh.

"What can I say? I'm pretty great." He grinned over at me and I shook my head. The table was a little quiet for a moment and I wasn't sure what to say really. Aiden however seemed determined to keep us talking. "You know that night, when I found you on the balcony?"

"Yeah?" How would I ever forget the night that changed my life?

"I couldn't believe it. I honestly thought it wasn't going to happen, that I'd be like Alpha Hudson from Alaska, twenty-five and still mateless. Then you were there, all wide eyed and fainting."

I put my hand on my face in embarrassment, "I was surprised."

"I know," he chuckled. "So come on, tell me more about you. I feel like we've barely scratched the surface, I know there's a lot more to you than what you portray." My hands tightened in my lap, how much could I divulge without giving away anything else? I mean, after all there wasn't much to me.

Scrambling for something I blurted out the first thing I could think of. "I like to paint, any kind of arty thing…I enjoy it."

"You looked like you did when we want to get those stickers for your mirror. We should have picked some stuff up for you."

I needed to get the spotlight off me. "What about you?" I asked, "Are you ready to be an Alpha in a few years?"

"In a *few* years, I want to try things first," he said eagerly. "College; you know all the fun stuff. Once I become Alpha my whole life will be this pack. Most next in line never bother trying life outside the pack, dad encourages it though. I'm allowed options, which is great. But I've made my choice. I'll be Alpha, just after I live a little."

I looked at him curiously. "You make it sound like a jail sentence."

He shrugged with a small laugh. "It kind of is. Dad dedicates a lot of his time to running the pack. It's a big pack and we deal with a lot of stuff. It's going to be a huge thing to take on." I nodded and found myself wondering if I would be able to handle the responsibility that came with being a Luna. "I'm just going to go into the back and order our dinner," he said with a smile. "Any preferences?" I shook my head, happy to eat whatever he chose.

As he disappeared I sighed, feeling relaxed as I stared at the condensation coming off the jug. I swirled my finger around on it, drawing little patterns.

When I focused more I noticed something odd, something that I couldn't put down to being weird accident or coincidence. My finger shook as I watched the water inside the jug moving in the same direction - up and down and in circles.

Hurriedly taking my finger back from the glass the water stopped moving just as instantly and I was left curious and a little scared. As I went to place my finger back to try it again the doors to the kitchen opened and Aiden came through.

I dropped my hand and smiled at him, trying to push what just happened from my mind. "What are we having?"

"A large pizza with the lot," he said proudly. "Minus anchovies."

"Don't like them?" I asked as I felt a little relieved, I didn't like them either.

"I don't mind them, but I saw you avoided them at dinner the other night." I looked up in surprise, realizing just how closely he must watch me for him to notice that. "So, besides art what else do you like?"

I found my thoughts scrambling, what else did I like? It's always hard when somebody asked you about your likes and dislikes, even a simple 'who are you' question leaves you wondering about who you actually are. "I guess reading," I murmured. How did I tell him I didn't really do anything back home? "I read a lot."

"I can't read. I mean I can read, obviously," he rubbed the back of his neck again and I bit my lip to stop from smiling. "I just don't have the patience to sit through a book. I flick to the end to see what happens, it's kind of like reading the whole book you just don't have to sit there forever."

"That's not reading, that's cheating," I laughed, shaking my head.

He shrugged with a chuckle, "maybe it is, and maybe it isn't. But I can guarantee I'll always know how a story ends. I'm better with movies, one hour or two, the whole story explained in one hit."

I nodded, "I can watch movies but when it turns into a series, or if it's a TV series I'm not so good. I get a little impatient with wanting to know how it will all really end."

Conversation between us seemed to flow; even as we ate we didn't stop talking. To be honest I wasn't sure if I had ever spoken this much in my life. He told me all about his childhood growing up and I skimmed over the details of mine.

"One time I went through a phase of burning ants with a magnifying glass. Mom thought I was going to become a serial killer," he joked. My cheeks hurt from smiling and laughing so much, the stories he told were so happy and carefree and so different from mine.

"Well you know they start out with small stuff like that, maybe I should be worried."

"You'd be the last person in the world I'd ever hurt," he told me, looking very serious.

I know, I thought. I'm starting to realize that.

As it began to get later Aiden sighed and said we'd better start heading home. I found myself dreading leaving the little bubble we had created here, would it pop once we reached home? Would our relationship feel this easy?

On the drive home I sat on the seat in the middle beside Aiden. It was nice to feel close to him. His hand rested on my leg as he quietly drove through the streets and in my relaxed state my thoughts drifted to my incident with the water.

Something wasn't right with that, and I knew it.

Not wanting to ruin the good mood I was in I pushed it as far into my mind as possible, instead deciding to focus on Aiden's hand on my leg, that would clear my thoughts. As we pulled into the compound the man at the gate gave us a coy smile and I looked away, not sure if I liked the way he watched us.

There was only one light coming from the house and I realized it to be Grace's room. Aiden pulled into the drive and shut off the truck, the air around us suddenly silent without the purr of the engine in the background.

Something had shifted between us I knew that, there was this new feeling, a new kind of energy. I found myself peeking up at him to find him already staring, and I suddenly felt self-conscious.

"Evelyn?" Aiden murmured as he shifted to face me as much as he could in the confined space. I shifted a little to face him, feeling I knew what was coming, and I wanted it to. He looked so good, smelt so good. He treated me like I was made of gold, like I was something so rare.

When his hand cupped my cheek it warmed and I felt my lips part as I gasped a little at the sparks on my skin. The air was thick with tension, an unanswered question. Did he want me to say yes? Please don't ask me, I pleaded mentally. Just kiss me.

If he asked, I would overthink it and no doubt come to a crazy conclusion and back out.

Just kiss me.

I wasn't sure if he could hear my thoughts, or maybe he knew I wouldn't say anything. As if he was testing my reaction he slowly leant in, his eyes darting from mine down to my lips and back up again. As he came closer I gained some courage and met him halfway and our lips came together like two pieces of a perfect puzzle.

The kiss was smooth, soft. It didn't feel rushed nor did it feel pushy. It was explorative, the way his lips moved. His arm snaked around my back and I briefly wondered if I was doing it right, I'd never kissed anyone willingly before.

I found my own hands on his chest; my heart felt like it was beating in my ears as I moved my lips with his, feeling fireworks going off in all directions. I was overwhelmed by how right this all felt, to be here in his arms.

When he pulled back a little my lips felt slightly swollen and my cheeks felt flushed. His own looked a little red. I felt bashful suddenly, looking down at the hands pressed on that shirt that made him look so great.

He felt firm beneath my hands, like a rock. I found myself wondering what he'd feel like skin to skin.

Feeling his finger lift my chin back up, my eyes followed the motion. His own were glowing amber, signifying his wolf was very close to the surface as he stroked my cheek. "I want to mark you so badly," he rasped. "I know you might not be ready for that, but Goddess, Evelyn you are amazing. I know I want to be with you forever."

I knew I was a goner, the way his eyes glowed that intense amber color. The way his hands tightened and relaxed on my waist. The way I felt so peaceful and calm with him, and at this very moment I knew I couldn't picture my life without him in it. However him marking me, that was a huge step, one I wasn't totally sure I was ready to take.

"Let's go in," he said with a smile as he kissed me one last time before getting out of the car and around to my side, opening my door with a grin.

Chapter Twelve

Waking up on Saturday morning was different, for a number of reasons. For one, I had never woken up with a smile on my face before, eager to start the day and see the people I lived with. Two, I was a little excited for the party this afternoon and three…well I don't know, I was just happy.

So was Grace it seemed as she barged into my room, modelling a stringy green bikini top. "Do you reckon this makes my boobs look too small?" She gave a spin and I watched as the material seemed to strain over her more vital areas. I was a little scared it'd fall off.

"Definitely not," I told her.

"Trey's bringing a junior," she muttered, disgust coloring her tone. "Goddess, he's disgusting."

My interest piqued slightly. I knew from watching the two of them, she and Trey didn't get along. Well sometimes they did and then Grace would flip out on him. Her problem was that he dated anything that walked and didn't wait for his mate. His problem was that he thought Grace was a frigid prude.

His words, not mine.

"Ugh, and I bet Katherine will be there, all breasts and gross." Grace flicked her hair with an eye roll. "She's such a cow to Hannah, I feel bad that Hannah had to mate into that family. Josh is an okay guy but he's a little too serious for his age."

I shrugged, "Hannah seems happy though."

"Hannah's always happy. So, tell me about your date!" She peered at my neck and gave a disappointed frown. "No mark?"

My cheeks went red. "He wanted to."

"Why didn't he then?"

"I'm not s-sure," I stammered, feeling nervous suddenly.

"I understand. It's a huge thing; it's smart you're waiting until you know for certain." She said, looking at me more carefully. "Have you told him anything about…Idaho?"

"N-not yet," I squeaked and I hated how panicked I sounded.

"You know you have to Evelyn. He'll see the scars one day, and he'll be a lot less angry if he didn't find them by himself. You know what male wolves are like."

"Exactly, he'll lose it and try killing Jonah."

She made a face and sighed, looking up, her gaze zeroing in on the broken light in my roof. "We'll have to get that fixed. It's so weird! I'm glad it didn't happen in my room, I would have lost it."

"Yeah," I said quietly, my memory flicking back to the light and then the water jug last night. "What time is the party?

"Lucy and Hannah are coming here at about one and then we're all going together, it starts at about two and then goes as long as the alcohol lasts."

"Is Aiden awake?" I asked, feeling eager to see him.

"Nah, he did a patrol after your date last night, he'll probably sleep until the party," she looked at me with a smirk. "You're all red Evie, were we naughty last night?"

"Don't," I groaned, embarrassed as she slapped my knee playfully.

"Ah, I thought I heard you girls, Evelyn your stuff came yesterday, I put it in the study. Only four boxes?" the Luna looked surprised.

"Four boxes?" Grace exclaimed. "Wow. Four boxes would just be my wardrobe."

I shrugged, feeling nervous again, hoping this wouldn't make her probe for more information on my life. "I didn't need much. I don't need much. I should call her and let her know I got them alright."

"Oh yes about that, we were thinking of getting you a phone." The Luna tucked her blonde hair behind her ears. "There's the new iPhone that's out, supposed to have really good reviews."

My eyes widened, those phones were overly expensive and I didn't need a phone, I'd never needed one. "Oh…I don't think I really need one," I mumbled, curling my toes under the blanket.

"Oh you do though," Grace said matter of factly.

"Not to worry Evelyn, we'll take care of it. Come down for some breakfast girls." The Luna left before I could argue and Grace began pulling me out of my bed. Aiden's door was open a crack and as Grace pulled me past the room I could see Aiden hanging off his bed, snoring.

Just seeing him had my mind flashing back to the kiss in his car and my cheeks once again felt warm. I really had to learn how to control that.

The Luna was scooping bacon and eggs onto two plates when we entered the kitchen and I sat down beside Grace who was scrolling through her phone contacts before settling on Lucy's number. I began to eat what was in front of me as she laughed down the line to whatever Lucy had greeted her with, before putting her on speaker.

"You girls should come over earlier," Grace instructed. "I can't choose what bikini to wear."

"Neither can I, I shouldn't have bought so many," Lucy huffed. *"Geoff practically vetoed all of them though, such a spoil sport, too bad there'll be humans at this party. He can't come."*

"You're so bad!" Grace laughed. "So, Evie and Aiden had a hot date!"

"Grace!" I exclaimed.

"Ooh! Evie, coming out of the shell?"

The Luna was rolling her eyes but smiling as she did the dishes; I myself felt incredibly awkward and wanted to fall into a hole in the ground. Aiden's mom did not need to hear this stuff.

"Okay I'll come earlier; I'll grab Hannah on the way. Apparently she stayed at Josh's last night and Kate was being a real shit, so she's a little upset today."

"I hope Kate ends up with someone far away from this pack, I can't stand the little-"

"Grace," the Luna warned, giving her a look before leaving the room.

"I'll be there soon, oh and Evie," Lucy's voice held a smile, *"be ready to be interrogated. You can't hide from all of us."*

The line went dead and I was left unable to finish my breakfast.

∞

"We are here!" Lucy shouted as she burst into Grace's room, a duffel bag over her shoulder. Hannah walked in behind her, her cheeks pale and her eyes dull as she dropped her bag on the floor and sighed heavily as she lay down across Grace's bed.

"How are you doing Hannah?" Grace asked sympathetically as she poked her shoulder. "Katie still being the devil?"

"I don't know what I ever did to her-"

"You're a low ranking member of the pack who got mated to the future Beta. That's enough of an insult in her eyes," Lucy pointed out. "She can't even find a mate, that'd also be what's made her hate you so much."

"I try so hard," she whispered, tears in her eyes.

I felt bad for Hannah, I knew how she felt - obviously on a larger scale, but I knew what it was like to not be accepted for who you were.

"Don't worry about her. Today is all about having fun!"

"She's going to be there," Hannah grumbled.

I was dreading that too, deep down I wished that something would come up that would make her not be able to go, then I could enjoy the day without her and so could Hannah.

"Alright, no more sadness! Help me choose a bikini!"

As Grace and Lucy leafed through all the bikinis I found Hannah staring at me strangely. When she caught me staring she smiled quickly. "Was your date nice?" She asked quietly, toying with a strand of her hair.

"Yeah," I smiled. "It was perfect really."

"Good," she said with a smile before making another face. "Hey Evelyn, I've been meaning to ask you...about Idaho, your mom-"

"Come on you two! Give us a hand or we'll never get there," Grace whined. Lucy sighed and went over and as my heart rate increased over her questioning me about Idaho I excused myself to the toilet, needing a moment to get myself together.

Backing out of Grace's room I bumped into something solid and turned around to see Aiden, looking freshly showered. "Hey," he grinned. I was a little surprised when he pecked me on the lips and then reminded myself not to be, this was going to become a regular thing now.

"Hey," I said shyly, feeling the nerves in my voice.

"You girls getting ready for the party? Grace's screaming woke me up." He did look tired as I looked at the dark rings under his eyes, clearly he had patrolled late.

"I'm scared she's going to try putting me in one of her bikinis," I admitted.

"If she gets too over the top just pull rank," he grinned at me. "The perks of being a higher rank than someone who is naturally bossy."

I couldn't see myself doing that but I nodded anyway.

"Evelyn! How long does it take to pee?" Grace shouted.

I cringed a little and Aiden grinned again. "I'm going to meet up with the guys…I'll see you at the party?" I nodded and closed my eyes when I saw him leaning in, eager to feel what our lips felt like together again. It didn't disappoint and my hands somehow made it to his upper arms, wanting to feel him again.

"Ev-" Grace pulled her door open and I pulled away immediately. Aiden's glare at Grace did not go unnoticed. "Ooh! I'll give you two a minute alone," she winked and shut her door again.

Aiden sighed before stroking my cheek. "See you later, beautiful."

I turned into a puddle of mush right there as he left and I found myself wandering back into Grace's room, all starry eyed. Getting through the rest of their escapades was easy enough, after seeing Aiden.

He called me beautiful.

I wanted the rest of the day to hurry up so I could see him again!

"No."

"What about-"

"No, I don't even know why I bought that!"

"This one is cute-"

"Nope."

"Lucy this is getting ridiculous," Hannah snapped.

"I think I'll wear the red one," she decided after having tossed it aside when she had begun this tiring game of swapping bikinis.

"Finally!" Grace snapped.

"We are all a little testy today aren't we?" Lucy huffed as she slipped behind Grace's dressing screen to change. "Sorry for wanting your advice!"

Grace rolled her eyes at Hannah and me and then sighed. "Sorry Lucy, we want to help. Really."

Hannah looked at me and shook her head and I smothered a laugh as Lucy pranced out from behind the screen, a sheer white playsuit over her bikini. Hannah took her turn to change, Grace was already dressed and ready, a green sundress over her bikini.

"I'm going to get changed," I announced as I got up off the bed.

"Oh, bring it in here. We still have to question you about your date!" Lucy looked at me eagerly and I just nodded quickly and left, having no intention of taking my things and getting changed in there.

I quickly pulled on the black one piece, making sure it firmly covered everything I wanted covered before pulling out the orange playsuit that the Luna had bought me. I liked the tassels on the shorts area; they bounced on my upper thighs as I walked.

Walking back into Grace's room Lucy pouted at me. "Evie! I'm still wanting answers."

I sighed and sat down nervously on the bed, eyeing Hannah who had changed into a pair of denim shorts and a loose white shirt. I hadn't done this before - girl talk. I'd never had anyone to talk to or anything this exciting to talk about. How much information did you tell? Were there rules to what you could say in front of your mate's sister?

"Evie," Lucy warned.

"Okay!" I conceded with my hands up in defense. Lucy could be quite scary. "We went to *Bella's-*" I looked at the girls who nodded; they seemed to know the restaurant. "We had pizza and we talked about a lot of different stuff. Then we came home."

Lucy looked at me blankly before asking, "That's it?"

Hannah crinkled her nose. "I expected more from him."

"Oh don't worry I saw them making out in the truck," Grace said casually as I whipped my head in her direction, horrified that she'd seen and even more horrified that she'd disclosed that information to the group.

"Ooh! Evie!" Lucy shrieked

"He didn't mark you though?" Hannah asked as she adjusted her shorts. "That's odd."

"He wanted to…I'm not - I don't know…just not yet," I finally managed as I toyed with the tassels on my playsuit shorts. The room was quiet and I knew from their point of view - as full-blooded wolves - they wouldn't understand my hesitation. Or maybe Hannah would, she was half as well.

"Well, that's cool you know. These things take time," Lucy said, smiling encouragingly. "We should get ready to go girls, we don't want to be the last ones showing up and I want a decent parking spot."

I was relieved for the subject change. Since Grace had brought it up earlier and then it had come up again now, suddenly Aiden marking me was all that was on mind, it felt like I was being hit over the head constantly. Trying to push it to the side I followed the girls down to the kitchen where we packed some towels and food.

Grace swiped a bottle of Wolfsbane from the cabinet with a cheeky grin and we headed out to Lucy's Jeep, watching as Trey pulled into the driveway in some sleek looking vehicle. He seemed proud of it as he got out and leant up against it.

"Ladies, we haven't stolen from the family liquor cabinet have we?" Trey asked as he eyed the bottle in Grace's hand. He shot her a wink and she wrinkled her forehead, the way she did when she didn't like something.

"Trey, haven't stolen any poor unassuming juniors virginity have we?" She mimicked as she eyed the brunette girl lounging in the front passenger seat.

"Where's Josh?" Hannah asked, cutting off Trey's retort.

"He's meeting us there." He looked pointedly at Lucy who rolled her eyes.

"I'm not going to drink too much, I'm seeing Geoff later."

"Oh okay," Trey nodded before looking at me, a grin spreading across his face. "How's it going Evie girl? I feel like I hear more about you than I see you."

I was taken aback, that he was speaking directly to me. What did I say? I didn't really know what to say, I didn't really know him. I just smiled nervously and looked awkwardly at the girls who were packing up the car.

I jumped in fright when a firm hand came down on my shoulder and I spun around quickly, giving myself a head rush as Aiden steadied me.

"Sorry," he said with a laugh. I took in his appearance, loose black swimming shorts and a blue shirt. "You okay Evelyn?" He asked, squeezing my upper arm.

Coming back down to earth I nodded quickly, swallowing the lump in my throat. "Ye-yeah," I stammered out. "Are you going with Trey?" I asked, as I tried to keep my head clear and not focus on the thumb that was rubbing in small circles on the exposed skin of my upper arm.

"Yeah, I guess. That girl better get in the back," he said loud enough for Trey to hear.

"Is she human?" I asked in surprise.

"Trey has no limits. We better get going, I'll meet you there." He kissed my forehead before letting me go and Hannah pulled me into the Jeep before I could get a breath in. "Drive safe!" He called to Lucy before getting into the now empty passenger seat in Trey's car.

"Alright!" Lucy said happily as she turned on her stereo, some random song blasting out. "Let's go have some fun!"

∞

The party was just gearing up when we arrived. Lucy pulled in beside Trey and from her car we could see the huge falls and the couple of barbecues and picnic tables set up. People were standing around, drinking out of that ever famous red plastic cup.

I watched as a boy ran up to a rope, swung and let go falling into the water with a yell. Music was blaring from somewhere and I felt nerves hit me in full force at all these people; a high school party and I was here.

"Let's find a spot," Grace said to Hannah as they ran off together, leaving Lucy and I with the things we had brought. Luckily Aiden and Trey appeared behind us and helped lug down the heavy cooler and fold out chairs. I carried the bag with all the towels.

"Jodie!" Someone shouted and the brunette who had come with Trey skipped over to them where they all giggled and pointed at Trey as he flexed his muscles deliberately, setting the cooler down.

Grace rolled her eyes and shoved her finger down her throat as he went over to the group of girls. Hannah went about setting up our chairs, eagerly sitting down with a sigh. I gingerly sat beside her, wondering if I looked like I fit in.

"Hey man," Aiden said behind me. I turned slightly to see Josh and him do that weird man handshake guys did before Hannah got up happily and embraced him.

"Where is darling Katie?" Lucy asked sarcastically as she rubbed lotion on her arms.

"She wouldn't come out of her room," he said with a shrug. "Said she wasn't coming."

"Oh, how sad." Grace's tone betrayed her real feelings however as she looked over at me with glee.

Hannah looked relieved as she sat down next to me and Aiden and Josh sat on the logs opposite us. I felt much better, from what I had seen of her fully clothed I could only imagine her bikini choices would be just as intimidating.

"When is Trey going to stop playing around with the human girls?" Josh muttered in disgust as he opened up a bottle of Wolfsbane. "It's sickening to watch, not to mention he turns eighteen in a month. What if his mate is in this pack and they find each other? She won't want anything to do with him."

"You know how he feels about that stuff man," Aiden said quietly. "Can't push him into it. You'll have to wait for it to all happen and he'll understand."

"Trey doesn't like the concept of the mate bond," Hannah explained. "He said it's his free will being torn away by some ancient curse."

"What he doesn't get is that the Moon Goddess only created it to guide us to the *right* person. He's a total dick!" Grace growled.

I nodded; realizing there was a lot more to this group dynamic. Looking around the party I noticed a lot of humans, they were very easy to pick out. They moved less fluidly than the wolves did, and they seemed to behave more boisterously.

There was a group of guys in letterman jackets so I took them to be the school jocks, a bunch of gorgeous girls near them as well. I assumed they were cheerleaders but I could be wrong. I noticed some people from classes I had as well.

The wolves were also very easy to spot, because half the time they were staring at us.

"Are we having a fire later?" Hannah asked excitedly. "I brought stuff for smores."

"Yeah we can," Josh said with a smile. The way he smiled at her nearly made *my* heart skip a beat.

"Well I'm *hot*." Lucy got up and slipped off her sheer playsuit, folding it on her chair. "I'm going to swim, Grace come swing off the rope with me."

"Evelyn, Hannah come on!" Grace pulled up Hannah and I felt myself seize up.

I hadn't intended on swimming at all today for another shortcoming I have. I couldn't swim for my life. "Oh - I'm okay for now," my voice squeaked.

"Alright! Come join us when you're ready!" The girls ran off and I watched as they waited for a turn on the rope. Josh got up and left so Aiden moved to Hannah's chair, sighing as he put the Wolfsbane bottle back in the cooler.

"We can't leave these hanging around. Humans wouldn't be able to handle it." He winked and took a drink out of his cup before handing it to me. "Did you want to try some?" I was unsure, I didn't know if I could take it. This stuff is for wolves. "You should be fine with even a cup to be honest. Just enough to relax a little."

I bit my lip, taking the cup from him and smelling the contents, making a face. "That smells so strong!" He laughed and put his arm over the back of my chair, angling toward me more. Cautiously I brought the cup to my lips, slowly taking a sip, squinting at the burn. It was warm in my throat and there was a strong taste I couldn't out my finger on. It warmed my whole body.

"Like it?" He asked as he played with the end strands of my hair.

"I'm not sure..." I said hesitantly as I held the cup.

"It'll grow on you," Aiden promised as he filled himself a new cup.

"Ahhhh!" My eyes followed the scream and I watched as Grace spun in the air before splashing violently into the water. When she came up it was almost like slow motion. Like the way Halle Berry walks out of the water in James Bond.

Plenty of eyes were on the gorgeous girl in the green bikini top and I noticed Trey stop talking to his date and follow her out of the water as she met up with Lucy who must have already had a turn because she was soaking wet.

Looking between Grace and Trey I wondered why it annoyed Grace so much that Trey didn't like the mate bond. Everyone did have the right to choose, and I respected Trey's choice. Briefly I wondered if maybe Grace had feelings for him but brushed it aside. Grace was so set on the mate bond she wouldn't let herself feel for anyone except her mate when she found him.

"You're deep in thought." Aiden broke off my gaze and I turned to him with a small smile, finding the guts to take another sip of the drink in my hand.

"I'm just watching."

"You haven't been to a party before, have you?"

Was I that transparent? "No...not really," I said quietly. Sure in Idaho they had invited me to one, but when I got there it definitely wasn't a party. Not for me anyway. I shook away that thought and focused back on what Aiden was saying.

"Anyway I just wanted to say...that color looks really nice on you," he looked awkward and I saw his cheeks were a little red. "You look beautiful."

My own lips tugged up at the corners as I felt a warm glow wash over me. "Thank you."

∞

"...I want to go all over the world!" Hannah declared to me as we reclined on our chairs, looking at the stars. The party was still going and it had just gotten dark. Grace was chatting to another group of girls with Lucy and the boys had gone off to cook some food on one of the barbecues.

"Really?" I asked in surprise. I never took Hannah for a traveler. Then again I didn't take her for a drinker but here she was, lying beside me in a whole other world. I myself felt a little dizzy but I was holding it together, I had declined a second drink from Aiden, one was definitely enough.

"Yep. I just want to get away!" She said seriously, sitting up and looking at me. "Away from Katherine, Goddess she's such a bitch. Sometimes I want to hurt her a little, with this," she opened her palm and a white glow came from it before she sighed. "But I'd lose my powers if I hurt anyone with them, for no real reason."

She lay back down and sighed sadly. "I don't know why she hates me so much. Josh and I fight about her all the time. Like always."

"People like Katherine can't live properly if they aren't making someone miserable," I told her quietly.

She nodded before rolling over to face me, her chair creaking. "Evelyn I've been meaning to ask you something." I felt nervous suddenly as she continued. "You never knew your dad did you?"

"No…my mother was-"

"I know," she said slowly as she closed her eyes tightly, clearly trying to fight the waves in her brain. "I'm just not sure about your aura, or your scent."

I frowned. "What do you mean?"

"I don't know," she said airily. "Your mom's story doesn't add up, how can a full blooded female wolf be overpowered by a human? Doesn't make any sense! You don't either, I get vibes from you."

"Vibes?" I questioned, sitting upright.

"Hey ladies!" Two drunken boys in letterman jackets stumbled over and I felt dread seep into my system. "Why are you here all by yourselves?"

"Pretty girls shouldn't be alone," one of them murmured as he took a hold of my arm. Panic near overwhelmed my senses as I was basically lifted up out of my chair. "You're new aren't you gorgeous?"

"Dude, let her go!" Hannah snapped as she got to her feet, wobbling slightly.

"Why?" He slurred as he pulled me closer and I felt my stomach turn as I squirmed to be released.

"Because that's my girlfriend," the air seemed to go cold when Aiden spoke; his words so concise and clear that it suddenly felt like it was just us four standing here, even the music seemed to fade out.

"Oh look, it's the Snob Squad." The jock took a swig of his beer and tightened his hold, effectively causing me to gasp in pain. My skin felt hot and not in a good way like it did when Aiden touched me. This felt like when Zac or Jonah had been all over me.

It felt like every bone in my body was rebelling against the jock. My heart hammered as I saw Aiden's eyes flickering slightly from light shades of amber and I knew his wolf was close to the surface. He was desperately trying to keep it together as he couldn't expose the pack to humans.

I wished I was a full blooded wolf, strong enough to push this guy to the floor. A normal she wolf could have. Not me.

"Let her go," Aiden growled sounding near animalistic. "Now!"

"I think you've had enough of her attention to be honest-"

It all happened so quickly I was surprised myself. Suddenly he was screaming in agony and releasing me and the hotness from my skin faded instantly. Aiden however was now ploughing his fist into the jocks face.

The crowd cheered loudly while some of the cheerleaders squealed. I didn't know what to do as I watched Josh struggle to take Aiden off the jock. I looked at Hannah for some guidance only to find her staring at me with wide eyes, like she'd seen something astonishing.

Josh finally managed to get Aiden off the boy on the floor who looked severely out of it. His friends swarmed immediately, carrying him off to their cars and hurling abuse towards the party before the music started up again and everyone acted like nothing had happened.

"What the hell man!" Josh shouted. "You could have killed him! Why would you lose control like that?"

Aiden simply ignored Josh and came over to me, taking my hand and leading me away from the party and from Lucy and Grace who had finally gotten through from the crowd.

Eventually we were alone where all the cars were parked and Aiden released my hand, growling in frustration. To be honest, I was a little scared as I watched his claws extending and retracting from his hands.

He was really worked up.

Suddenly he was in front of me, his hands on my waist. "Did he hurt you?"

"No," I lied weakly.

"I heard you gasp," he said. "I know he hurt you."

"Aiden it's okay, he let me go."

"It isn't okay!" He snapped. "No one should be touching you without your permission. No one should touch you except me! You shouldn't be getting hurt."

"It's fine," I murmured. I'd had worse; a drunk human squeezing my ribs was the least painful thing that I had ever experienced.

"You don't get it Evelyn. You don't know what went on in my head when I saw the little prick touching you. My wolf near lost it and I nearly shifted. I've never lost control like that in my life. I've never punched a human. I could have killed him." I remained silent as I let him calm down, knowing I'd probably only aggravate the situation if I told him I was fine again.

"I'm sorry."

He looked at me incredulously. "Why are you apologizing?"

"If I was stronger I could have practically flicked him off and you wouldn't lose control. You wouldn't have to feel like you needed to protect me." Once again I felt doubts about our relationship surfacing. This event only proved that Aiden would have to spend the rest of his life not only watching over the pack but me as well. I could never be independent like the Luna.

The space around us was quiet minus the background noise of the music in the distance. I stared at Aiden's shirt and realized he hadn't gone swimming today. Had he not gone because I hadn't? Was I holding him back again?

It took me by surprise when he lifted my chin and softly kissed my lips. In his aggravated state I would have expected something rougher. He seemed calm now, careful. His hand ran up my back as the space between us closed and became non-existent.

This kiss was different to our first. I didn't feel the need to analyze my every move as I kissed him back, running my hands up his arms and to the base of his neck, enjoying the feel of safety and peace his presence brought me.

When he pulled away he took my hand in his and brought it to his lips, closing his eyes. "Don't talk yourself down," he said quietly. "I like you because you're different Evelyn."

His words gave me something to think about has he gave me one last peck before taking us back to the party.

Chapter Thirteen

THE REST OF THE NIGHT went smoothly after that. We had a little camp fire and Hannah handed out the marshmallows. Everyone seemed to be enjoying themselves, although, people did stay away from our group.

Trey and Grace were actually laughing together, his date nowhere in sight. Lucy was lounging on her chair looking up at the sky looking like she was on a totally different planet. Aiden sat so close to me I could hear him breathing, but if it made him feel better then so be it. Plus I enjoyed being close to him anyway.

By the time we got home it was half past one in the morning and I was supremely exhausted. We made as little noise as possible coming in knowing that the Alpha and the Luna would be asleep, though with their sensitive hearing it was inevitable they'd hear us.

"Dad's going to stomp all over you when he finds out what you did to that human," Grace whispered as we all climbed the stairs. "Josh will tell him, you know that."

Aiden sighed behind me, seeming annoyed with Grace. "I'm going to tell him anyway, keep out of it."

I knew Aiden was going to get in trouble with the Alpha, from what I'd seen he gave Aiden a lot of responsibility and expected excellence and Aiden seemed to live up to those expectations…before I came. If I hadn't been at that party Aiden wouldn't have punched the jock out. He wouldn't be in trouble with the Alpha.

"Hey Evelyn?" Aiden asked quietly when we reached the landing and Grace slipped into her room. I looked at him nervously, noting the tired look in his eyes. "Do you want to watch a movie or something? I'm not ready to sleep."

I was definitely ready to sleep but I didn't want to say that to him. "Sure."

I thought we'd go back downstairs to their huge theatre room but instead he took me by the hand and led me to his room, which was surprising because I hadn't been in it yet. It was a basic looking room, not overdone or anything.

A double bed donned in black blankets and pillows was pushed up in the far side of the room, a black chest at the end of it. A large chest of drawers sat beside the door which no doubt led to his walk in robe and on top of it was a huge TV that was surrounded by DVD cases, either open or shut. There was a messy desk up against the wall opposite the end of the bed, his computer screen nearly the same size as his TV.

"Do you approve?" He asked with a smile as I looked away from his dark blue walls.

"Yeah," I laughed. "It's…surprisingly neat."

"Why wouldn't it be?" He asked as he went through his DVD collection.

Shrugging I sat on the edge of his bed, feeling a little nervous about being in here. I wasn't sure why really…I'd been in Laurance's room once but that was just to take him dinner when he'd been studying and I hadn't stayed in it long.

I'd never been in a guy's room before.

"All guys are messy right?" Aiden smirked as he showed me a DVD case. *Iron Man*. Nodding both my approval to the movie and to his comment I decided to get more comfortable, putting some of the pillows up against the wall to lean on.

Aiden joined me on the bed and sighed, stretching out his legs and yawning. Pulling out a bag of potato chips from his bedside table he offered me some before pressing play on the movie and I finally felt myself relaxing as well.

∞

Why was it so bright? I'd never woken up to this much light in my room before. Burying my head under the pillows I closed my eyes again and sighed. Morning always came so quickly, why did it feel like night time was over in a blink of an eye?

As I slowly peeled my eyes open I took in the bedding that did not match the ones on my bed. These were black, not cream. The walls were a dark blue and not the creamy white ones in my room. Sitting up hurriedly I took in the lit up room that was Aiden's - however he was nowhere to be seen and I was fully tucked under the blankets.

I didn't even remember falling asleep in here.

"Ev-ah-leeeen!" Grace chanted down the hallway, pushing open Aiden's door she grinned at me. "Did you and Aiden have a little sleepover?"

"Uh-"

"Mom wants to see you, she's in the kitchen." Grace left the room and I quickly got out of Aiden's bed - making it - before hurrying to the kitchen. I wouldn't keep The Luna waiting.

"Oh Evelyn," she smiled as she looked up from her laptop. "How was the party?"

"It was fun," I said nervously as I sat down at the bench with her. Had Aiden told her about the confrontation he'd had with the human?

"I'm sure it was. Those kids think we don't know what happens at those parties. I think they forget that we once partied at the falls as well." She winked before opening the drawer beside her, pulling out a white box.

As it came into view my mouth dropped open at the iPhone displayed on the front of the box. "Luna I-"

"Claudia," she reminded me.

"C-Claudia I can't accept that...that...that's an iPhone."

"Well it's not just any iPhone. It's the iPhone six," she proudly presented it to me and I took it with shaky hands. Jada had an iPhone four. Mom wouldn't buy her the new model, yet here I was with it in my hands. "Greg said it was sixty-four gigabyte, whatever that means."

"The Alpha-"

"Yes he went and got it, he knows more about that stuff then I do. Because you don't have a pack link or won't be able to establish one you do need some form of communication, if there was an emergency or something like that." She got up off her chair and went to the fridge. "I'm honestly surprised you don't own a phone already, how did you stay in contact with your mother if you went out?"

I traced the pattern of the phone, biting the inside of my mouth. "I didn't go out…" Not unless I wanted to be chased and abused.

"What about when you went to school? Grace texts me at least a dozen times during the day."

I was too busy hiding and running to my classes, taking out the time to text wouldn't have been an option. My lack of response seemed to confirm something for the Luna as she watched me with interest, slicing up some fruit.

"This is really great," I said quietly looking at the box, too afraid to open it.

"Well Grace will help you set it up," she said coming over and giving my shoulders a squeeze. "And then you can call your mother on your brand new phone."

∞

Grace had a ball setting up the phone and logging in everyone's numbers. She downloaded a whole bunch of apps she had on her phone as well as putting on a bunch of her favorite music. When she gave it back to me I had a text from Trey, Lucy and Hannah.

I felt nervous, I didn't text.

Trey: *Hey Evie baby! Catching up with the times are we?*

Lucy: *This is so exciting!*

Hannah: *I need to talk to you. Can we meet up out the front of yours in ten?*

Hannah's message made my heart skip a beat slightly as I watched Grace tapping away at her phone with a bored expression. Sliding off Grace's bed I thanked her and slowly walked downstairs, texting back Hannah.

Sure…

As I reached the front door the phone vibrated in my hand and I nearly dropped it in excitement when I saw Aiden's name pop up on the screen. Pressing the green phone button I put it to my ear.

"Mom gave you the phone already," he sounded like he was smiling and his voice coming through the receiver made me feel giddy. *"I wanted to give it to you."*

I found myself acting like a shy schoolgirl even though he couldn't see me. "Well if it helps you're the first phone call."

"Do you like it?"

"Yeah…I'm not sure I needed it though…"

"Dad wants you to have communication with us; you can't make a pack link so a phone is the next best thing."

"I could have bought one…I should get a job actually, I need to pay back your mom for the phone and-"

Aiden's laugh down the end of the line cut off my rambling. *"Any money you give her she won't accept Evelyn. She was horrified you didn't have your own phone to begin with. Don't think too much into it…just enjoy it."*

As I saw Hannah walking up the street my stomach tightened. "I have to go, Hannah's here."

"I see how it is," he teased. *"That's fine, I'm with Trey anyway. We had a patrol this morning and now we're fixing up his car. I'll be home soon."*

"Okay," I said quietly, not wanting to hang up on him. Mainly because I wasn't sure I wanted to have a serious conversation with Hannah and for the fact that I found myself missing him even though I saw him last night. "Bye."

"Bye Evelyn, I lo-bye yeah. Okay see ya." The phone cut off after Aiden's voice seemed to choke up as he scrambled out his final words. Maybe Trey was taunting him. Frowning I looked for a pocket before realizing I was still in my playsuit from the party.

Hannah showed up in some jeans and a pale blue shirt, wearing a nervous expression. "Hey Evie," she said quietly as she sat down on the floor by my feet. Following her lead I sat beside her, ignoring the buzzing my phone kept making, signaling texts.

"Hey…"

She looked at me with a hesitant smile. "I know you're probably wondering why I wanted to meet up…I wanted to ask you this last night and I couldn't and then I saw what I saw and my head near exploded." I looked at her in confusion, wondering where she was taking this. "Evelyn, your birth father…could there be a possibility he wasn't human?"

Huh?

Where did that come from? I thought this was going to be about my past, maybe she'd seen a scar or found my behavior in general suspicious. "Mom said he was. I believe her, the pack did."

The next smile she gave was polite, not a real one. "Maybe they lied though?"

"What do you mean?" I asked. Lied about who had raped her?

"Evelyn last night…that boy had a very strong hold on you. Aiden didn't know how to get you out of his hold without hurting you in the process and then suddenly he just let you go?" Hannah picked at the grass before staring at me. "I think you made him let you go."

"I don't know what you mean…" I got up off the grass, brushing off my clothes. "He let me go."

"Because you made him."

"Made him how?" I found myself becoming frustrated, feeling fears about myself surfacing. Questions I had and answers that I gave myself that I deemed to be unrealistic and stupid. Yet Hannah was going in that same direction.

"I felt your aura Evelyn, it was bristling. It felt like I was touching the sun, it was so hot. Then he dropped you like you had burnt him." My mouth felt dry as I took in her words. I didn't do that, I know I didn't. "Evelyn you aren't a wolf but you aren't half human either. There is something else going on here."

"W-what?" I asked in disbelief. "No my pack made it quite clear what I was and no one here has picked up on any scent that differs from being a half-blood…"

"Because wolves can't pick up the scents of witches Evelyn," Hannah said in frustration. "I think you're part witch and so does my mom. You can do things I can do and your aura makes so much more sense now. Why it was so hard for me to work my own magic on you. When is your birthday?"

My head felt dizzy as I looked at Hannah. Was she trying to be mean or was she being serious? Was she setting me up like they did in Idaho? Suddenly I felt very nervous that the big game of me being Aiden's mate was coming to an end and this might be the final draw card.

I could expect to be back in Idaho and become the laughing stock for the rest of my life. My skin prickled as I felt tears well up in my eyes as I realized this was all a big game and I had fallen into it again. I felt so stupid!

"Oh great. It's our two future females, both as weak as the other." We both looked to the curb to see Katherine standing there, all dressed up and nowhere to go. She held a bunch of files in her arms as she regarded us under her heavily made up eyes. "Oregon is going down the gutter, what the Moon Goddess is thinking I have no idea."

"Of course you have no idea," Hannah spat, visibly distressed. "She's the Moon Goddess and you aren't even on the same level as her."

Katherine's eyes went tight, and I saw her clench the folders in her arms before she seemed to take a calming breath and flashed us both a fake smile. "Just because the Moon Goddess chose you, *Evelyn*," she said my name like it was something sour. "That doesn't mean you're necessarily right for Aiden."

For a fully-fledged wolf she sure spoke lowly of her creator.

"If the Alpha heard the blasphemy you're sprouting right now-"

"Katherine, hello!" The Luna came out from the house with a tight smile. "I assume your mother has sent you over with the files I asked for."

"Yes Luna," Katherine bowed and immediately became two sizes smaller than the giant she had been mere seconds ago. Walking past us she handed the files to the Luna.

"Anything else then?" The Luna asked, staring her down.

"No. Not at all - uh, see you guys at school." She walked away like a dog with its tail between her legs. I found myself wishing I was as strong as the Luna; all she had done was look at her.

"Are you girls okay? I thought I heard shouting before."

I looked at Hannah from the corner of my eye, her revelations coming back to the forefront of my mind and I put myself back on guard, wondering the Luna's façade of being an accepting woman was going to drop as well. Hannah had clearly already cracked and was trying to get into my mind.

"We're fine, Luna, uh I have to go. I'll text you Evelyn." She smiled weakly before quickly leaving and I was left on the lawn outside, wondering whether or not I'd reply to her.

∞

Gym.

My palms sweat as I stood next to Lucy and Grace. Hannah stood on Lucy's other side but I made no contact with her, not since what she had said the other day and she knew I think, not to badger me with it either.

I was stressed enough as it was as I stared at the long climbing ropes dangling from the ceiling and old terrors ran across my mind like a slideshow. Back in Idaho, Jonah had tugged my rope when I was right at the top and with his superior wolf strength had torn it right out of the socket.

Hello, broken leg.

Hello, fear of heights.

I jumped when two hands positioned themselves on my waist but by the feelings that went through my body I knew it was Aiden. Suddenly my fear just seemed to ebb away as he kissed my cheek.

"Okay class, today we are rope climbing. You're all going to partner up; we'll do some demonstrations first. I want you to actually *try*," the gym teacher emphasized the word *try* and I wondered if she'd be as callous as the gym teacher back home.

This one was human though, so maybe I'd have better luck.

"Partner?" Aiden said to me with a grin and I nodded quickly, not really wanting to go with anyone else. As the teacher went through the best techniques to get up the rope I lost focus on her and instead focused on the circles Aiden made with his fingers on the side of my hip.

It made me tense to think just under his fingers and my shorts was that darn scar.

Suddenly people around us began jumping onto the rope, laughing and flailing around in the air before sliding down. Realizing we must have started I looked over to where Grace effortlessly pulled herself up the rope while Lucy texted on her phone below it.

"Do you think the teacher will notice if I don't climb the rope?" I asked Aiden quietly as I turned to face him. He smiled down at me before leading us over to the rope. "Maybe you should go first."

Aiden let go of my hand and took the rope in a firm grasp. He could probably climb up it one handed. Gym for werewolves must be so boring. He did climb it with one hand and I watched as the jocks from the falls party stood on the other side of the gym, scowling in our direction.

I quickly looked back at Aiden who dropped from the very top, landing with a loud thump that caused everyone to look over.

"Mr James, please be sensible," the gym teacher called out with a glower.

"Your turn," he said enthusiastically as he positioned the rope in front of me.

I didn't want to. My hands felt so slippery that I thought I wouldn't be able to hold on. My legs felt weak and I knew I wouldn't have the coordination to actually use my legs and my hands to get up this thing.

I didn't want to fall again.

"Come on Evie!" Lucy said with a wink as she dropped to the floor. "I've been up twice already."

"We'll have to rotate out soon." Grace was looking at me curiously, no doubt trying to piece together more of my past. Realizing my hesitation might lead to unwanted questions I took the rope from Aiden's hand.

"Just grasp it a little ways up and then jump," he directed. Doing as he said I clung the rope and jumped, making sure I was on securely. I'm not going to say he didn't help me because he did push me up a little ways before I was too far.

As I used every bit of energy in my body I knew Hannah had to be helping me. Rope climbing had never felt this easy before. As I reached the top I heard some cheers below me and I couldn't help the grin of satisfaction that formed on my face as I got ready to climb down.

Something happened in that split second.

There was a shout, a chorus of screeches as something hard hit me in the head and in my shock I release the rope and was suddenly plummeting down toward the ground. A squeal echoed through my ears before I made impact with something hard and a bit of the wind knocked out of me.

I gasped in terror as I was lowered to the floor by Aiden. My heart was pumping wildly and I was embarrassed to feel tears forming in my eyes.

"What the hell are you idiots thinking?" Grace was shouting at somebody.

"Thank God you caught her Aiden. Henderson! Myles!" Both boys looked up at the gym teacher, not looking at all sorry. "My office, now!"

Looking to my left I saw Katherine on the floor and I wondered what the heck she was doing down here. The glare on her face made my skin cold and I looked back at Aiden who stared down at me in worry.

"Are you okay?" He asked, "Did I hurt you?"

"Hurt her? You saved her from broken bones Aiden! I can't believe those assholes!" Lucy was practically bristling and Hannah looked ready to cry. My hands were shaking as my body seemed to pulse with adrenaline.

"You hurt me," I heard Katherine mutter as she got up. No one paid her any attention and I think that made her angry because she stormed out of the gym.

"What happened?" I asked quietly as my hands still shook.

"The boys from the fall party," Grace spat. "They kicked a volleyball at you."

"Aiden caught you," someone called out, sounding awed.

I looked back at Aiden and found myself smiling. No one caught me last time. Feeling a rush of different feelings I did something I never thought I'd do. I leant in and kissed him. I made the move not him.

When I pulled away my face felt red and I watched as people seemed to scatter away. Aiden looked at me with a grin.

"Wow."

∞

"How dare you even look in his direction!" A cold voice hissed into my ear as her claw like hands dragged their way down my scalp and neck to the back collar of my shirt, yanking it backwards before slamming my head down onto my desk.

I saw stars, I felt my nose clogging up with blood and my head pounded from the impact. I wasn't looking! My mouth wouldn't work, no words could come out.

I wasn't looking.
I wasn't looking.
Please.

Enveloped in a darkness of physical torture I awoke screaming and clutching the back of my head, wondering if I could feel the fleshy claw marks. I couldn't but I knew the scars were well hidden beneath my hair.

"I wasn't looking," I thought to myself as my eyes clogged up with tears and my nose dripped.

When would the nightmares stop?

"Evelyn?" My door burst open and Aiden stumbled in looking half asleep. The dream immediately disappeared as a wave of calm washed over me as Aiden came over. The usual safe-like bubble I got when he was around came back.

Also it was hard to focus on why I had been so freaked out seeing as he was standing in front of me in just some loose sweat pants.

"Evelyn? Are you okay?" He sat down on the edge of the bed, a worried crease between his eyebrows. "You were screaming."

I couldn't tell him why, I'd have to tell him everything.

Suddenly I felt like Heather's claw scars were visible and not hidden under my thick mane of hair.

"I'm fine," I croaked out, my voice hoarse. "Bad dream."

"You have those a lot," he muttered and I looked at him with a frown, not remembering disclosing that information to him. "I check on you after I do patrols. You're always murmuring or crying."

I'm sure my face drained of color. Had I said anything in my sleep that would lead back to Idaho? Grace's voice was chanting over and over in my head. *You have to tell him everything.*

"Evelyn?" Aiden's voice was quiet and I hesitantly looked at him, holding my hair out of my face as exhaustion hit. "I really like you Ev," his voice was cautious and I could see a tinge of red in his cheeks as he spoke. "I'm not stupid, I know you've gone through some things and I'll say what I always have, I'll wait. But you're going to need to open up one day and tell me everything; you have to let me in."

I was stunned as he kissed my forehead and left the room, the door shutting with a gentle click.

"But you're going to need to open up and tell me everything; you have to let me in."

Let him in.

Don't let him in

Leave.

Stay.

I was so tired of all this indecision, all my worries and doubts and I was tired of being afraid. It was so draining all the time. So what was I to do? Flopping back down in my bed I found new tears in my eyes only this time it wasn't fear but frustration.

Frustration with myself, frustration with Hannah and whether or not she really did sense something which led to confusion and frustration with my mother. I felt so angry I wanted to break something.

I knew I had to prove Hannah wrong, I needed to get one less worry off my mind. Looking around the room I wondered what I could do that could put my mind at ease and get her off my back. Flicking my gaze up to the roof I stared at the ceiling and to where my light once was, now missing the globe seeing as I shattered the entire thing.

There it was.

Okay if this worked I'd believe her. I'd believe myself. If this worked then I had a lot of questions for my mother. Raising my hand I rolled my eyes at myself for even trying, before closing them and thinking about the broken light itself. Imagining it wasn't shattered, nothing was broken.

It was a light.

To my shock and horror, the room lit up and judging by Grace's angry snarl so did the rest of the house.

Chapter Fourteen

"I can't go any further." Puffing I stopped running and hunched over, resting my hands on my knees as I sucked in glorious breaths of air. Aiden ran as fast as a leopard and even with my extra capabilities I couldn't keep up. We'd been running for what felt liked ages and I hoped it was because that meant we could stop soon.

"Good job, we made twenty minutes without stopping." Aiden sat on the floor, not really looking fatigued but I think he acted like he was for my benefit. He did have a small sheen of sweat on his forehead but I knew it'd take a lot more than a jog to make him really sweat. He could probably run for miles. "Jet said we needed to work especially on your hand to hand combat, which is good. I'd rather teach you than him anyway. He's good but he wasn't trained by my dad."

"Jet is terrifying," I muttered as I thought back to the male coach we had at training. He'd been scarred horrifically when he'd been captured by rogue wolves. His face, his arms…any bit of exposed skin.

"To you," he laughed as I sat beside him.

"To anyone who isn't your size." Plucking at some grass I squinted into the distance. We were positioned on a hill that overlooked the pack compound. I was trying to find our house. I gave up eventually and went back to thinking about Jet. "We had someone like him back in Idaho," I said quietly.

"Oh?" Aiden's voice piqued with maybe too much interest. Then again I hardly divulged much Idaho information to him.

"Yeah. Only he wasn't caught or anything. Apparently - from what I managed to hear - a rogue that had been caught broke free and really beat him. Probably the same way the rogue was beaten," I wrinkled my nose in disgust at some of the stories I'd heard. "This rogue wasn't as bad as the others. Apparently he'd never had a pack before. He was born into it."

"A rogue is a rogue. They're all the same," Aiden said bitterly and it was the first time I'd ever heard him talk that way.

I know there was a lot of stigma and drama when it came to pack wolves and rogues. Maybe I related to the rogues better because I felt like one my whole life. "W-well," I stammered feeling myself losing confidence. "H-he was different."

"He attacked that guy you just told me about."

"He was tortured," I said feeling heat rising in my cheeks as my palms began to sweat.

"He was a rogue."

It was just so…so…this was infuriating. Not all rogues were evil. They couldn't be. The rogue I had met…the one that had scarred his torturer, he was friendly. I helped him escape. I'd been hiding near the border after Jonah and his friends had been chasing me.

The rogue had stumbled over, bleeding and battered. I didn't know who he was or what he was, I couldn't get his scent after all. All I knew was that he looked like a male version of me. Terrified, abused and emotionally drained. He had the opportunity to escape and I didn't. So I helped him.

Sam.

Closing my eyes I found myself realizing I'd barely thought of him since being here. Then again after the beating I had received when they followed his tracks to me, made me too scared to ever think of him again.

"Do you know if this border goes to an ally pack or neutral?" The pale red haired man asked me, his eyes frantic as his wounds slowly healed before my eyes. I'm sure my reflection mirrored his and he stepped towards me, his arms outstretched. I stepped back and got ready to run. "Please!" He cried frantically. "They will kill me."

My hands tremored nervously and I looked at where I was standing. If he went North he'd reach the Montana border, and Idaho were on neutral terms with them right now, however if they caught him…I grimaced. To the East was Wyoming but the packs main base was Casper so he had a better chance of sneaking through and then going South to unoccupied lands.

I hesitantly relayed the information and he nodded frantically as he listened. "Thank you. Thank you so much…" He squinted at me and I licked my dry lips nervously.

"Evelyn," I uttered.

"Thank you Evelyn. I'm Sam. I'm never going to forget this."

Then he was gone.

"I'm ready to run again," I muttered as I got up, shaking that memory from my head. I didn't even wait for his reply as I set off at a cracking pace. That conversation was another reminder why pack life terrified me so much.

∞

Sitting in Math with Lucy is always funny. She'll do anything to get under Mr Collins' (it feels too weird calling him Geoff) skin. She spends more time hiking up the edge of her skirt or stretching her arms back so her chest pops out.

I'm sure some of the other boys in the class enjoyed it.

They seemed like such an odd pair. To me Lucy was a wild person, a free spirit. From what she had told me about Geoff I'd constructed a fairly serious man in my head. I saw him as someone with his head in the books, someone who wouldn't try human drugs to see if they had any effect on you.

Lucy was insane.

I hadn't seen Hannah in a few days and the fact she wasn't responding to any of my texts now had me concerned that I had offended her. Or maybe she was giving up the rouse of being my friend. It was only at lunch when I found out that she and Josh were taking a couple of days in wolf form.

I knew a lot of wolves did that. Sometimes they just needed it, the animal in them growing too wild from being contained; if they were out for an extended period of time they'd be less edgy.

I felt slightly strained with Aiden after our discussion on the hill. He seemed like nothing was wrong but I had this new fear inside me. Something I hadn't felt before. I'd never openly expressed my views to anyone, was I allowed to do that? Have an opinion different to his?

Heather had always agreed with Jonah, from what I saw she never had her own original idea, even before they found out they were mates. Is that what you did? Just agree? Because I didn't and couldn't.

If I didn't have the same view on rogues as he did would that make me a bad Luna? Would he be able to carry out whatever duty he had to with them, if I was always in the background silently disagreeing with him?

The bell rang and I was glad to get out of the class, who knew what Lucy would do next. I headed off to art alone, my mind jumbling before a pair of well-manicured feet encased in strappy sandals appeared in my view and didn't move.

Following those feet up strong but feminine looking legs to a white skirt that seemed way too short and a terrible blue crop top I came face to face with Katherine whose pretty face was marred by a terrible scowl.

"You're in my way, *half-breed*." The hall was virtually empty with only two or three students loitering but they barely paid us any attention. Definitely human.

There were plenty of things I could say to her:

"There's more to this walkway than this pathway." Or, *"Maybe you're in my way."* Instead I just apologized and moved out of her way and she scoffed, pushing my shoulder.

"They say you're the future Luna. You have the makings of an Omega. Your offspring will be just as pathetic as you and this pack will never have a strong Alpha after Aiden. So many people see the flaws in your relationship." She pruned her decadent long black hair and sighed, "Aiden and I were planned to be together. Alpha James wanted to keep this pack strong; your arrival ruined it all!"

"Well I'm sorry," I said quietly and I watched as her eyes narrowed. "The Moon Goddess chose me, not you. I'm sorry that you can't accept that. I hope you find the wolf she chose for you, but it's not Aiden and it never would have been!"

I'm not sure where I gathered the strength from… to walk away like that, to turn my back on her and carry on to my class.

Maybe it's because I knew she couldn't physically touch me. She'd sign her own death certificate if she did. I felt stronger somehow, I didn't know if it was because my relationship with Aiden was growing or if it was just me.

All I know is that I never would have attempted that in Idaho.

Lying on my bed later that day I kept looking at the broken light in the ceiling. The Luna had put it down to the fact it was faulty - after I had managed to turn on every light in the house. Someone was coming to fix it tomorrow.

I knew now it wasn't faulty. I had done it, just like I had done it with the jug of water on my date with Aiden. There was something within me as Hannah said, and I was hoping she'd reply to my desperate texts soon.

Today was wolf training so I couldn't attend that seeing I couldn't shift. Instead I was supposed to be meeting Aiden who was going to take me through the combat stuff. I'll admit I was nervous about it. Things felt weird after our talk on the hill, even if he didn't think things were.

Even though I was feeling nervous about us my stomach still fluttered when he walked into my room dressed in his casual training gear and I couldn't stop the smile that automatically spread on my face.

"Hey," I murmured.

"Hey beautiful." I flushed and felt my nose wrinkle as I dropped my eyes to the bed.

Me? Beautiful?

"Are you ready to get started?"

"Yeah." Quickly I got up from the bed, ignoring the phone and following him from the house to the large backyard outside. In the class we mostly had bags, only a few people actually fought each other. Did he expect me to hit him? I don't know if I had the courage to take a swing.

"Okay so first we'll work on your stance and stuff. You need to be steady on your feet, in the end how your carry yourself will determine whether you win or lose a fight and in your case, if you're fighting another wolf…you won't heal. You need to be extra careful. They're strong, but you still have some wolf strength, use it."

This class was a little different to Jet's. The whole time Aiden was there, moving my body, positioning me, basically using any opportunity he could to touch me even when he didn't need to. I wasn't going to say anything.

He showed me how to move, so I stayed steady. He even shoved me randomly a few times to see if I was focusing, most times I made it. He was strong. After about two hours we called it a day, he was happy with what we had done and I felt it went better than the classes I took with the girls.

Lying on the grass beside Aiden we stared up at the expanse of blue sky and a chill went through the air. It was going to be Fall soon. I wonder what they did for Halloween here.

In Idaho everyone dressed up like humans. I guess it was funny but it lost its originality after the first few thousand times they had done it.

They'd have this big Halloween party for all the teenagers and a big group of kids would go trick or treating. I'd done the trick or treating as a kid, mom always took me. The parties…I'd never been, I used to hear them from my room.

"That's a very thoughtful looking frown on your face," Aiden said quietly beside me.

Feeling a little sassy I pursed my lips and said, "Well I'm in thoughtful mood."

"So am I."

My skin prickled; hopefully his thoughts weren't going to lead to any questions I didn't want to answer. "What are you thinking about?"

He huffed as he rested his arms behind his head, staring at the sky. "The future really, what I want to study at College. How much free time will I get before dad wants me to take over from him? I'd like to see some of the world. I have a friend in Italy; his pack is one of the largest in the world. Known him for ages."

My interest was gained, not a lot of wolves mingled with packs outside of America. "How did you become friends?"

"Exchange program," he laughed. I looked at him, seriously? "No, my cousin found her mate when she was traveling. Family was pretty happy about it, a neutral alliance with an international pack, not an easy feat."

"Why are you allied with Alaska?" I asked, remembering my old packs confusion over it. "Did he really want just free booze?"

Aiden snorted. "When you're one of the most powerful packs in the world, if you want to ally with someone for free booze you can do it. Plus we aren't the worst pack to be allied with either."

"But he's so far away."

"He moves fast. You've heard the stories."

"Yeah I heard the stories," I said. "A lot of packs don't like him."

"He does some questionable stuff," Aiden admitted. "No one ever takes him to the High Council though so, if they really wanted to stop what he does they could. They're just scared now. Alpha Hudson doesn't follow the rules. Why would he? He comes from a line of rogues."

Oh not rogue talk again. We needed to steer clear of conversation that went this way. "He's like twenty-five right?" I murmured, squinting at a cluster of fluffy clouds.

"Yeah. Crazy he hasn't found his mate yet." I shrugged, those things happened in due time. As the clouds moved I watched as they formed into a shape. It sort of looked like a duck really. I looked at Aiden hesitantly, biting my lip. One side of his face was lit up by the sun; the side closest to me was shaded.

I liked his features, they were strong. He looked like an Alpha, not like Jonah. Jonah still looked like a boy really. He was too pretty as well, his hair was always perfect. I felt my eyes widen as Aiden turned his head to face me with a grin. I felt my own smile creep on my face.

"You look beautiful in the sun," he murmured as he got up and rolled onto his stomach, resting up on his arms. "Your eyes almost look amber from the light." My breath caught when his finger went to the scar at the top of my hairline. "How'd this happen?" He asked.

I swallowed, feeling my pulse quicken, frozen to the spot. "Can't remember," I lied. I could hear the lie, it didn't sound like a casual answer and I watched as his lips pressed together, like he was deciding whether or not to push.

Please don't.

"You look healthier," he said as he grazed his hand down my arm. I felt my skin break out in goose bumps from the action and I wondered if I did look healthier. I barely noticed my own body; I made a point not too. "I think my mother put herself on a mission to fatten you up."

I let out a genuine laugh at the Luna. She was a great woman. The kindest Luna - the only Luna - I'd ever met besides Larissa. She could never match up to the woman here. "I think I'm naturally thin though."

"I think so too, but that won't stop her."

Another gust of chilled air came through the yard and I shivered, making a face. "It's going to be cold soon."

"You don't like the cold?"

Oh boy did I not. When the weather got colder in Idaho the attacks just seemed more brutal. I'm not sure why, maybe they were bored because the bad weather would stop them from other activities. Jonah's favorite game was to push my head in a puddle and see how long I could hold my breath.

"No," I said quietly. "I hate Winter."

"Me too. I hate running patrols in the rain, it's so cold. Plus trying to catch a scent and stay on it is the hardest part. I broke my leg falling down a cliff one year; the rain was so hard I didn't even know where I was. Healed in five seconds but still, hurt for that moment."

I felt myself startled at the idea of him injured and had to reassure myself that he was fine. I assumed our bond was getting stronger; these weird feelings had been starting to attack me a lot more lately. I sighed and toyed with the hem of my shirt. "I fell through weak ice when I was skating one year." Well fell isn't the word I'd use, pushed onto the ice was more like it. I can still remember that freezing water, and the thought I'd never make it out.

Aiden frowned, as if he'd just experienced those same emotions I'd felt earlier. "Well…no lake skating this winter then." His voice was grim, but there was a hint of humor and I found myself smiling up at him weakly.

Just as he leant in a bustle of voices came around the side of the house, some started wolf-whistling. Ha, *wolf*-whistling. He rolled his eyes, giving me a cheeky grin before getting up to his feet pulling me with him.

∞

"*Go on half-breed, skate!*" *Heather pushed me onto the weak looking ice and I yelped in fear as I felt it shift beneath me. It hadn't been a very cold winter and this ice could crack any minute. I was light but I wasn't that light.*

How could I skate? I wasn't even wearing blades. Of course they couldn't care less, I knew what they wanted and I knew their wish would come true. Feeling a cold lump hit my head I grimaced and raised my hand, only to be attacked by another and another vicious snowball attack.

Laughs could be heard from the shore as I moved further and further out until I was in the middle of the lake and out of their range. Eventually they got bored with me just standing there but none of them wanted to come onto the ice to get me, so they gave up and left.

I was still frozen to the spot, terrified if I moved it would crack and I'd fall in, but it was starting to get late and I couldn't stay here all night either. Calling for help did nothing, anyone who recognized my voice would probably walk in the other direction.

I trembled in the cold air, feeling myself crying before I knew it was even happening. My tears were hot compared to the wind whipping across my face and I rubbed my nose as that started to drip as well.

Death by icy lake.

A big gust of wind caused me to stumble backwards and that sickening crack of the ice breaking was enough to send my stomach into my boots as it gave way and I went under.

I sat up hurriedly in my bed clutching my chest as I breathed heavily, gasping for much needed air as I pulled myself to the realization that I was in my bed and not sinking to oblivion.

Forcing myself to lay back down I found my thoughts drifting to other horrible things that had happened in Idaho and I couldn't turn them off. This just happened some nights, I'd sit there and think and wonder about what caused them to have so much hate for me, besides my status.

They truly despised every inch of my being.

I didn't end up getting much sleep that night and I was exhausted by the following afternoon when Hannah finally showed up in my room while I poured over homework. Aiden was patrolling and I had training in an hour.

"I had no phone access, I'm so sorry!" Hannah quickly gave me a hug. "So…you sort of believe me now? I promise you I wasn't taking the mickey or anything. I genuinely believe you've got a little something going on there."

I nodded at her, pointing at my light. "That's definitely broken and I turned it on using my mind. I also switched on the rest of the house too. Then the Luna said it was probably faulty so I don't know. What if…what if it is faulty and I was just pretending to do magic?"

"Like when people say the lights going to turn green and it does, then they think they're Sabrina?" She made herself comfy on my bed and I nodded firmly.

"Too many things I've done have all been coincidental. Except for the water jug on my date with Aiden."

"So you feel you need to prove it to yourself then?" She asked me. "That's okay so did I. When mom said what I could do and what I was capable of I laughed at her, until I actually started doing it. I can't do as much as she can because some of my genes are stained by the wolf gene. Something makes me think though that maybe that side of you is more powerful than the wolf side of you though, which is crazy. Witch genes aren't as dominant as the wolf gene."

Another defect, I thought. Typical that'd be my case. Why couldn't I just be half like Hannah? At least I'd be able to shift then.

"Maybe you can try doing some of the exercises I do," she suggested as she dug through her book bag. She pulled out an old leather bound book, the pages inside falling out a little. "This is my family's book. Each of us get one each generation. I'll lend you some pages and just try - only when you think Grace won't come barging in."

I nodded slowly as she handed me ones she thought I could do. Some of them looked weird, and some required me to say the words. I crinkled my nose instantly for some reason. It felt silly. Everything I'd done had been in my mind.

"So when does this not be a big secret anymore?" Hannah asked hopefully.

I bit my lip and put the notes she gave me in my bedside drawer. "When I work out what's wrong with me and when I talk to my mom. She'll know more than I do."

"Are you a little pissed she's lied to you for years?"

I frowned. "She might not have known."

I knew Hannah wanted to say something else, but she wisely didn't because I knew I would jump to my mom's defense straight away. She couldn't have known she wouldn't have let me go through so much if she had, surely.

Suddenly my door flew open and Grace and Lucy flew in, all dressed for training and both beaming. "You guys want to go see a movie tonight? There's a new comedy out. Starts at seven so we can wash up after training and then go."

The movies? I mused inwardly; I hadn't been since I was six. Jada kicked up a stink every other time after that, so I just stayed at home to save my mother the hassle. I'd seen people from the pack go all the time, it kind of made me sad to miss out on it.

"So are we going?" Grace asked.

I nodded and so did Hannah, both of us smiling. I remembered that Hannah hadn't been friends with Grace and Lucy long. Only since becoming mates with Josh had they all struck up a friendship. I guess for her, being invited out somewhere was like being accepted.

It felt that way to me.

Today's training was a weights class. The instructor Ralph was built like a tank and I watched as girls set up their bars with huge amounts of weight. Five pounds was enough for me. Hannah loaded up her bar and winked at me, wriggling her fingers magically.

Ralph had to help me a lot. He had to fix my posture, my stance and not to mention, spot me. My arms were aching by the end of it and I felt like I had been hit by a semi-trailer.

I guess this would be another class to work on with Aiden.

I met Aiden outside the training grounds, he'd worked up a sweat doing whatever class he'd just been in and I was admiring the way his muscles shone with the combination of the setting sun and the sweat. I wondered how much weight he could lift. If girls in my class were doing six hundred pounds then he could do a lot more.

I happily accepted the offer of a piggy back home, my legs were way too sore to even think about walking those fifteen minutes back to the house. Grace had to beat Trey into giving her a piggy ride home but she finally beat him into submission and he rolled his eyes as he lifted her off the ground.

I thought I saw him smile a little though.

So when we finally got home I had a quick shower and found myself excitedly going through my wardrobe to find something to wear. I'd never had this kind of excitement, only when we had got ready for the falls party. This is another thing that had been missing from my life, friendships and doing things.

I settled on a pair of blue jeans and a gray stretch cotton shirt before pulling over a creamy sweater that ended near my upper thigh. I rolled the sleeves up a little as they were long, before I pulled my hair up in a ponytail and slipped on a pair of black boots that the Luna had bought me.

As I made it to the hallway Grace was still in the shower so I hesitantly walked to Aiden's door, knocking lightly. I hoped he was dressed. He opened it with a smile, shirtless but wearing a pair of dark jeans. I did my very best to keep my eyes on his face.

"You look great," he said as he went over to his drawers. I slowly walked into the room, enjoying the smell that invaded my senses. He smelt fresh, like a warm summer evening mixed with light rain. I wasn't sure if that was even a scent but I thought it was.

Sitting on his bed I watched his back muscles ripple slightly whenever he moved his arms in his drawers, looking for a top to wear. Finally he settled on a gray one and pulled a black and gray hooded jacket out from his closet.

"How do I look?" He asked with a smirk.

Like a Calvin Klein model, I wanted to say. Thankfully I have a filter between my brain and mouth. "Great," I managed and also copying what he had said earlier. I offered a smile to compensate for my lack of originality.

I was taken by surprise when he leant down; resting his arms either side of me, his face now level with mine. He looked at me for a second before catching my lips in his. I felt like I could kiss him forever. The feelings that went through me whenever we kissed were nearly addictive. I found my hands on either side of his face, feeling a slight prickle of stubble under them.

His right hand ghosted over my neck, his thumbnail grazing over the skin between my neck and shoulder and it tickled. I giggled into his mouth and pulled back, my smile mirroring his. I'm sure my flustered cheeks did as well.

"Come on love birds, I'd like to make the movie on time!" Grace yelled from the other side of the door.

Aiden shook his head and stood up straight again, stretching out his hand. "Come on, the last thing I need is her in here, ruining the smell of this room." I blushed a little, knowing my scent would linger here for a while. I guess his wolf would enjoy that.

Taking his hand I followed him from the room, my enthusiasm lifting even more when I realized I could get popcorn.

Chapter Fifteen

"Well, I've seen better movies." Grace dumped her box of popcorn into the bin and stretched her arms out above her head. "So incredibly cliché."

"You picked it," Trey pointed out.

Grace made a face at the back of his head as we all walked further into the mall. Aiden walked beside me, my hand firmly in his as we followed after everybody. Much to my surprise Katherine had come along with Josh, her brother. Hannah had texted me a heads up. Now Katherine trailed ahead alongside Lucy, talking like they were the best of friends. Lucy's tight smile said it all.

Our confrontation was still fresh in my mind and I didn't miss the backward glances she gave. I didn't get why she was here, Grace and Lucy had given clear indication on how much they disliked her. I stared at the back of Josh's head. Sometimes I think he let Katherine get away with a lot, for instance, the way she treated Hannah.

"Who wants to go to the arcade?" Grace called out as she stopped underneath a neon flashing sign. "I want to play air hockey."

"Yes!" Lucy shouted as she happily walked faster toward Grace - leaving Katherine to totter around in her strappy heels. Unfortunately, she slowed enough to walk beside Aiden.

"How did you like the movie, Aiden?" Katherine practically purred as she played with the ends of her hair. The sounds of the arcade got closer and I hoped she'd disappear when we arrived.

"It was alright. Bit of a chick flick. Typical seeing as it was Grace's choice." Aiden looked down at me and smiled and I gave him a weak smile back, my hand marginally tightening on his. "You look like you enjoyed it," he said to me.

My cheeks went red and I shrugged. "It was good."

Katherine looked between us quickly, like she was trying to think of something to say to get the attention back on her. She must have figured something out because a moment later she opened her mouth. "What about that movie we saw…" and it went like that even as we entered the arcade. Katherine went on and on about all the different movies she'd seen with Aiden, even going as far as to grabbing onto his arm.

An ugly little monster reared in my mind and I realized I was starting to get jealous. I also wanted her damn hand off his arm. As I looked around the arcade I spotted Trey and Josh playing some sort of gun game, Grace was at an air hockey table with Lucy and Hannah.

"Oh Evelyn, let's play this one," Aiden said enthusiastically as he pulled me towards a console in front of two car seats. It looked like a racing game. Katherine was left in the entrance and I was glad for it, I'd play any game Aiden wanted to as long as Katherine stayed far away.

The only problem was I didn't get how it worked at all. I couldn't even drive in real life, let alone something on a machine. It was all interactive, you could feel the chair shake and move around whenever you rammed into something or turned too sharply.

I think Aiden lapped me twice and when I made it to the finish line he was waiting and watching my console as he'd beat me to the end already. When I came up as the loser my lip twitched. Very fitting. Aiden helped me out of my chair and went through a recap of the whole race, including how many times I hit things.

Aiden went off toward Trey and Josh and I wasn't interested in their shooting game so I went to find Hannah and the others. They were shooting basketballs into hoops, Grace cursing wildly every time she missed.

As I noticed Hannah's very concentrated face I knew she was using her magic to make the balls go in the hoop every time. Hannah was declared the winner and Grace ranted that she'd never play with her again.

"That wasn't fair!" Grace complained loudly.

"You agreed to go against me," Hannah said smugly.

It surprised me when Katherine came over to us as we lounged by the basketball game, talking. Well the girls talked - I listened as they gossiped mainly, however conversation ceased when Katherine made an appearance.

"*Katie,*" Lucy said sweetly. "Why are you here tonight?" I looked at Lucy, my eyes wide. She was so blunt, so to the point…how awkward. I even noticed Katherine's cheeks tinge a little and I felt uncomfortable. "You've made it abundantly clear what you think of all of us, so we're a little confused as to why you came out with us."

"Or maybe not entirely confused," Grace said, her eyes flashing.

"Is it your turn to say something now?" Katherine said with a look of nonchalance as she stared Hannah down. Hannah visibly shrunk and kept her mouth shut while a catty smile formed on Katherine's face. "You know, I was wondering the other day why the Moon Goddess would choose such a weak girl to be the future Luna. Then I realized we already have a future weak Beta female. Wolfsbane is clearly going to the *dogs.*"

"It's a wonder you stick around," Lucy said airily as she loaded up a new basketball game. You'd think from the tension Lucy's calm façade would have been proven fake as she started shooting hoops, however her throws only seemed more determined.

"Aiden will see what he's missing eventually." Her words left an awful taste in my mouth and I couldn't help but look at her. She looked at me scornfully. "What? You think that just because you said some words to me I'd be giving up? You're pathetic, Evelyn. Aiden will see that eventually and then you can go back home to Idaho where you belong." Her eyes flickered amber as a nasty smile plastered itself on her face. "Jonah says hi by the way."

My nose crinkled in both disgust and fear as Grace looked at me quickly before back at Katherine. "Why are you speaking to the future Alpha of Idaho? Who has a mate by the way! Then again obviously that wouldn't stop you."

"We met at the party; it's none of your business anyway. Our packs are allied and I'm a Beta of this pack. I can talk to whoever I want." With that she promptly turned on her heel and went toward the race car game, giving me a look before sliding into the empty seat beside some random guy.

"One day I will tear a strip off her," Grace seethed. We all looked at her in surprise. You couldn't just tear a strip of a wolf. You really had to have a good reason for it. It tore their rank and everything and if Grace did it just because she didn't like someone - well the consequences for her would be astronomical.

"I didn't know you'd talked to her," Lucy said to me.

My mouth felt dry as all the girls turned to look at me. "I just t-told her that…if the M-Moon Goddess chose me then…then she needed to stop."

Grace growled under her breath. "I really want to call her the S word."

"You've been cursing all night, why stop now?" Hannah muttered.

Grace briefly glared at Hannah before puffing out her chest. "I've reached my swear quota. I'll call her one tomorrow."

∞

"Did you practice anything from the book?" Hannah asked me as I handed it back to her. We were in the middle of the woods. It was the first time I'd been this far out in the territory, and I felt a little nervous.

"No," I shook my head. "I'm sorry…it felt weird. It felt like…like it wasn't m-mine to use."

She nodded as she slipped the book into her bag. "I had a feeling it would. That's okay. Those books are created through generations of our different blood lines. Usually it won't work in the hands of someone who isn't part of that specific family."

"So why did you give it to me?" I asked, bewildered.

"I wanted to see if you could use it anyway," she shrugged.

"Okay, so we are here today to test you out a bit more...have you spoken to your mom yet?"

"No... I haven't had any time to call her. I will." Truth is I had time; I just didn't want to have that conversation because the questions I had to ask may have answers I might not like...and she might not like the questions.

"That's alright, it would just help a little...it would give us more of an insight into what you are...we'll get to that. So when you do stuff...how have you done it? What do you do?" She looked at me eagerly, a notepad ready. Was she going to study me? "Mom's going to read over what I write and see if she can work you out," she told me.

"Your mom knows?" I nearly shouted in shock.

"She's cool Evie; she isn't going to say boo to anyone."

"Hannah...I didn't want anyone to know," I protested quietly.

"Evelyn just trust me," she pleaded. "Mom is a genius, if I can't figure you out she can. Come on." I gave her a long look before sighing, signaling my defeat. She nodded seriously before gesturing at me to pick up from where we had left off.

"I guess...I just focus on what I want. Then I kind of picture myself doing it."

"Like leaving your body in your mind?" She murmured as she bit the end of her pen. I shrugged, that sounded like what I was trying to say. The truth was, I didn't know how I did what I did.

"That time on my date with Aiden though, I didn't even know what I was doing at the time. I wasn't even focusing on the water it just moved with my finger." I had something I couldn't necessarily control...this whole thing was confusing.

Hannah stopped suddenly, her face going white like she had seen a ghost. Her nose crinkled in disgust and I watched as her eyes glazed over as she used the pack link. Why was she using the pack link? Why did she look so scared?

A twig snapped behind me and I spun around quickly, backing myself toward Hannah who gripped my arm frantically.

Three dirty looking wolves were standing in front of us, a stone's throw away. I knew by their unkempt look they were rogues. Judging by Hannah's nose she would have smelt their disgusting scent that a rogue supposedly carried with them.

"I've called the Alpha," she whispered shakily in my ear. "Do as I say, at all times."

I shrieked as one of them jumped at us, the scariest looking one on the right. Hannah pushed me behind her at the same time she flicked her wrist and the wolf contorted in mid-air, pain lacing through his features as he howled violently. Hannah flicked it again and I watched as the wolf's neck snapped and he fell limp to the floor.

The other two by this point looked really pissed off. Rogues didn't believe in packs however they did have a few small groups they travelled in; they still bonded like regular wolves. If Hannah killed their friend or worse, their leader, we were screwed.

Hannah obviously felt more confident in her human form. I'd never asked if she could do magic in wolf form. Probably not, she seemed to need her hands most of the time. The other two still hadn't made a move however they had started circling us, and I got the gist of their plan.

One would take Hannah and the other would take me. Hannah had a better chance of getting out of this intact. If a wolf got me I was toast. There was a yelp and looked over Hannah's shoulder quickly to see she had taken down another wolf.

Then she shifted.

That was the most terrifying feeling of my life. I'd never had someone shift so close to me before but I was flung into a tree and I groaned from the impact I made with my head. Feeling blood trickling down my face I watched as two snarling wolves went at each other.

Hannah was a little smaller than the rogue and her beautiful cream coat was getting muddied and bloodied up. Every time she yelped my heart lurched in my chest. With one violent swipe with the rogues paws Hannah was flung into a tree and I shouted in horror as she made impact before falling onto the floor, not moving.

The rogue then turned its evil looking eyes on me and my breathing quickened as I was posed with life or death. How many times in my life had this feeling ran through my body? I never got used to it.

I wasn't a violent person; I didn't want to hurt the rogue in front of me, regardless of whether he wanted to kill me.

The wolf stalked me, each time I watched his claws dig into the earth I had the terrifying image that they would soon be digging into me. I didn't know what to do. He had this look on his face like he'd won already; he knew he was going to get an easy kill.

So many people had looked at me like that in my life.

Looking back down at his huge paws I noticed they were now near buried in the thick leaves that surrounded the tree I was under. I also saw some pretty impressive roots that had started protruding from the ground. A weird tremble went through my body as my mind seemed to come alive.

The branches started to move slowly, creaking even at the effort to do so. This was an old tree, a powerful tree. Taking a leap of stupidity and trust in myself, I did what I thought I'd done once before with the light.

I used my imagination. It was better to give it a try than to die with the thought of, 'Oh no, what am I supposed to do?' Focusing on the devilish creature before me I observed briefly he was getting way too close now. My focus moved to the roots and I closed my eyes, shaking nervously.

He could jump any minute and that would be the end of me.

Shaking that thought I saw what I wanted to happen. Those roots would come up from the ground, wrap around the rogue and trap him. That's all I needed. I'd done it with the light switch; maybe I'd even done it to Jada that day in the dress shop.

Focus, trust yourself.

It seemed too quiet, my skin prickled and my mouth felt dry as I waited for my death to come.

The ground suddenly seemed to shake as I kept playing the scene over and over in my head and my eyes flashed open. They felt warm suddenly, but I had to ignore that. I knew I was focusing and judging by the way the ground shook beneath us I knew what I was trying to do was working.

Which confirmed all my fears, that I was still a deformity and that there was something else going on with me. In a sickening crunch I watched as the root shot up from the ground at the same time the wolf snarled and launched itself at me.

Changing tactics and knowing I had no time to trap him I pictured the wolf in mid-air and the root curled itself backward and flicked him away as if he were nothing but a piece of dirt on my hand. All that was heard was the thump as the strong root made contact with the wolf and the yelping winded sound that came from him as he was flung far off into the forest.

The moment I broke focus the root dropped back to the earth and I fell over as the ground shook beneath me. I looked over at Hannah who had come to and must have watched the whole thing with wide eyes. She was naked, from shifting and I hurriedly pulled off my cardigan and gave it to her.

I looked down at the two dead bodies, seeing as they had shifted back when Hannah had killed them. It surprised me to see one was a woman. She looked just as unkempt in human form as she did when she was a wolf.

"Evie," Hannah whispered as she gripped my arm. "That was insane...your eyes..." Her bewildered speech was cut off as we heard pounding paws approaching and I looked at Hannah.

"Say you killed all of them," I pleaded quickly.

"Evelyn! We can't lie about you anymore...this is insane. I couldn't even control a tree!"

"I didn't control a tree I used it!" I said frantically. "Hannah just say it was you."

"Evelyn!"

"Hannah," I begged. "Please." She looked at me sideways before sighing and nodding her head, she didn't look happy though.

Suddenly a group of fifteen wolves entered the space we were in and took in the situation. Aiden shifted almost immediately and I didn't even get to see what his wolf looked like. I nearly squealed in surprise when his naked body took form and I averted my eyes. Didn't these guys stash clothes anywhere? I was suddenly swept up in his arms and any embarrassment I was suffering from catching a glimpse of…well that embarrassment heightened.

"Are you okay? Did you get hurt? Why are you girls even out here?" His words were rushed and it was possibly one of the only times I'd ever seen him losing his cool, calm and collected façade he had on. He showed his age at this moment.

All the wolves shifted and I felt like I couldn't look anywhere. Everyone was naked. I mean in the wolf community nakedness is normal, it just happens when you shift back. I however had not spent much time around shifting wolves in Idaho, therefore my eyes and mind was very, very virginal. Until now.

"I was showing Evelyn some magic," Hannah lied smoothly. She'd have to be convincing, if the Alpha picked up on her scent, covered in guilt and dishonesty he'd lose it. "I needed space for what I wanted to show her."

"Why'd you lie about going to the mall?" Josh demanded, his features etched in worry as he inspected her. I noticed she had dried blood on her skin however any wounds she may have received had healed before they had all arrived.

"Evelyn and I weren't sure if you guys were cool with her coming out into the territory."

"You are both so far out! What if there had been more? How did you even manage to take out three mature rogue wolves Hannah?" Alpha James looked at her with tight eyes and I knew my lies were putting her in the firing line for serious punishment.

"We lost track of how far we came out," Hannah mumbled lamely, her cheeks red.

"Hannah you're on a shifting ban for five days. For a further ten you can shift, but you will be required to state where you're running and for how long you're running for to the head patroller. Evelyn," Alpha James sighed and ran a hand over his head and I kept my eyes on Aiden's chest. The safest spot for my poor eyes right now. "This could have gone so badly for you girls," The Alpha muttered. "It's good to know your training actually works. Hannah I want you in my office and I want a fully detailed report on what happened here."

"Yes Alpha," her voice trembled and her eyes watered a little.

"Dispose of these bodies," he ordered a man next to him, who I remembered to be the Beta from the ball. "Everyone else besides me, Aiden and Josh - run a full border perimeter. If you see any rogues, don't hesitate just take them out."

Everything else happened so quickly and before I knew it we were back at the pack hall. Aiden finally got some clothing on so I was able to look at him again. Hannah was taken to the Alpha's office and Aiden took me home.

My mind was bustling. I had definitely done something, there was no coincidence now. Which means my mother lied when she said it was a human who attacked her. The rest of her bloodline was pure, there were no gene mutations or anything, it was all wolf.

"You have no idea what went through my mind when Hannah showed me what she was seeing. A rogue wolf walking right up behind you and you didn't even see it coming," Aiden's fists clenched and unclenched on the wheel. "We rarely get rogues, something isn't right. I don't get why you two went out so far, Hannah should know better."

I felt sick to my stomach for Hannah. She was copping the full brunt of it, but my mouth couldn't form the words I needed to say she had nothing to do with it. That I was the big liar, keeping a huge secret.

When we arrived at the house the Luna ran out straight away, wrapping me in a hug. "Goddess, Evelyn I was so worried. You need to call your mother right away and tell her you're okay."

Mom, I had to call mom.

When Aiden finally let go of me I escaped to my room and sat in the center of my bed, my finger hovering over the call button for my mom's number. How was I supposed to ask her what I needed to know? How would she take it? She couldn't lie now, there was no way I was half human.

I pressed the call button.

"*Evelyn?*" My mother's voice answered after two rings and I knew she must have been waiting by the phone. "*Evelyn are you okay?*"

"I'm fine," I whispered as my voice cracked. My emotions hit me all at once and I realized how close to death I had been. What if I hadn't been able to lift those roots? Hannah and I would have been ripped apart.

"*Evelyn-*"

"Mom..." we spoke at the same time and there was a brief awkward silence. "Sorry, you go."

"*No, you go.*"

My stomach clenched as I took a breath and willed myself the courage to say what I needed to ask. "Mom...something's wrong with me."

"*What do you mean? Did the rogues hurt you?*" Her voice was frantic and I knew she would have lurched up to a standing position had she been sitting down. "*I'll get on the first flight over there Evelyn, I'll come see you.*"

"No - no mom I'm not hurt," I said hurriedly.

"*Why do you think something is wrong with you then darling?*"

"Mom...I'm," I swallowed the lump in my throat. "I'm doing things...s-stuff I c-can't explain. M-maybe I've been doing this stuff for a while...I o-only just realized I was actually doing it...I-"

"*Honey you aren't making any sense,*" she murmured gently down the line.

"I - God..." I huffed in frustration. "Who is my father?" The line was silent, like deathly silent. The only sound that gave away she had heard what I said was her sharp intake of breath, like I had sucker punched her. "Mom?"

"*Evelyn...h-honey, you - you don't have a f-father. I was r-raped,*" her voice cracked and I felt instantly bad for asking about it. Maybe that was her true story...maybe I was just some sort of huge mix of weird genes.

"Mom…I'm sorry…"

"*I've got to go darling,*" her voice cracked and it was my turn to feel winded this time. "*I'll check in with you later. I love you.*" The call shut off and I fell forward in both shame and frustration. If that's what she said I believed her, but it still didn't explain *me*.

What was happening?

∞

"I'm really sorry Hannah," I said quietly on the phone. She had called me the moment she'd finished her report with the Alpha. "I feel terrible."

"*It's alright, really. The ban will fly by and I don't usually run by myself anyway so really it was a lenient punishment. The fact that he thinks I killed all those rogues has impressed him though, so it kind of makes me sound a lot tougher than I am. Maybe Katherine will get off my back.*"

"Josh looked mad."

"*He was just worried. We're all okay now. Your face when Aiden shifted though, I thought only tomatoes could go that red!*" Her attempt to find humor in the situation worked and I found myself blushing again.

"I'm not used to so much nudity."

"*You should get used to it. Once Aiden marks you you'll spend more time out of your clothes then in them.*"

"Hannah!" I squealed down the phone.

She snorted with laughter before she sobered up. "*We can't keep it a secret forever Evie. We really need more help here and the fact your mom is sticking to her story…*"

"It might be the truth."

"*It doesn't make sense Evelyn and you know it. I know you love your mom but she is definitely hiding something serious.*" What she said made sense, my mom's answer to my question made me feel ashamed yet curious. Because it didn't sit right.

Aiden walked into my room at that moment and I hurriedly ended the call, biting my lip nervously as he flopped face forward onto my bed. I wasn't sure if he was going to say anything or just lay there. I continued to just sit and stare at him, waiting.

Shimmying down beside him he slowly opened his eyes. "I really freaked out today."

I nodded, "I know. I'm sorry."

"If you were marked I could track you better." His arm went over my back and I dropped my eyes to the sheet. I knew he wanted to mark me; he'd wanted to mark me since our date. I didn't want him marking me until I told him everything about myself. Maybe he'd change his mind about me if he knew my past. If he marked me he was stuck with me forever.

"I won't go into the woods again," I told him, changing the subject.

He made a face. "Well I was hoping you'd want to…I wanted you to see my wolf, I realized today you hadn't actually seen it yet."

My interest piqued and a bubble of excitement ran though me. "Okay!"

He laughed at my excitement before leaning over and placing a kiss on my lips. I couldn't describe how much I enjoyed kissing Aiden. It always felt so warm, and I liked touching his chest. He had a nice chest.

Really he had a nice everything to be honest. I was a little surprised when his hand ran over my thigh, squeezing my hip. That was new. His hand went to my neck as he deepened the kiss and I felt myself getting lost in the feelings he could evoke within me.

It didn't feel cheap, my skin didn't crawl. I remember when Jonah had shoved his tongue in my mouth in a disgusting drunken haze two years ago. It was horrible, if Heather knew what he had done to me…

Noticing Aiden had stopped his affections I blinked my eyes open to find him staring down at me with a grin. "You're in another place again."

"Sorry," I said sheepishly.

"Doesn't give me much confidence, I want your mind blank when I kiss you."

"Oh trust me, it does go blank," I blurted out. He cocked a brow and my face felt hot. "L-like I mean uh…I'm just…"

"Knock, knock!" Grace called from outside the door. "Dinner!"

"Saved by meatloaf," he joked as he helped me up. Laughing nervously I straightened my clothes and made to leave, surprised when Aiden didn't budge from his spot. "Evelyn?"

"Yeah?"

"Keep Friday night free okay?" My stomach twirled a little as he squeezed my hand. "We have plans."

"Okay," I breathed out, feeling flustered. Another date? I had to plan an outfit with Grace.

Chapter Sixteen

"So my eighteenth is coming up," Trey said solemnly from the other end of the table at lunch. "I'm joining the big leagues. College, graduation and a mate. Goddess, my life is going up in smoke!" He grumpily picked at his food and I looked at him in interest.

"Don't be such a baby." Lucy poked her fork in his direction. "The way you behave the Moon Goddess has probably written you off and you won't have a mate anyway."

"He's just scared because now he knows he's in for some real shit when his mate finds him. How are you going to explain you didn't wait for her?" Grace asked with a satisfied smirk.

"I don't need to explain anything. I am a free agent until I get put under some crazy ass spell that forces me to pretend I'm in love with someone." He picked up his tray and left, dumping it roughly in a bin and scaring a bunch of freshman girls.

Josh scowled in his direction and set his fork down. "The way he blasphemes...I swear..."

"Grace you shouldn't rile him up," Aiden sighed as he pushed his empty tray away.

She flicked her hair and rolled her eyes. "I'm pointing out the bluntly obvious. Anyway for his surprise party I'm thinking no theme no nothing, keep it casual and full of booze."

"Very Trey," Lucy agreed as she wrote in her notebook.

"Aiden you're going to have to take him out and then lure him back to the house."

"You girls sound like you're planning his murder," Hannah laughed. "There isn't much to it. *'Hey man, let's go for a run. Yeah man, I'm up for it. Hey man, let's go play Xbox for a while at mine. Sick as bro.*' Not that hard." Hannah switched to male voices so comically that I found myself giggling at her.

"Typical women, have to make it all so dramatic."

The bell rang and everyone began getting up. Hannah came to my side and squeezed my shoulders. "Heard from your mom yet?"

I shook my head, biting my lip. "I tried calling last night but she didn't answer…what if I've really offended her?"

"Offended who?" Lucy asked as she came to my other side.

"Our art teacher," Hannah said quickly. "What have we got next?"

"Gym," Grace whined as she dumped her tray in the bin.

I was nervous to go back in there, thankfully we hadn't had any more episodes with the jocks but falling from that rope had scared the life out of me and I didn't want anything else to happen. Feeling Aiden take hold of my hand I relaxed immediately, at least he was in this class with me.

∞

Grace wrapped her jacket tightly around her, blowing hot air into her hands. "It's starting to get a lot colder. Thank the Goddess we don't do patrols, imagine patrolling in winter."

We were walking to training, today was combat and Aiden and I had been working on it a bit so hopefully I had improved some. He didn't go easy on me, and he expected me to really hit him which was always a little hilarious because it must have felt like someone threw a pebble at him.

Katherine walked ahead with her friends and they all shot dark looks over their shoulders.

"Sometimes I wonder how Kate's wolf feels about how she acts," Grace murmured. We all looked at her and she continued. "Well, I mean naturally your wolf wants to obey your higher command right? The fact she completely disregards her superiors must really drive her wolf nuts."

"Unless her wolf is just as bratty as she is."

"No…I can see the fight in her eyes," Hannah said. She tucked a stray piece of blonde hair behind her ear. "When she goes on at me for instance…her wolf acknowledges that now I'm her equal however she refuses to accept it. Sometimes her attacks are really half-hearted."

"Well she better watch herself, I'm getting sick of her crap."

Grace seemed in a really bad mood today and everyone kind of looked at each other before entering the training compound. In my opinion I think it had to do with Trey - usually whenever Trey and Grace got snappy at each other she'd be in a mad mood for the rest of the day.

"Alright, everyone put your stuff down and let's get started." Jet rubbed his hands together, his crazy muscles bulging, the man could snap me in half if he desired. "For the next few weeks we are doing a lot more partner work. I'm going to spend a week on matching you with someone your speed and then matching you to someone more capable of taking you down." Great, I'd be eating the floor for the next four weeks I guess.

"I hope I get Katherine," Grace hissed.

Jet went through a long list - no Grace didn't get Katherine much to her annoyance but poor Hannah did. I ended up with a red haired girl who looked friendly but her strong body looked very intimidating. Looking over at Hannah she smiled at me calmly, I guess she felt she could take Katherine. She probably could.

As Jet went around critiquing I spent my time blocking a lot of very rough attacks, I nearly thought the girl hated me before she stopped and began showing me how to stand, where to put my arms, how to block. I even managed to hit her once - I apologized profusely afterward.

Hearing a shriek everyone stopped as Hannah waved her hand and Katherine fell to her back, and stayed there. Hannah's hand hovered over Katherine's body, like super glue keeping Katherine pressed into the floor.

Eventually she let go and everyone clapped, but Katherine got up looking furious. "How is that even hand to hand? She can't rely on some pathetic witchy gene to get her through a tough situation."

"Well from what I heard, she took out three rogues using that *pathetic witchy gene* Katherine." Jet looked at her darkly. "You can use whatever is at your disposal. Hannah has flaws but she knows how to use her other gifts to get her through."

Katherine spluttered, looking ready to hit someone before storming out of the room, making very sure to slam the door roughly. From the corner of my eye I saw Josh in the other training room, frowning after her before getting back to his workout.

As the class came to a close Jet pat me on the back. "You're coming along really well. I see a lot of Aiden's moves when you strike which is good. Keep on working with him; you'll be up to scratch in no time."

"Thanks," I murmured shyly. Searching for my bottle in my gym bag I absentmindedly listened to the girls chatting, before they were interrupted by a high pitched voice.

"Hey guys!" I looked up to see the red haired girl I trained with.

"Hey Carrie," Grace said warmly.

"I just wanted to let you know that the Halloween dance is coming up! You guys are coming right? It's mostly a fundraiser for the Prom so…"

"Yeah, totally!" Grace said excitedly. "I've actually got the best costume in mind. Oh my Goddess, I have a brilliant idea! Evelyn you and Aiden should partner costume."

"Huh?" I asked, confused.

"Like go as…Cat Woman and Batman or - or, oh my Goddess! Red Riding Hood and the Big Bad Wolf. That's brilliant right?" Grace looked at Lucy and Hannah enthusiastically who nodded with excited eyes.

"Josh and I can go as Mario and Princess Peach!" Hannah shrieked.

"Katherine could go as the Hunter because she likes butting into things that don't concern her." Grace was still on Aiden and me.

"The hunter technically saves the day though," Lucy said thoughtfully.

"That's also what I wanted to say," Carrie cut in on Grace with wide eyes. "I heard from Sammy who heard from Karla who heard from Jenny that Katherine is planning on asking Aiden to the dance…which is weird because we all know Evelyn is his mate and then she said that he hadn't marked her yet so it didn't count. She's been saying some pretty horrible stuff about you Evelyn."

"Like what?" Grace asked through gritted teeth.

"That Aiden wasn't really interested in her - that he's been coming to see her when he's supposedly on patrols. The fact he won't mark her because he really wants to be with Katherine. How they'd still be together if she hadn't come here-"

"Carrie!" Grace said suddenly, looking at me with wide eyes. Oh but I had heard it.

I felt like I had been punched in the stomach, my mouth felt dry and I felt really stupid. "A-Aiden dated Katherine?" I squeaked as I conjured the raven haired beauty in my mind. She was stunning, flawless…how could I compete with that?

Was I even competing with that? Was he really seeing her like Carrie had said?

"He was," Lucy admitted softly. "Only for like a few months then he realized what an idiot she was. He broke up with her in April when he turned eighteen. He realized he was being an idiot by seeing another girl when he could meet his mate any minute."

"He and Trey were really stupid. Well Trey still is stupid, Aiden grew out of it. That's when dad started giving him more pack responsibilities. Evelyn, Aiden would never be seeing her behind your back. She's like mud on a boot compared to you." Grace's eyes were earnest but I wasn't so sure.

I wanted to leave and I wasn't sure if I wanted to see Aiden. I felt really awkward and embarrassed and I wasn't sure how to handle myself around him right now.

"Hey Evie, uh, if we're still going to do that art assignment tonight then we need to leave now. I have a time limit before mom sends people home." Hannah gave me a confident smile as confusion washed over me. What assignment? Then I realized that she was giving me an escape.

"Okay, yeah. I'll uh, I'll see you at home…" I waved at Grace and hurriedly slipped from the hall like someone shot a firecracker up my butt. I walked beside Hannah numbly and she stayed quiet. I'm glad she wasn't trying to make me feel good like the other girls. It didn't help. I felt like a huge idiot.

As we reached Hannah's modest looking home I smiled at its simplicity. It was closer to the outskirts of the compound - being that her family wasn't very high up in the rankings of the pack, but it felt homely. The front housed a huge blossoming garden, the house itself was brown, and the window panes were white and at the end of an overgrown pathway sat a proud white door.

"Your house is lovely," I murmured as I followed her to the welcoming front door.

"Thanks, mom loves to garden."

She pushed open the door and called out before frowning. "Guess mom's still working. Okay let's go upstairs and help you out because you look like someone killed your kitten."

The house was decorated in earthy colors, it looked mostly rustic and I felt a few things were being held together with magic they looked that old. Hannah smiled as she passed me and motioned that I should follow her upstairs.

Hannah walked to the door across from the landing and pushed it open walking in, so I followed her. Her room was serene. The walls were a light olive green color with an intricate vine design on the wall where her window sat. A rustic looking double bed sat in the middle of the room with unmade covers and it squeaked when she threw her bag on it. The rest of the room housed the essentials, a wardrobe, and a chest of drawers and of course a lot of girly clutter which was to be expected.

"Okay, so no one told you Katherine dated Aiden, but I'm not kidding it was literally for five minutes. I mean I didn't hang out with the group until June, when Josh found me, but I still heard and saw a lot. Everyone thinks Aiden panicked under the pressure his dad put on him so he kind of rebelled a little, then he realized how dumb he was and he dumped her."

"She clearly hasn't gotten over it then."

"A girl like Katherine? No way. She thought she was going to be the next Alpha Female. She lorded herself around the pack like she was Lady Godiva; and then when he kind of just gave her the flick she lost it. Then when Josh found me she got even worse, like she couldn't believe that someone below her in rank was now her equal."

"She's so pretty," I mumbled as I eyed the mirror above her drawers.

"So are you."

"She's a Beta."

"You're the chosen one from the Moon Goddess, you win."

"Why didn't anyone say anything?" I rubbed my forehead, "I mean I guess it doesn't matter. It was before I even met Aiden… before I even believed I'd have a mate, but no one said anything at all…like hey just a heads up…" I trailed off and picked at her duvet.

"I get where you're coming from," she agreed. "I'd want to know as well."

"If Aiden would date a girl as gorgeous as her, as pure as her…why would he want to be with a girl like me for the rest of his life?" I felt genuinely confused. Here was this purebred beauty queen practically throwing herself in his direction yet, he stayed with me.

Hannah looked at me, her mouth dropped open. "Evelyn, don't limit your self-worth. Why do you let yourself be defined as someone who isn't important? That's just crazy talk. You're the girl that was destined to be in his life forever."

"Katherine would be a better Luna than me," I whispered. My inner insecurities began to rear their ugly little faces.

"She'd be a power craving psychopath and this pack would fall apart. She's not made for that title, you watch her be mated to someone who's just a regular wolf. The Moon Goddess isn't an idiot. She knows who we are before we're born. Who we will be, what we will do."

"She'd let him mark her."

Hannah bit her lip before asking a question that I felt like she'd wanted to ask for a while. "Why won't you let him mark you?"

I felt the tears welling up in my eyes, my vision blurring. "If I get marked I'm trapped here, I won't be able to leave. I got to leave Idaho; I might not get that choice if it happens again."

"I know Idaho were crazy blood purists Evie…it isn't like that here. No one here besides Katherine has a problem with you." She touched my hand, her eyes wide. "Listen Evie…Grace told us some stuff about Idaho that you told her." I felt the color drain away from my features and I watched as Hannah quickly jumped to Grace's defense. "We were all being nosey and she was trying to not say anything…she didn't tell us everything but what we heard…"

I got up off the bed, quickly trying to reign in my emotions. "I need to go."

"Evie, please…"

I was out of there quickly and she did follow me to the front gate before leaving me to go. I had no idea what part of the district I was in but I was happy to be lost anyway, I didn't want to go home just yet, I didn't want to face Aiden and now I didn't want to face Grace.

If she had told the girls stuff then what had she told Aiden?

Fumbling with the iPhone in my hand I dialed my mom's number and once again got her voicemail which isn't what I needed right now. I needed her comforting voice, to tell me everything was going to be okay, like she always did.

"Mom," I croaked out. "I d-don't know why y-you won't take my calls but I need to talk to you," my voice wobbled. I felt crazy emotional and I briefly wondered if I was having a wave of PMS.

I walked for ages and I felt like I was going in circles. Nothing looked familiar and my phone had died. I was feeling better however; I had come to the comforting conclusion that if Grace had told Aiden about my past he would have gotten rid of me by now.

Him dating Katherine was a big deal though and I knew it was something we had to talk about…the way I'd felt when I found out, part of me was glad I didn't have the ability to feel the whole bond because I didn't know if I could handle anything worse than what I had.

As the sun began to set I heard the familiar sound of Aiden's truck behind me and I slowed my walk before I stopped as it pulled up alongside me. Hesitantly I turned and stared at him through the wound down passenger window as he looked at me nervously, the only sound in the street was the engine.

"You dated Katherine," I murmured as I ran my finger along the door.

"Honestly it meant nothing Evelyn I swear. I had a moment of insanity; I thought too much was being expected of me. Some hard words with dad straightened me out - you could hardly call it dating really."

I swallowed the lump in my throat and admitted the horrible truth. "She's better for you than I am."

The engine cut off so abruptly and his door slammed so violently that I fell back into the door of the truck. Aiden appeared in front of me looking close to shifting into his wolf. His eyes glowed from amber to brown and I knew his wolf was close to the edge.

"How can you even say that?" He demanded, his cheeks a little red. "Dammit - Evelyn you are everything!" I looked down but he quickly lifted my chin, holding it in place so he could look me in the eye. I felt it wobble in his grip. "You need to hear this, you have to listen. You're the only reason I wake up in the morning, the only reason I bother doing anything. I don't know who I was or what I was doing before I met you. You are the center of my world."

"Aiden," I mumbled weakly.

"It drives me nuts how you see yourself Evelyn. How you see us and our relationship, like I'm going to walk away at any minute. You don't want to open up with me, share with me. We're supposed to be partners…" He held my face in his hands, his eyes desperate. "I am falling crazy in love with you and I'm scared that you won't love me back."

I felt cold when he released me and I was left to take in his words…his admission. He paced back and forth a couple of steps before shaking his head and getting in the truck. I quickly hopped in and we drove back to the house in silence, he got out before I could say anything. He just told me he was falling in love me and I said nothing.

Nothing.

As I sat in the front seat, alone for the next hour, I came to the conclusion that I had been majorly stupid…and I needed to fix this.

It was past midnight as I hesitated outside Aiden's door. His light had only switched off ten minutes ago so he had to still be awake. I wasn't sure what I wanted to say…or I did I just didn't know how I was meant to say it.

My hand lightly touched the handle before it sprang back and I bit my finger nail before running my hands through my hair in frustration, giving up and going back to my room, closing the door as quietly as possible.

"I am falling crazy in love with you and I'm scared that you won't love me back." His honest words ran across my mind like it was on a flashing neon sign. They echoed in my ears and I couldn't focus properly. We both had fears then, I was scared to tell him my past in case he didn't want me and he was scared of me not wanting him.

So this should be easy to solve right? Communicate, talk to each other. That's easier said than done.

I flopped down onto my bed and shut off the lamp so I was in darkness. I didn't want to be hurt…I'd experienced some of the worst pain in my life but I knew if Aiden decided he didn't want this it'd ruin me. He'd truly break me, like so many people have wanted. Feeling my eyes flutter close I welcomed the presence of my mind going blank as I drifted to sleep.

"Evelyn? Are you in there?" *Aiden's smiling face waved a hand in front of me and I blinked, he looked a little blurry. "You're so hard to reach, get out of your mind I have to talk to you." Suddenly his face transformed, into a man I had never seen in my life before. He had brown almond shaped eyes; his hair was brown and long, reaching his ears.*

"Who are you?" I mumbled hazily, my voice sounded like it was underwater.

"Someone who can do things like you," he said gently as he took my hand. I looked down at our joined hands, noting all the tattoos that went all the way up his arm until I couldn't see under his sleeve.

"I don't do anything."

"That's not what I've heard," he said with a small smile.

"Who are you?" I repeated.

"Wake up Evelyn," he murmured as he stroked my forehead. *"Wake up."*

"Wake up Evelyn," the Luna murmured gently as I felt her hand ghost across my forehead. "You'll miss school if you sleep any longer." I squinted my eyes into the morning light, surprised to see the Luna above me in her dressing gown. "Friday mornings are always the hardest aren't they? Well, along with Monday. Breakfast is ready so get dressed darling."

She left the room and I was left to pull myself together, but I felt exhausted, like someone had sucked all the energy from my body. Getting up I stumbled slightly as my head rushed and the man's face popped back into my mind again.

What the heck kind of dream was that?

I dressed quickly in some gray jeans, a white sweatshirt and I pulled a black jacket on before quickly brushing my teeth and tying my hair up. Going downstairs I hoped to see Aiden but he wasn't there. Grace sat on her phone and smiled at me nervously.

I wasn't sure how I felt with her just yet but I offered a small smile in return as I ate the food on the plate given to me.

"So you and Aiden are having a little date tonight?" The Luna asked me kindly. My confused face must have surprised her and I remembered he had asked me to keep Friday clear. "He asked me this morning to make sure you were ready by five."

"This morning?" I asked, feeling hopeful. Maybe he didn't hate me after all.

"Oh yeah, he's been putting some thought into this one. He's working today with his father so he won't be at school."

"Oh." So the next time I see him after what happened last night would be our date? Great way to set the mood, I could already feel my nerves creeping in.

Grace and I walked to school in silence. I wasn't sure what to say and I knew Hannah would have given her a heads up that she had told some of the stuff. Someone had worked some magic overnight because the school was plastered with posters for the upcoming dance and ticket prices.

The entire day was tense and I felt sick to my stomach, by the time art came around I felt like ditching it. Hannah and I walked side by side, she had looked like she'd wanted to say something a couple of times but then seemed to stop herself, holding back.

When Katherine appeared in our pathway, and it definitely did not look accidental I felt a cloud of dread above my head.

"You thought you were so smart yesterday," she harped as she towered over Hannah. "One day you won't have the safety of a classroom, I swear to the Moon Goddess I will-"

"Stop it!" I snapped angrily at her as I shoved her arm off Hannah's shoulder. Hannah's eyes were wide as she stared between Katherine and I. Suddenly I felt like I had made a very big mistake as Katherine's scary glare ended up on me.

Her glare faltered somewhat though and she shuffled back a few steps as she looked at me open mouthed. Then suddenly she was gone, like a dog with her tail between her legs.

"What was that?" I wondered in disbelief. I thought she was about to beat the living daylights out of me.

"Evelyn your eyes are glowing amber!" Hannah exclaimed as she pulled me into the girl's bathroom. She shoved me in front of a mirror and I balked immediately, before I stopped and saw my reflection.

My eyes were amber.

They felt like warm liquid, like they had in the forest that day with the rogues. Hannah must have read my mind because suddenly she was raving on about how she wasn't crazy and that she had definitely seen it in the woods.

"Katherine's seen it Evelyn, you won't be able to hide this much longer."

I nodded as I watched my eyes dim back to brown and I immediately turned from the mirror. "I know," I sighed as I shook my head. I guess my decision had been made for me, how much longer could I have hidden it anyway?

"Evelyn, Grace feels really bad," Hannah started.

"I know," I murmured as I cut her off.

"She hasn't told Aiden, she swears."

"I know."

Hannah looked at me for a moment before smiling softly. "You're going to tell Aiden everything aren't you?"

I bit my lip and sighed. I needed to be careful with what I told Aiden, how much I could hit him with in one go. "Not all at once. I'm telling him about what we've discovered first. The other stuff - it can wait a little longer."

"No worries. How are you two? Grace said it was pretty tense last night."

"It was…it still is, but I've given everything a lot of thought. I know what I want with my life and who I want in it and the idea of not having Aiden…the way I feel when I think about it is enough for me."

"Well you guys have a lot to talk about on your date then."

"Yeah," I sighed. "Yeah we do."

Chapter Seventeen

GRACE HELPED ME GET READY again; thankfully she didn't try and force me to look in another mirror which was good. This time she had dressed me in a pair of dark gray jeans, a white shirt and a cream knit cardigan, reminding me it was getting colder now. She even threw in her favorite black booties to complete the outfit.

Leaving my hair down and letting her do whatever she wanted to my face, my mind swam with the conversation Hannah and I had and Aiden's confession last night which we still hadn't talked about. I hoped we resolved it before the date, I didn't know if I could handle and awkward drive to wherever we were going.

How did I bring it up?

"All done!" Grace popped her brushes into the little cup on her dresser and smiled at me. "You've got gorgeous cheekbones Evie, and I'd kill for them. In fact your whole face just looks great; I think I'm getting a lazy eye."

I shook my head at her. I'd never taken a lot of time to deeply examine my profile, I hardly looked like my mother which would lead me to the hazardous questions of why I looked so much like the man who raped her. My features may be gorgeous to Grace but they threatened my life every day in Idaho.

"Alright, Aiden's downstairs I can hear him breathing, he sounds nervous." She cocked her head using her super hearing. "His heart is beating really fast."

Maybe he was feeling as awkward as I was; at least it wasn't only me.

"Alright well, thanks…" I practically whispered.

"Goddess, even *your* heart is beating a million beats a minute…are you and Aiden all good?" Oh no, I did not need Grace prying when Aiden could hear her. I gave her a quick nod and made for the door, ignoring her worried glance as I quickly left her room.

"…Well take this and put it in the truck okay? Don't be too late either, you have a patrol at two and no one can cover for you." The Luna handed Aiden a picnic basket as I reached the top of the stairs and they both looked up. "Oh Evelyn, you look very pretty." Aiden kind of shifted his weight from each foot, his hand tight on the picnic basket. He wore black jeans and a loose blue shirt. He pulled off casual so well. "Okay you two, have fun, I'll leave the front door unlocked."

Hesitantly I walked down the stairs, sliding my hand on the railing as I watched my feet, listening to the Luna disappear. When I reached the landing I slowly peeked up at Aiden whose face was tense and awkward. He rubbed the back of his neck - like always - and opened the front door, gesturing for me to go first.

I guess we weren't going to sort this out before the date.

∞

Maybe I was supposed to say something, I thought for the umpteenth time as we continued to drive in silence. He had laid it all out last night, maybe he thought I didn't care…which wasn't true because I did care, more than I knew. Opening my mouth and shutting it again I realized I was starting to look like a fish. If I didn't know what to say the best idea was to say nothing, right?

Suddenly we pulled off the road and onto a dirt track that led into the forest and for a brief, paranoid moment I thought he was bringing me out here to kill me. Not too far in the distance I could see a shimmering of lights and I leant forward in interest, wondering what it was.

Aiden slowly pulled the car to a stop near the entrance of a clearing and I could hardly believe my eyes at the sight before me. Candles were everywhere; in jars hanging from trees, on the floor on rocks - on any available surface a candle had been placed.

A rug was filled with cushions and twinkle lights hung from a scattering of trees above the clearing. It was beautiful. I looked over at Aiden to see he was no longer in the driver's seat and neither was the picnic basket. The door to my side opened and I looked at him, happy to see him smiling even if it was small.

Taking his offered hand I slid out, shaking my head in amazement. "Aiden this is…this is beautiful. You did all this?"

"I can't take all the credit, I did have help." Leading me further to the elegant setting he motioned to the picnic rug and I sat down, looking up in wonder at the lights that looked like tiny stars. Amazing. Not far off I could hear water trickling so we must be near a river or the falls, all I knew was the whole area looked amazing and I felt unbelievably special.

After all the doubt I'd given him, the way he laid out everything last night, and he still did this for me. It scared me how close I was coming to ruining us; I needed to just open my mouth and say how I was feeling.

"Aiden-"

"I'm-"

We both stopped and laughed nervously, not sure who should go first. When I went to open my mouth again he spoke so I quickly shut it. "I'm sorry about last night…it wasn't fair to lay all that on you. I promised myself I wouldn't do that, I wanted to be patient and let you realize things on your own-"

"Don't apologize," I said quickly. "What you said…you have no idea how much clarity you gave me. I'm glad you got angry. I'm glad you told me how you felt," my voice was starting to get quieter. "I f-feel like I've made a big mess of us." My voice cracked and tears of frustration welled up in my eyes, angry I couldn't keep my emotions in check.

"Don't cry Evelyn," he groaned. "I didn't want to make you cry, you haven't made a mess of us. We're both new to this, the intensity that comes with finding your soulmate is a big thing, we both have to work through our feelings…we arrive at stages of our relationship at different times I get that." He pulled me into his arms and I was glad for it, I could hide my embarrassment.

Taking a breath and swallowing my nerves I broke the peaceful silence. "I do like you," I admitted. I was so quiet I could barely hear myself, but I knew he'd be able to. "So much it's starting to scare me." Because I don't want to lose you, ever. He stayed silent as he held me and we sat for ages in each other's embrace, staring into the darkness that wasn't illuminated by candles.

Sometimes there was the odd rustling in the bushes, or a candle would go out because of some wind. The air was getting colder and it brought with it that smell of Fall, I didn't quite know how to describe it but it just smelt like Fall.

"I had a dream about you before I met you." His confession threw me and I leant back and looked up at him, enjoying the way his eyes glowed in that amber color. His wolf must be fairly close to the surface. "I never saw your face, just your hair really."

"How'd you know it was me?"

"The feeling I got when I looked at you. I knew the only way I'd feel like that was if my mate was around. Then I saw you on the balcony, the same long brown hair and that same feeling. I couldn't believe it." He smiled down at me, shaking his head. "And then you wouldn't believe me." Sighing I rested my head back on his chest staring back out into the mass of trees.

It was quiet once more and I had plenty of opportunities to break the silence and tell him what I needed to, before he found out through the grapevine. Maybe I could show him, it was easier than saying it. I wondered what I could use to demonstrate what I couldn't say. How would he react when he saw it?

Something else that made me different.

Pushing down the fear I eyed the flickering candles around me, a nervous idea forming in my mind as I willed myself to calm down and focus on what I wanted to do. It wasn't long before I felt that warm glow in my eyes and I took a shaky breath.

"Aiden?" I whispered.

"Yeah?"

"I have to show you something."

He was quiet for a moment. "Okay?" Leaning back and sitting upright I watched as his eyes widened as he stared into my amber filled ones. "Evelyn, your eyes-"

"I know."

"You don't have a wolf…"

"I know. Hannah and I…we think it's something else, something a little more…" I bit my lip and hesitated before waving my hand and the clearing became pitch black, all the light provided by the candles disappearing. Waving my hand again the clearing once more lit up and the lights danced once more, shadows glimmering on the trees.

I felt the warm glow evaporate from my eyes and I looked at Aiden nervously, waiting for his reaction. He looked shocked to say the least; it kind of reminded me of Hannah. This reminded me. "Hannah didn't take out all those wolves that day. I helped."

"Why didn't you say anything? How long have you known you could do this?"

Putting my head in my hands I mumbled, "I didn't want to be any more different than I was. I tried to ignore it, but then I just kept doing things like blowing up the light in my room…lifting roots from the ground…I'm scared of it. I called my mom and asked her…about my father…I haven't heard from her since."

"Your father obviously isn't human." We were quiet once again as Aiden processed what he had just seen. "What else can you do?" That surprised me. I thought he would flip out, think I was just becoming way too much to deal with. It was like he read my mind. He took my hand in his and brushed a stray hair off my forehead. "Evelyn, this is really cool. I mean, where were you when we were lighting all these candles?"

That made me laugh a little and I snuggled back into his side. "I still have to find out why I am the way I am though…mom obviously hasn't shared the full picture with me."

"If she doesn't answer your calls I'll get my dad to ring Idaho and get her on the phone. If she's been lying to you about who you are…" His voice trailed off and I could feel him shaking his head. The rest of the date went smoothly after that and I was relieved to get it off my chest. We ate the meal that had been prepared by the Luna and when the night was over I got the honor of shutting off all the candles.

I knew though, that by telling Aiden I was now officially opening a whole new can of worms.

∞

"So your mother wasn't assaulted by a human then?" Alpha James sat at his office desk with a thoughtful look. The Luna stood beside him; regarding me with interest while Grace looked betrayed I had only told Hannah. "It makes sense…we were all confused as to why she couldn't fight off a human, for her age she should have possessed some werewolf strength."

"So you're sort of like Hannah then?" Grace asked.

"A little I guess…she uses more words though, I do more with my mind."

"I don't know why you refrained from telling us for so long, Evelyn, and your mother had no information for you at all?" The Luna asked.

"She said I had no father…"

"Well I mean, who keeps in contact with their rapist?" Everyone in the room turned to look at Grace, mostly with glares. I found myself chuckling at her bluntness. "Look I'm sorry for how I said it, but it's true, you don't really expect her mother to know anything about Evelyn's father do you?"

"If Evelyn really is part witch then her father would be a part of a coven, we know there's only five in the US-"

"There are too many drifters though son," Alpha James cut Aiden off. "It's rare to find a group of witches that actually live together. Not after the covens were attacked anyway. It's not like Evelyn has any other scents either. You can only smell half her wolf side, there's nothing else mixed with it."

"You can't smell Hannah's witch side," Grace stated. "We can't scent witches remember? Maybe that's why Evelyn smells so plain."

"Well we aren't sure Evelyn is a witch," The Luna reminded. "She can do a thing, that doesn't necessarily put her into a group. There are plenty of unknown species out there that remain hidden and if only half of Evelyn's scent is showing up…"

"Then maybe someone's cloaked her?" We all looked at Grace and she continued. "It could be possible that maybe the man who did father Evelyn didn't want it leading back to him."

"That would mean he was around for the nine months she was being carried, he'd have to have known about her." The Luna looked frustrated. "It doesn't make sense for him to be around if her mother was in fact, raped."

"I can try asking my mother again, if she'll take my calls…" I trailed off in doubt.

Everyone's faces in the room shifted as their eyes glazed over and I realized they were in the pack link. Suddenly the Alpha looked at me in surprise, "I don't think a phone call will be necessary Evelyn."

"What do you mean?"

Everyone looked at each other, Grace was grinning. "I think we're about to get some answers."

"What?" I asked in confusion.

"Your mom has just arrived at the border."

∞

"Mom?" I was stunned as she walked up to the front door, looking like she hadn't slept in a few days, her clothes were wrinkled and her hair needed a brush through it. "Mom what are you doing here? Not that I'm not happy to-"

"Look at you sweetheart," she said happily as she stroked my cheek. "You've put on some weight, and you look so healthy, so happy."

"Where's everyone else?"

"Well they don't really know I'm here. Well they would by now, but I needed to see you face to face." She sobered up her excited expression and looked at me with sad eyes. "Evelyn we need to have a very long talk. I'm not sure you're going to be happy with what I'm going to tell you."

"I've notified Alpha Hess that you're here Beta Maria. It would have been nice for our patrollers if you had informed us you were coming. We're on high alert because of the rogue attacks, I'm sure you heard." Alpha James' eyes were narrowed on my mother and I watched her visibly shrink.

"I'm sorry for showing up unannounced, but what I had to talk to my daughter about could not be done over the phone, nor can it be done in front of all of you-"

"Mom...I'll tell them anyway, come inside. You can have a drink...maybe a shower?" I looked at The Luna who nodded, stretching out her hand. "Go with Claudia mom, and then we can talk afterwards, okay?"

Mom looked at me strangely before giving me a small smile. "This place has been good for you, I can see that." She followed the Luna inside and I was left to think about her words before Grace shook my arm.

"Thank you for not sending us away, I would have died if I didn't get to hear what she had to say."

"You would have listened from another room Grace," I pointed out as I followed her inside. Aiden and the Alpha had disappeared somewhere and judging by the Alpha's response to her arrival I would say he wasn't too thrilled to have her here. I was happy though, to see my mom. It felt like it had been forever since I saw her that night at the gathering.

"Are you nervous for what she might tell you?"

"A little." Truth be told I was really nervous, she said I might not like it, but I wanted to know and I knew that I had to just take it in and go from there.

"How much else did you tell Aiden last night?" Grace gave me a look and I frowned in confusion. "Did you tell him all that stuff you told me?"

"Oh...no not yet."

"You know you'll have to soon-"

"I know." I quickly walked inside and toward the sitting room where I saw glimpses of the Luna setting it up. She had an array of biscuits and cakes on the table with a large pot of tea. "I'm sorry for the way my mom turned up…I haven't heard from her in a few days - didn't imagine that this is what she was doing."

"Oh that's fine sweetheart. Your mother is welcome here anytime; we'll put her up in the spare bedroom, no worries at all." She came to stand in front of me, a genuine smile on her face. "How are you feeling? You've had an interesting couple of days; I can't imagine it's been easy telling us all what you've been going through."

You don't even know the half of it, I thought. "I'm fine…mostly surprised my mom came all this way. I thought I'd really upset her when she stopped answering my calls."

"Yes," she tucked a strand of hair behind my ear. "How are you and Aiden sweetheart? I noticed you were both a bit off yesterday, even before the date." A noise in the doorway had us looking over to my mom freshly showered and in new clothes - possibly loaned from the Luna. "Ah, I knew we'd be almost the same size, come sit down and have a cup of tea Beta Maria."

I didn't miss the odd expression on my mother's face as she walked into the room and sat on the sofa. I immediately sat beside her, happy to just be in her presence again. I had missed her smell, the calm feelings she gave off. I always felt at peace when I was with her.

"How's everything back home?" I asked as the room slowly filled with Aiden, Grace and the Alpha. I wanted to relax her a little bit, she looked extremely tense. Whether this was from the presence of the Alpha or she was gearing up for our big conversation. "How's Jada going with training?" Grace made a face at me when Jada's name came up and I gave her a quick look.

"She's fine. She's much better at controlling herself these days - a lot calmer." Probably due to my lack of being there, I thought. Mom rubbed my knee. "Laurance has been practicing with the pack doctor, not anything really technical but he has a real knack for it."

"Oh that's good; he was always reading those huge books."

"Yes." The room was once again gulfed in tense silence and I felt like I was holding my breath as I flicked a glance at each individual in the room.

"Well I guess polite pleasantries are officially over." The Alpha broke the silence, much to my relief. "We were having an interesting discussion with Evelyn before your arrival, Beta Maria. She has found herself able to do things she can't begin to explain."

"Her eyes glow," Aiden said quietly obviously still reeling from what I had shown him last night.

"She took on rogue wolves," Grace looked at me with admiration. "She hasn't been training with us long enough to have done it physically."

"She cut off the power to the house." The Luna gave me a fake-stern look and I bit my cheek trying to hold in a smile.

"So we gather she isn't half-human. So this goes back to you, Beta Maria. I'm just going to come straight out and ask it, just to clear any possibilities. Was Evelyn's father a human?" The Alpha watched her carefully, maybe trying to detect a change in her body language, to see if she was lying.

I watched my mother rub her forehead. She seemed really agitated and I knew her silence and the way she didn't look up from her cup was starting to get to the Alpha. I'd never seen her be this disrespectful to a higher rank in her life.

Finally she looked up and stared at me. "I need to discuss this with Evelyn alone first. This has nothing to do with anyone right now, except for me and her."

The Luna bristled, I could notice her demeanor changed instantly at mom's harsh tone. "On the contrary, Beta Maria, this now concerns all of us. She lives under our roof, is mated to my son, will be birthing the future Alpha's of our pack - we would like to know what is in her blood and who it came from."

"Mom…it's okay." I put my hand on her shoulder. "They have a right to know as well."

She looked at me with glistening eyes, her lips thin as she nervously ran her finger along her lower lip. "This was hard enough to work myself up to…to come here and t-tell you what I have to t-tell you. Oh Evelyn," she put her head in her hands. "I was a very, very foolish young girl."

I frowned and looked around the room, to everyone else's reaction. Mostly they just looked impatient. "What do you mean?"

She swallowed audibly as she looked back up at us all before looking directly at me. "Evelyn, you have to promise me that you won't think of me differently. Well, maybe you will. I guess I can't ask you to do that. M-maybe you could just promise that one day you could forgive me."

"Forgive you for what?" I was starting to freak out now; a whole range of scenarios were running through my mind. Was I adopted? Was I a botched abortion? She never wanted me and that's why the pack hated me so much? "Mom you have to start talking."

"You know I was originally from the pack in Indiana?" She asked and I nodded eager for her to continue. "The pack was bordered with Ohio - unclaimed wolf territory so rogue ran rampant throughout that area, our borders were really tightly controlled, considering." She took a sip of her tea and took another breath. "Ohio has a coven of witches that live quite close to the Indiana border. We didn't talk to them and they didn't dare try and cross the border either."

"My friends and I were a little uh - wild, back in the day. We did everything we weren't supposed to, including running along the borderline." The Alpha snarled under his breath at the idea and mom went on. "One day I was just out by myself, in our territory, I went to rest by the lake and I saw him. Standing in our territory like he owned the place, he wasn't human. No, he gave off no scent that I knew he possibly couldn't be."

"So a witch?" Grace asked her eyes wide.

"Not exactly," mom worried her lip between her teeth. "He had sensed me long before I had, he just never left. He moved the water with his hands, made it do things no witch could do." My mind immediately flicked back to the jug on my date with Aiden. "Naturally I was ready to take him down, until he turned around, greeted me by name and made me shift."

"Made you shift?" The Luna gasped.

"Yes. He just, waved his hand and I felt the tremors going through my body, I could feel my bones contorting and suddenly I was human again and I hadn't made it so. He did. He gave me a robe and I obviously demanded to know who he was. He told me exactly where he lived in Ohio - like he fully trusted me not to tell my father."

"Did you?"

"No. Never," her eyes looked wistful suddenly. "Cornelius, that was his name. He was possibly the most handsome man I had ever met, so well read, and so sophisticated. It was different being around him, most male wolves were so violent, always beating their chests. He was so calm." She looked at me with very serious eyes. "You know some packs have different laws, penalties right?" It was such a change in topic I found myself blinking at her before finally nodding. "Well, here goes. We started a relationship, I would sneak out to see him, and he would show me his magic. Goddess, it was fascinating. Then we'd talk, about the future, what we both wanted out of life. He was to inherit his family's coven; I wasn't sure if I even wanted to go to College."

I felt like I was maybe catching on to where this could be going. "Mom?"

"I fell in love with a man who wasn't my mate. Goddess, I did love him Evelyn, so much it hurt. It thrilled me that I had fallen in love with a man outside some age old bond. One night it just happened, we made love and when it was over I realized what a mistake I had made. Indiana has strong laws on this stuff."

"If you sleep with someone who isn't your mate both parties can be exiled, only to different parts of the world," Aiden sounded like he had recited that from a book.

"Well in some packs that's the case, in other packs they have a trial and your punishment is decided by the people. A lot of the times it was execution, people take the Moon Goddess' bond very seriously." Mom rolled her eyes a little and I winced, she was in the wrong room to do that.

"Why wouldn't we take the bond seriously? It's the purest entity ever created, one of our most direct links to the Moon Goddess herself!" The Luna looked furious and Alpha James put his hand on her arm.

"Go on," I managed to say.

"Well I told Cornelius how what we had done was wrong. Very wrong. My wolf was already losing it inside my head, I felt like I was going crazy. He was…surprisingly helpful though, he agreed and cloaked my scent. He made sure it stayed unchanged seeing as I was no longer a virgin. I thought all was well. Until I missed a period."

The room was deathly silent and I felt betrayal well up inside of me. "You weren't raped?" I whispered as I stood up.

"No Evelyn, I wasn't. I was a naive seventeen year old girl and I slept with a man who wasn't my mate. When I told him he was over the moon and I was terrified, if my family found out about this I would be in big trouble. I could already smell my own scent changing." She grabbed my trembling hand. "He said he'd help me, and he did. We created the story and he cloaked your entire birth and then when you were born, cloaked your scent. He said it would be as strong as his if not stronger seeing as you were half wolf."

"Why did he help you do that?" Grace demanded. "He didn't want to be in her life?"

"No he did, but his coven…if they found out he had been with someone outside of his clan…" She shook her head. "He was betrothed to someone; he's married to her now. They have six children."

My stomach flipped, I had six half-siblings? Did they look like me? Did I look like them? There were people in this world that shared my appearance? "I'm dizzy," I groaned as I put my hand to my head. Aiden was by my side instantly, guiding me to a chair - away from my mother.

"They wouldn't have accepted you Evelyn. Cornelius said you wouldn't get any of his powers, that the wolf side was more dominant than his. His clan…they weren't normal witches those people. They were way more involved than that, they could do things that sent my mind into endless wonder. They had very pure bloodlines. The fact their eldest son and the man soon to take over had had a child with a wolf? No, it wouldn't have been good for him either."

"This is so messed up," Grace said hysterically. "Like seriously messed up. Who lies about being raped?"

"Grace," the Luna warned.

I felt calmer beside Aiden, his arm was around my shoulder, rubbing small circles into my arm and I could start to focus again. "How does Michael come into all this?"

"Michael," mom laughed and shook her head. "Michael…I met him at a pack gathering eight months into my pregnancy. He - he was so angry, he thought I had been unfaithful."

"Which you had," I pointed out, feeling angry. Mom looked at me in shock, and I realized I'd never spoken to her like that in my life. I felt like she deserved it though. "So you told him your big lie and he swallowed it, you went to Idaho and lived happily ever after and I got to enjoy living with a pack that hated me because of your lie and the fact you couldn't keep your pants on."

"Evelyn!" The Luna gasped.

My breaths were heavy and I felt that same liquid warmth reach my eyes. It was happening again. I looked at my mother and she gasped in shock, pointing. "That's what he did," she practically whispered.

I felt anger, pure anger. Anger I had never felt before. Even through all my pain and suffering I had never felt this anger, but it was justified. The woman who I went to for comfort when I had spent the day with my head down a toilet - she had all the answers. She lied to me my whole life, kept me in that place and let me get hurt.

A chorus of shattering glass around me snapped me out of it and as I felt my eyes go back to normal I noticed the shattered coffee table, TV cabinet and china on the floor. Everyone looked at me in shock and I doubled over in horror at the glass shard in Aiden's ankle.

He seemed surprise as he leant down to slide the piece of glass out. I felt my stomach turn and my body grow hot as my heart raced. The room began to spiral before my eyes as my head felt like liquid on my shoulders.

"Evelyn?" The voice came out garbled as I tried to see who said it, before darkness cloaked my eyes and I fell to the floor with a bang.

Chapter Eighteen

"Half-breed! Half-breed! Half-breed!" The circle chanted around me and I stood small in the center, thirteen years of age and terrified. I was shoved roughly from my left side and fell into a set of arms that roughly pushed me back in the same direction before I was being shoved around like a ball.

"You don't have the right to be here!" Thirteen year old Jonah snarled in my face, still managing to look horribly scary at that age. "No one needs your type here."

"Look at yourself!" Heather grabbed me by the neck. "You don't look like your mother, you're evil. No wolf, no senses. Nothing. You're a defect that shouldn't have happened."

"Ugly!"

"Kill yourself!"

"Don't make a mess when you do it!"

My mournful scream hurt, it was so loud people covered their ears. I didn't want to be here, someone take me away from this. Help me, please. I can't stay here, I'm going to die. They'll kill me. Maybe I'll kill me.

I'm scared.

"...Her life is my entire fault. She never had it easy, ever and I'm not sure how much she's told you either. Evelyn is very tight lipped on those things." I could hear my mother in the background as my mind still swam; I didn't want to wake up yet.

"She hasn't disclosed much." That was definitely Aiden and I could hear the tension in his voice, I could feel his hand holding mine which sent comforting feelings through my body. "I'm not an idiot; I'm not going to push her into telling me anything. Even though she told Grace."

"Don't be so sulky Aiden," the Luna ordered. "Girls talk better to other girls, you are both in a relatively new relationship, laying out all your cards is daunting."

The room was quiet so I decided not to eavesdrop any longer and face the music. Slowly I opened my eyes and stared up at the ceiling, noting my broken light. I ran my hands over the fabric and groaned a little as my muscles felt stiff.

"Oh Evelyn!" The Luna exclaimed. "You do make a habit of fainting sweetheart."

Only when I don't want to face things, I thought.

"Evelyn, honey?" Mom brushed her hand over my forehead and I looked at her, curious at how she had lied for so long. It was insane, how many other people knew about how I really came to be? Had she ever told anyone in confidence or had she lived with it her whole life?

What about my father? He was this blurry image in my mind my whole life and I usually had him in a circle of curiosity and disgust, disgust in myself for how I was brought into the world. Disgust I barely had my mother's genes and seemed to look like a stranger I had never met but everyone hated. My thoughts on myself mirrored the thoughts that I had for my father, that my mother had to go through so much and then have me, a constant reminder every day.

It was all a lie though, and that's what really hit me hard. My whole self-perception was now warped and blurred like the man in my head. Who was I? I don't know. I know who I was, but it was easy now to change that. I wasn't a monster because the man who fathered me wasn't. He was a man who fell in love with the wrong woman.

"Evelyn?" My mother snapped me out of my mind and I looked at her in the eye.

"I want to meet him. My Father, I want to meet him." Her lips thinned and she seemed to lose some color in her cheeks.

"Evelyn I'm not sure that's a good idea-"

"No," I cut her off. "Maybe it isn't, because maybe he won't want anything to do with me. I have six half-siblings, and maybe they don't want anything to do with me, that doesn't matter. I've got experience in dealing with that." I sat up in my bed and put my head in my hands. "You have dropped a serious bombshell on me mom. You've lied to me my whole life about who I am and how I got here…there are people out there that look like me, that can do what I do."

"Can't blame her for being curious," Grace interjected. "I would be."

"You need to tell me how I can find him, where he lives," I demanded.

"Evelyn…" Mom sighed and rubbed her temples.

"Let's all calm down for a moment. Evelyn if you arrange a meeting with your father we need to have a big discussion. You'll be leaving pack territory and possibly crossing other territories; there is a lot to figure out, not to mention if…"

"If he wants to meet me," I finished quietly as I curled my knees up under my arms. That was a sad thought, and like my mother said earlier - I wouldn't have been accepted there either. Well I didn't want to live with them; I just wanted to meet my father. Didn't I deserve the opportunity to understand who I was? Why I am the way I am? Because living in confusion and misery for so long has got to earn me the right, surely.

"I think we all need to take a breather and we'll talk more over dinner. Evelyn you need to rest I think, you're looking very stressed. You've had to take in a lot today." The Luna got up from the foot of the bed. "I'll come wake you when dinner is ready."

I probably wasn't going to sleep but I nodded anyway, trying hard not to look at my mother. I wasn't sure how I felt about her right now, and I couldn't look at her until I knew. Everyone besides Aiden left the room and he squeezed my hand. Looking over at him I sighed, feeling the tears well up as his eyes softened.

Taking me into his arms I cuddled into him, just wanting to be enveloped and hidden from my life. I didn't want to face it right now, I needed this. I needed his comfort, his touch that calmed me so much and slowed my overactive brain.

I was crying before I knew it and using his shirt as a tissue. He didn't care, he just held me tighter and whispered words of comfort. My whole life was a lie and it wasn't my lie. Yet it was a lie that hurt me for so long and left me with so much emotional bruising and physical scarring.

It was a life I had never chosen but had to make do with.

It was also a life that led me to Aiden and I think that would be the only time I would be thankful for being alive. Meeting Aiden had helped me in ways I had never imagined; I felt like maybe I could finally start to heal, that I always had him no matter what.

He's the only honest thing in my life, and the thought made me cling to him tighter as my sobs quietened to sniffling and the few stray tears that came off and on whenever my thoughts got particularly dark.

The room slowly got darker and before long the dusk light was drifting through my half open curtain. My tired tear stained eyes drifted over to my covered mirror with disdain, bloody mirrors had been the bane of my whole existence. Mirrors showed me what everyone called me; mirrors showed me the monster I saw in myself. I didn't have a monster though, my mother did. She just let me carry some of that weight.

"I want her to go," I whispered into the dimly lit room, my voice cracking from the lack of use and the thickness left over from crying. "I want her to give me my father's details and then I want her to go."

"Are you sure?" He asked hesitantly.

"Yes."

"Okay, I'll let my father know, he's not happy with her at the moment anyway." Aiden's voice was terse and I knew he wasn't either. Lifting my head off his chest and feeling my ear had been pressed into the side of my head I rubbed it and then looked at him. He stared back at me with weary eyes before brushing his thumb over my cheek and dabbing a tear from the corner of my eye.

"Thank you for being with me," I whispered. "If I didn't have you…"

He gave a small smile. "I know what you mean, I can be having the worst day and the moment I see you…hear your voice, it's amazing what you can do for me. That's why mates were created, so no one would ever be alone forever, so they don't have to shoulder all their problems by themselves. Evelyn I will be here for you through all of this."

His words were a relief and I nodded, wrapping my arms around his neck and burying my face into his shoulder. With Aiden by my side, I could get through anything.

∞

Mom was in shock, I think, as she stopped by the front door. I had received a scribbled phone number and an address from her and she looked at me with this look of betrayal that made me feel guilty for asking her to leave. I had to remind myself why I was doing that.

I felt sad to see her car leave but the heaviness I felt with her presence faded which brought me comfort and better clarity on my thoughts. I once again disappeared to my room and spent the entire day doing homework that was running dangerously overdue.

Aiden joined me at some point with his but neither of us talked about the crinkled piece of paper on my nightstand that possibly had a lot of answers behind it.

Come Monday morning the weather perfectly fit my mood, it was overcast and horrible and the air had a dampness to it that suggested rain. Grace was complaining about how it was ruining the texture of her hair the entire ride to school and I found her whining enjoyable, it took my mind off my crazy weekend.

Everyone must have known about my mother's arrival and I doubted Grace could have kept all that a secret either. My phone died at some point and it's not like I used it anyway, I'm fairly sure it's under my bed.

Hannah smiled at me when we arrived and pulled me into a gentle hug, squeezing my shoulders. Lucy gave me a wink and Josh awkwardly pat me on the back which was funny and I cracked a smile. Everyone sat down and began talking and it moved to Trey's surprise party and I realized he was missing.

"Where is Trey anyway?" I asked.

"Whoring," Grace muttered under her breath before smiling at everyone. "It's basically just going to be in our basement.

Plenty of drinks and food, some cake. It'll be a fun night anyway."

"I cannot be bothered being educated today." Lucy occupied a whole bench to herself as she lay across it, her blonde waves spilling over the edge like a honeycomb waterfall. "I have no motivation, I'm feeling like I should ditch."

"My feelings mirror yours," Grace said suddenly.

"No one is ditching," Aiden said firmly. "It's only like seven hours, deal with it."

"You're so boring!" Lucy grabbed her bag and stormed off in a huff.

Hannah shook her head and said, "Geoff and her had a fight. He wants her to move in right? After graduation, and she wants to go to College straight away. She feels like she's being forced to grow up because he's older than her."

Grace frowned and said, "She's allowed to go to College, this isn't the fifties, he doesn't own her."

"I guess he's just afraid of losing her."

"They're mates Hannah, he can't lose her. She'd be in physical pain if they weren't together, oh I got it. So he'd have to go with her!" Grace's eyes widened as the light bulb hit before she frowned again. "So why is he mad about that?"

"Because he has a good job he doesn't want to leave?" Josh interjected.

"She has the right to experience College."

"I didn't say she didn't, I'm just saying you can understand why he'd be hesitant."

"He'd get it back," Grace countered as she narrowed her eyes at Josh. "I mean how did he get it in the first place? He was young and fresh out of College yet somehow he got a teaching job? All someone would have to do is pull the same strings they pulled the first time."

"Let's not talk about a situation that doesn't concern us," Aiden said finally and I was glad he spoke. I felt awkward discussing people and their personal lives. I didn't know Lucy well enough to hear all this.

I was relieved when the bell rang and I followed Hannah to art after giving Aiden a brief kiss goodbye. I still felt funny when he kissed me in front of other people; I wasn't sure about how I felt about PDA.

"So how are you doing?" Hannah asked me as she linked arms. "From what I heard your mom dropped Hiroshima on you."

I laughed a little and bit my lip. "At the moment I'm a little bewildered and still trying to wrap my head around it. I'm unsure about what I should do next and I'm scared my mom hates me a little so…I'm not feeling great but I don't feel terrible, which is good I guess."

"I just can't get my head around it really so if you're managing then hats off to you, because I would be hiding under my bed, revaluating everything."

I didn't say anything; I wasn't really sure what to say. I'm not managing and I know it, but I guess I had gotten so good at squashing down how I really felt that it didn't show on me physically. I was glad for that; I didn't want Aiden to get worried.

I really relaxed in art that day. We had started a new project recently. We could paint whatever we wanted as long as it had depth…meaning. My canvas had been blank for two weeks, I didn't know what I could paint, I came up with a void every time I tried to think.

Today though, it felt effortless to do a light outline of what I wanted, the pencil just moved without needing my brain to overthink it. I put away all my worries, fears and doubts and found myself feeling the most content since being in Aiden's arms after everything had gone down.

I wasn't sure what the drawing would be, maybe it would be nothing, but it was coming from within me.

Later on after school we had all gathered on the front lawn, waiting for training. Everyone talked about this and that, Hannah was doing her homework and Josh's at the same time which made me laugh, especially when she told him to watch what she did and if he got distracted she gave it back to him.

"So…the Halloween Dance!" Grace said loudly when chatter had died down.

"Why are we talking about this stupid dance when we haven't even planned my party?" Trey sulked. "That's it, none of you can come."

"Your birthday is after the Halloween dance, therefore its level on the priorities list is low, now shut up." Grace clipped him over the back of her head before looking at Hannah. "You wanted to go as Princess Peach right? And Josh could be Mario."

"Why those two?" Josh complained loudly as he fell backwards.

"Come on, it'll be fun!" Hannah tugged on his arm and pulled him back up. "Don't be such a spoil sport."

"I'm not going," Lucy announced loudly. "Geoff and I are going to have our own party, seeing as we can't dress up together."

"Aw!" Grace pouted, "That sucks."

"Yeah well we can't go together can we? And I'm not going to watch him chaperone all night while I pretend I'm having a good time, so…"

"Alright." Grace looked a little put out but her face brightened when she locked eyes with me and I didn't like the twinkle she got. "Evelyn is going to be Red Riding Hood and Aiden is going to be the Big Bad Wolf!"

How original, I thought to myself.

"Really?" Aiden asked as he peeked down at me to gauge my reaction. If he didn't want to do it I was fine with that, it was kind of boring to go as something you basically were in real life. "I kind of wanted to go as the Hulk really."

Lucy's eyebrows rose. "Can we paint you green?"

"Oh my Goddess! Evelyn can go as Black Widow! Why don't we all go as Avengers!" Hannah was near squealing her idea by this point and Grace nodded seriously obviously agreeing.

I looked up at Aiden who just smiled and shook his head. I didn't know what an Avenger was and I wasn't really interested in dressing up like one. Everyone began getting up and dusted themselves off, still talking about what to go as. Aiden took my hand in his and I found myself lightly holding onto his arm with my other free hand, enjoying the closeness with him.

"You've been quiet," he commented. "Don't you want to partner costume with me?"

I laughed as an idea formed in my head. "Well someone already asked me to go with them to the dance and dress up as Salt and Pepper shakers so…"

"What an offer, how did you turn him down?"

"I'm allergic to pepper."

"You couldn't be salt?" Aiden asked with a smile on his face.

"He wasn't willing to give it up," I laid on the fake pout and Aiden snorted. "Really though…for the costumes…" I bit my lip and walked faster as I leant up to whisper in his ear. "Their ideas aren't really my cup of tea."

"Ha! Don't let Grace hear that." We kept walking and I listened to the others behind us, not picking up on what they were saying but I could feel eyes on me. Sometimes I felt like a science project here, I felt like I was always being watched and assessed and then people would compare notes. Or I could just be paranoid. "So what do you want to go as then?" Aiden asked me as we crossed the street and headed toward the compound.

I bit my lip and wondered if it was silly. "A 1920's flapper."

"A what?" He asked, sounding a little baffled.

"Y-you know, those girls in the twenties who wore those cool dresses and head pieces and gloves and stuff. String pearls and even a feather boa." Okay maybe it was stupid, he didn't even know what it was.

"That is such a good idea!" Grace said beside me suddenly. "I love it! Trust Aiden not to know, he doesn't know a lot of things." She pulled out her phone and typed quickly before shoving it in front of Aiden's face. "That, big brother, is a flapper."

He looked like he had a light bulb moment as he recognized what it was. "Oh! Got it! That's cool."

"Aiden you should go as a gangster!" I found myself rolling my eyes a little; he already said he wanted to be Hulk and judging by the look on his face, that idea hadn't changed. "Evelyn, did you just roll your eyes?" I was surprised she saw it and surprised I got sprung as she looked at me in wonder.

"A-a little," I squeaked. She gave me a look as if to go on and I found my palms started sweating and I knew Aiden would feel it. "W-well…Aiden wants to go as the Hulk…we d-don't have to partner costume just because we're mates."

The area was quiet as Grace processed the information I had just given her. Personally I was waiting for a smack for speaking out against her. Sure Grace had never been violent with me in the past but I never would have rolled my eyes back in Idaho. I guess it showed how comfortable I was getting here.

"Amen!" Lucy whooped. "Oh Evelyn, you surprise me every day. Come on guys, we have some hard-core cardio to get through!"

∞

Exhausted from training I wanted nothing more than to fall on my bed and just sleep forever. Those people ran on some sort of weird energy levels that just never seemed to wear out. I was thankful for Hannah's help whenever I started getting too slow. I found myself too tired to even eat all of my dinner.

I showered quickly, just wanting to be in my pajamas and do some homework while Aiden had his patrol. Pushing open my door and flicking on the light - which had finally been fixed- I stopped mid-step as I saw the two wrapped gifts sitting on my pillows.

Frowning I walked slowly into the room and shut the door, not sure if this was a weird trap or prank. Did Grace get some sort of dangerous animal and wrap it up for me to open and set up cameras in my room? Was it my birthday? No, it definitely wasn't yet.

Why were there presents on my bed?

Then it clicked, it had to be mom. Maybe it was a peace offering although I wasn't sure if I was supposed to forget everything because of some gifts. Giving up on trying to guess and letting my more impulsive side take over I picked up the largest one, testing its weight.

It felt funny. It was thin but it was large, maybe the size of one of my bed cushions. Something rattled around inside the packaging and before I knew it I was slowly peeling the paper away from the gift inside. Out slid a packet of art pencils and an eraser and as I finished opening the rest of it I realized it was a sketchbook.

A smile broke out on my face and got so excited I nearly forgot about the smaller gift that was also on my bed. Dropping my eyes I noticed the white envelope that must have been hiding under the sketchbook. Picking it up I quickly opened it, hoping for a clue.

The front of it was plain white with a simple red heart in the middle of it and straight away I knew it was from Aiden. Opening it I held my breath, wondering what he wrote.

Dear Evelyn,

I told you I'd get you the art supplies. If you haven't opened the next gift then you should stop reading. If you opened the other gift before you read this then I've just spoiled what the next present is, so…good job Aiden.

I laughed and put the card down before picking up the other gift, admiring the dark purple wrapping paper and the little pink bow. The gift fit in the palm of my hand and I couldn't begin to guess what it was, so I did what I do best and tore it open enthusiastically.

The box was pure white with a black ribbon on it. The logo was embossed in silver with the name Murray & Co. I'd never heard of them and but I assumed it was jewelry and I felt nervous to undo the ribbon and see what was inside.

Slowly I tugged at the black material and lifted the box lid off, peering inside. My breath nearly knocked out of me at the sight. A band - which I believed to be white gold - housed a row of five stones the size of my pinkie fingernail. What got me though was the color of them. They were definitely amber and they glinted almost magically under the light in my room.

I felt nervous taking it out of the box and placing it over my wrist before pushing the band together and sealing it. I was surprised it even fit my wrist, either Aiden had a good guess or he had somehow measured my wrist without my knowledge

It looked even more beautiful on. Slowly I sat down on the bed, admiring it. Feeling the card beneath my butt I tore my eyes away from the extravagant bracelet and drew my eyes back to his card.

Whichever one you opened first I'm sure both made you happy. I hope they made you happy. You said you enjoyed art and Hannah said you make some really nice stuff in your class, so the book is for you to do whatever you want with it. The bracelet…I saw it and straight away thought of your eyes when we first met. You had that amber ring - which we now understand - around them, and the color reminded me so much of it. I also wanted you to have something of me on you.

This is hard, I'm better at telling you how I feel than writing it. The bracelet should be indication enough of how I feel about you Evelyn. When you walk into a room I have to remind myself to breathe. When you talk to me I have to think about what I say so carefully in case I say something stupid and embarrass myself. You are the best thing to ever happen to me, and I'll never take you for granted.

Aiden

I quickly wiped away the few tears in the corner of my eyes as I looked back down at the shining bracelet on my wrist, absolutely in awe of the precious stones that sat grandly on it. It was absolutely beyond beautiful.

Knowing I still had a mountain of homework to do I got started, although half my thoughts were now side-tracked on the gorgeous bracelet which had taken up residence on my wrist.

My eyes did flicker occasionally to the crumpled piece of paper that still sat on my nightstand. I still needed to talk to the Alpha before I seriously got in contact with my father and I knew I had to prepare myself for the fact he may not even want to meet me anyway. I knew though that before I met my father I had to tell Aiden everything. There was no way I could leave him fully in the dark on my life when I embarked on this next journey. My only worry was how he would take it? How would he think of me? Would our relationship change?

I had to get it over and done with though, it ate at me every day and every time Grace gave me those looks of 'hurry up', I got nervous he'd find out from her instead and I didn't want that. How did I tell him though? Would I show him the scar and see how he reacted or just blurt everything out in one hit?

How would he handle it? Did I tell him about how Jonah and Zac would touch me when I didn't want them to? Or would that drive him all the way over the edge? If I was going to tell him everything did it include that?

Would he want to be with me if he knew that another guy had touched me? Would I be his Evelyn or damaged Evelyn?

Jumping at a tap on my door I looked up from my book and happily took myself out of my thoughts to see Aiden in the doorway looking tired. "I'm surprised you're still up," he yawned as he made his way into my room and falling face down on the bed. Glancing down at my phone I saw it was half past one in the morning. Had I seriously been worrying for that long? I had to have fallen asleep at some stage.

Shaking my head I looked back at the bracelet on my wrist and smiled, moving my lips to his ear. "Thank you for my presents, and the card."

He blinked his eyes open. "No one can see the card, ever. Last thing I need is Grace making fun of me. As for your presents…I'm glad you liked them."

"I love them."

He gave me a strange look, an emotion I hadn't seen before crossed his eyes as he leant up and stroked my cheek. "I love you Evelyn." I froze. He loved me? He just used the 'L' word, and he didn't even know my whole story. He gave me a nervous smile, "I've freaked you out."

"N-no." My voice was breathy and too high.

"I'm just being honest with you, it's better you know how I feel then you trying to guess. You don't have to say it yet; you don't even have to feel it. I'm just telling you I'm in love with you." He lifted my chin up and looked me in the eye. "I love you."

His words should have made me happy, and deep down they did. However the big ugly monster in my mind was more dominant tonight and I found myself shaking my head. "You can't love me Aiden." No one can love me.

"Why can't I love you?" he asked with a grin on his face, flopping face forward back on the bed.

"Y-you don't know everything ab-about me," I stammered as my throat began to feel tight.

"I will in time." His voice was muffled in the mattress as he stretched his arms out and pulled me down on my back beside him. I lay there tense, coaching myself up to the words I needed to say to him.

"You need to know now." My voice was quiet and every nerve in my body was on alert as he slowly lifted his head, his eyes red. "You need to know everything and then you can tell me if you really love me." I took a breath and went on. "Aiden I - in Idaho…I received more th-than just basic ridicule and verbal abuse."

He frowned and sat up, pulling me with him. "What do you mean?"

I looked away from him and to my covered up mirror, willing myself to keep it together. You told Grace, you can tell Aiden. "There was a group of them…the Alpha's son and his friends. They hurt me for being a half-breed. A lot. When we were kids it started out as just being shoved around on the playground or having my lunch stolen, you know kid stuff. Then when I turned eleven and didn't get my wolf…they really upped it. I went home every day with some sort of injury…broken arm, missing tooth…one time someone stomped on my face and I was in the pack clinic for a month."

"You heal slower," his voice was raspy and I saw him shaking a little.

"We got older…the attacks became more brutal with each phase I missed. My head got stuffed down a toilet so often that sometimes I thought I was going to smell like one for the rest of my life," I cracked a weak smile and looked at Aiden's dark expression nervously. "Aiden?"

"Just…keep talking."

I felt like I could possibly throw up with what I was going to tell him next. "They touched me," my voice nearly inaudible as I looked down at my hands in my lap. "Jonah and Zachary w-would do things…uh and then J-Jonah found his mate so h-he stopped." A bit of a lie but I could feel Aiden losing it.

Looking at him anxiously he said nothing. He sat stiff as a board, staring straight at me in such an intimidating way that I thought I was going shrink down five sizes.

Guessing I should just go on I slowly slid off the bed and stood beside him. Raising shaking hands to them hem of my bed shorts and folded them down along with my underwear, allowing that horrible scar on my hip line to show.

"What is that?" His voice was lethal, dark. He'd never sounded like that before. I made to cover it but Aiden's hands went over mine tightly as he stared at it before lifting a finger and tracing over the white scar. "H."

"Half-breed," I whispered.

"Half-breed," he echoed as his eyes suddenly lit up amber and he let me go as his claws came out. "You have more scars?"

I swallowed thickly. "A few."

"Where?"

"Nearly everywhere."

"Did you fight back?" He asked tightly.

"In the beginning. In the end it only got worse if I did."

The room was silent and cold, I'm positive I heard my own heart beating it was that silent. I wasn't sure what to say and Aiden was saying nothing. He looked ready to explode though. Was he mad at me? Was he mad at the Moon Goddess for giving me to him as a mate or was he mad at Idaho?

Please Aiden say something, I pleaded in my mind.

"They're dead." He said simply as he got up from the bed and I watched in horror as his eyes glazed over and he communicated through the pack link.

"Aiden!" I called out to him, but he was obviously focusing on what he was telling everyone. Hearing a chorus of violent growls throughout the house and a bunch of echoing howls outside Aiden's eyes went back to normal only they glowed with amber.

"I'm going to destroy Idaho. I will burn the entire pack to the ground. I am going to make those weak, fucking little asshole *pups* wish that they had never laid a hand on you in any way!"

A chill ran down my side and I nearly choked on my words. "Aiden you can't tear down an entire pack…there's innocent children…not everyone was involved. I've moved on…I'm not there anymore, I'm safe here."

He smiled at me softly only it didn't reach his cold detached eyes. He pressed a surprisingly warm kiss to my lips before pulling back. "I love you Evelyn, if you thought that was going to change when you told me, it didn't." He held my chin in his hand firmly. "Please do not try and stop me from doing this."

He then left the room and stormed past a stunned looking Grace who still looked half asleep while I stared after him in despair.

I just sentenced Idaho to death, and a chilling thought crossed my mind.

I'd sentenced my mother to death.

Chapter Nineteen

I'VE BEEN IN OREGON FOR precisely a month as I looked at the calendar. October twenty-fifth, I shook my head and found myself wondering where all the time had gone. It hadn't felt that long at all. The last few weeks had been utter chaos after I had told Aiden about my past. He wanted to go straight to Idaho and burn it to the ground.

The Alpha, however, put his extermination plans to a halt, and told him he couldn't just take down a pack the way he planned on doing it. I guessed Aiden's plan was to get all his best fighters and storm Idaho, which obviously was a bad idea but through his rage he didn't see that.

I had to sit down with the Alpha and Luna and talk them through my life, Aiden sat in and listened and he got just as angry as the first time, even going as far as breaking one of his mom's vases, which she was not pleased about.

Everyone knew now, including the pack. People stared at me with wide eyes or looks of pity at school and I did my best to just not look in their direction. Katherine had left me alone for a while which was nice and according to Hannah she hadn't spoken to her either. Either Katherine had grown a conscience or something was definitely up.

Hannah and I had been working more on the magic I had, which was fun when it was controllable. I had managed to make most of the stuff we were working on explode. I had worked out though to distinguish between the heat levels in my eyes to know when something was close to being obliterated.

Things had been so crazy that I hadn't even addressed the other problem in my life and the crumpled up piece of paper that housed my father's details still sat on my night stand, glaring at me and burning a hole through the wood.

"Just call the number!" Grace was frustrated with how long it had taken me. The Luna had been kind, not wanting to push it but I knew the Alpha wanted me to call him as well and I understood why. We had no idea what I really was and I guess it made him nervous.

"Every time I try - I just can't press the call button."

"You're going to have to eventually and when you do it will be one less thing off your plate and a whole brand new perspective." Lucy flopped down on Grace's bed. "I wish all I had to worry about was a father I never knew of."

"Geoff still pissy you're going to College next year?" Hannah asked gently as she rubbed Lucy's shoulder.

"Yep. But I don't care, he got to go and have his fun and so can I. I'm not even leaving the State for crying out loud. I told him I was never going to take a back seat in our relationship. I'm not a wifey and I'm not doing the kids thing until I know I'm ready. I'm still young and he needs to get that through his head."

"I don't know where he gets off. Like seriously, telling you not to go. Thank the Moon Goddess I am still mateless." Grace made a victorious face and sat at her dresser, picking up her tweezers and plucking stray hairs in her brows.

"You can't evade it forever, one day you'll meet your mate and you'll wonder why you were so against it," Hannah was all matter of fact as she sat up. "It's not that bad."

"Yeah, if your mate is your age and wants to go to College *with* you."

"The way my grades are it will be a miracle if I get into College. You know mom's making Trey tutor me? How did he ever end up being smarter than me? Seriously, I mean Trey?"

"Trey may act stupid but he isn't *actually* stupid," Lucy commented. "He got me through Chemistry last year." Grace muttered something under her breath and went back to focusing on her brows. Lucy made a face at Hannah who grinned. "Have you guys noticed Trey hasn't been dating anyone this past month?"

I had in fact noticed that, and I was surprised Grace hadn't said anything about it, seeing as she always had something to say about Trey and his love life. Her spine stiffened though as she continued plucking. Lucy winked at me and I realized she was teasing her. So did Grace actually like Trey then?

"His birthday is like nearly two weeks away, maybe he's panicking."

"Good luck to him if his mate is in this pack. All the girls think he's disgusting for how he's behaved these last few years." Grace set down her tweezers and pulled out her tray of nail polishes, concentrating closely on the different colors. Maybe a little too closely.

"Trey is such a smooth talker; he'll get himself out of the doghouse. I remember that time when he was dating all three girls at once…remember?" Lucy said as her eyes lit up when Hannah nodded enthusiastically. "They all found out and he ended up getting them to hate each other instead of him, and he dated them for like another two months before he dumped them all at the dance."

"He is insane," Hannah said giggling. "You have to admit, he is good for a laugh."

"He's a joke!" Grace spat as she got up and stormed from the room.

The girls looked at me wide eyed but still wore matching grins. "You guys are mean," I said quietly.

"Grace has been in love with him for years, she just won't admit it."

"She told me in fourth grade she prayed every night that they'd be mates when they turned eighteen," Lucy whispered quietly.

I bit my lip nervously. "If they end up being mates I do not want to be around for that. Grace would lose it."

"I would film it. What a hilarious memory to look back on."

Hannah laughed at Lucy before looking over at me. "So, how are you and Aiden doing…after everything?"

I scratched behind my neck and sighed. "Well…I mean nothing's changed between us I guess, but he's been spending a lot of time with the Alpha…I haven't really had much time with him. I'm scared they're planning something."

"You can't blame him for wanting to rip Idaho apart though." Lucy sat up on the bed, "I want to rip them apart. Who even hurts someone for being a little bit different?"

"I can't believe you went through all that, everyone thinks you're one of the strongest people in this pack - emotionally. They're really behind you for being Luna. Like at first people had their doubts but after hearing about everything you went through…" Hannah shook her head. "You have a large fan club."

Better than having a hate club, I thought. "It's just so different here; I still get surprised by how different everyone here is. When I first came here and the Luna acknowledged me…and then Grace smiled at me - I was so shocked."

"They were that bad?" Hannah asked quietly.

"Worse."

"Have you spoken to your mom since she's been here? Did you tell her you told Aiden?"

"Nope, I don't know how to pick up the phone to her either. I have two parents in easy contact and I can't bring myself to do it."

"Are you scared he won't want to talk to you?" Hannah asked gently.

I was afraid. What if I called this man and he didn't even know who I was? Or he didn't care, which is a high possibility. How would I feel if my father and half-siblings wanted nothing to do with me? "It's so weird that I have more siblings. I never would have imagined it."

"Hopefully they're more tolerable than Jada." Hannah wrinkled her nose, "Grace can't stand her."

"Maybe they'll look like you, seeing as you have more of your father's genes than your mom's. That'd be kind of cool." Lucy sighed and looked around. "Speaking of Grace, where did the moody bitch disappear too?"

Hannah's eyes glazed over as she searched the pack link and she smiled as she came back to us. "She's running for sure, but most of her link is blocked, I only saw scenery."

"We still have to go shopping to finish getting the stuff for our costumes!" Lucy groaned. "Why did she go running?"

Grabbing the phone vibrating underneath me my heart skipped a beat as I saw Aiden's name and a half message below it. Quickly I opened it; glad actually had the phone on me for a change. *Dinner tonight?* It read. Not passing up on that opportunity I quickly texted back my approval. We hadn't been on a date since that one in the forest so many weeks ago.

"I know that smile. What does lover boy have to say?" Lucy winked at me.

I blushed a little. "Nothing, we're just going out for dinner tonight."

"Grace's shifted. She said be ready to leave." Hannah scooped up her bag and gray knitted cardigan. "Time to costume shop!"

∞

Dress shopping was a very fun affair, and it pulled Grace out of her dark mood. We raided the best fancy dress costume shop in town and everyone found what they were looking for. I think I made a convincing flapper. The dress was shimmery and black with silver tassel bits. The head piece was black with a silver feather and my feather boa was bright pink - just to give it some color.

"All you'll have to do is just buy some cheap pearls and you're set. I can style your hair that night; I've been watching a couple of tutorials online on how to do it." Grace had settled on dressing as a Greek Goddess and was sifting through the mass amount of togas.

"We should get Aiden's body paint while we're out," Lucy called from somewhere in the shop. "His costume is so easy, green paint and some purple shorts."

By the time we made it home it was nearly five but Aiden was nowhere to be seen so I quickly slipped upstairs and changed my clothes. It was getting a bit colder so I slipped on some black jeans and a white stretch cotton shirt, pulling a light pink cardigan over the top of it. I quickly ran a brush through my hair and pinned a few strands back and deemed myself ready.

A couple of steady knocks sounded on my door and I turned around instantly, a smile on my face as Aiden entered the room. He had been looking really tired lately and I know the Alpha had been giving him more patrols since I'd dropped my life story bombshell on him. I assumed it was to burn some of the anger and excess energy out of him.

"Hey." I walked over to him and rested my hands on his shoulders. "How are you?"

"Better now," he mumbled as he wrapped his arms around me and pulled me into a strong embrace. I sighed in content and relaxed into his arms, enjoying the closeness. I think he was enjoying it to as he pulled back and caught my lips in his, weaving his hand into my hair. My hands slowly grazed up to his neck as I reciprocated, my mind going a little hazy. He pulled back and looked at me before placing a kiss on my forehead, then my nose and then my lips. "I'm sorry I've been so busy."

"It's alright. You have responsibilities." My voice was all airy and breathless and I could feel the flush in my cheeks.

"Goddess, you're perfect." Aiden leant back and stared at me, making me feel self-conscious. His eyes caught the bracelet he had given me and he ran his fingers over it. "You are perfect Evelyn, everything about you is perfect."

"Aiden," I mumbled as my cheeks heated and I dropped my eyes to the floor. He had to stop saying stuff like that. Perfect was a serious word and I was far from perfection.

"Believe it, beautiful." He placed a kiss to my forehead before pulling back. "Come on. Let's go out."

As he turned to leave I took in his light blue button down and black dress pants and I found my gaze lingering on his broad back before I shook myself out of it and concentrated on moving my feet behind him. We past the dining room where the Luna was setting the table and she called out a goodbye to us.

Aiden opened the door to his truck for me and I hopped in happily. It always smelt like him in here and even though the seats were worn and torn in some places, it was comfortable to be in. I wondered if my scent lingered in here, and did he enjoy it just as much as I did?

"We haven't done this for a while." Aiden put his arm over the back of the chair and pulled out of the drive, giving me a cheeky smile. "We're going to *Bella's* if that's alright with you?"

"Yeah that's fine." I was just happy to have some proper time with him. Between training, school and his patrols and the fact he'd been locking himself in the Alpha's office lately I'd barely had any time with him in ages. As we pulled into *Bella's* I noted looked relatively busy tonight, unlike the night when Aiden had got the whole place to ourselves.

"I'll get your door," he said as we stopped. He hurried around to my side of the truck and pulled the door open, giving me a hand down from my seat.

"Thank you." My voice was all breathy and I wondered if the nerves I got when I was around him would ever leave. I wasn't sure I wanted them to though, I felt alive with him, not numb like I used to.

Entering the restaurant I was unable to distinguish between wolves and humans but whenever Aiden nodded at a specific family or couple, I took that they were from our pack. A girl with caramel colored hair and green eyes smiled at us. "Do you have a reservation?"

"Yes, it's under Aiden James."

"Ah yes. If you'll follow Elizabeth here, she will guide you to your table and be your server tonight." I looked to see the awkward looking teenager, her red hair pulled back into a tight bun and her pale skin looking illuminated against the black uniform.

Taking Aiden's hand I followed him between the tables before we reached a private looking booth. It was set up beautifully and Elizabeth removed the reserved plate from the table. "I'll be back with your menus," she squeaked before scurrying away.

I slid into the booth as Aiden gestured for me to sit before he sat across from me, moving the small vase of roses from the middle of the table so that there was nothing between us.

Elizabeth was back quickly, carrying a glass bottle of chilled water, two glasses and the menus.

"What would you like?" Aiden asked me as he opened it.

I looked down at the menu, glancing over the pizza section before looking at the pastas. I nearly salivated over the endless selections. "Maybe the risotto to start…and the spaghetti and meatballs."

He grinned over his menu at me like he was enjoying some inside joke. "And dessert?"

"Oh!" I flipped the menu over and the large piece of chocolate mud cake stood out instantly. "The mud cake."

He closed his menu and took mine. "Exactly what I wanted." Elizabeth came back soon after and Aiden relayed our order to her as she scribbled on her notebook furiously before once again darting away toward the kitchen. Aiden poured me a glass of water and I sipped it gratefully, it was warm in here.

"We bought your body paint today," I remembered. "All you need are purple shorts."

He shook his head with a smile. "I better win best dressed."

"They have a competition?"

"Yeah I think there are Best Couple Costume and Best Character, Best Dressed in general and Best Prince and Princess. Grace is determined to win Best Dressed this year." He frowned and said, "Do you know if anything is up with Grace? I haven't seen her much lately but she's been weirder right?"

"Um…I guess. She got a little angry today before we went shopping, but we were talking about Trey and that usually does it, right?" I took a sip of my water, wondering if I had missed anything in Grace's behavior. She had been a little more testy than usual lately.

We got through our first course and continued light chatter but there was something underlying in the air. There was a slight tension between us. Maybe it was because we hadn't really talked in depth about what I had told him and the fact that he'd been on a war path which myself and the Alpha had somewhat contained. Something was definitely up though and by the time it was our second course, I decided to ask him.

"Is…is everything okay, with us?" I asked quietly as I stared down at my pasta.

"What do you mean?"

Maybe I was looking to into things, I was stupid for even asking that questions. "Doesn't matter, don't worry."

"Evelyn," Aiden said my name in such a way it had me looking up from my food and into his trapping eyes. "You can ask me anything. What's up?"

I awkwardly moved my pasta on the plate and cringed a little when I heard my fork scrape it. "You've been…I feel like you've b-been *too* busy since…well what I told you," I said so it quietly almost didn't hear myself.

"I had to be," he said just as quietly. "Evelyn you have no idea how angry I was when I heard all that. I almost lost control and an Alpha should never lose control. I asked for more work, I wanted to respect your wishes, you didn't want any deaths, I wasn't going to do that to you. I just needed time to process."

"So you're feeling better about it then?" I asked hesitantly.

"No." His voice was strong and I felt nervous. "Part of why I asked you here tonight Evelyn…was to talk to you away from the family. My father and I have been talking about everything you told us. He wants us to go to the High Council and call for a hearing with Idaho."

My palms began to sweat as I set down my cutlery and pressed my hand against my legs. "A h-hearing?" I squeaked.

He nodded, watching me. "Evelyn if you won't let me take them down physically, then I'll have to do it the second best way, but Idaho cannot be left to behave the way they do. What if someone else like you is born into their pack?"

They'd be killed, I thought. The only reason I survived so long was because my mother was a Beta. "So this is what you've been doing with you father? Planning a hearing?"

He nodded and took my hand across the table, running his thumb over a bracelet. "The High Council has requested that you take the stand and tell your story as you told me." High Council? I felt dizzy and weak. I'd heard of these council hearings, they were massive.

"I don't want to." My hands were shaking as I looked up at Aiden. "I was ready to put it all behind me Aiden, telling you…I was s-supposed to tell you and then it wasn't meant to matter to me anymore. It was going to go away."

"Well it hasn't has it?" He asked with a frown. "You're still having nightmares."

My face paled and I looked down at the table. "I don't want to," I whispered again. I felt angry suddenly, that he had taken it further without telling me. That he had shared my story outside of the pack. I watched as a crack appeared in the glass bottle of water and I quickly tried to get a handle on my emotions. I took my hand out of his and shakily brushed a loose strand of hair from my face.

"Evelyn." He looked even more tired suddenly; his eyes even glowed a little. "You won't let me do my duty and defend you. You won't let me go and kill them, you won't do a trial…you don't understand how angry my wolf and I are and it needs to be sated in some way because the anger that's in me is consuming me. If something doesn't get done about this, my wolf will take over."

"Aiden…" I sighed and worried my lip between my teeth now feeling guilty he was going through pain over it. I knew how male wolves were about their mates; I'd seen how crazy protective they were over them. Some wolves would lose it if you so much as looked in their mate's direction. I felt bad for causing him pain…but to stand up in front of Idaho? Call them out on everything they had done? I had not expected our evening to go like this. I had been excited to finally spend some quality time with him and enjoy each other's company. He'd only asked me out to drop this bombshell he'd been working on.

"Evelyn?" Aiden asked, trying to get my attention.

"I don't feel well." I quickly got up from the table and found myself hurriedly going in the direction of the bathrooms where I found the first available toilet and hurled up my first course. The idea of confronting Idaho? Jonah? The Alpha? It sent another wave of nausea over me.

"Are you okay in there?" A voice asked in concern.

"I'm fine," I croaked.

"If that's an indication of what the food is like then I'm not sure I want to eat here," another girl said as the doors swung open and they left. I found myself laughing a little but I'm fairly sure it was because I was already hysterical.

Flushing the toilet I wiped my mouth with some paper before going over to the counter and standing with my head over the sink. Hearing a knock outside the door Aiden's voice drifted through, saying he'd take us home. Exiting the bathroom I nearly bumped into him.

"Are you okay?" He asked as he rubbed my upper arm.

"I uh, just need to get home." Get home, have a shower and then hide under my blankets like none of this was happening. He nodded and sighed and I followed him from the restaurant and toward the truck, enjoying the cool night air on my flushed face.

The ride home was silent and uncomfortable and by the time we pulled into the driveway I was glad to be home. I opened my own door and got out, heading up to the front door. The moment I opened it I was faced with the Alpha, the Luna and Grace.

"Evelyn, we have to talk." By the look on the Alpha's face, I knew I wasn't going to be hiding in my bed anytime soon.

∞

"Evelyn, their behavior needs to be dealt with. They have broken so many laws not only in their treatment of you but by the sounds of some of the things you have told us, plenty of others as well. Idaho is led by an unstable Alpha with purity values that are so heinous you have to wonder if he was a result of inbreeding." The Luna put her hand over mine, "I know the idea of going to the council is scary and stressful but what happens if they end up with another innocent victim like you? Do you want somebody else to go through what you went through?"

"No." My voice was quiet and my face was already stained with tears by this point. I'd had the same speech from everyone now; the Luna was the most gentle with it. The Alpha had been pretty much 'pull it together and suck it up'. Grace had been as gentle as possible but with her passion came loud volume and boisterous gestures. "I wouldn't have said anything if I knew this was going to happen."

"What was that?" The Alpha asked, though with his excellent hearing I think he just said it for affect. "Why Evelyn?"

My hands shook as they covered my face and I swallowed the lump in my throat. "I've revisited my past too many times. I told Aiden out of respect for our relationship and everyone else only f-found out because he l-lost it. I was ready to m-move on from it."

No one said anything for a while and I was getting exhausted, mainly from all the crying. Eventually the Luna suggested we pick up the conversation tomorrow and I was more than eager to leave the sitting room and go upstairs.

Aiden followed me up, saying my name periodically while I didn't bother replying. I was upset with him, I decided. He couldn't just leave it alone. It had been so hard to tell him and now he wanted me to tell a room full of Alpha wolves and High Council members. When I reached my door he caught my wrist and I turned around grudgingly.

"Evelyn," his eyes were pained. "You need to understand why we have to do this…"

I shook my head and as much as it pained me to do so, took my wrist from his hand. "I don't need to understand anything right now," my voice was surprisingly cold and I nearly gave myself a chill. It gave me an ache in my chest to shut my door on his face but I knew I didn't want to be around him right now.

Lying on my bed I buried my face in my pillows and allowed the sob party to recommence.

I'm surrounded by violence. Everything was a blur of color but you could make out the figures of wolves fighting each other, snarling and ripping chunks of skin and flesh from their opponent. I stood in the center of the violent field, surrounded by mangled bodies and injured wolves waiting for death to take them.

"This is on you," a voice ghosted in my ear. I looked around to find the source however I saw no one, there were no more blurred fighters, just countless bodies lying naked and bleeding over the clearing floor.

"You should have said nothing," the voice whispered again.

"Evelyn!" The familiar sound of my mother's panicked shout had me whipping my head around as I watched Aiden prowling toward her. "Evelyn!" She cried again and I tried to move my feet, screaming in frustration as they wouldn't move. As the silver blade cut through my mother's neck I averted my eyes.

"You bring death and suffering."

Suddenly the dream shifted and I was standing in what looked like to me the main street of the Idaho compound, only it was nearly unable to be recognized. Buildings had been ransacked, windows smashed. Fires consumed houses and people ran through the streets screaming, shoving me this way and that way.

"Shouldn't have said anything," the voice crooned once more.

"Evelyn, I'm going to kill you." My eyes widened as Jonah appeared in front of me, his hands around my throat, grasping tightly. I felt the sensations, the air was being cut off and I felt like my head was swelling, my eyes popping. "What did I say about opening your mouth?" He growled.

Just as I thought this was the end Jonah disappeared and instead I was in front of Aiden who was coated in blood as he stroked my cheek. "I did it to defend you," he murmured as a strong smell circled us. My gaze dropped in horror as I found we were standing on top of and surrounded by rotting corpses. "This was all for you."

All for you.

All for me.

"Evelyn," a cool and calm voice broke through torment surrounding me and Aiden had disappeared. Instead a man stood a few feet away dressed in a dark green robe. "Be wise, if this comes to violence there will be no survivors."

"Who are you?" I asked quickly as I squinted my eyes at him, trying to make out his face. He seemed so far away yet sounded so close.

"I'm the past you are scared to look into and the future you avoid."

"What?"

"Be wise, Evelyn." A force shoved me roughly and I felt like I was falling into a never ending oblivion as darkness closed in.

My heart lurched like I was falling and I realized I was as I landed on the floor, clutching my chest and pulling the blankets around me tightly. My breaths were loud and uneven as I tried to pull myself away from the dream and back to reality.

Rubbing the back of my head in pain I noticed I'd hit my head on my nightstand. What I noticed more however was the crinkled note in my hand. The note my mother had given to me. Slowly I peeled it open and grazed my eyes over the scribbled words, dropping it in shock as I saw words scribbled beneath it.

Be wise.

Chapter Twenty

ALL OF US WERE A comical looking lot as we posed in front of the Luna's phone as she snapped a picture of us all dressed up. It was a group of characters you probably never would have put together in the same room really.

Aiden was dressed as The Hulk and it did look impressive, he even managed to sort of mimic the trademark angry half snarl-glare look that was always painted on the action figure. Grace was dressed up very dramatically as a Greek Goddess. Hannah had talked Josh into dressing up as Mario so she took the role as Princess Peach. Grace had commented that Katherine should have dressed as the ape that always kidnapped the Princess. Trey decided to go as Frozone from The Incredibles.

"You guys look great," Lucy said with a smile as she stood beside the Luna.

"I wish you were coming!" Grace whined.

"Nah, been to enough school parties. Geoff and I are going to spend some time together, you guys have fun."

"Alright everyone, smile and look at me!"

"Seriously, looking at Evelyn makes me feel like we could walk into the twenties at any moment, how did you do her hair so well Grace?" Lucy came over once the Luna finished taking her pictures and marveled at Grace's updo she had created.

"Evelyn wouldn't even look in the mirror!" Grace complained, "All that hard work and she won't even check it out."

"I'm sure it's perfect Grace," I said for what felt like the fifth time.

"We better leave before we're late." Aiden saved me and he gave my hand a squeeze which helped. The mirror thing - that still hadn't been sorted and none of them knew the real reason why. Glancing up at Aiden as we walked I decided I'd never tell him why. He might blow that out of proportion as well.

Yes, I was still a little mad. Frustration and fear fuelled my anger, the idea of standing up in front of the High Council and my old pack made me feel sick to my stomach. I didn't want to do it but it looked like there was no way out of it. It was that or Aiden was going to have Idaho ripped apart.

Be wise, the note had said. That confused me as well and the dream had scared me so much I nearly flushed the note down the toilet. I had made a decision though. Tomorrow I was going to call my father and would scratch the one less thing off my list to have a panic attack over.

That dream troubled me because I had a deep down niggling feeling that the man in the dream was my father. How else would that message have gotten on the note with his details which my mother had given to me? Because it hadn't been there before.

"Earth to Evie," Grace waved her hand in front of my face. "Time to go chicken!"

"Oh." Coming back to the present I filed out of the room with everyone, heading to Aiden's truck. Grace was riding with Trey, Hannah and Josh. I was happy to be going separately in Aiden's truck; at least I wouldn't be cramped.

Plenty of kids were walking the neighborhood with their parents, carrying their buckets with high hopes of having them filled to the top with candy. The Luna had stocked up on a full container of treats to give out to the young wolves that visited.

Leaving the compound behind us we neared town and once again we were flooded with kids running across the street and shouting excitedly to one another. I remember watching all this from my bedroom window in Idaho, now I was out in it.

The exciting atmosphere was contagious and I gave Aiden a full smile when he looked over at me. When he smiled back his white teeth stood out hilariously on his green skin and I couldn't help the laugh that escaped. "You look so funny."

"The Hulk is meant to be scary," he grumbled with a pout, looking back at the road.

"Just don't smile and you'll be fine," I assured him. We approached the school and my excitement grew at seeing everyone dressed up. Girls I recognized from training and from the hallways waved at us as we got out of the car. Grace latched onto my arm immediately, beaming.

"How cool is this, hey?"

"Pretty cool," I agreed as Hannah approached us.

You could hear the music blasting from the school and as we followed the heavily decorated hallways and paths we found ourselves at the gym. A girl dressed up as a vampire was handing out tickets to people who hadn't previously purchased them. With an irritated glance at ours she waved us in. She clearly wasn't happy she was on the door and I watched as she sourly yanked the vampire fangs out of her mouth.

The gym was bustling with dancing bodies and decorations. Cobwebs had been hung across the ceiling with spiders either on them or dangling. Lit up pumpkins were bundled in corners, windows had Halloween themed fake window covers over them, looking all cracked and eerie.

There was a DJ up on the stage along with a couple of people dancing and I saw Katherine with her friends. Her costume was exactly what I had thought it would be. All sexy and revealing, and I wasn't really sure what she was trying to be, unless she was going all BDSM.

"Let's get some drinks!" Grace shouted over the music as she pulled Hannah and I toward a table filled up with all kinds of candy. Next to it was a refreshments table with a very large questionable looking bowl of punch which was surprisingly unattended. "Get a whiff of that Hannah, this has so been spiked."

"Oh!" Hannah laughed and ladled some liquid into her cup. "It won't do anything for us; we should have brought some Wolfsbane with us."

"What about Evie?" Grace asked with a frown. "She's not full wolf."

"Yeah but she isn't human either, she's got some weird bloodline so how would we know if it would work on her?"

"How about I take a cup of this punch," I suggested as I took the cup from Hannah's hand, "and I drink it. Then if I feel like the alcohol is actually getting to me I can let you know and we can stop talking about me like I'm not here."

"Whoa! Evie Bear is feisty tonight!" Grace made a claw like motion at me and 'meowed' and shook my head with a smile and smelt the contents of my drink.

Yuck.

"Bottoms up, tough girl." Hannah clinked our cups together and I took a sip, deciding it didn't taste too horrible. "Look at Kate."

"I swear I saw that costume in the sex shop last week."

We both looked at Grace with raised eyebrows. "Pray tell what you were doing in the *sex shop*?" Hannah asked.

"Lucy wanted to get some stuff for her and Geoff."

"Okay, too much information, you could have just said I was with Lucy," Hannah rubbed her temples. "It makes sense Katherine would buy her costume there. Her last ditch effort to shove her body in Aiden's face."

"Last chance?" I asked.

"She's going to be seeing her Grandmother, from her mom's side. They live in the Utah pack. She's going over Christmas break."

"Josh isn't going?" Grace asked as she refilled her cup.

"No, he's doing extended training with Aiden. You know what the holidays are like for those two." Hannah touched my shoulder and said, "They literally disappear. You only see them when they want food, sleep or…"

"Or what Hannah?" Grace asked with a wink.

"So Evie." Hannah flicked her hair over her shoulder. "When is Aiden going to mark you?"

My eyes widened and I decided to busy my mouth finishing my drink. "Oh uh…"

"Another?" Grace laughed as she took my cup and refilled it. "Really though sweetheart…it's starting to become talk of the pack these days. People are slightly concerned but mostly confused, plus it lets Katherine spread her venom and some people believe the crap she says because Aiden hasn't marked you."

"I guess I haven't thought about it much…my minds been so preoccupied."

"I wonder what it's like to only feel certain amounts of the bond."

"It's weird," Hannah murmured. "I mean I did feel strongly for Josh because I did get a lot of the wolf qualities but never the way Lucy or your mother, Grace, described it. I didn't get the itch, or the constant heat."

"Aiden is always looking at her neck."

"He does?" I asked, surprised.

"Evelyn, he is a full blooded Alpha wolf. His number one urge would be to mark you, he's just a good guy and he'll wait. It probably kills him though. That's probably why he's so grumpy all the time." Hannah emptied the rest of her cup. "Can we dance now?"

"Dance?" I asked in alarm. "No I can't dance."

"Come on Evelyn!" Grace whined. "Dance with us!" Oh God, I could already feel the mortification rising and I hadn't even *tried* to dance yet. My hands were grabbed and I was pulled into the throng of people who danced and laughed with each other. Grace started swaying and moving my arms, giving me a nod of encouragement.

"Come on Evie, show us some moves."

I felt stiff and awkward and all I wanted to do was find an escape to get myself out of this situation. As Hannah and Grace got more involved in their dancing I finally seized the opportunity to get away, shrieking in surprise when I bumped into a wall of green.

"Running away?" He asked with a grin. He sniffed the air suddenly and looked at me. "Have you been drinking?"

"Huh? Oh no, the punch was spiked but it hasn't done anything to me so…" I trailed off with a shrug.

"So you don't want to dance?" He asked as he played with a loose curl from my updo.

"Not really," I mumbled. Have mercy on me Aiden, I don't dance.

"So you won't dance with me at all tonight?"

"If the music was five paces slower and I could actually move in time, then you'll get your dance." Judging by the look of the DJ and the stuff he played, I doubted he had anything that wasn't some sort of remixed song on his list.

He gave me a cheeky grin, leaning in to whisper into my ear. "Is that your roundabout way of asking me to slow dance with you, Miss Wright?" I felt my cheeks go hot, feeling caught out even though I technically hadn't thought of it that way, of course, now I did. "Wait here." He left me in the middle of the dance floor and I frowned as I watched the back of his head approaching the stage before he leant up and spoke to the DJ.

He started walking back towards me after doing a 'man-shake' with the DJ. The song came to an end and a slow beat came over the room. "Time to slow it down for you love birds out there, and even if you don't have a love bird, there are plenty of lovely ladies to dance with here tonight."

"Something in your eyes makes me wanna lose myself..." I quirked my brow at the DJ, surprised he'd even have a song like this. Aiden's green body blocked my view of the DJ and he gave me a grin. "It's about five paces slower," he murmured as he took one of my hands and placed it on his shoulder. I felt both excitement and nerves as I placed my other hand on his other shoulder, his own slipping to my lower back.

It was a moment I knew I would remember forever. How perfect it felt to be in his arms, dancing to this song. The people around us disappeared in my mind; it was just Aiden and I swaying easily in the middle of the Gym. I really looked at Aiden in this moment, like my eyes had been opened properly. The feelings for him that I'd managed to hold back overwhelmed me. This man in front of me, accepting me for who I was and am. How did I ever get so lucky? What had I done to deserve him?

I let out a surprised laugh when he got one of my hands and twirled me away from him before spinning me back. We were closer now, my free hand on his chest as I steadied myself. His thumb grazed over the hand he held as he swayed us and I smiled softly up at him.

"*…it feels like I'm all the way back, where I belong."* The song slowly died out and I freed my hand from Aiden's and placed it on his cheek, leaning up to press my lips to his, hoping to convey in some sense everything I felt for him in that moment.

Pulling back I looked up at him with new eyes.

I loved Aiden.

∞

"It was the cutest thing I had ever witnessed in my life!" Grace was filling Lucy in on the Halloween Dance as we walked to training, of course bringing up Aiden and I dancing. "Should have seen Katherine's face when they kissed, she looked ready to kill Evie."

Lucy was laughing as she nudged my arm. "So they tried to make you dance?"

"I can't dance like *that*," I grumbled.

"You're so cute Evie!" Grace laughed.

Entering the training room I groaned in horror that today was cardio. Girls were setting up their treadmills or were already completing a slow walk. Since training with everyone though I had been getting a lot fitter and according to Grace I had more 'meat on my bones' as well as some muscle. I didn't really care about that, I was more concerned with just being able to keep up with everyone.

"Alright girls, are we ready?" Sharon boomed over the microphone, and I desperately shook my head no but she didn't see, not that it would have mattered much anyway if she did. She'd still make me run until I was ready to pass out.

By the time the class was finished I was sweating and had taken about five breaks in between while all the girls had powered on. I felt like I could hear my heart beating as I rested my head on the treadmill, groaning in pain.

"I didn't help you today, you did really well!" Hannah clapped me on the back and helped me off, handing me a towel to wipe my face with.

"That's good I guess." Sluggishly I ran the towel down my face, wrinkling my nose when I smelt my body odor. "I need a shower."

"How bad do you think it is for us? We have super sense of smell and right now I feel like I'm in a bath of sweat, like a literal bath." Lucy wrinkled her nose and we all slowly made our way from the gym, stretching any tense muscles.

"Kind of glad I don't have to worry about that." Grace and Lucy walked ahead leaving Hannah and I to stroll along the streets, I couldn't believe those two still had the energy to walk any faster than snail's pace. It did give me some time though, with Hannah which was what I needed, and I wasn't sure if what I wanted to ask could be asked over a text message. "Hannah?"

"Mm?" She hummed as she stretched her arms out behind her back.

"Josh marked you right?"

She stopped stretching and looked at me with a glint in her eyes. "Yes…right here." She pulled aside the thick strap of her singlet and I saw the two brown puncture holes, fully healed.

Twisting my fingers I looked at the floor. "Does it bother you that you can't mark him?"

"I can. I mean my teeth in human form are blunt, I had to mark Josh when I was in wolf form."

"Oh." Duh, idiot. Not everyone is like you.

"You want Aiden to have a mark from you though," she said what I struggled to and I nodded slowly. "It can be done. You could probably do it, but it's something you'd have to ask…your father about."

I nodded to myself. "I was thinking of calling."

"Really?"

"I think I'm ready."

"Good. Good for you Evie, I'm glad." She wrapped her arm around my shoulders. "Whichever way it goes you know you have everyone's support."

I nodded and I felt the sickening nerves rising again. As everyone parted ways to get home I fell into step with Grace, listening to her talk about school and whose outfits she didn't like. Really my mind was far more consumed with the fact I had admitted out loud I was going to make contact with my father, which meant I was actually going to do it.

I had to do it.

With Aiden out on a patrol and the Luna cooking dinner I made my way upstairs and had a quick shower before slipping into some gray leggings and pulling a loose white shirt on. As I made to leave the bathroom I spied myself in the foggy mirror. I didn't wipe the fog away, I wasn't sure I was ready to look at the girl in the mirror yet, but for the first time in my life, her silhouette didn't scare me.

Maybe because I knew the man I came from and looked like wasn't in fact a monster. Would I eventually be comfortable enough with myself, that I could wipe the fog away?

"Evelyn, dinner!" Grace called outside the door.

Jumping I hit my elbow on the shower screen and I grunted at the tingles that ran up my arm. Quickly I exited the bathroom and made my way downstairs, enjoying the cooling feeling of the cold hardwood beneath my warm feet.

"It's just us tonight; Aiden and Greg are running an extended patrol." The Luna gave me a hug. "How was training tonight?"

"Oh it was okay, I think my stamina is getting better." Taking a seat I looked down at the pasta dish in front of me and my stomach growled in anticipation. "Um Claudia?" I asked as I picked up my fork.

"Yes Evelyn?"

"I'm going to call my father."

The Luna smiled at me, and took my hand across the table. "Good, I'm very happy you're reaching out to him Evelyn. It sounds like you have a lot of extended family. Whether or not it works out or not doesn't matter in the long run. You tried and you did what was right."

"I'm sure it will be fine," Grace added. "What kind of father doesn't want to meet their child?"

"Let's stick with a phone call first," I suggested. I was not ready to meet the man and I wouldn't entertain the idea, I had to try and get through a phone call and even then I wasn't sure if I had the guts to do that.

"How have you been feeling lately, about the hearing and everything?"

I sighed and suddenly felt off my food. "I still don't want to do it."

"What are you afraid of...it's fear that's stopping you, right?" The Luna picked up her fork and began eating again and I felt slightly more relaxed that maybe she wasn't fully concentrated on me. "Are you afraid that your offenders from Idaho will try to hurt you? Or that they will deny it?"

"I guess if they deny it...t-then I have to try and prove it."

"The scars are evidence enough," Grace grumbled.

"They could say I did them to myself."

"So you're worried that they won't believe you, and they'll get off and you'll be left with people thinking you're a liar?" The Luna was very good at putting my feelings in order. I guess that's why she was Luna after all and I wondered if I'd ever be as good as her. Would I ever be able to help other people? "Evelyn even if it comes to that, we know the truth. This pack knows the truth and that's all that matters. Packs like Idaho have a way of crumbling, you can't raise a pack on violence and expect it to sustain."

"Alaska is raised on violence," Grace pointed out.

"Not with each other though, only to anyone who isn't an ally. Alpha Hudson maintains a strong pack; everyone is family - as it should be. Cross that family and yours will be wiped out. I very much like his ideas."

"He's the Alpha who has the pack of rogues, right?" I remembered Jonah and everyone going on about it when they saw him at the gathering. He was a giant; I wouldn't ever want to be in the same room with him.

"Yes, that's the one. Technically they aren't rogues though, seeing as they're a recognized pack now." The Luna looked at our plates and then at me. "Well I'm going to clear up, Grace is going for a shower and Aiden isn't due home for another hour. If you want a private moment for this call, now would be the time to do it."

"It isn't too late?" I asked nervously.

"It's seven o'clock Evelyn." Grace gave my shoulders a squeeze. "You'll be fine."

Grace disappeared as well as the Luna so I reluctantly made my way upstairs and towards my door. I felt like I was walking toward my doom and maybe I was being dramatic but I wasn't sure how I'd react if he said he wanted nothing to do with me. Closing the door behind me I made my way over to my bed, grabbing the phone and sitting on the edge, nerves eating away at me as I took the now very crumbled paper off the nightstand.

Slowly I tapped in the number, my finger hovering over the call button. Just press it Evelyn, get it over and done with. Out of the way, you'll never have to worry about it again. My palms were sweaty and my breaths were a little quicker as I pictured all the worst possible scenarios.

"Why would you think I want anything to do with you?"

"Don't ever try and contact me again."

"You aren't welcome in this coven."

I swallowed the lump in my throat and my hands shook. Shutting my eyes I pressed the call button and slowly raised the phone to my ear, my chin quivering. It felt like it was ringing forever and I wanted him to answer and at the same time I didn't.

"Hello?" A female voice chirped down the line. My breath caught and I didn't know what to do or what I should say. *"If you're trying to make a prank phone call you haven't done a very good job, you didn't block your caller ID."*

"I...uh..." My voice cracked. "Is...C-Cornelius there?"

"Cornelius?" The woman sounded like she was frowning. *"What do you want with my dad?"*

I was speaking to my half-sister. I nearly dropped the phone as I tried to maintain some composure. "I uh...he called me today and I missed it. H-he wanted me to give him a call back." Nice lie Evelyn. The last thing I wanted to do was say, 'Oh hey there, I'm your half-sister and I'm trying to find my father'.

"Oh sure okay. Dad! Your phone rang!" There seemed to be a shuffling and I heard a man's voice in the background and once again my breath caught in my throat.

"*Hello?*" That's what my dad sounds like. His voice was smooth, warm and inviting. "*Hello? Is anyone there?*"

"Oh!" Shaking my head I swallowed the lump in my throat. "Uh…I uh…I'm Evelyn," I blurted out.

The phone was quiet and I could hear was his breathing as he processed what I had said to him. "*Maria's daughter,*" he finally said and my skin tingled a little nervously. He said Maria's daughter, not his daughter. Prepare yourself Evelyn. "*She's finally let you call me it seems.*"

That seemed slightly positive. "Sh-she told me everything, about you two…I didn't know about y-you until a m-month or so ago." My voice was all jittery and my hands shook and I was scared I'd drop the phone.

"*And the dream helped your decision to call me?*"

I sighed in relief at the fact I wasn't crazy and he had come to me in my dream, and I'd like to know how he even did that. "Y-yes."

"*Why did your mother wait so long to tell you about me?*"

I scratched the back of my neck. "I uh…never got my wolf. I got your powers instead."

The line once again went quiet and I wish I had a chord or something I could fiddle with. "*I had a feeling this would happen. Especially seeing as I've been able to trace you. I know you had some power but obviously it's not underlying anymore.*"

"Trace me?" I asked.

"*Even though we've never met Evelyn, I am your father. We're connected, that's why I can come into your dreams. I've kept a link on you your whole life. You're living in Oregon now, correct?*"

"Y-yeah…wow."

"*We have a lot to talk about. I'm sure your mother has told you her side of the story…would you be interested in hearing mine?*"

My heart thumped erratically for a moment. Curiosity however won over and I said, "Yes I would," before I could help myself.

"*Do you want to come to me or shall I come to Oregon?*"

"Oh I um, I have to speak to the Alpha first. Um…"

"*That's fine. Call this number again and let me know when and where, I'm very flexible.*"

"Okay," I breathed out.

"*Alright. It was nice hearing from you Evelyn.*"

"Oh...yeah...you too..." I muttered awkwardly. "Um...bye."

"*Goodbye.*"

I sighed in relief when the line went dead and I fell backward on my bed, trying to absorb all the emotions I was feeling right now. I called my father and he wants to meet me. Sure the conversation was a little stiff but we didn't know each other. I even spoke to my half-sister even though she didn't know who I was.

Jumping up I couldn't help myself as I did a little dance of excitement, stopping in surprise as Aiden watched me from the doorway. "Don't stop on my behalf, I was enjoying that. Was that the chicken dance or the sprinkler?"

Even though I did feel slightly embarrassed I ran up to him and threw my arms around his neck. "That was neither of them. It was the 'I just called my father and he wants to meet me, dance'."

"Really?" He asked with a big smile. "Evelyn that's so good. I can't believe you called him."

"Neither can I."

"So when are we going there? I'm not sure if dad would want an unknown witch on pack lands that's all."

"Yeah I didn't think about that. You'll come with me?" I asked hopefully.

"Absolutely. I'm with you on this every step of the way Evelyn." I felt incredibly lucky to have Aiden and I was even more excited now that I wasn't going alone. This was happening; I was going to meet my father.

I leant up and placed a kiss on his cheek. "Thank you."

"No worries, beautiful."

Chapter Twenty-One

SITTING AROUND THE DINING TABLE the Alpha spoke to my father over speakerphone as the trip was arranged. Aiden and I would be going to Idaho along with the Luna who volunteered herself. Our little party also included the Luna's two guards (I never even knew she had any) and the three Aiden had assigned to me. I thought three guards was a little overkill but according to Aiden 'my safety is everything'.

"Two days is all we can give. We have a lot going on, which I'm sure Evelyn will tell you about," The Alpha looked over at me and I sighed internally. I'd have to tell my father about Idaho as well? And the trial? "Not to mention they have school."

"That's fine Alpha James. Two days is more than I thought I was going to get. My entire family is very excited to meet their sister." My insides warmed and Grace shot me a happy smile from across the table.

"We were led to believe there may be some aggression toward Evelyn. Her mother said Evelyn wouldn't have been welcomed in your coven." The Alpha was asking all the tough questions and I could understand why, he didn't want a repeat of Idaho.

I didn't either.

"Yes. We have a lot to talk about, especially Maria. Have no fear, there will be no harm coming toward Evelyn. She is very welcomed in this coven and there is a lot of anticipation about her visit." His voice sounded honest and I instantly believed him.

"Okay well, Evelyn's plane leaves tomorrow. It's a four hour drive to Portland and then she'll take the six hour flight to you. "

"No worries, we'll be waiting at the airport. I guess I'll see you tomorrow Evelyn."

"Yeah," I said breathlessly, feeling my excitement rise. "I'll see you then."

"Thank you Alpha James. I look forward to meeting your son and your Luna on this trip as well."

"Goodbye, Cornelius." The Alpha hung up the phone and sent a rare smile in my direction. "I like your father, he has respect."

"So, how are you feeling?" The Luna asked me eagerly, rubbing my arm.

"Nervous, excited and a little sick, so much is happening, I can't think straight."

"I wish I could come!" Grace groaned aloud again.

"Grace." Alpha James shot her one look and she clamped her mouth shut. Aiden squeezed my hand under the table and got up and I followed suit, eager to go and chat his ear off about how excited I was.

"Don't stay up late you two; we have a very early morning." The Luna stood up and kissed us both and I quickly took her into a hug, which I think surprised her a little.

"Thank you for helping. And coming tomorrow, it means a lot."

"Oh Evelyn, it's no worries at all. You're another one of my daughters now, I care about how all this goes for you. Enjoy the moment; don't let the nerves freeze you up too much, okay?" She squeezed my shoulders and gave me a soft smile before taking Alpha James and leading him to the kitchen.

"I'm going for a run!" Grace announced.

"It's late. Don't stray too close to the border," Aiden ordered.

She rolled her eyes. "I'm going with Lucy and Trey. I probably won't see you guys so have fun!" She pulled me into a tight hug before punching Aiden's arm. "Safe flight." As the front door slammed Aiden and I made our way upstairs to his room where he flopped down onto his bed.

I moved to sit next to him, leaning my head back against the wall. "This is so insane. What if I look nothing like my siblings?"

He pulled me down to rest beside him and placed his head on my stomach. "You'll look like your father then. You have to look like someone and it isn't your mother or Jada or Laurence. I wouldn't worry about that Evelyn."

"I can't believe I'm going to meet my real father. All this time I had a monster in my head, a man who had hurt my mother. Turns out he wasn't a monster." I'm not a monster, I added as an afterthought. "If I had never come here none of this would be happening."

"You still would have gotten your magic though," he murmured as he grazed his hand along my side.

"Yeah I guess. Still I think it's happened much faster here than it would have back home. Mom may have never told me the truth. Do they even know I'm leaving Oregon to go to Ohio? I'm going to be flying above Idaho tomorrow. If they knew I was going to Ohio mom would have had to have told them the real story."

"We can make a stopover in Idaho. It shouldn't take too long to decapitate Jonah." His voice was like steel and I instantly regretted even saying the word. "When I become Alpha the alliance will be null and void. I think dads even heading that way now."

"That would kill them. They really wanted this alliance."

"Without our alliance Idaho would eventually fall anyway. They don't have many friends. They're constantly thwarting off rogue attacks. Our alliance with them has recently boosted their security, but I hope they don't get too comfortable." Aiden lifted his head slightly to look at me and I noticed the dark circles under his eyes.

Cupping his cheek I sighed, "You need more rest."

"Sleep doesn't exist these days," he grumbled. "I'll sleep when I'm Alpha."

I laughed out loud, shaking my head. "No you won't. Alpha's barely sleep."

"You have such a beautiful laugh Evelyn." His eyes were warm and the air in the room seemed to shift slightly, becoming slightly hotter. Maybe it's because my cheeks went hot.

Trying to divert the attention off myself I picked at a loose thread on his shirt. "Why do you always call me Evelyn when everyone calls me Evie or some sort of variation?"

"Do you want me to call you Evie?" He asked his tone light. He knew I was changing the subject as he shifted his body further up mine until we were eye level.

"N-not really," I stuttered.

"Do you want a pet name, Evie-Bear…Evelyn-Boo?" He teased as he stroked my cheek.

"Aiden!" I laughed as I crinkled my nose. "If you ever want me to answer you I'd suggest not ever saying those names again."

"Evie-Bear," he repeated with a grin and a cheeky glint in his eyes. Pursing my lips so I wouldn't laugh I stubbornly ignored him, looking to the side of the room where the TV was. "Evelyn-Boo," he chuckled and I ignored him. Well, until his fingers dug into my sides and I screeched as he tickled my ribs, grabbing my flailing arms in one hand and holding them above my head.

"Ah! Aiden!" My laughing increased as breathing became hard, he grabbed my kneecap and squeezed which caused me to squeal even louder as I twisted this way and that to try and release myself.

"What was that? I can't tell if you're talking to me or not." His assault ceased and I was left gasping for air beneath him, feeling tears in the corners of my eyes from laughing so hard. Honestly I was afraid I was going to wet myself. Catching my breath I looked up at him with a nervous smile, feeling hyper aware of my hands still held above my head. "You are perfection," he murmured. "I love you Evelyn."

Giving me no time to respond he caught my lips in his, kissing me slowly and thoroughly like he was savoring the moment. He released my hands as he cupped my cheek, deepening the kiss and my own hands went to his waist as I allowed myself to open up to feelings he evoked within me.

I kissed him back just as passionately, reveling in the fact that this man was mine, no one else's. He was mine to touch, mine to love, mine to be mad at, and mine to be happy with. His lips trailed softly over my jaw and I felt slightly embarrassed with how loud my breathing was. I jumped a little as his lips connected with the skin where my neck and shoulder met. My heart rate increased at the prospect of him marking me. I felt him graze his teeth along my neck and I shivered at the delicious feeling.

Not really knowing I had been doing it, Aiden's shirt was now bunched up under his neck and he whipped it off over his head before settling his lips back to mine, a little more rougher this time. His flesh on my hands felt hot, and tingles shot through my palms wherever I touched him. I felt his hands at the base of my shirt, slowly lifting the material and I wondered if I was comfortable with it. As it neared the fabric of my bra Aiden pulled back and looked at me, waiting for a yes or no.

I found myself nodding lightly and I lifted myself up off the bed and allowed the shirt to slide over my head. I felt nervous. I'd been in front of him in my swimsuit but they had covered the scars. With just my bra on, the scars on my stomach and sides were visible. Feeling his finger under my chin I looked up at him and he softly grazed his lips along mine and I found my nerves settling.

It surprised me as I rested back onto the bed, when his lips made contact with my chest and down the valley between my breasts which had me clutch at his arms as hot feelings flowed through me. His kisses became scattered then, on my stomach. He moved across, up and down and I rose up on my elbows, my breath catching in my throat as he kissed each individual scar.

As he kissed the last scar he looked up at me. "You're still perfect."

I blinked away the tears that wanted to fall. Instead I allowed him to lift the blanket from under us and wrap us both up in it, hiding my face in his chest as my heart seemed to grow five sizes.

Taking a deep breath I kissed his shoulder. "I love you, Aiden."

∞

Even though it was six in the morning I woke up fresh and alert. I felt my face slowly light up as I moved closer to Aiden's warm body, feeling the chill of the air on my bare shoulder. The Luna had just knocked on the door and I heard Aiden grunt.

"We have a plane to catch and a very long drive," I reminded him as quietly as possible as I ran my fingers across his scalp.

"If you keep doing that I'm going to fall back to sleep," he grumbled as he rolled all of his weight onto me, burying his face back into the pillows.

"Aiden," I gasped as the wind near knocked out of me. What did this guy eat?

He finally rolled off me and I sucked in as much air as possible. He smiled down at me. "You stayed here all night."

I felt shy suddenly, my cheeks felt warm. "I did."

He gave me a quick kiss before rolling out of bed and fishing around on the floor. He produced my shirt and I gratefully put it on. "Did you want the first shower?" He asked as he pulled his already packed bag onto the bed.

"Yeah." Before I could leave Aiden's arm snaked around my waist as he pulled me in for a hug. I contentedly rested my head against his chest, enjoying the feel of his hands rubbing up and down my back.

"I love you," he said with a carefree smile.

I smiled back up at him, feeling my body go warm. I escaped quickly then to my room and grabbed some jeans and a knit sweater. I showered quickly, knowing we had to hit the road very soon in order to make our flight. I was in my room pulling on my boots when Aiden poked his head in.

"Ready?"

"Yeah!" I sounded a little breathless, probably from my excitement and the fact I had been rushing around. I zipped up my small bag, making sure I had my essentials before following Aiden from the room, a bounce in my step.

"Oh good, you're both ready. I was scared you might still be in bed." The Luna had her bag in her hand. "The men are waiting outside; we need to leave now if we want to make our flight. Got everything?"

We both nodded and she smiled and rubbed Aiden's arm before descending the stairs and opening the front door. Grace was definitely still in bed but the Alpha was outside with what I assumed to be our *guards*.

"Charles, Vincent." The Luna smiled at two men, both looking near identical with their short buzz cuts and intimidating muscles. They must have been her regular guards. "Evelyn this is Louis, Seb and Citra." I looked at the other three, all seemingly young but still scary looking. Citra was the only girl on our guard team, but I didn't underestimate her, she wouldn't be here if she wasn't good.

"Hi," I waved shyly and the two boys grinned at me while Citra just nodded, keeping her eyes on every move I made.

"Have a good flight son. Contact me immediately if you need anything." The Alpha pulled Aiden in for the 'man-hug'. He pulled back and moved to me, surprisingly taking my hands into his. "Good luck Evelyn, I hope you find what you're looking for." I didn't look when he moved to the Luna, you only needed to *hear*.

"Alright, let's get this show on the road." One of my guards who I think was Seb grabbed mine and Aiden's bags and put them in the back the large 4WD that waited for us on the street. As we made our way toward the vehicle the Luna got in with her two guards. Aiden and I climbed in and Seb got behind the wheel with the other guard up the front. The rest of them climbed into the back row.

As we pulled away from the curb I was overwhelmed with nerves. This was really happening; I was going to meet my father, my family. By this afternoon I'd be in Ohio and a piece of my life would be put in the correct spot.

"So, you excited to meet your dad?" I think it was Louis who asked me that.

"A little," I said quietly.

"I remember when I met my dad for the first time." I looked at Seb in confusion and he smirked at me through the rear mirror. "My mother isn't my dad's true mate. They both kind of just had me and then dad met his actual mate and they split. Dad lives in the Colorado pack now, with three of my half-siblings."

"And your mom?" I asked curiously.

"I stayed with her; she was heartbroken when he left. I met him when I was six, a bit of a meat head if you ask me. I haven't spoken to him since. Of course it was stupid of them to even get involved with each other."

We stopped in at a diner to have a quick breakfast. The Luna seemed more excited than I did as she babbled to me about how great it felt to get out of Oregon. "I've been there for so long! What a breath of fresh air."

"Remember when she first came?" One of her guards said, I'd already forgotten both of their names. "She got so many people punched it was a joke."

I raised my eyebrows in confusion. "Huh?"

"The Alpha was very protective over our Luna here. If someone so much as looked in her direction…" her guard rubbed his chin. "I swear to this day it still clicks."

"He's not bad anymore," the Luna said defensively. "He was young and short tempered."

I found myself laughing and they all looked at me. Shrugging I said, "I find it hard to picture the Alpha young." It was true, he was terrifying and he had that air about him that he had always been this stern and old forever. The Luna just laughed and paid the bill and we all went back to our car to continue the drive to the airport.

"Do you reckon your dad will try and give me the talk?" Aiden asked with a smirk.

"I doubt it. He barely knows me; he doesn't seem like the type either." Well, I hoped he wasn't the type that would. How awkward would that be?

"Should have heard the talk I got from Janie's father. He said if I consummated the relationship he would personally desex me." Seb shuddered and I made a face at the mental image. "Obviously that didn't happen and I'm fairly sure he still hates me, but what can you do?"

"I don't know if I could go through with it with a threat like that hanging over my head," Louis commented, glancing up from his phone.

"Wait until you meet your mate Louis, it will change your prospective. I was honestly willing to lose my balls to just be with her once." Seb seemed proud of himself and my cheeks heated a little at how he talked so openly about mating.

Aiden seemed to sense my discomfort and he changed the subject. "How far off are we?"

"I'd say about two hours," Louis yawned. "I hate long journeys."

It was a long drive and I forgot how long it actually was. The last time I'd taken this route I'd been on the way to Oregon for the gathering. I'd never expected to leave the territory again after I'd met him. It even felt weird that I'd be flying over Idaho. At some stage I had fallen asleep against Aiden's shoulder because he was nudging me awake and offering to carry me to my seat on the plane.

I was eager to just sleep for the whole plane ride so the trip would go faster but suddenly I was wide awake and my mind was in overload. In six hours we'd be in Ohio and I was going to be meeting my family. What if they decided they didn't like me? Would I have wasted everyone's time dragging them over there? I had six siblings; surely one of them would have to hate me right? What if my own father decided he didn't like me? What about his wife?

"Hey," Aiden said quietly next to me. "Are you okay?"

"Uh huh, yeah…sure." My voice was high pitched and I sounded like I was lacking oxygen. "Promise me something?"

"Anything."

I smiled lightly and rested my head on his shoulder. "Please don't leave me at all throughout this whole trip." I knew if I had Aiden by my side I would be okay. He would look after me and he'd pick up the pieces if it all went to hell.

"I promise. I didn't plan on it anyway." He took my hand in his and brought it to his mouth. "Just relax; it's going to go great." I allowed my body to relax, watching the end of the air hostess' safety presentation. Her next words undid all my relaxed feelings.

"Ladies and gentleman please fasten your seatbelts as we begin our ascent out of Portland, Oregon."

I felt sick, there was no turning back now, this was it.

∞

I clung to Aiden during the landing, not enjoying the sensations or my ears popping. I doubt my death grip felt like much to him but I did apologize afterwards. It did take some coaxing to actually get me out of my seat and I was all too aware now that I was going to be meeting my father within the next ten minutes or so.

"Do I look alright?" I whispered to Aiden for the tenth time.

"You look beautiful Evelyn. If you'd look in a mirror you'd believe me."

"I must say Evelyn, you do travel well. Not a hair out of place." The Luna was smoothing her blonde tresses down and her cheeks were slightly flushed. "I cannot wait to have a nap."

I followed them through the airport at snail pace, practically dragging my feet as nerves and fear ate at me. This was really happening now. It was like finding my mate all over again. I never thought I'd get a mate but I did. I never thought I'd know my father but here I was, taking tiny steps towards doing so. But what if he hated me? I'd had luck with Aiden, he actually liked me. Well he loves me, but would I have that same luck with my father - or my family?

"Aiden wait," I quickly said as my feet planted to a standstill.

"Evelyn?" He asked in concern as he stopped walking and came to stand in front of me. I could feel the tears welling up and I felt stupid for crying. "You guys go ahead, we'll follow after." He used his Alpha tone and I knew he was worried, so now I felt bad for making him worry. When the others left I let the tears freefall.

"I don't know if I c-can do this," I sobbed out as I rubbed my eyes with my sleeves. People walking past us briefly stared but continued on which I was glad for, this was humiliating enough as it was. "We should go home."

"Evelyn," Aiden sighed and pulled me into his arms. "You know you'll regret it if we do."

"I'll regret this more if he decides he doesn't like m-me or want me i-in h-his life," I stuttered out as I tried to control my breathing. "Please Aiden, can we just go back? Can we?" I turned to leave but he stopped me, gently pulling me back to him.

"Evelyn." His voice was quiet and I stared at the floor, feeling my lower lip trembling. "Look at me Evelyn." I hiccuped and slowly raised my eyes to meet his, sniffling my nose. He cupped both my cheeks in his hands and wiped the falling tears away with his thumb. "He wants to meet you Evelyn; he's made that very clear. You want to meet him. A piece of your life is about to make sense. Listen, it doesn't matter how all this goes. It doesn't matter if your half-siblings don't love you, or if you father doesn't love you."

"Yes-yes it does!" I blubbered. "What if they're like Jada? I can't handle my hair being cut off in my sleep again. Or - or what if dad is like M-Michael, what if he sees all my flaws and personally puts me b-back on a plane back to Portland."

"That isn't going to happen Evelyn. If anyone touches your hair I will kill them."

"What if they brought me here to finish me? Mom said that th-they wouldn't h-have accepted me. What if I'm some really bad mixed b-breed and they've led me here under false pretenses and they're really p-planning my execution!"

"That's a lot of what ifs, Evelyn."

"I would say you watch too much TV, my love." I stopped my proverbial flow of speech at the familiar voice that broke into my panic attack. That voice very much mirrored the one on the phone and I peeked around Aiden's broad body slowly to see if it was who I thought it was. "I have no intention of murdering you sweetheart. Nor do your sisters and brothers."

He was a sight.

The man who'd been a blurred figure my whole life was standing in front of me, clear as day. His tan skin that matched mine, his mess of brown hair atop his head which curled in some spots and had visible grays poking through. What struck me were his eyes, and how I had those eyes. This was my father, and so far he wasn't a monster.

I had been waiting for this moment my whole life, and I was suddenly overwhelmed with emotion for the man before me, my father. We just stared at each other, as if we were both trying to match up to the other, spotting either marks or body shapes that mirrored our own. I couldn't describe the feeling that ran through me as I looked into his eyes, the eyes that matched my own, it was like home. Slowly he held out his hand and I swallowed, taking it in mine dazedly.

"You must be Cornelius," Aiden outstretched his hand to my father who turned his attention to Aiden, releasing my hand with a smile as he looked over my mate.

"You look like an Alpha," my father commented as he assessed Aiden. "I've met a few in my time. Why are you all so large? Never mind that. Evelyn, have you finished panicking? We have a forty minute drive to Lyons and I have a very eager family waiting to meet you." My eyes were wide and I could barely form a word as I took some stumbled steps forward, grasping Aiden's hand as I continued to take in all the features I believed I shared with him.

We were quiet on the way to meeting up with everyone else. I was still stunned to know I was walking beside my father right now. My father was next to me, within arm's length and I was too shocked to do anything except stare.

People walked everywhere, mostly looking tired and sipping on coffee. They pushed and shoved but Aiden took the most of it, shielding me from flailing bags and screeching people who greeted each other enthusiastically. By the time we got outside I gratefully took in a breath of fresh air. I followed them to a large van where the Luna's guards were already putting the bags in. She waved at us in excitement. "We thought you got lost!"

"Nothing like that. Evelyn thought we were planning on killing her is all." We reached the van and he touched my shoulder which sent a wave of what felt like cool water through my veins. I felt my eyes glow and I widened them in reaction to the magic coming up so quickly. "Well, you do have my powers it seems, and you are my daughter. You wouldn't have felt that otherwise." Everyone climbed into the van and I took a seat beside Aiden, taking in the old smell of the vehicle.

I relaxed a little as Aiden put his arm over the back of my seat and kissed my head. "See? Nothing to worry about."

"Y-yeah," I whispered.

"I'll have to apologize for what's waiting for you at home. If my daughters had their way the entire coven would be here tonight. They are a little excited to meet their long lost sister. They've been waiting for this for some time." He looked at me through the rear-view mirror and I frowned.

"Th-they knew about me?" I asked quietly.

"You'll have to speak up, mouse, I don't have werewolf hearing." He shot me a smile and I gripped Aiden's hand. The Luna repeated what I had said, seeing as she was up front next to him. "Oh yeah, they knew. Everyone knew. Not a secret one man can keep to himself. That's a whole other story; we have a lot to talk about."

The Luna and my father talked up the front and I looked back up at Aiden for some reassurance. He smiled at me and shook his head before flipping out his phone and texting Josh, I think. My phone was in my bag in the back of the van and I wished I'd had it with me for something to do with my hands. At least I could focus on something other than not trying to make eye contact with my father in the mirror. This was so weird. And it was crazy to think over the border was my mother's old pack. My grandparents and her sister still lived there. I'd only met them once but they hadn't been too friendly either.

"How's school for you Evelyn?" My father asked, trying to make conversation, which left me feeling hopeful.

"It's okay. It's s-school." I tried to appear relaxed but my voice said otherwise. Aiden squeezed my hand and I felt a little more courage. "I like art."

"That's good. Sienna, one of my eldest, she is an exceptional sketcher. I hope she pursues it professionally, she could go a long way." A name! I grasped at the information. I had a half-sister called Sienna.

"How did your wife take all of this?" The Luna asked him quietly, but I managed to pick up on it.

"She was thrilled for me. She knew about Evelyn, I wasn't going to lie to her about my life before her." We passed a sign and he announced that we were about ten minutes of out Lyons. My palms felt slightly sweaty and I tried to calm myself down. I didn't need a repeat of the airport in front of my siblings.

"So you don't live in a compound?" The Luna asked him with interest.

"No ma'am. We all live around the area, my house is central though as I am its leader. We feel we are little more inconspicuous that way. People would label us as a cult if we lived how the wolves do. I mean, the way we dress for starters…" My father tapped the wheel, "it works for us."

"It's so interesting. I haven't been outside the pack in a very long time. Fascinating to see how others live." The Luna beamed at me and said, "You could have grown up here Evelyn."

I bit my lip. If I had grown up here, would my life be a mirror image of my life I'd had in Idaho?

We pulled into a gravel track lined with thick trees and it was almost too dark under their cover. I noticed a few lights strung from branch to branch and I had to admit it looked beautiful. As we reached the end I spied a modest looking double story house with a wraparound porch. I could make out the green shutters on the windows and the green front door. There was a vegetable patch off to the side, but what really hit me was the amount of different flowers growing everywhere.

"My wife is obsessed with flowers. She doesn't care that they make me sneeze." I almost laughed however the sound was choked in my throat when I noticed the swarm of bodies exiting the house. One…two…three…four…five…six…seven, gosh.

As the van pulled to a stop I tried to discreetly take in the swarm of people outside. Three girls with identically flowing brown hair stood in pale green, blue and pink dresses that hung from their shoulders delicately. The three boys each wore black slacks and loosely tucked in dress shirts. The older looking woman on the end I assumed was my father's wife. She was beautiful. She herself had dark brown hair but her eyes were a piercing green which complimented her tanned skin.

I let everyone exit first before Aiden turned around to me with an encouraging smile and helped me down. We were on the side where my family wasn't and he squeezed my upper arm. "I'll be with you the whole time."

I took a calming breath and nodded. "Okay, here goes."

As we came around the side of the van I took in the expressions of each of my half-siblings. They all wore excited smiles and I looked at the Luna who gave me a thumbs up. "Everyone…this is Evelyn," my dad introduced. "Evelyn this is Sienna…" he pointed at the girl in the pale pink dress, and her eyes twinkled as she gave me a small wave. "This is Jasmine…" the girl in blue made a small squeal in the back of her throat as she danced on her toes. "Gabriel and Christian." He gestured to the two older looking boys who both gave me warm smiles.

"Sienna, Jasmine, Christian and Gabriel are quads." My father's wife said gently to me. I nodded with wide eyes as I wondered how that small woman had given birth to four children all at once. Someone give her a medal.

"Then we have our twins, Aliyah and Phoenix." The girl in pale green immediately flung herself on me, wrapping her arms tightly around my neck. I stared wide eyed over her shoulder at Phoenix who gave me a small wave and adjusted his shirt.

"I'm so happy to meet you!" She whispered in my ear. "I had dreams about you, and you look exactly like the girl."

"Oh…" I was beyond stunned at this reception.

"Aliyah let the girl breathe." My father's wife disentangled Aliyah from me and held out her hand. "I am Stella. Welcome to our home."

I shook it hesitantly, making sure it wasn't weak. "I'm Evelyn…this is my mate Aiden."

"She has a boyfriend!" One of the girls squealed. I couldn't remember her name at all.

"No she has a mate, stupid." Aliyah snapped. "Totally different."

The other rolled her eyes. "It's like the same thing. And don't call me stupid!"

"Then don't be stupid!"

"Mom are you just going to let her call me stupid?"

"Girls" My father snapped. They both shut up instantly. "I'm going to direct our guests to their quarters and let them freshen up before dinner. When I return this petulant behavior will not be present, will it?"

"No dad," they both murmured in unison.

"Good." He tuned to smile at us, gesturing toward the house. "Follow me."

∞

"I just met my family," I whispered to Aiden once we were alone in our room. I didn't have enough room in me to be surprised by the fact we were sharing a room, I was still in shock by the amount of half-siblings I had.

"And they didn't try to kill you," he said with a laugh. I made a face and he stopped laughing, instead he came over to me. "You have to admit, he walked in at the perfect time. I wasn't sure what else I could say to make you not get on the first plane out of there."

"I'm glad I didn't," I admitted.

"Make sure you two get some time alone. Some of this stuff… some of the stuff you two need to talk about is personal. I want you get everything you need out of this trip. Don't let your fears stop you."

I nodded slowly, sitting on the edge of the bed. "I have a lot of sisters. I can't remember their names is that bad?"

"Seeing as you met them all in the span of five minutes of arriving - I'd say no it isn't. I can't remember them all either." Aiden opened his bag and rifled through it before producing a toothbrush and he walked into the joint bathroom. Now that I was calming down I wondered why my father hadn't put us in separate rooms, maybe he didn't think it was his place. Not that I minded, I slept with Aiden last night and it was probably the best I'd slept in my whole life.

The room itself was idyllic, kind of like the rest of the house. Gentle pastel colors were used throughout the entire house. The room itself had pale blue walls and flowing white curtains. My father had said not to try shutting the windows because they didn't budge. I was a little weary of insects coming in, hopefully they'd put some kind of bug repellent spell on the windows. The double bed was wrapped in white and blue blankets and the furnishing were all white wood with paint chipping off them. Some of this furniture had to be older than I was.

Aiden came back into the bedroom with a weird smile. "It's strange being out of Oregon, I've rarely left the pack before."

"I've done more traveling in the last few months than I have in my whole life." This definitely was not how I saw my year going that's for sure. I was going to finish out my senior year and escape to more human occupied areas. Now I had no idea what I was going to do after graduating. Aiden wanted to go to College so I guess we'd do that, but after that it would be all pack business. It was daunting to know in a few years I'd be a Luna.

"Last night really meant a lot to me," Aiden said quietly beside me. "You have no idea how I felt hearing you say you loved me." I felt my cheeks go warm as I looked up at him, wishing I had my hair down to hide my face. "Thank you, for giving me a chance."

"Thank you for being so patient with me," I murmured. He gave me a small smile and I couldn't resist closing the distance between us and placing a soft kiss to his lips. "I love you," I said with a shy smile.

He grinned at me and pulled me into his side. "I love you too."

Chapter Twenty-Two

"So how does the whole mate thing work anyway? I mean we don't get any werewolf exposure here. We only hear things." Sienna looked at me over thick framed glasses that she hadn't been wearing earlier. "It's all love at first sight right?"

I made a face at her and looked at Aiden who smirked. "Well Evelyn fainted when she met me; I was that much of a shock to her."

"Evelyn was under the impression that she wasn't going to have a mate," the Luna explained as she rubbed my hand. "So when she met Aiden she got a little overwhelmed by it all."

"Why did you think you wouldn't have a mate?" Phoenix asked me, setting down his phone. "You're half-wolf, you're surrounded by wolves. I mean it's all magnetic really isn't it? That's really how it all works."

I shrugged, not really wanting to get into the reasons why. "I just wasn't sure it was going to happen, but it did. I'm lucky."

"So your kind doesn't have the mate thing then?" One of the Luna's guards asked from his corner in the room.

"No. It's funny isn't it? Werewolves have mates, vampires have their brides, but Morgana decided to jip out on her own kind," my father said shaking his head. "Although I'm happy we don't have it. I think it's a little too simple in my opinion."

"Too simple?" The Luna asked politely as she sipped on her tea.

"I never could get my head around it. Once a wolf reaches a certain age and looks into the eyes of someone they may have been around their whole life, they suddenly love them? Even though they never looked at them once beforehand?" He set down his teacup. "Not that I don't respect my own creator, I do so immensely. But, it wasn't a very fair decision for her to make."

"You're looking at it all wrong dad," Aliyah murmured from behind her book. "She created one being and split the souls. They're half of each other. They don't discover it until they're fully matured wolves because their human side is too weak… it is simple, but it's pure genius. I love the idea, plus it takes out all that rubbish of being messed around with by silly boys. "

"Aliyah is having boy troubles," Sienna whispered to me.

"Yeah. One of them stole her crayon." That was Gabriel then, who looked over at his sister to see if it got a rise out of her.

"Ha-ha, I'm fourteen and it doesn't make sense for me to have boy troubles. Good joke Gabriel, you should do stand-up comedy."

"You have to be funny to do stand-up," Jasmine put in quickly, glaring at Gabriel as Aliyah stormed out of the room. "Really Gabriel, give her a break. If I recall correctly, I remember you had girl troubles at fourteen."

"What can I say? All the ladies want me."

"Gabriel go and apologize to your sister," Stella ordered. He grudgingly got up and dragged his feet as he left the room, loudly calling out Aliyah's name. "You're having a real experience here Evelyn; imagine if you grew up with all of them. You have two siblings in Idaho, right?"

I felt a little shocked by the mention of Idaho but I quickly nodded at her. "Yes, um, Laurence and Jada. They're the same age as Aliyah actually."

"What are they like?" Sienna asked with interest.

"Wretched," Aiden put in before I could talk. I looked at him with wide eyes as Sienna stifled a giggle. "The girl was under some ludicrous impression that I was going to be mates with her friend. And if not her friend, then her. Thank the Moon Goddess it was Evelyn."

"Were you close with them?" My father asked me, regarding me with curious eyes.

"Oh...um, not really. They uh, did a lot of wolf stuff...I wasn't really involved with all of that." I sipped my tea to avoid talking any further and hoped that the conversation would switch. Sadly it didn't and there was only so long someone could gulp their tea before it disappeared.

"What about Michael?" My father asked as he leant back in his chair. "What was he like?"

Just the name made me shiver slightly and it didn't go unnoticed by Aiden whose fists slightly clenched on his knees. "He was busy a lot. You know...being a Beta and all, I didn't see him much. He wasn't my dad so; he didn't have too much to do with me." I put my head down and looked in my cup and I could feel everyone exchanging glances.

"What about your powers?" Sienna asked suddenly. "Dad said you'd been having some trouble controlling it."

"Oh, yeah it's been strange. It wasn't until recently I actually started believing that I actually had something. It was only with the help of a witch back home; she showed me sort of what I had...but somehow mine feels a little different to hers."

"Different?" My father asked, leaning forward in interest.

"Yeah...she does a lot out of books and she uses words. I don't...I kind of just used my mind." They all looked at me with disbelieving glances and I touched my neck nervously. "What?"

"Nothing...it's just...dads the only one here who never needed to learn from books. He used his mind from the start as well." Jasmine looked at me with a big smile. "This is so cool. Not a lot of us can do that. It takes a lot of power for it to happen."

"Mom said your eyes glowed?" I asked, hoping that would explain why mine lit up.

"They do. Yours do as well?" I quickly nodded, feeling excited I had an answer to a question.

"She took down a rogue wolf with her magic," Aiden mentioned and once again all eyes were on me and I wanted to hit him a little for putting me into the spotlight like that.

"You can do a lot more than what you're already doing though, Evelyn. With the gift we have - anything is possible. I can move the water up from the earth into the sky. I can move plants, trees and if I really wanted to, mountains. There's no limit, unlike ordinary witches." My father got up and went to the bookshelf by the fireplace and skimmed his fingers across various titles before pulling out a weathered looking leather book. "This was my grandmothers. She was like us - the first one of us. You can borrow it, you'll learn a lot."

I accepted the book and ran my hands over the soft but worn out leather. *The Diary of Cecelia Amara Ahasverus.* The lettering was fading and almost difficult to read, but I managed, and I admired the last name. "Ahasverus?" I murmured aloud.

"That's our family name. It's been around for a very, very long time." Jasmine said. "You'll get a massive history lesson in that diary. We all had to read it. Our great grandmother does not hold back, let me tell you."

"Yeah you read *everything* in that thing. We never got *the talk* because it's in that diary." Phoenix shuddered, "I'm so glad those days are over."

I looked down at the book apprehensively and back up at my father who shook his head. "It isn't that bad. You'll find great enjoyment out of it; you'll understand when she talks about her power. They were too immature when I gave it to them."

"I'm sorry but no one wants to read about their great grandmother's sex life!" Jasmine said indignantly as she stood up. "It's weird!"

"Jasmine we have heard this speech a million times. Sit down; you're ruining the peace and quiet." Stella gave her a warning look and Jasmine sat down quickly.

"Actually, Evelyn." My father hadn't taken his eyes off me. "I was wondering if you'd like to go for a walk."

A walk? I looked at Aiden and he nodded at me, offering me a smile of encouragement. Nerves churned in my stomach as I slowly nodded and got up from my seat next to Aiden, suddenly feeling any security I had drifting away.

"Okay."

I gave Aiden one last look before we left the room and ended up on the porch outside. I could hear Seb and Louis following, but slowly. I wasn't sure how far we walked but we ended up walking down the driveway under the canopy of trees and surrounded by the little twinkling lights. It was like a mini universe in here.

"I have to admit Evelyn I was surprised to get a call from you. When you told me Maria had told you everything I was shocked. She vowed to keep the secret until her deathbed. It would have been bad news for her if her pack had found out she'd slept with one who wasn't her mate." He looked at me thoughtfully. "You look a little like her. I have to say though you do share much more of my features."

"I know. I was reminded of that every day."

"Hm?"

"You know…because I didn't look like mom and because of her lie of how I came to be…I was out casted for it. My appearance just seemed to make things worse."

"Yes. That lie. I was disgusted when I had heard it, and the fact you were raised believing that." He shook his head. "I had to wait for you to come to me. I felt you'd never want to speak to me or know me with that sick story in your head."

"I hated you for a very long time," I admitted quietly.

"I'm aware. I would too if I grew up not knowing any better." He shook his head and sighed tiredly. "Your mother, what a woman, but she was a little insane to be honest. Sometimes I feel like she used me to get a child. She loved the attention your mother."

"Really?" I never really got that from her. Although, thinking back, she did start a lot of fights with Michael over how the pack treated me and in result her. Was that her being attention seeking or did she genuinely care? She was my mother, she had to care.

"I cloaked you to save my own skin. The last thing I needed was an army of wolves ripping apart my coven. That's why you have no scent. That's why everyone believes you were half human, because that's how I made you smell."

"Wow," I said, crinkling my nose.

"I can uncloak you if you want. You might shock your mate with the scent change though."

"Really, it doesn't affect me anyway. You can leave it on. I'm not sure I can handle anymore change right now." We continued walking and I felt myself growing more comfortable in his presence. It was a little exhilarating that I was walking side by side with my father right now.

"We need to discuss your life in Idaho. Aiden said there is a rather important hearing that will be happening soon? You're going to be giving evidence of mistreatment?" His voice was a little tighter then, the same way Aiden's got when he got angry. "I always warned Maria that if she took you, you'd never have a good life."

My skin prickled slightly. "Well what other choice did she have?"

"She could have let me have you."

"She said I wouldn't have been accepted here either," I muttered as I kicked a rock.

"Yes, well that's where I call another load of bullshit from your mother." I looked up in surprise and he looked at me seriously. "My coven was more than willing to take you in Evelyn. We never discriminated against interracial couplings. They just wouldn't have let me marry her; I was already betrothed to Stella."

"She would have been found out if she carried to full term and then suddenly I disappeared," I said quietly. "Her whole cover story was gone and she'd be charged with adultery."

"Yes," he murmured. "So to save her own skin she allowed her first daughter to suffer. Lies have a way of coming out Evelyn, and it's all going to come out at this hearing. You've gone through your first seventeen years of life suffering for no reason."

"Aiden wanted to kill them," I admitted in a whisper.

"I would have helped. It angers me Evelyn, you have to understand. You're my child and I should have done more. I'm so thankful for the trip you took to Oregon. Meeting Aiden was probably one of the best things that could have happened to you. He's a strong minded young man, as a young Alpha should be. I'm glad you have him."

"So am I. I will always be thankful for that trip." We walked along quietly and my thoughts drifted to Aliyah and her supposed boy troubles. "Aliyah is allowed to date at fourteen?" I asked curiously.

"Aliyah is so far my only child that isn't promised to anyone. She is taking full advantage of that fact. There is another boy; in a coven from New Orleans…I am discussing a betrothal with their leader. She's not going to like it."

"Why? I mean I don't want to sound rude…but why are they *promised* to people?"

"It's more about creating stronger alliances. With a lot of covens falling apart it's important to have brothers everywhere. The others understand this and have agreed wholeheartedly, however Aliyah believes the idea is archaic. I am dreading our conversation." He looked tired and he ran a hand down his face. "Aliyah is a tough one to crack. I find her emotions most difficult to read."

"There's always one," I murmured. "Especially with so many siblings, there's always that one who runs on a different grid than the others. She'll understand better maybe when she's a little older."

"I had always wondered when none of my children had attained those special powers if you would receive them. I was nervous for it; I was convinced that your mother's wolf genes would override it. When I got your call I knew it. You look a lot like my mother; in fact you and all your sisters share a very strong resemblance."

"They're twins and quads," I shook my head trying to sort it out in my mind. "Why wasn't I apart of a set? I mean wolves usually have up to about three children at a time, so that mixed with the fact-"

He stopped me before I could go on. "Twins are not on my side, my wife Stella - her whole family is twins. Twins, triplets, quads. I knew what I was in for when I married her. The fact that you didn't come out in two surprises me. Your mother is a wolf after all, maybe it was our mix."

"Well I don't shift," I shrugged.

"Well in my opinion you have a better deal. Sure shifting into a wolf may be exciting, but a wolf can't set multiple brains into a meltdown can they?"

"Send a brain into meltdown?" I was beyond intrigued.

"Well while our magic is pretty, we can do more than just play with the elements Evelyn. We are capable of some serious destruction. You'd do well to learn your magic to use a defense and an offense, seeing as you can't protect yourself from wolves physically, you don't have their strength. However, one thought could have blood coming out their ears and their eyeballs popping out of their skulls." I shuddered and made a face and he laughed at me. "I do want you to learn it though Evelyn, you're going to be a Luna one day, a Luna of a very important pack. You need to be able to defend your pack and yourself."

I swallowed the nervous lump in my throat and nodded. "How do I learn?"

"Well it's all in the mind isn't it?" He asked me, and I hoped he didn't expect an answer because I had no clue. "Watch." His hand moved so quickly and the tree beside us shot up into roaring flames, the heat coming off it making me cringe back. "All I did was picture the tree on fire."

"So weird," I marveled as he put it out. "I don't get the whole concept of it. Just using your head and it happening..." It was so confusing to me, it seemed so fake. There had to be more to it.

"Evelyn, our family traces a direct line back to Morgana - or as the wolves call her, *Moon Goddess*. The creator of all things magic and supernatural. Obviously our bloodlines are tainted but sometimes - in our case - some of the powerful magic sneaks in. The Ahasverus name is famous not only for our talent but for the fact that the Moon Goddess/Morgana is our ancestor, directly." I watched in awe as he flicked his palm open and a lone flame sat flicking above his open hand. "Try it."

I bit my lip nervously, I wasn't sure if I could do this. Especially in front of my father, talk about being put on the spot. What if I wasn't really magical anyway? I held my palm out, noting how it shook slightly as I focused on what I wanted. Fire. Heat. I pictured it shaped like a ball, a myriad of red, orange and white. I pictured my hand heating up as the flame would grow to the size of a tennis ball.

"Amazing." I opened my eyes and yelped in surprise at the ball of fire in my hand and I looked at my father who beamed at me. "Throw it in that dry field over there and before it hits the floor turn it into water."

"What?" I asked in shock. "What if I don't make it to water in time? I'm not setting the place on fire!"

"I'll stop it before it gets out of control. Come on Evelyn, stretch your limits. Anything is possible, remember." He gestured for me to go and I shut my eyes with a squeal and threw it. "Open your eyes Evelyn!" I tore them open quickly, craning my neck as the flame flew into the air and I watched it descend from the sky. "Well now would be the time to make that water…" he muttered dryly.

Shaking my head I focused on the fire ball falling closer and closer to the dry grass and I pictured myself creating water, my body feeling cool as I felt like it flowed through my veins. I felt the chill really hit me as coolness ran down my fingers and I watched as the flame became nothing, hearing a splash just in time as it hit the floor. My heart thumped as I took a relieved breath.

"Wow."

"You will have no problems learning how to use your magic. You're a natural. As for the defensive stuff and offensive, practice on your mate, he'll heal quick enough just don't kill him." I looked at him in outrage and he laughed. "I joke, but it wouldn't hurt to train with that witch friend of yours back in Oregon."

We slowly began walking back toward the house and I felt myself eager to get back to Aiden. I wondered if the bond would be stronger when he marked me, it had to, everyone said it would be. It just bothered me I wouldn't be able to mark him, my teeth were not as sharp as a wolves. I looked at my father sideways who stared down at the floor with a thoughtful look on his face. Dare I ask? Was I even able to mark him somehow? If I could apparently melt someone's brain then surely I could put a mark on someone's skin, right?

"Your thoughts are so loud. You have so much energy coming off you right now, what do you want to know Evelyn?"

"Oh!" Feeling slightly caught out and even stupid for asking I twisted my hands together nervously. "Well…uh…Aiden and I…I'm going to - Aiden's going to mark me soon. I just um…it's," I huffed in frustration. "I can't mark him!"

"Yes you can," he said simply. "It will hurt him, briefly. Same for you when he marks you, but you can mark him Evelyn. Plenty of witches mark their wolf mates."

"Oh." I frowned and then waited for him to go on, when he didn't I raised my hands. "Well how then?"

He sighed and we stopped walking. "Place you hand wherever you want the mark to be, imagine whatever you want it to look like. Nothing too intricate, you don't want to make your mate pass out from pain, because believe me, it does hurt. Stella marked me and I near collapsed."

"Witches mark each other?"

"We mark our husbands, wives and children. We even have coven marks to easily identify one another."

"Ha, cool." I nodded my head slowly and we began walking again and I began thinking about what I would make my mark look like. Did I just use my initials? I didn't want to do anything too fancy I might hurt him. It was an exciting prospect though; I was going to be able to mark Aiden.

∞

"I keep trying to imagine what my life would have been like if I had lived here," I murmured quietly to Aiden as we lay in bed. I could hear crickets chirping outside and as peaceful as it was, I was scared I was going to wake up with bugs in my bed; I had been assured however that that would not happen. *"Trust me Evelyn, if that happened, I wouldn't be sleeping in this house,"* Aliyah had said as we all got ready for bed. "It makes me sad that I missed out on so much."

"There's no point thinking about it. Just think about now, you have your family who all love you." He kissed my shoulder.

"In the past few months you have gained two extra mothers, two fathers and six siblings. You've got so much more to look forward to, worrying about what could have been will only take away the joy from now."

"You're right," I conceded as I turned in his arms to face him. "I made a fireball today."

"You have got to show me that. What else did he say you could do?" He looked like an inquisitive child and I laughed at him.

"Melt someone's brain out of their ears," I said as I made a face. That did not sound particularly appealing and I doubted I would ever need to do that to another human being. He made a face like he looked impressed and I shook my head at him, crinkling my nose. Grace would probably suggest I melt Katherine's brain. We settled into comfortable silence and I watched as his eyes gradually closed as he relaxed and I bit my lip as I wondered on whether I tell him about the fact I could mark him too.

He looked so peaceful, I hadn't seen him so rested since I had been in Oregon and I assumed that was because he wasn't out running a patrol until three in the morning. How he even got through school was beyond me, if I was him I'd crash at the lunch table and wakeup the next day. I marveled at the fact that somehow he was all mine, no one else was ever going to have him besides me.

I would get his smiles, his hugs - his kisses…and his love. I felt incredibly lucky and thankful in that overwhelming minute and I found myself thinking maybe all this time the Moon Goddess had given a damn about me.

"I can feel your eyes on me," he grumbled tiredly as he peeked them open slightly.

I blushed at being caught. "I'm sorry."

"What are you thinking about?"

"You," I admitted. Taking a breath for confidence I found myself saying, "My father told me something." He waited for me to go on and I bit my lip, dropping my eyes to his chest. "He said I can mark you." He seemed to wake up a little more now and I nearly laughed at his eager expression. "I'm ready

Aiden. I'm ready for you to mark me…I have been for a while now."

He seemed hesitant as he asked, "Are you sure?"

I nodded and shuffled closer to him, placing my hand on his cheek. "Where do you want your mark?" I asked, feeling slightly nervous. I watched as he inaudibly swallowed and I was glad he was as nervous as I was. I watched as he sat up slightly and peeled off his shirt before pulling me up with him. Gently he took my hand and placed it where his neck met his shoulder.

"Here." His voice was steady but his body trembled slightly as his eyes glowed dull amber, his wolf fighting to rise to the surface.

"It might hurt a little," I warned quietly. He nodded once and I knew he was waiting, to see if I would really do it. Biting my lip I climbed into his lap, which seemed to surprise him slightly and I straddled his hips, feeling my blood rush at our closeness, our noses just inches apart. His hands rested on my thighs and I knew I would have to focus very hard on making this mark and try and ignore the sensations his hands created as they glided up and down.

I closed my eyes to concentrate as I imagined an E and an A elegantly entwining itself together, connecting us. I heard him hiss in pain and I felt my hand getting hotter as the mark made itself permanent. My mind felt like it was being split slightly and I assumed that was because the connection was being made. As the heat from my palm ceased I slowly opened my eyes to look at Aiden, removing my hand at the same time.

"That did hurt," he said a little hoarsely and I noticed he had been gripping my thighs a little as he released his grip. "I feel it," he murmured as he rubbed his neck. "I can feel it in my head."

"So do I," I whispered. It felt odd but I knew it would be heightened once he marked me. I closed my eyes instantly as he cupped my cheek, his thumb lightly grazing across my cheekbone. I loved it when he did that. His lips on mine seemed better than it ever had been, the connection between us buzzing as we both got a taste of how the other felt. His lips grazed down my jaw and below my ear to the skin between neck and shoulder, the same place as his.

"This will hurt. Not as much as yours though," he muttered. I smiled a little and I could feel him smiling against my neck. His teeth felt sharp as the grazed along the skin, his canines were elongated and I felt nervous that if they felt sharp now, how would they feel lodged in my neck?

"Oh!" I gasped as he sunk his teeth in. I could hear the flesh break and my stomach turned slightly from the sensation as Aiden's canines dug in deeply, deep enough to leave his mark. It hurt and my normal instinct made me want to wrench my neck away, only in doing that I'd probably just tear my flesh open even more. Gritting my teeth together and digging my nails into Aiden's shoulders I waited for him to release my neck and when he finally did I sighed in relief. He pulled back and I was a little shocked to see my blood on his lips.

"I'm no vampire," he murmured as he ran his thumb over the mark and my entire body seemed to respond as jolts of electricity ran up and down my skin. My mind was twisting itself, making room for the bond that was now growing in my head. I felt like I was getting a firsthand experience at least half of what Aiden felt when he'd seen me for the first time.

Everything felt so right, this was all meant to be. We were meant to be. "You're perfect," I murmured aloud as I found myself getting lost in his brown eyes. He didn't have time to respond as I caught his lips in mine, relishing in the new feelings that consumed my body as the mark on my neck tingled, making itself known.

He pulled away for air and shook his head at me. "Goddess, Evelyn. I love you."

"I love you too," I murmured softly before I leant back in and kissed him again.

∞

"Make sure you call and visit. You are always welcome here," Stella pulled me in for a hug before she released me and moved on to chat with the Luna. I hugged each of my siblings who had put my numbers in their phone and vice versa. Their hugs felt real and warm, I still felt astounded they had accepted me into their family.

As I reached my father I smiled at him. "I'm glad I came, thank you."

"I'm glad you came as well. And I will be at that hearing."

"You don't have to," I protested. "Really its fine."

"Evelyn I'm going to be there. I want to get a good look at all those disgusting animals your mother chose over you." He took my hands in his, his eyes boring into mine. "Call me often. I have a lot to teach you. Don't be a stranger." I nodded, knowing it was futile to even argue with him. I was surprised as he pulled me in for a hug but I hugged him back, feeling warmth spread throughout my body. I was hugging my father.

Pulling back he squeezed my arms and released me and I turned to climb in the car the Luna had hired to take us back to the airport. She had insisted on not making my father drive all that way again.

It had been an amazing visit; the highlight had been this morning though. I had come out for breakfast after being the last one awake and all eyes had dropped straight to my neck. The Luna had clapped her hands gleefully and began planning how many grandchildren she would have; my siblings inspected it with curiosity. My father looked at Aiden coolly and I did worry slightly about the whole brain melting thing.

Sitting beside Aiden he squeezed my knee and I smiled up at him. "Thank you for coming with me." He just kissed my forehead and I turned my attention to the figures outside as the car began to roll away. Waving goodbye I felt sad to be leaving, but I knew that it wouldn't be the last time I'd see them.

I felt incredibly lucky as I rested in my chair beside Aiden as I came to the realization I had two families now.

Chapter Twenty-Three

"He marked you!" Grace squealed as she dove on me, looking near psychotic. "Oh my Goddess! I am so excited, this is so great! I'm so happy, you have no idea!" She was bouncing on her knees as she inspected the mark, running her fingers over it. It surprised me when the mark didn't jolt or throb as she touched it. It tingled whenever Aiden or I touched it. "Wow. Does it hurt?"

I laughed and brushed her fingers away. "It hurt when it happened, but not after. Now whenever I touch it just tickles a little."

She made a face and wriggled her eyebrows. "What about when Aiden touches it?" My face went red as I thought about the warm feeling I'd get all over my body if Aiden so much as ghosted his hand across it. "Ooh lala!"

"Grace!"

"Okay, I'm sorry; I'm just so excited for you. Can you imagine the look on Katherine's snarky little face? She's going to hate you so much more now!"

"Thanks for that, I feel really good about going to school tomorrow now." Inside I felt queasy, what would her reaction be? She'd made it fairly clear she wanted Aiden and the only thing she had over me was the fact he hadn't marked me yet. What would she be like now that I wore his mark and he had mine?

"Well, what did you naughty little mates get up to in Ohio, hm?" Lucy pranced through the door giving me a naughty wink with Hannah following behind, a huge smile on her face. "I smell a freshly marked girl, actually that scent is really strong."

"Well her mate is an Alpha, of course it's strong." Hannah gave me a hug, and whispered in my ear, "So happy your back."

"It's good to see you; I have a lot to tell you." I couldn't wait to talk to her about the stuff my father had taught me, and of course, to go through the diary together. I'd like a witch's perspective on that one. Lucy and Grace looked at me in a way that said, what can't you tell us? "It's magic stuff," I said quickly.

"Oh!" Lucy waved her hand dismissively. "Yeah we can't help with that."

"So, come on, the mark? How did it happen?" Hannah gave me the same eager look Grace had been giving me prior to their arrival and I felt nervous as I thought about how to tell them without having them make me feel more awkward.

"Well…we were going to bed and then I was thinking about what my father had been saying…I had asked him how I could mark Aiden and it was pretty simple. Aiden was just falling off to sleep, he looked so…peaceful…perfect…" I trailed off and I smiled at the memory. "He caught me staring and I told him I was ready."

"Oh Ev!" Lucy squealed as she clapped her hands together. "This is so exciting!"

"It's totally official now. There's no backing out, this is it. Forever." Grace looked at me sadly, "I'm sorry it was my brother." The girls all squawked with laughter and I smiled but deep down, even though it was a joke, I wasn't sorry. I would be forever thankful that it was Aiden that night on the balcony.

"So it's Trey's party tomorrow night," Lucy said as the girls calmed down. "I'm so keen for him to find his mate and have her beat the crap out of him for being such a womanizer. I can't believe he's seeing that freshman. It's like he just doesn't care."

"Oh so now people agree with me," Grace muttered as she flopped back down onto her bed.

"Well yeah, I mean, he's eighteen tomorrow. The chances of him finding his mate are pretty dang high!" Lucy frowned and said, "Imagine if he does find his mate tomorrow? How is she going to feel?"

"She'll reject him," Grace said firmly. "I would."

"She'd have to kill him," Hannah pointed out. "A lot of people don't reject their mates, even if their past is sketchy. No one wants to murder their other half."

"Alpha Grieg's did it," Grace stated.

"He was a psychopath to begin with," Lucy said shaking her head. "And his own pack murdered him anyway."

"His mate won't kill him," Hannah said calmly. "She'll be hurt and she'll make him work for her, and he'll learn the value of mates. Trey has a lot of growing to do, finding his mate will make him grow up *very* quickly."

The room felt silent as everyone seemed to drift into their own thoughts. I was pulled from mine when my phone buzzed under my leg. My heart skipped a beat when I saw Aiden's name, and I could feel the wide smile on my face.

"Hello?" I answered, ignoring the girl's quick glances at me.

"*Hey, what are you up to right now?*"

"I'm just with the girls," I murmured as I moved to sit on the edge of the bed.

"*Can I steal you from them?*" His voice held a tone of excitement and my interested piqued. "*I want to show you something.*"

"Okay!"

"Gee, don't ask us," Lucy joked.

"*Meet me out the front!*" He hung up and I quickly got off the bed.

"I'm going to go," I said with a smile and the girls all shook their heads at me. "I'll catch you guys later!"

"Text me!" Hanna ordered. Giving her a quick nod I made my way downstairs and out the front, not even surprised to see Aiden already waiting for me. He was only wearing a pair of gray shorts, and not that I minded the view he just usually wore more clothes.

"Hey," he grinned as he pulled me in for a hug. I melted into his arms instantly, enjoying the warmth that ran through my body. I giggled when he grazed his hand over the mark and pulled back, giving him a look.

"It tickles."

"I know." He pecked my nose and pulled back. "So I wanted to show you something."

"Yeah! What is it?"

He looked nervous and he was rubbing the back of his neck. "Well…if it was okay with you I…I want to show you my wolf." Oh! I did not expect that, though coming to think about it he had mentioned it a while ago; we'd just gotten caught up in so much stuff. I definitely wanted to see it.

"I want to see it," I said and I could hear the excitement in my own voice.

His shoulders slumped in relief, he even looked surprised. "Well we can go somewhere more private, you might freak out when you watch me shift. It's a little…well it's a lot of bone contorting that's for sure." I made a face and he laughed. "You never watched anyone shift back home?"

"Mm…Not really. I was kept away from all that stuff."

"Well this is going to be an experience then. Hop in the truck, I'll take us to a good spot." Following him to his truck I was bouncing with excitement. I was more kicking myself for not having asked to see it earlier. Aiden drove too slowly in my opinion, but that could have just been because my excitement was at an all-time high. We ended up where we had had our little outdoor picnic date, which I thought was cute and a little sentimental.

As he pulled the truck to a stop he turned to face me. "This could be a little weird for you to see…just don't freak out or run. If you run my wolf will want to chase you. He'll be more in control than I am…I'll be more toward the back of his mind, kind of like how he is in mine right now."

"Okay…" I felt a little nervous now. What if it ate me?

I came to stand in front of the truck as Aiden walked a small distance away from me, giving me a nervous grin. I guess he was scared for my reaction, the last thing I wanted to do was offend him if I freaked out. "Alright, here goes."

Here goes, I echoed in my mind. His body shook lightly and I watched as the tremors seemed to increase. The ground beneath his feet even seemed to vibrate. His legs popped first, contorting in an almost sickening angle that near had me passing out. How did the human body allow that? I squeaked as his back popped and he was falling face forward as his arms bent at weird angles. All I could hear were pops and clicks that made my ears bleed and my skin crawl.

Suddenly as if his skin shredded from his body a grand looking wolf stood before me. Shifter wolves were on average slightly larger than an actual wolf. However, Alpha wolves - even Beta wolves had a bit of extra size advantage. I estimated my head would reach his neck.

His fur was a dark brown; it looked soft to the touch, almost shimmery. There were random flecks of white around his legs and belly but he was mostly brown, his eyes were glowing rich amber and I knew this was his wolf I was dealing with now.

I held my breath as he slowly walked toward me; each thud of his paws matched the slow thud in my heart. He seemed to get taller as he approached me and I realized it was because I had sunk to my backside on the floor. I watched wide eyed as the wolf slowly sunk to the floor and on its belly, crawling across the floor toward me. This was crazy. I flinched as he nudged my foot and I searched his eyes wildly, trying to find Aiden.

I nearly choked on air when he rested his giant head into my chest, a low grumbling sound in his throat. Hesitantly I raised my hand, noting it was shaking and placed it softly on the side of his neck, marveling at the softness of his fur.

"A-Aiden?" I whispered and I watched as his eyes flickered open and he stared at me, the glow of the amber slowly dulling as his eyes became the warm brown I was used to. He nudged my hand and I assumed it was because he wanted me to continue what I was doing.

We must have sat out there for ages, because the air got chillier and the light became dark, but the marvel over Aiden's wolf never got old. When he got up and went behind a tree I waited in the dark nervously, before he finally emerged in a different pair of shorts than the ones he'd had on before. It was no secret wolves stashed clothing around their territory in case of an emergency.

I was surprised at how cold my skin was against Aiden's when he pulled me in for a hug and I eagerly soaked up his warmth, feeling tired. "That was awesome," I yawned against his chest.

"You looked ready to faint."

"I thought I was going to. It looked painful."

He laughed and said, "It hurts the first time. The pain is unbearable but after that it gets easy. Like changing clothing really, it's effortless."

I shuddered. "I'm glad I don't shift."

"So you liked him then?" His voice was hopeful as he pulled back to stare at me and a harsh gust of wind came into the clearing.

"Y-yeah!" My teeth chattered. "But we need to get home before I freeze to death!"

∞

"Evelyn, can I see you in my office?" Alpha James asked as we all finished up dinner. I don't know why but a sense of foreboding ran over me as I swallowed the last of my pasta. What did he want to see me about? My father? My mother? It sort of clicked though that it was about the council meeting. As Aiden squeezed my hand and the Luna gave me a comforting smile I hesitantly followed the Alpha toward his office - the one place in the house I hadn't seen yet.

What a mess. There were files all over his desk, papers spilling out of filing cabinets and a disorganized bookshelf that seemed to house more rubbish than books. His proud looking desk sat in the center of the room and I sat on an available chair in front of it, feeling my palms sweating.

"Evelyn, the reason I wanted to speak to you privately is because…the High Council requested a fully written statement from you, outlining your treatment in Idaho." He leant back in his chair and ran his hands down his face, he looked exhausted. I wondered how much strain this hearing was putting on him and the pack. "As was Aiden's request we have cut ties with Idaho, they are no longer allied with us."

"Oh!" That would make Alpha Hess ruthlessly angry, I would not want to be around to face his wrath on that topic.

"It is believed your mother has told the truth to her pack and her mate. Things are not looking good in Idaho right now. This trial…it could become a lot more than just a trial." He looked at me with heavy eyes and I felt confused. What more could it become? "We are sensing that Idaho may try and attack us."

"Why would they do that?" I asked with a frown. "They don't even have the numbers for that kind of attack."

"Since we canned the alliance we have had a number of rogue sightings on the borders. We've caught a few and they said they were paid off, but by whom they won't disclose to us."

"Idaho?" I asked, feeling my skin crawl.

He nodded tightly. "You know the ins and outs of Idaho better than we do. Is this something they'd be capable of?"

I thought hard. Alpha Hess always wanted his own way and if he didn't get it, there was hell to pay for. He didn't care much how his actions affected those around him and if his nose was out of joint - and it probably was - because the alliance had been scrapped, then he would retaliate with rage. I was nervous that this rage would soon be directed at me.

"I think so," I said calmly. I felt anything but calm, suddenly I felt like me opening my mouth had caused a very big problem. I should never have said anything.

"I believe he was scouting when he came to the gathering. I feel he wants my territory not an alliance. Did you ever have any kind of indication that that's what he was after?" He looked at me, hoping I had answers, the truth was, I didn't.

"I wasn't really allowed to listen in, a lot of the stuff that went on I never knew much about, it wasn't my place to know anything. I'm sorry…I wish I could tell you more." I bit my lip as brief disappointment flittered across his features. "A-Alpha Hess was always a little weird to me - mostly scary but weird. He seems to enjoy confrontation, and he loses control very quickly."

"Every Alpha enjoys confrontation, but the lack of control doesn't surprise me. Alpha Hess was always unfit for the position, just as his sniveling son is. The pack will only end in its own demise because it had poor leadership." I nodded and the room fell silent and I looked around it nervously. "How are you and Aiden?"

What? I looked at him in surprise and thought I almost spotted a ghost of a smile on his face. He wanted to talk to me about Aiden? Wasn't that the Luna's area? "Uh…good, yeah."

"You both completed your marking."

"Y-yes." This was so weird.

"So you have accepted him as your mate?" he asked happily, even though he knew the answer. I just nodded and he smiled at me genuinely. He looked a lot more like Aiden when he smiled. "I'm happy it was you. I'll let you go now; Claudia said she'd help you with your statement. I'm going to need it within the next few days."

"O-okay!" I got up quickly, gave an awkward wave and dashed for the door. What an odd conversation, I was surprised he'd even asked about Aiden and not to mention that was the longest conversation we'd ever had, and half of it wasn't even about my old life or Idaho. Interesting.

My phone buzzed in my hand and I smiled to see it was a message from Sienna, a photo attached. I opened it, nervous to see what she had sent, only to laugh at a freckle circled on her face. Going back to the text I read: *'we have the same freckle in the same spot! How cool is that!?'*

I laughed and texted back. With a smile on my face I climbed the stairs and headed toward my room, thinking about my new family and how many similarities I shared with them. I'd always thought I'd been alone in the looks department, that no one shared any features with me, except the man I'd thought to be a monster. The reason I'd despised and feared my own appearance as well.

As I entered my room my eyes immediately flickered toward the covered mirror and with a burst of courage and even self-acceptance I found myself standing in front of it, peeling off the stickers piece by piece, watching as my reflection came into view. And I looked, I looked hard. I caught my eyes first, and I noted the flecks of hazel mixed with the deep brown color. I noticed the amber glow that Aiden claimed he saw, and I assumed it was my magic because I could feel my body humming. I noticed the freckle that Sienna had found, just below my left eye. The scar that started at the edge of my hairline and disappeared under my long brown mane, that had the same texture as Jasmine's.

I shared my father's nose, it wasn't too long, but it wasn't short either. It had a small bump in it, barely noticeable, only if you looked hard enough could you see it. I had thick lashes and I knew I received those from my mother, along with her plump lips. My form was small but I had gained weight since being here I noticed, even some muscle. I decided I shared both my mother's lithe figure and my father's long legs.

This was Evelyn. But not Evelyn Wright, I was never Evelyn Wright.

I am Evelyn Ahasverus.

∞

"Ooh! Very nice!" Lucy pinched my backside and I let out a squeal as she pranced around in her heels. "You look a little saucy tonight Evie."

"It's Grace's," I said quickly as I pulled down the hem of the chiffon halter she had stuffed me into. It was a deep red, and very flowy. I was glad the party was being held in the basement and not outside because I didn't need the pack to see what was under the dress.

"It's Evelyn's now; she wears that way better than I do." Grace popped her mouth open as she applied her mascara. "Aiden's kept Trey out of the area all day; he won't shut up about starting the party already. Most of the guests are in the basement already so we better hurry."

"I've barely seen Aiden all day," I mumbled.

"I didn't see Josh either. Grace, you kidnapped our mates." Hannah fluffed her blonde locks and twirled around in her blue strapless dress. "How do I look?" She gestured to the diamantes down the sides, biting her lip nervously.

"Hot!" Lucy cheered. "Here is to a good night, and getting supremely drunk!"

"Amen!" Grace dropped her mascara and pushed her breasts up in her white midriff before running her hands over her leather leggings. "Dang, I look good."

"I wish I had that confidence," Hannah laughed.

As everyone finally deemed themselves ready for the party we made our way downstairs to the basement where I could hear music already thumping. The front door was wide open and people were pouring in, all carrying a bottle or two of Wolfsbane. The Luna watched carefully from the hall and I watched as all the wolves entering bowed their head in respect and flashed the odd wink in her direction. It was cool of her to let them drink. I wasn't going to touch the stuff but it would be fun to see them all like that.

As we made our way into the basement I was overwhelmed by the heat of so many bodies and I could smell the liquor. "When is Trey arriving?" I said loudly to Grace and she waved her hands.

"About ten minutes or so!" The music shut off and Grace hoisted herself up onto a table. "Alright everyone! Shut up!" The talking voices and laughter dimmed as Grace stood proudly above us. "Aiden and Trey will be arriving in about ten minutes, so I don't want to hear a sound. This is supposed to be a surprise. No one even sneezes, got it?" There was a mumbling through the crowd and she got down, straightening her top. "This is going to be so good."

The silence seemed to go on forever and I could see frowns forming on people's faces as they texted whatever they wanted to say out loud but couldn't. "Grace…"

"Sh!" She hissed at me. "They're coming!" Someone killed the lights and it sucked I was the only one who couldn't see in here. I don't even know why they bothered; Trey would just smell them all anyway.

"Someone baked a cake right? I can smell it, it's so good!" I heard Trey's voice and I was relieved he was finally arriving; I'd get to see Aiden.

"There's no cake man," Aiden laughed at him. "Just a lot of Wolfsbane."

"Surprise!" Everyone suddenly shouted and the lights flicked on. Trey didn't look surprised but he did smile widely as he scanned his eyes over the crowd. My eyes found Aiden's immediately and I beamed at him. He left Trey and pushed his way through the crowd, pulling me into a bear hug.

"Finally," he grumbled into my hair. Pulling back he kissed me, his lips felt amazing against mine. "You look great," he muttered as he toyed with the hem of my dress.

I flushed a little and murmured, "Thanks."

"No. Nope. Not happening!" Grace shouted suddenly. I turned to face her and I saw Trey holding her arm, his eyes desperate. "Get your *filthy* hands off me!" She seethed as she ripped her arm from his grip.

"Grace!" He pleaded as he reached for her again.

"Oh my Goddess…" Hannah whispered beside me. "No way." It clicked then, the way that Trey stared at Grace and the tears of frustration in Grace's eyes. They were mates. Her biggest fear had come true. She stormed from the room quickly, but not before giving a well-aimed kick to Trey's leg.

"Well shit," Josh commented.

"You can say that again…" Lucy's eyes were wide and I noticed Mr Collins standing next to her - Geoff. He wasn't my teacher at this party. "I knew it would happen though."

Aiden's expression was tight as he stared at Trey. "You need to leave her alone for a while," he said as he stopped Trey from following her. "If she chooses to reject you, I won't stand in her way. We all warned you what would happen if you found your mate within this pack and she knew what you had done."

I felt sorry for Trey as his eyes held a pained expression. The room held a mixture of sympathy and smugness; everyone knew what Trey was like. "I need to see her."

"You don't get to see her until she wants to see you." Aiden's voice was firm and I watched with wide eyes. Protective big brother or what? "That's an order."

Trey's face morphed into an angry snarl. "You can't *order* me not to see my own mate! How would you feel if your father ordered you not to see Evelyn?"

"I didn't sleep around before I met her," Aiden said coolly. He did however draw me that little bit closer, so Trey's words had had some effect on him. "I'm ordering you for your own good. If you go to her now she will reject you."

I jumped in fright as Trey punched the nearest thing to him, which happened to be a wall. He took a quarter of the brick away on his knuckles. "This parties over!" He stormed angrily from the basement. Everyone looked around at each other awkwardly, before sighing and slowly filtering out of the basement.

"I was looking forward to tonight," Lucy grumbled.

"We'll do another party when everyone's calmed down," Hannah sighed as she took Josh's hand. Katherine slinked past then, sneering at me before she looked to where Aiden had marked me. The fabric of my dress concealed it but I knew she could pinpoint it by scent. With one last withering glare she to left the room before Aiden led me upstairs as well.

At the top of the landing we met the Luna who looked at Aiden with worried eyes. "Aiden, what on earth is going on? Grace refuses to come out of her room and Trey near ripped a hole in my front door. How can those two be fighting *again*?!"

"Well…"Aiden looked at me and shook his head. "Trey realized Grace is his mate."

The front hall was silent as the Luna took a moment to absorb that information, a frown on her face. That frown slowly morphed into a look of concern as she looked upstairs in the direction of Grace's room. "Well, that's…complicated isn't it?"

"Complicated isn't the word I'd use. Messed up, but at the same time insanely enlightening." I looked at Aiden in confusion as did the Luna. He rolled his eyes, "Grace has always been aggressive toward Trey when he was dating random chicks. I think deep down her wolf has identified him as her mate for a very long time. We all just took it that they hated each other."

"Ha!" The Luna shook her head and sighed. "Makes sense, I better notify Greg. He is not going to be happy."

"Trey made his own bed. We warned him, everyone did." Aiden shrugged, folding his arms and looking stern. "I have no sympathy."

I sighed and bit my lip. "Maybe I'll go and talk to her."

Aiden placed a kiss on my forehead. "I'll find Trey and talk to him. As irritating a the whole situation is - and the fact that I'm not thrilled he's my sisters mate, he'll be tormenting himself. But I do want to actually see you tonight."

"Me too," I said with a smile. "We'll work something out."

With that I made my way upstairs, wondering how I was supposed to say anything good enough that would hopefully comfort Grace. She'd be so angry and so hurt. I'd never had to do this before, talk to someone about their feelings. Reaching her door I hesitated before slowly tapping on it, trying to make it as light as possible.

"W-what?" The voice croaked out followed by a loud sniff. Taking a breath I pushed the door open and walked in, closing it behind me. Grace lay in a heap on her bed, under her blankets.

"Grace?" I whispered as I came closer.

"There's n-nothing you c-can say Evelyn. It won't change this." Slowly sitting down on her bed I bit my lip. She was right. All I could do was be here for her. So I lay down next to her and closed my eyes, sighing out all the tension from my body. Some party. "W-why me? Of a-all people!"

She was talking. I thought of my response as carefully as possible, I had no intention of wanting to make the situation any worse than it was. "I'm not going to sit here and pretend I know what you're feeling. I don't. The situation is crazy...but I have to ask...you had an idea right? That maybe he was..."

She was silent for a while; I watched the clock on her wall and counted four and a half minutes before she replied. "I thought about it. I n-never understood why I got so angry when he dated. The others did, but I just seemed to be angrier than they were. I'm so stupid."

"You aren't stupid Grace," I said quietly.

"I don't want him," she said, trying to sound firm. The crack and wave in her voice however said otherwise. There was still hope to mend this. "H-he sure doesn't want me. He doesn't w-want a mate, he never has." With that confession another round of tears rolled out as her words echoed within her and I felt awful for her.

"I think he does want you Grace."

"Only because his wolf does, he doesn't want me. Aiden and his wolf want you; only Trey's wolf wants me." She looked up at me and I took in her tear stained face. "I hate the mate bond. It's awful. There's no choice."

"Well there is," I pointed out.

"I can't kill him."

The room was silent again and I once more found myself racking my brain for something to say. My mind drifted back to the conversation I'd had with my family back in Ohio, to what Aliyah had said. *She created one being and split the souls. They're half of each other. They don't discover it until they're fully matured wolves because their human side is too weak… it is simple, but it's pure genius.* I looked back down at her. "You don't hate the mate bond, you never have. You hate Trey and its understandable, but you love him as well."

"I don't love him," she snapped.

"Yes you do Grace. Why else would you be on his back all these years. I've been here a few months and I thought something was up with you two." I kept my voice soft but it was strong, firm. "You can try and make this work, or you can live in misery…but fully accepting your mate," a blissful smile ghosted across my lips. "It's the best feeling in the whole world. I can understand a little how you're feeling, when I found out Aiden had seen Katherine I was angry and upset. Obviously he didn't…you know, but Trey's an idiot and everyone knows it. You'll be the best thing to ever happen to him."

"Damn right I would," she grumbled. "It just makes me angry at the idea of how many little sluts he let touch him. I don't feel special. When we mate I won't feel special, he's done the same thing with a dozen girls. How will I be any different?"

I bit my lip and sighed. She was right in a way; I could understand completely where she was coming from. Taking her hand in mine in found myself saying, "You're his mate."

Chapter Twenty-Four

"WHAT A NIGHTMARE." Aiden was lying next to me in my bed as I ghosted through my grandmother's journal. I looked up at him with a small smile, happy he was finally talking to me about the Grace and Trey situation. "I'm happy but I'm not."

"Understandable."

"Why did it have to be my sister? Of all people Trey could be mates with, it's my sister."

"At least you know him..." I knew that was the wrong thing to say as soon as I said it.

"Exactly, I know what kind of guy he is. He's my friend, but he has no values and no morals." He groaned and buried his head into my stomach and I had to bite my lip to stop myself from laughing. Even if it hadn't have been Trey who found Grace to be his mate, Aiden would still have a problem with it. She's his little sister.

"I think Grace would be good for him," I said calmly.

"She's too good for him."

I rolled my eyes. "No what I'm saying is, she could change him. She's strong willed, she won't take any of his crap. You'll see a massive improvement in him as a person." Aiden grunted but he had nothing else to say - because I was right. Grace could whip Trey into shape very quickly.

"She'll accept him," he muttered.

"Yes she will."

"She better make him stew for a little longer though."

I ran my fingers across his scalp. "She will, it's Grace."

"Hm." He didn't say much else after that and not long after his breathing slowly began to even out. Picking up the diary again, I immersed myself in the words of my grandmother, embarrassed by some of the things I was reading with Aiden so close.

I find that my magic is stronger when I'm with William. Maybe it's the amount of emotion he evokes within me. I can only practice when my emotions are high…boy are they high when he's around. No one understands how I feel for him. He's my soulmate. The other night proved that, every touch…my body has never felt more alive than when he…

I widened my eyes and slammed the diary shut. Don't need to know, don't need to read. Why couldn't my father have bookmarked the sections that would be useful? This diary was a case of dodging sexual exploits so far. The amount of men she's claimed to be her soulmate was ridiculous. I was excited though, to meet up with Hannah this afternoon. Now I know how I can actually use the magic I have - and the fact that there really were no limits…the possibilities were endless.

My mood dropped though when I realized I hadn't even started writing the victim statement for the council. Truth is every time I sat down to try I just couldn't. I didn't want it on paper forever. In my mind it was able to disappear…on paper and in the hands of the council it would be there forever. Not to mention I knew I had to call my mother. By now the council would have contacted Idaho and she would have had to have said something by now.

I received multiple messages a day from my new siblings, and I usually called my father every night, but I'd had no missed calls from my mother since she'd come and told me the truth. Maybe she was ashamed, but her silence didn't help with my inner turmoil.

My bedroom door flew open suddenly and Aiden jumped up instantly, a scowl on his face directed at the intruder. Hannah held her hands up, her face going from a big smile to a scared gasp. Slapping Aiden's arm I pushed him over and he fell off the side of the bed.

"Ready to train?" I asked her as she stared wide eyed at a disorientated Aiden on the floor and then back at me.

"Y-yeah…sorry if I interrupted…"

"I was getting ready to text you. He fell asleep on me. Really was that necessary?" I asked him as he got up, rubbing his head.

"Sorry," he mumbled at Hannah. "I was in a deep sleep. Don't go too far into the woods this time."

"It's all good. We're going to the training field. No one's using it today." Hannah looked ready to go, her eyes shone with excitement. I was pretty excited to see what else I could do to. Picking up the diary from my bed I slipped it into my nightstand and turned to face Aiden.

"Maybe you should go and talk to Grace," I suggested softly. "You haven't directly spoken to her about it yet, it could help." He sighed heavily and leant down, kissing me on the forehead before shuffling from the room. It must be hard to be torn between wanting to kill one of your good friends, and resisting the urge because in the long run, it would kill your sister.

"Okay." Hannah rubbed her hands together, looking eager. "Let's get going!"

∞

We stood on the edge of the training field, closest to the thick wood behind us. At least here if I did something too crazy no one would get hurt. It worried me that I may be able to hurt someone unintentionally. Hannah made sure to keep an eye on me at all times. After relaying what I had done in the field with the fire and water with my father, Hannah demanded to see it. She stared open mouthed and wide eyed, even screeching when she thought I wouldn't get the water on it in time.

"This is crazy. Not only do you have magic but you can manipulate elements. Make a small sand tornado or something. Nothing huge, keep a reign on it if you can." I gave her a worried look, just imagining I'd end up creating a huge tornado and wiping out the town. "I'll stop it if it gets out of hand," she promised me.

"Okay…" I whispered hesitantly, twisting my hands within each other. Just focus, and focus on keeping it under control. I didn't want to be known as the future Luna who wiped out her own pack because she couldn't control her magic. Did I pick up sand? Did I just start from the ground?

"Don't overthink it too much Evie, remember, it's like your dad said, no limitations. Okay?" She gave me an encouraging smile and I nodded at her, steeling my feet and straightening my posture.

Raising my hand over the small patch of sand beneath me I closed my eyes. I knew what I wanted, how I wanted it to look and how big I would let it become. I began moving my hand above the earth in small waves, feeling an energy thrum through my body, my palm tingling and my eyes began to glow. I heard Hannah let out an excited squeal but I pushed that to the back of my mind, focusing on keeping it all under control.

"It's working!" Hannah shouted. Opening my eyes I nearly jumped in fright at the dirt that spiraled around in a perfect tornado, its height just above my head. I let out a triumphant grin. "Make it move!"

Biting my lip in concentration I raised both hands, and motioned them toward the left. My heart skipped a beat when the tornado moved with it. It didn't take long for me to have full confidence and control. At some stage it did begin growing larger, which freaked me out so with a flourish of my hands I flattened it, and closed my eyes as the sand quickly began floating down to the ground in huge clumps.

"Ev, that was brilliant."

"I know!"

"I wish we could practice your defensive techniques." Hannah pouted. "I guess if it ever comes down to that, you'll just have to have faith in yourself that you can actually take them out. You did it to the rogues."

I frowned. "I don't want to ever have to use my magic like that."

"No one - well, anyone with a conscience - wants to hurt people. Just know that as a future Luna you may have to. Some people don't give a crap about the mate bond. If a wolf challenges you, at least you know you'll win. I wouldn't want to go up against what you can do. No thanks."

"Do you think Katherine would challenge me?" I asked, deep fears creeping into my mind.

"No." Hannah sounded firm, which helped my nerves. "As much as she had a thing for Aiden, she does want her own mate. She's a bitch but she does have values I guess. She leaves in a few days anyway. Finally."

"Hopefully she finds her mate and doesn't come back," I muttered hopefully.

"See that dead flower?" Hannah asked suddenly. Looking to where she pointed I nodded. It wasn't so much a flower as it was a weed. "Bring it back to life."

"What?" I asked, crinkling my nose. "That's ridiculous I doubt I'd be able to do that. I may have some special powers but I'm not the Goddess or Morgana or whatever names you want to give her."

"Just out of curiosity. Come on." Hannah nodded at me encouragingly, and I sighed in defeat as I walked over to the weed-flower and crouched next to it.

"I feel stupid already."

"Don't. Feel the concentration and remember *no limitations*." I feel like Hannah was going to start taking on my father's words as her motto.

I held my hand just above the dead plant, and I was surprised to feel nothing. I usually felt some kind of tingling, or energy. I guess seeing as it was dead it would give off nothing. Taking a breath I closed my eyes. I wasn't sure what I was supposed to picture here. I didn't know how to give life back to something. I just imagined what it would look like alive. The leaves would be green and not a graying crunched up appearance. The small flowers showed evidence they had once been white, with flecks of yellow toward the center, now it was stained brown.

So I pictured it healthy and alive. Its petals and leaves gently fluttering whenever the wind skimmed across it. The way it would move toward the sun and close up when the sun went away for the night.

My palm tingled.

My heart rate spiked.

I focused myself and as I felt the plant brush my palm I knew it was coming back.

"Oh my Goddess," Hannah whispered. Opening my eyes I moved my hand away and there the little weed sat, alive and looking healthier than the rest of its companions. I looked up at Hannah who shook her head in disbelief. "Crazy. How do you feel?"

I felt normal. "Fine."

"Excellent. Bring this back." A dead rabbit landed at my feet and I shouted in shock and jumped away.

"Hannah!"

"It's alright. You can bring little Thumper back. Give it a go. I didn't kill him, I promise."

"You just happen to have a dead rabbit on you?" I demanded as I stared down at the brown hare in dismay.

"No. I have werewolf sense of smell. It's pretty fresh. Come on, try. You brought a plant back."

"That was a plant, not an actual thing with a heartbeat!" I felt stressed out now, it didn't feel right but I couldn't leave it dead now that it was in front of me, and part of me didn't trust Hannah hadn't killed the poor thing. She didn't say anything, just sat on the floor in front of me and waited. I grumbled when I noticed she had just sat on the plant I had only brought back to life moments ago.

"Come on," she urged.

Shaking my head with a frown I looked down at the pale brown bunny. It had a small white bushy tail but he was just plain brown, good for camouflaging. I ran my hand over his fur, silky in some places but rough with dirt in others. There were prickles and leaves stuck under its stomach and I picked those out first before Hannah made an impatient sound in the back of her throat. I shot her a look before looking back down, taking a breath and hoping for the best.

The only way I felt I could do this was to focus on my heartbeat. Mine was racing a little and I took some deep breaths to calm myself down. I felt like I could hear it beating in my ears. Placing my hand more firmly over the rabbit and to where

I thought its heart was, I closed my eyes and pictured its heart pumping in rhythm with mine.

Thump. Thump. Thump.

I pictured blood running through its body, the careful movements of its stomach as it inhaled and exhaled. The way its nose would wriggle constantly. Cleaning itself with its tiny paws. It's heart. Thump, thump, thump. A huge wave of dizziness moved over me then and the creature beneath me suddenly sprang to life, looking at Hannah and me before tearing off into the woods.

"NO WAY!" Hannah screamed. It sounded like she was underwater though and I looked at her with heavy eyes, my head throbbing. "Evelyn?" She garbled at me. She probably said it quite smoothly but I could barely make it out.

The world moved and I was on my back, staring up at the sky before blackness swept in.

∞

"It's over exertion I think. Hannah used to get this all the time when we first started training her," a familiar voice said above me. "Her vital signs are good and I see no damage on any of the scans. I think she gave up too much energy."

"She brought an animal back to life," someone snapped incredulously.

"Yep. That was pretty amazing."

"Then she faints. Obviously it's not right."

"Aiden, she's part witch plus much more according to Hannah. Her mind became overwhelmed. She's healthy, there's no damage been done to her. You can talk to her father, if it will make you feel better. He might have better answers than me. I can just reassure you she is fine."

I felt fine. I didn't feel sick, just well rested actually. Blinking my eyes open I took in that was definitely in the pack clinic. I had a drip in my hand. "Aiden?" My voice was a little croaky and I cleared my throat.

"Oh, Evelyn!" Hannah gasped with a smile.

Aiden looked at me with concern, brushing my hair from my face. "Are you okay?"

"Yeah, I'm fine. What happened?"

"You were training with Hannah," he told me. "You brought a rabbit back to life?" There was a hint of worry in there but I could hear some awe as well. It was pretty cool.

"Then you fainted," Hannah told me with a grin. "Freaked me out a bit, your eyes like, rolled back into your head."

"Can I please have the room?" Aiden asked calmly, though his irritation was evident. The room cleared out and I recognized Hannah's mother as she dragged her daughter out of the room. I looked back at Aiden who continued looking at me in concern. "Please don't do that again. Don't overstretch your magic, Evelyn you've been out all day."

"All day?" I asked, with wide eyes.

"You were as pale as a ghost when they brought you in. I don't want to see you like that again, even if you are fine now." His face crumpled, "I thought…"

I took in the gravity of the situation suddenly. Aiden's paleness and the way his lower lip was curled hit me right in the stomach. I decided then and there not to ever do it again, lest Aiden look at me with this expression. Sitting up in the bed I wrapped my arms around his neck. "I'm sorry."

He held me a moment longer before pulling back and kissing me on the forehead. "Let's go home."

The pack doctor discharged me and it was funny to find myself being in the clinic by my own actions. The other times I had visited in Idaho were because somebody had done something to put me there. This time it was my fault, and to be honest it felt a little liberating. Aiden treated me like I was a fragile doll the whole way home. Putting me in the truck, helping me out of the truck.

"Aiden, I love you. But you need to let me walk to the house. I'm fine, I promise." He stopped himself from picking me up again and settled on placing his hand to the small of my back. I'd let him have that.

The Luna grabbed me in a huge hug the moment I entered the house. "Oh, Evelyn!"

"I told them not to worry," the Alpha said as he came to the front entrance. "But they all lost it. Your father has been calling though; he wants to speak with you urgently." I nodded at him and disentangled myself from the Luna's grasp. "Have you written your statement?"

"Oh heck, no I haven't. I'm sorry."

"We can work on it after dinner," the Luna said beside me, squeezing my hand.

"I'll need it by the morning. I have to send it tomorrow." He disappeared back down the hall and I assumed he was going back to his office.

"I should call my dad," I murmured. Aiden followed me upstairs to my room and I climbed onto the bed, taking my phone off the stand and leaning back against my pillows. "He's going to be all protective isn't he?" I asked Aiden, who was settling in beside me.

"Probably."

I called his number nervously, and he picked up on the first ring. "*Evelyn?*"

"Yep. It's me."

"*Are you okay?*" He asked me urgently, his voice laced with worry.

"I am. I promise. Hannah and I were just training and we stretched my magic too far."

"*How far is too far?*"

I bit my lip and clutched Aiden's arm. "Bringing a rabbit back to life?" He was silent on the other end, not saying anything. My heart began thumping. "Dad?"

"*That's very dangerous Evelyn. You can't do that. Promise me you'll never do that again.*"

"I promise. I already promised Aiden I - why's it so bad?"

"*Evelyn when something is dead, it's dead. You go against nature by bringing it back. It's just not right. You used your own life force to breathe life into something else. Please don't do it again. You could very easily end up killing yourself.*"

"Oh." My mouth felt dry as I took in the gravity of his words. It made sense and even back at the training field I hadn't felt right doing it. "Will the rabbit be okay?"

He chuckled and told me, *"The rabbit will be fine. Trust you to worry about the rabbit and not yourself. It's just a precaution Evelyn. You should never interfere with life and death."*

"I feel fine though."

"You fainted though didn't you?" I didn't answer and he went on. *"Evelyn the only reason you're okay is because it was a small enough creature. If you brought say, a human back to life, you can very much kiss yours goodbye. Don't meddle with it, that's all I'm saying. This should all be in your grandmothers journal."*

"All I've read about so far is her sex life." Aiden gave me a look and I stuck my tongue out.

He sighed, sounding tired over the line. *"From about the middle of it, she gets into the magic. The earlier pages are her when she was younger. She liked to date."*

She liked to do more than date, I thought to myself. "Okay."

"Alright. I have to go. Call me tomorrow with an update on how your feeling."

"Okay," I said quietly. "Goodbye."

"Goodbye, Evelyn."

Ending the call I put the phone back on my nightstand and flopped back down onto the bed. Aiden threw his arm over my stomach and I placed my hand over it, tracing my fingers over the birthmark on his arm. I rolled to face him, eyeing the mark I had placed on him, and then eyeing off his very nice chest.

"You're so beautiful," he murmured, running his thumb over my cheek to my lips, ghosting across them. I'd never not be embarrassed when he called me beautiful and the tell-tale signs of blushing showed up as my cheeks went hot. Leaning in he kissed me, drawing me in closer as his arm curled around my back. My body hummed as our lips touched and my mark tingled, especially when he ghosted his palm over it. I squeaked in surprise when he rolled us over and I was straddling him. I felt exposed and nervous as he stared up at me with hot eyes, his thumbs ghosting across the skin of my thighs.

Leaning down I briefly kissed his lips, before pulling away and finding the mark I had created. Kissing the mark unleashed a whole new Aiden. I guess his got the same reaction mine did.

He growled lowly in his chest and rolled me beneath him, gripping my thigh tightly as he kissed me thoroughly, passionately. Our tongues dueled for dominance and I felt like every-everywhere he touched me set my skin on fire.

A knock on the door and the Luna telling us it was dinner had me pushing Aiden off me faster than you could blink as I was terrified she was going to come in. Aiden just laughed next me, his hand on his stomach as he tried to calm his breathing. I ran a hand through my hair, feeling hot and flustered. It didn't help when Aiden quickly pecked me before pulling me up off the bed and leading me from the room. I needed a moment of him not touching me to get my thoughts in place. When he let me go outside his room so he could get a shirt I managed to take a breath, however it didn't help as I watched him put it on, his muscles moving deliciously.

Thankfully by the time we made it to the dining room my cheeks didn't feel so hot and there was a nice jug of ice cold water on the table. Grace sat looking sullen beside her father, not looking the least bit interested in the meal. She did look at me though as I sat down. "How are you feeling?" she asked.

"I'm fine."

"Sounds like you were more than fine five minutes a-"

"Dinner is served," The Luna interrupted Grace and gave her a warning look as she set down a bowl of mashed potatoes. My face felt red and I refused to look at Aiden across the table, but I could feel his eyes on me. "What time are you meeting Trey, Grace?"

My eyes widened and I looked at her before looking at Aiden who looked just as surprised. "You're meeting Trey?" I asked.

"It wasn't my idea," she grumbled. "I'm sick of having missed calls on my phone. I can't do anything on it without his stupid caller ID popping up. We're going to *talk*." Her tone was sour and I knew Trey was in for a mouthful.

"Aiden I need you to run patrols until two," The Alpha said. "Hunter's mate is going into labor." Aiden nodded and my mood sunk. He wouldn't be in bed till late. I made up my mind to just sleep in his until he got home.

"And we have to get that statement written," The Luna said to me. "How in depth does it need to be Greg?"

"It needs to detail as much as you can remember Evelyn. In great detail. These are very big accusations, not only will they cross examine you, they'll cross examine all your offenders."

"Great," I muttered quietly as whatever appetite I'd had started to slowly seep away. So after dinner as Grace sulkily left the house to meet Trey and Aiden left for his patrol, I sat with the Luna at her laptop, recounting hideous events that I'd never wanted to go over.

…As I dressed for gym in the change room Jonah Hess, Zachary Keenan and Ben Maxwell entered the room. They proceeded to remove my clothing and force me to touch them. They touched me, roughly grabbing at my breasts. This was my punishment for talking back to Zachary Keenan.

"So help me I will kill those boys Evelyn," The Luna whispered beside me.

"It wouldn't change what happened," I told her calmly as I swallowed the bile in my throat and stopped typing.

"It'd make me feel better."

"Are you sure you want to write this with me?" I asked quietly. "It gets worse."

"Yes. I'm not going to let you relive this alone." She rubbed my shoulders. "Keep going."

…Jonah put Heather and me into the training pit. We were instructed to fight until someone conceded. Obviously it would be me, however I knew if I conceded there'd be no point. Heather beat me quite violently; she bruised my vocal chords for three days as she strangled me. This was my punishment for not receiving an A on Heather's history assignment.

It took near ten pages as I went through everything I could possibly remember. Various sexual attacks, violent beatings, my hair being cut off, the scarring, the 'H' carved into my hip which the Luna photographed and added to the statement. The numerous broken bones which should be in the pack clinic records. Looking at it all on paper, realizing so much had happened to me had me crying in the Luna's arms by the end of it.

If it hadn't been for Aiden I'd still be there, living it every day.

…I don't presume to know why I was abused the way I was. It happened from a young age and I am sure there are things I'll never remember because I was too young. My belief was I was hurt because I was different. I was hurt because my mother convinced the pack I was a product of rape. I was hurt because I had no wolf qualities, so where did I fit in? I was hurt because I wasn't like everyone else. I was easy to pick on, weak. Only being with the Oregon pack and my mate Aiden, I found that my differences are celebrated. I make the pack stronger by just being me, and accepting who I am. I am stronger because I am surrounded by people who believe in me. Idaho thought they could break me, maybe they think they did. I think they made me stronger, which I doubt was never their intention. Their cruelty doesn't live on in me and even though I will have those heinous memories forever, I also have the ability to forgive them. If I don't I'd be no better than they are, and they win. Here's something for you Idaho…you'll never win against me.

"That gave me shivers," the Luna said beside me. "You're a strong girl Evelyn; you'll make a terrific Luna."

"I hope so," I said with doubt. "I'm scared I might fluff it up."

"Everyone learns with it. I made plenty of mistakes. But you have the strength and the courage that I never had in the beginning. You're coming into the job a lot wiser than I did." She gave me a hug before getting up. "I'll send this to Greg, you go get ready for bed, it's quite late."

"Grace isn't home yet," I said with a small smile.

"Hopefully they'll both get over themselves. I didn't believe for a minute that she was sick of seeing his caller ID. Nice excuse though, just very weak." The Luna gave me a wink before she began saving the document and emailing it off to the Alpha.

Stumbling up to Aiden's room and I fell down on his bed, feeling extremely exhausted. What a day. The statement seemed to be the one that really took it out of me. I was surprised at how much I had remembered and by how much I had buried. It left me thinking about Heather of all people, Jonah's mate.

How did she feel knowing that Jonah had touched me the way he had? She knew what went on, even if she wasn't present for those moments. She heard things; she saw when Zac would feel me up in the actual class. Grace could hardly forgive Trey for his transgressions before their mating so how did Heather overlook it all? Trey's exploits had all been willing, I had never been willing. Her mate sexually abused another woman and she was content to be with him. She'd even go as far as to throw herself at him during lunch and then look at me with a smug stare.

My mind flittered back to the statement.

…Jackie Morris held me down by my arms as Heather Cooper cut my hair from my head. This was punishment because she thought I wanted her mate.

…Jonah Hess locked me in the janitor's cupboard and proceeded to spray flames under the door.

…beat me into submission because I wouldn't bow at his feet.

…strangled me because I talked back.

…broke my ribs for looking in her direction.

…slammed my head into a desk, raking her claws over my scalp, causing a scar from my forehead under my hairline.

…threatened to kill me if I spoke a word of his sexual assault.

I found myself hiccupping sobs on the bed, suddenly feeling very alone. I'd been alone for so long, Aiden had been a light that pulled me out of my own darkness. If I ever lost him I don't know what I'd do. The only times I ever felt truly safe was when he was with me. I cried for a long time, but it felt good. The statement was important and now having written it all down I understood why Aiden wanted to tear through Idaho and wipe them out.

"Evelyn?" Aiden's voice broke over the sounds of my sniffling and hiccups. It couldn't be two already. He knelt above me, a worried expression on his face. "Are you okay?"

"They're sick," I choked out.

"Who?" He asked quietly as he pulled me into his arms. At once I felt comforted, and I curled into him.

"Idaho. They can't get away with what they did. They can't do that to anyone else. I won't let it happen." I would die before another person was hurt for no reason. Just because they were somebody no one else could really understand or accept.

"They won't. This trial is going to expose them to scrutiny from every pack in America. They won't get away with it Evelyn."

I nodded, taking a calming breath. "They won't get away with it."

Chapter Twenty-Five

THE HEARING WAS SCHEDULED FOR the 30th of November. I was relieved it wouldn't interrupt our Thanksgiving. We had school today before we got the four day weekend off over Thanksgiving. I'd invited down my father as well as my siblings and Stella. After giving the statement to the Alpha all talk in the house lately had been on the hearing. I was glad to escape to school or training with Hannah - even the hard-core training with the others was a welcome escape.

Hopefully I would have some days of peace during the holiday before it all came to a head on the coming Monday. I'd been feeling the pressure lately, concentrating on other people's problems helped, but not when I was alone at night with nothing else to think about.

I stood in front of my mirror, eyeing off my reflection. I'd borrowed a nice cable knit sweater off Grace and I'd stuffed that over one of Aiden's shirts which I had tucked into some high waisted jeans. Aiden probably wouldn't even know I was wearing one of his shirts. Throwing on some deep brown boots I picked up my bag, patting at the ponytail I had put my hair into.

"Hey." Aiden stood in my doorway, wearing a black sweater and deep blue jeans

"Hi," I said with a small smile, walking over to him. He took my bag like always and put it over his shoulder.

"Are you alright?" He asked, taking my hand in his. "You've been quiet lately."

I shrugged and sighed. "I'm as good as someone who has to stand in front of the High Council and be cross examined could be. I just have a lot of thoughts right now. Kind of tired of every conversation being about it. Tired in general."

Aiden made a sheepish face. "We have talked about it a lot. It'll all be over soon."

"Yeah." I hope so, I thought. I couldn't take much more of the anxiety it was giving me. "Is Grace coming with us today?"

Aiden made a face and started to lead me out of the room. "No, Trey's picking her up."

"That's good!" I exclaimed. "At least they're sorting themselves out, I hadn't heard much from her about it in a few days so, I'm happy they're working their relationship out."

Aiden grumbled under his breath and I rolled my eyes at the back of his head. Now he was all grumpy because he would be losing his sister soon, and he wasn't happy about it. I was though; I was scared of trying to figure out what I could and couldn't say around Grace.

"Mom's stressing about Thanksgiving," Aiden chuckled as he threw our bags into the car. "She's nervous to put a meal on for your family."

"Why?" I asked.

"She wants to make a good impression. She kind of sees herself as your unofficial mother I guess, she cares a lot about you, so in turn she cares about your family." Aiden gave me a smile and I felt warm from the idea that the Luna cared so much. "Have you heard from your mom?"

My lips thinned as the dark cloud that had been chasing me for the past few weeks reappeared. "No. I'd assume Idaho had the Summons by now."

"They have, Alpha Hess has spent the past two weeks calling."

"Ha." The truck fell silent and I stared gloomily out the window. The sky matched my dark mood and I knew we were in for same rain later. My thoughts drifted back to my mother. Maybe I should call her. Was she waiting for me to call her? The thoughts that had been dancing around in my mind for the past few weeks were once more invading. We pulled into the parking lot and I sighed, grabbing my bag, ready to get out. Aiden caught my arm however and I turned to look at him.

"I love you."

And just like that, my day was good again. I wasn't really able to construct a proper reply without mumbling and getting all bashful, so I settled for a peck on his cheek before getting out of the truck. Almost immediately I was swept up by Hannah who was screeching.

"Kate's gone!" She whispered in my ear. "The whole Thanksgiving weekend. I can actually be thankful." I snorted and put my hand over my mouth. "Josh doesn't understand my enthusiasm."

"He's blinded by her," I stated, adjusting my bag on my shoulder. "Has Grace arrived yet?"

"Yeah. Look over there." Hannah pointed toward the tree with the wrap around bench and I saw Grace, sitting on her phone with Trey just staring at her like a lost puppy.

"Wow."

"I know."

"She's really making him work hard, look, it's like he doesn't even exist."

"That was my idea," Lucy piped up next to me. I jumped in fright, falling back into the truck door with a thump. Aiden came around immediately, followed by Josh.

"What was that?" Aiden asked, looking at his truck.

Rubbing my elbow I frowned at Lucy. "That was me."

"Look at all his ex bimbos though," Hannah whispered conspicuously to me as she dragged me toward them slowly. I looked in each direction Hannah pointed; smiling a little wider at all the girls who stared longingly at Trey. "It's amazing."

We reached Grace and Trey, he didn't even look up however Grace set her phone down with a smile. "Hey girls," she got up and pulled me in for a hug and then Hannah and Lucy. "Cold this morning hey?"

"Yeah," Hannah said awkwardly. "Uh…hey Trey, how are you?"

"I'm good. I bet you're great considering Kate's gone." He gave Hannah a wink and she nodded enthusiastically, watching as Josh and Aiden came closer to the group.

"Well I hope the plane crashes," Lucy said loudly, sitting beside Grace.

"Whose plane crashes?" Aiden asked.

"No one's." Hannah glared at Lucy whose lips curled up in a naughty smirk.

"We should go up to the falls tonight," Grace suggested as the bell rang. "We could get a fire going, roast some marshmallows, and prepare ourselves for an onslaught of family time."

"Thanksgiving will be quieter for you this year, hey?" Lucy nudged Aiden who shrugged.

"Not really. Evelyn's father and her siblings are coming."

"It's a good distraction for mom. She won't have any time to think about grandma or grandpa." Grace smiled softly at Aiden before looking at me. "Evelyn saves the day again." I just stared at her and she decided to elaborate. "Our grandparents passed within days of each other after Christmas last year. Mom's sister is staying in Kansas, and she usually brings a lot of people with her, so if your family wasn't coming, it'd be just us."

"The pack doesn't get together?" I murmured, remembering all the times Idaho used to set up the hall every Thanksgiving and Christmas.

"Not for Thanksgiving. Christmas is a *huge* affair. It's awesome."

"Hey! The bell rang five minutes ago you lot, get a move on!" A grumpy looking woman in her mid-fifties scowled at us, and she kind of reminded me of the witch from Hansel and Gretel with her pointy nose and freakishly thin pointed fingers that directed us toward the school.

"I cannot wait for a break from this place," Grace grumbled. "I'm so sick of being shouted at."

The entire day everyone moved around with no motivation. Even the teachers looked ready to pack it in. I guess everyone was keen for the few days off that Thanksgiving would bring. That didn't stop the teachers from handing out nice big assignments though, and I stressed about trying to find the time to even do them. Thankfully only one was due the first day back. I was happy to see Aiden at lunch, sliding in beside him at the table I looked at the mountain of food he had got us and settled on a sandwich. He could eat the rest, and he probably would.

"So we have to sketch a what?" Hannah asked next to me, her eyes frantic.

"Something we see over the break. It has to have meaning and then we have to give a talk about why we chose this specific image."

"Crap."

"Yep," I sighed. I hadn't done any sort of oral presentation since coming here, we'd had heaps in Idaho. Sadly I knew I wouldn't be able to escape it for long.

"What are you going to draw?" Aiden asked.

"No idea. Maybe a turkey. 'This has meaning to me because I was super hungry and in that moment, all that mattered to me was eating the delicious bird.' How's that?" Hannah grumbled. "I do not understand why we have to do homework over the break, seriously."

"How many days left of this torture? I live to graduate." Lucy flopped her head down onto the table as Grace went through her phone, searching for the countdown she kept.

A shadow came over the table and we all looked up, spotting one of Trey's old girlfriends. Her black hair was pulled back into a sleek ponytail, her legs were encased in tight black leather leggings and I eyed off her chunky shoes, noting the gold stubs around the toe area. Imagine being kicked by those. Her breasts were practically stuffed into her tight 'shirt' and I briefly thought of Heather and how these two would get along.

"Trey," she cooed, all breathy. Grace's eyes snapped up instantly, zoning in on the pale hand that rested on Trey's shoulder. "Where have you been baby? I haven't heard from you in ages."

"Get your filthy little hand off him, or I'll do it for you. Trust me, you won't like it," Grace growled, standing up and I noted she was a centimeter or two taller than ex-girlfriend number whatever. Trey shook her hand off his shoulder and rose to settle Grace down.

"Grace ignore her," Trey pleaded. "She means nothing."

"Who do you think you are?" Leather pants snapped. "And Trey, what? I'm not good enough for you now? So you go and screw this flat chested nobody?"

Grace lunged for her, Trey quickly interceding and copping Grace's hand to his cheek instead. "Move!" She snarled, "I'm going to rip her hair from her head!"

Trey's ex laughed obnoxiously. "Okay, sure." She flicked her hand dismissively in Grace's direction and I knew Grace would be seeing red by now. This girl was human; however Grace's wolf would be beyond insulted by now.

"Don't worry, I'll do it." A screech came from leather pants as Lucy roughly yanked on the girl's ponytail, twisting it around in her hand and forcing the girl to be half bent backwards as Lucy hissed into her ear. "Get the hell out of here and don't come back."

"Get off her, bitch!" Another voice shrieked and I gasped as a small Asian girl grabbed Lucy's hair from behind and dragged her backwards, effectively dragging little miss leather pants with her.

"What the hell!" Hannah shouted. Lucy swung around with her free hand and back handed her attacker. Trey lost focus on Grace and suddenly she joined the brawl and before long legs and arms were flailing and violent slaps could be heard. I only hoped the girls kept an eye on their strength, they could kill those girls if the hit them to hard.

"Aiden stop them!" I shouted, worried for the two humans in the scuffle.

"There's blood!" Hannah yelled.

Aiden seemed to be shaken from his surprise at what had occurred in front of him as he pulled Trey up to stop the fight. The cafeteria was still a chorus of shouts and I watched with worry as Aiden and Trey pulled girls off each other. People cheered it on with glee, finally something interesting for them, I bet.

"What is going on here?!" A voice boomed and I turned to see Principal Hill. Looking back at Grace and Lucy I stared in amazement as the two girls grinned at each other, Lucy holding a black hair extension. They didn't even have a scratch, no doubt any injuries they got had healed already. "My office now!"

∞

"No phone. No laptop. No shifting. Nothing," Grace whined in training. "Still wouldn't take it back though, I feel great. Seriously, I've always wanted to hit one of his little skanks. Now I have and I feel better."

"She has a concussion," I reminded her, feeling bad as I thought of leather pants, whose name I found to be Alison. Her eye had already started swelling when the principal intervened and her hair - her fake hair - was on the floor, revealing quite short locks.

"She deserved it. If she didn't want a fight she should have kept her mouth shut," Lucy said calmly next to me, hi-fiving Grace.

My skin itched with anger. They could have handled the situation way better, they were ten times stronger than those girls. It could have been solved without violence. I didn't know how they could feel so content having such weak opponents.

"When I ripped out her hair-"

"Guys," Hannah murmured next to me.

"It felt so good. Maybe people shouldn't try and think they're all big, just because her cup size is bigger than mine. Like seriously-"

"Shut up!" I shouted, standing up. "Just shut up! Really? Do you feel satisfied? Sure she ran her mouth a little, but you hit someone weaker then you…you hit them when they were down! What the hell?"

"Evelyn you don't feel the whole mate bond, you don't get what it's like when someone touches your mate." Grace's face was red as she folded her arms. "You didn't spit the dummy when Aiden beat those jocks."

"Don't try and feed me that rubbish," I snapped, addressing her first rant. "I know how I feel when I think of Kate's hands on Aiden. I could easily break them with my mind if I wanted to. But I don't, because I have self-control and I trust the man I'm mated to. Lack of self-control, that's all I saw today." Picking up my bags, feeling my blood rushing I walked to the exit. "And Aiden never gloated after he beat those guys up, because he knew it was nothing to be proud of."

"Evelyn!" Lucy called after me.

Slamming the door shut I walked towards home, feeling the cold air biting any exposed skin. I didn't grasp how they could feel proud of their actions. Sure, Alison's words were rude, but it didn't warrant the beating that followed. The other one only got involved because her friend was in trouble...Lucy hade made the first aggressive move.

"Evelyn!" Hannah was beside me, nearly tripping over her training bag. "That was awesome. No one has ever given those two a talking to."

"I don't see how they think their behavior was warranted."

"It wasn't," Hannah agreed. "Trey had Grace restrained, Lucy started it."

"I know."

"I didn't know you were so angry."

I slowed my walk and turned to stare at her. "Unnecessary violence makes me angry. It didn't have to go that far today. I'm not talking to those two until they apologize to those girls."

"Going to be a quiet Thanksgiving for you and Grace then, she won't do it."

I shrugged. Grace hardly acted like an Alpha; she set a bad example for any younger wolves in that cafeteria today. Violence wasn't the answer and it didn't have to be. I didn't even understand why Lucy got involved.

"I've never seen you angry. You're kind of scary. Want to go blow stuff up?" She looked at me cheerfully and I shook my head and stopped, taking a calming breath.

"No," I said softly. "I'm going home."

"Okay..." Hannah looked at me with worry and I shook my head and began walking again.

Was I justified with my anger? I felt like I was. It didn't seem fair to me that they fought people who were massively outmatched and they were happy about it. Didn't deep down they feel a bit of remorse for the battered appearance of the girls? Maybe the humiliation they felt? Maybe werewolves were incapable of remorse unless it was to do with their own kind.

Reaching the house I went inside, welcoming the warmth that encased me. I heard clanging in the kitchen so I made my way toward it, spying the Luna leafing through the fridge. "Evelyn!" She smiled at me as she shut the door, carrying a variety of greens. "You don't look happy," her face dropped.

"I guess I'm not," I murmured as I picked up an apple and rolled it around in my hands.

"Why aren't we happy?" She asked me, leaning over the bench and resting her head in her hands. "Is it to do with what occurred today at school?" I nodded and she sighed. "Well you've left training before it's even started I see. I assume you tired of Grace's chest beating."

I looked at her in surprise. "Yeah."

She shook her head and her face morphed into disappointment. "That girl…I wonder about Grace sometimes. She possesses qualities any Alpha wolf does but there are no Luna qualities about her. It makes sense she has been matched with a normal ranked wolf. I'm not happy about today at all; I've already been in contact with the other girl's mothers."

"Are they okay?" I asked, putting the apple down in front of me.

"Well praise the Moon Goddess the girls didn't use all their strength otherwise we'd be looking at a murder trial. They fought humans, and that's inexcusable to me. I can understand fighting another she-wolf; I've done it plenty of times. Humans? No. Big no. They're so fragile, and we have so much physical strength as a species. When Aiden beat that boy at the falls party he got into a terrible amount of trouble, I feel Grace needs the same punishment.

"What happened to Aiden?" I asked curiously.

"Unfortunately I'm not allowed to say anything." She looked at me and said, "Those girls won't understand Evelyn. Not until they've been beaten by someone stronger than they are." The Luna shook her head and pulled out a knife, starting to chop the vegetables. "I'm sending them both to apologize once they get here. Greg is furious."

"Oh."

"What time does your family fly in tomorrow?" The Luna asked me with a smile. She had asked me this a few times already today, but remembering her stress Aiden had told me about, I calmly reminded her it was at nine in the morning.

"So you and Aiden will pick them up and then come here? I hope some of the siblings don't mind bunking up. Seeing as you sleep mostly in Aiden's room or vice versa, you okay if I give the room up for a few nights?"

"Oh yeah, sure." Aiden's bed was comfier anyway.

"So many of them," she laughed aloud, sounding flustered.

"Do you want any help cooking tomorrow?" I asked, biting my fingernails. With my six siblings, plus my father and Stella, along with the Alpha and Luna, Grace and Aiden and me...thirteen of us. "I really don't mind."

She looked at me in surprise. "No one has ever cooked with me on Thanksgiving."

"Oh!" I felt my cheeks heat up. "If it's your thing that's okay, I just thought with so many people...and so many being my family-"

"No its fine sweetie, I'd love the help. No one has actually offered to help before, ha!" She smiled warmly at me before turning to the stove and putting her chopped up vegetables into a pot.

"Okay," I said smiling. I was kind of excited to help. I used to help mom make it back home, well sort of. She cooked, I kept her company. She'd never let me touch anything. Sliding off my stool I put the apple back in the bowl and made to leave; only the Luna stopped me.

"Evelyn?"

"Yeah?"

She smiled at me. "I'm very glad you're going to be the next Luna. This pack is going to be in very good hands." Feeling my cheeks flush from the compliment I quickly left the room, smiling at her airy laughter.

∞

"It's too cold to get out of bed," Aiden mumbled into my hair. "He's magical right? Why can't he get a flying carpet and fly here."

I snorted, "Aiden."

"It's four in the morning. I much prefer going to bed at this time than waking up to it." He rolled himself on top of me and I wheezed from his weight. "Five more minutes."

"I c-can't breathe!" I gasped, pushing at his shoulders. He chuckled on top of me and I frowned, wishing I had the strength he had just to push him off me. Like flicking away a mosquito, that's how it would feel. I was surprised when I heard a crash and Aiden's weight disappeared. Hurriedly I looked to the floor to see Aiden groaning, holding his stomach. "Aiden!" I dove out of bed and too his side, helping him up as he tried to catch his breath from being winded.

"When did you get *that* strong?" He wheezed, slowly getting to his feet. "I won't do that again."

"I'm so sorry!"

He chuckled and rubbed his eyes before pulling me into a hug. "Don't be, now I don't have to worry about anyone being stronger than you. Your magic still confuses me. Anything you think, boom."

"It's strange. I probably should have read more of the diary; he'll ask when he comes. I'm going to get him to show me the important stuff; I don't need to hear about a stranger's sex life, no thanks." Even thinking about some of things I read made me feel uncomfortable. We dressed quickly and warmly. No one else was awake and I envied them as we found ourselves in a borrowed minibus from one of the pack members.

"Do you want to drive two hours and then I will?" Aided asked with a yawn.

I bit my lip and looked at him hesitantly. "Uh…I don't drive."

"Huh?" He looked shocked. "Really?"

"Y-yeah…never learnt…" This was embarrassing.

"Wow. Okay well, we'll work on that." He nudged my arm with a grin and started the van while I was left to die in a bubble of shame. I wanted to sleep badly but I knew it wasn't fair on Aiden, so I stayed awake, singing repetitive cartoon tunes over and over in my head. We stopped for some takeaway breakfast and Aiden got a large coffee with three extra shots.

Traffic was a nightmare the closer we got to the airport. Aiden exercised his road rage several times and I had to bite my inner cheek to stop myself from laughing at some of the insults he came up with. By the time we pulled into the airport I was glad for him to take a break. We were here about an hour or so early so we went inside and Aiden found himself another coffee to chug down. My phone buzzed in my hand and I thought it might be my father, announcing their arrival. My heart stopped when my mother's name popped up.

"Mom?" I answered, feeling my hands shaking. Aiden became awake instantly.

"*Evelyn. I just wanted to wish you a happy Thanksgiving sweetheart.*" Her voice sounded tired, and I felt my eyes watering. I'd almost forgotten how it sounded. "*I thought one of us should break radio silence. Especially today, the day where I'm reminded of all the things I am so thankful for.*"

"I just didn't know what to say," I breathed out. "I was confused."

"*I know. I would have been too. Which is why I'm sure you think it's a good idea to have a trial. Let me advise you against it sweetheart. Nothing good will come out of this besides two packs with bad blood for each other.*" Her voice was thick, and hosted an undercurrent of warning. I shook my head though, still resolved with my decision.

"The hearing is a good idea, mom. Idaho needs to learn how to treat people." The line was silent and I shook my head, feeling suspicious. Did she only call me to stop the hearing? Did Alpha Hess put her up to it? "Everything is in my statement."

"*Everything?*"

"All of it. My real father is going to be there, as will my half-siblings."

"*What?*" She demanded down the line, any kind of fatigue she had disappearing from her voice. "*Evelyn I have not told them about my past.*" I gaped at Aiden in disbelief as he frowned, his super hearing picking up on her words. I couldn't believe it. "*Evelyn, this would ruin my entire relationship with my children and my mate.*"

Our relationship didn't matter, clearly. "You need to tell them," was all I said as I hung up. Aiden shook his head, taking my hand in his and pulling me into a hug. Taking a heavy breath I felt a headache coming on and I knew there was going to be no escape of 'the hearing' conversations this Thanksgiving.

"Hello *sister*!" Arms tore me out of Aiden's and wrapped themselves around my neck. I was pushed between my half-siblings, wrapped in air crushing hugs before I finally found my way to my father, who hugged me much more gently.

"Your aura is quite dark," he commented.

"Mom rang just then," I told him. "She hasn't told the truth yet."

"Is she stupid?" Jasmine asked matching the disbelief Aiden and I had shared moments earlier. "Did she think that with the hearing like three days away she was going to be able to keep it a secret?"

"She wanted me to stop the hearing."

"Fat chance," Aiden muttered.

"So much gloom, so early in the morning!" Stella sighed. "Come on, let's forget about all the drama and head to your compound. It's Thanksgiving today. Nothing besides happy things is to be spoken about." Thank…Morgana? Thank the Moon Goddess? I was still yet to decide which one I chose to thank. Thank whoever for Stella.

The drive home seemed shorter than the drive there and I knew once we got home Aiden would do a patrol before taking a nap. He looked exhausted. All the girls rambled in excitement as we entered the compound. The boys looked around in vague interest, but the girls were way more caught up in it. Pack members scurried along everywhere, carrying covered dishes. Some driveways were piled high with cars, while others were bare.

"So many people!" Sienna exclaimed.

I was sitting next to Aliyah who stared out the window gloomily. I remembered back to my trip, where she had been having guy problems. Did that still exist? She didn't look happy at all. "How have you been?" I asked her quietly.

"Just peachy," she grunted. "I've been promised to someone, check it out." I stared at the brown intricate looking design on her forearm, admiring it until it was covered. "It's really set in stone now that monstrosity is on my arm."

"She had to break up with her true love," Gabriel mocked.

"Piss off *Gabby*!" Aliyah snapped, giving him the finger.

"Gabriel!" Stella warned from up the front.

"Is he nice?" I asked tentatively, scared she may bite my head off.

She flipped her hair and sighed. "Yes, he's nice. That's the problem; I can't even hate him properly."

"Oh."

"He lives in a coven in New Orleans. We're getting married when I turn eighteen and I have no say in it, because my family are barbaric and outdated." She screwed her face up at the back of our fathers head as he sat up front with Aiden.

"Enough Aliyah," he groaned from the front seat. "Just leave it alone for one day. One day."

"Oh I'm sorry," she scoffed. "It's only the rest of my life that's been taken away from me, but whatever. One day of no complaining sure. I have the next seventy odd years of my life to bitch and moan about it right?" She was met with silence and she resumed staring out the window and I hoped we'd be home soon so I could escape the tense atmosphere.

Pulling up to the house everyone piled out and Stella began complimenting it immediately. I remember when I first saw this place. It seemed like an age ago now. We unpacked their luggage and I heard the front door open, the Alpha, Luna and Grace coming down the front steps. The Luna grabbed Stella straight away for a hug, much to her surprise before she moved onto my father.

"Lovely to see you all again!" She exclaimed. She took charge of introducing everyone to Grace and the Alpha, saving me from doing it myself. Everyone looked a little overwhelmed being in the Alpha's presence and I was glad I wasn't the only one.

"You have a lovely home," Stella commented as we entered the house.

"Thank you," the Luna smiled. "I'll show you all to your rooms. I hope you don't mind sharing. Then we can all sit down and have some lunch. Evelyn, I have two pie crusts in the oven, they're ready to come out. Could you do that for me please?"

"Sure!"

"I'll meet you in there soon; I'm just going to speak with dad." Aiden kissed my head before following his father and I gave Grace a glance before heading toward the kitchen, my mouth watering at the smells coming from it. Taking out the two trays from the oven, I carefully set them down on the stovetop.

"Evelyn," Grace said from the doorway. I stayed silent, lifting the crusts carefully and placing them on the cooling racks the Luna had left out. "Please talk to me Evie."

"Have you apologized to the girls?" I asked tightly, already annoyed I'd broken my no talking rule.

"Yes. Lucy and I went last night. And I meant it, truly. When I saw them…I do feel awful Evelyn. I know I could have handled it a lot better than I did. It's just; Trey and I are still shaky. Seeing her like that with him, and the way she spoke to me-"

"You need to stop making excuses," I said quietly. "You can't expect punching someone to solve all your problems. Trey and you still have problems right?"

"Yes."

"So hitting those girls didn't fix anything."

"No. I get that. I have said sorry though, and I truly meant it. Please don't ignore me." Her eyes were wide and I was surprised to see them slightly welled up. I sighed, knowing anger or the silent treatment would never be my thing anyway, and it was hard enough to ignore her when she came home last night.

"Okay," I sighed.

"Oh thank the Goddess!" She ran around the kitchen bench and threw her arms around my neck, squeezing tightly. "I'm so happy. I really did not want today to be spent like that. Not when you have so much going on as well."

"Yeah, well, no dramas today. Just fun family time, okay?"

"Definitely!"

∞

"Well I truly could not eat another bite," my father said with a smile. The table that had only a half hour ago been piled high with food now stood empty, with either bones or leftovers people couldn't eat. The Luna looked happy and I was glad I had helped her. The entire day had been fun and relaxing. My sisters got to know Grace and Aiden spoke more with my brothers. At some stage my father had gone into the Alpha's office, and I knew they were talking about the hearing and the phone call from my mother. I was glad they took it to another room.

"Well there's still pie for later," the Luna announced with a smile. "I think you should all have a little break first. I forget not everyone has the appetite of a wolf. When Evelyn first ate with us I was worried she had an eating disorder."

"I suppose you're feeding two beings?" Stella asked as she pointed at her head. "I still am so awed by the fact you have another being within you. Such an interesting concept."

"It's interesting until it doesn't shut up," Grace said. "Seriously when it wants something, it won't be silent until it gets it."

"You've had my Jasmine here in love with the idea of soulmates," my father laughed. "It's all she wants. I must admit after watching the way Evelyn and Aiden are together, it's quite inspiring. You move like you're one, like magnets."

"Or the fact he like, never takes his eyes off her," Sienna said with a giggle.

Blushing under their scrutiny I tried to think of a way to change the subject. Using whatever first came to mind I said, "I helped make the pie." The table laughed again and I sighed, jumping when I felt Aiden's hand on the small of my back. It was private, intimate and comforting.

"Well I'm so glad you could all make it. Thanksgiving was going to be very quiet this year otherwise."

"Well seeing as we couldn't make Christmas, we definitely had to do this. My first Thanksgiving with my dear Evelyn. And many more to come, I hope." I smiled over at my father, growing warm from his words.

"Definitely."

"Let's move to the sitting room," the Luna suggested. Everyone murmured their approval and began getting up. The Luna started collecting dishes but I stopped her.

"I can do it," I offered.

"Yeah mom, rest a bit. Evelyn and I will do the dishes."

The Luna gave Aiden a look of surprise and I assumed it was because he didn't offer often. A smile threatened at my lips but I held it together. "Okay," she said unsurely. "Thank you."

The rest of them moved to the sitting room and Aiden and I cleared the table, and I stared silently in dismay at the pile of dishes that gathered by the sink.

"We can put some in the dishwasher and some we'll have to do by hand." Aiden held up gloves and a tea towel. "Wash or dry?"

"Wash." We slowly worked through the dishes, and I admit I went slower than I needed to. One, because I enjoyed just being with Aiden, alone. Two, because the longer I took, the slower the hearing would come. As much as I wanted to keep it out of my mind it found very annoying ways to just creep right on in again.

"We could drop them all and then we don't have to do them," Aiden suggested as I handed him a plate.

"That's a great idea," I laughed dryly. "I can drop your mother's favorite dishes and she can hate me."

"Not possible. You could reject me and she'd probably still love you."

"Well that's not possible either," I mumbled. The idea of rejecting Aiden almost as insane as dropping all his mother's favorite dishes.

"I was worried you might, at one stage."

"I know," I said quietly as I stopped washing. "I was worried I might as well."

"Then you realized what a stud you got landed with." I laughed and took off my gloves, taking his hand in mine. I placed it over my mark and sighed at the peaceful feelings that flowed through my body. "I'm glad you didn't."

"So am I." I couldn't imagine my life without him now. The idea of letting him in my life in the beginning had been so terrifying to me that I was ready to run for the hills. Now it felt like I'd fall apart if I didn't have him. I took a step closer and ran my fingers over the mark I had placed on him. "I'm glad we took our time though."

He swallowed loudly and I held in my smile. Leaning up I placed a feather light kiss on his lips, pulling away only slightly. "Goddess, Evelyn. I love you," he said quietly as his hand snaked around my waist. "I thank my lucky stars every day that you're in my life."

"So do I. How much changes in a year, hey? Last Thanksgiving I was left at home while they all went to the gathering to celebrate. Now I'm here, with you, surrounded by people who care about me. It's a surreal feeling."

He stroked my cheek and I closed my eyes, leaning into his touch. "You'll never be alone again," he promised. "This is our first Thanksgiving. How's it shaping up?"

"Great so far," I grinned. I watched as he produced a small blue box and I frowned as he scratched the back of his neck nervously.

"I got you something…a couple of days ago actually. I just was waiting for the right time to give it to you."

I laughed and ran my hand down my face. "You have to stop buying me things."

"You have to get used to it," he smirked as he pressed the box into my palm. "Open it."

Slowly I lifted the lid, gasping at the gorgeous stud earrings inside. Immediately I looked down at my wrist, noting the stones on the earrings matched the stones on my bracelet. "Aiden…it's beautiful."

"You're beautiful," he murmured. "You'll only make them look better."

Oh swoon! He had a way with words tonight.

"Thank you," I giggled out. He kissed me again and I fell into it, allowing myself to get swept up in the feelings he gave me. I couldn't be happier in this moment or more thankful that my life was where it was right now.

Happy Thanksgiving, Evelyn.

Chapter Twenty-Six

"Beta Ward will be staying behind to run the pack in my absence. We each have five of our packs best fighters assigned to us. As much as I trust the High Council, I don't trust Idaho, especially after pulling the alliance." The Alpha adjusted his tie and looked at me. "Evelyn I hope this trial brings justice for you, hopefully the council will proceed with an open mind and unbiased judgment."

"I wish we were coming," Lucy pouted as she pulled me in for a hug. "Stick to your guns, if you need a pep talk, call me." She released me and I was pulled into a choking hug by Hannah.

"Be careful and don't let them into your head, okay? Your dad's going to be there and so will your siblings. That's already a big fat in your face to them. You've become so strong since being here Evelyn, remember who you are when you get on that stand. You aren't a punching bag for Idaho; you're the future Luna of Oregon and a dang powerful witch." She kissed my cheek and squeezed my hands before stepping back beside Lucy.

"We shouldn't be more than two days," the Alpha informed us. "We can't be away from the pack any longer than that, especially with all these rogue attacks recently."

"We'll keep the borders tightly patrolled, Alpha." Beta Ward bowed his head and I wondered how such a respectful and decent man could have fathered a child like Kate.

The two vans pulled up that would be taking us to the airport and I found my palms beginning to sweat at the idea of leaving the safety of Oregon and having to go and face the members of Idaho. I'd thought once being here I would never have to see them again, now here I was, on my way to testify against them. I could vomit.

Most of the pack had gathered to see us off. Members I hadn't even met yet gave me comforting words and pats on the back. Following Aiden I got into the first van along with Grace, Sienna, my father and Aliyah. The Alpha and Luna climbed into the second with Gabriel, Phoenix, Jasmine and Christian. Then came the guards which filled up any available seat. I couldn't even find it in me to wave at Hannah or Lucy as the van pulled away. I felt like I was driving towards my doom.

It was funny how small I felt. These past few weeks I'd felt so much stronger, more capable. The idea of confronting my past had me curling into a ball and wanting to pretend it wasn't happening. It was funny to me, the power that people had over you. You could be so much stronger than them physically, but the emotional torture they put you through was enough to make you incapable of being who you are when you're in their presence.

"Your heart is beating so loud," Aiden whispered into my hair before pressing his lips to my head. "Breathe Evelyn. You're going to be fine, and I will not leave your side the entire trip." Nodding shakily I rested my head on his shoulder, willing the pains in my stomach to go away. I was safe with Aiden.

"…Just don't see why mine had to be set in stone? All the others are promised but they didn't get branded!" Aliyah's voice was in a hushed whisper toward the back of the van and I craned my ears to hear what was being said.

"This is an alliance marriage Aliyah. The other girls are only loosely promised because the details haven't been figured out yet. He's a lovely boy, I wish you would just try and get to know him. He calls you all the time and you never answer. He is trying Aliyah." Sienna's calm words were met with silence so I assumed Aliyah was contemplating what her sister was saying.

"I wish mine was set in stone," Jasmine moaned. "I'm exhausted with all this waiting."

"Yeah, well you're marrying into a family of snobs."

"Well he isn't one," Jasmine defended. "I'm glad we have arranged marriages, saves me the trouble of useless, time wasting dating. At least if I decide he sucks there's really no way out and I have to live with it."

"How many Alpha's are going to be at the hearing?" One of the guards asked Aiden. He looked to be about twenty-five; copper locks tossed about on his head and had a few days worth of stubble on his chin. His green eyes flickered to my watching ones and I dropped my own to my hands.

"We have no set number. Apparently this hearing has been big news throughout the packs. You'd be surprised how many packs want to have 'talks' with Idaho regarding their alliances. Even Alpha Hudson is coming down."

Copper locks widened his eyes in surprise. "Really?"

"Yeah. Though judging by his words he's really only passing through. Apparently he's down here on other business. I can only imagine."

"Well you'll hear about it in a few days. He's either tearing down a pack or causing some kind of other chaos. I can't believe the council lets him get away with so much. It's insane to me, if any other pack behaved the way he does…"

"Well he doesn't believe he's under our laws. His lineage is rogue after all. He doesn't have an issue with us and I'd like to keep it that way. He's a good ally to have." Aiden shrugged and asked, "Who would go up against Alaska anyway?"

"Not me. He doesn't even take planes," copper locks said, shaking his head. "They say he moves so fast in wolf form, that he's a blur."

"He's more wolf than human, everyone knows that. It would not be a good idea to put him in a flying box." This was another guard and I remembered his name to be David. He took off his cap and ran his hand over his bald scalp. "I spoke with his Beta at the gathering. Twenty-five, still mateless. Apparently he's been searching."

"Goddess help the poor woman that ends up with him," copper locks laughed.

Conversation died down after that and I was a little annoyed it did, it kept my mind off the fact that I'd be boarding a plane to South Dakota in less than an hour. I was left to just swipe left and right on my phone, trying to keep myself occupied when really it just let my mind go into overdrive.

They would all be there. *All* of them. Anyone who had been mentioned in that statement would be there. Someone would be questioning me, looking for lies, trying to poke holes in my story. I was comforted by the fact that there was no way I could lie to them, they'd smell it. They would believe me, I was just worried for how much of the statement they'd read out. Aiden got a very watered down version of my life. Anyone who hadn't read that statement got a watered down version. Not to mention the thought of seeing my mother. How was she? She should have told Michael by now the real story behind my conception.

Did the pack know? Did any of them now feel guilty of my treatment? Or did they still feel justified because I was still a half-breed? Surely now with it going to a hearing they had to realize what they had done was wrong. There wasn't any way they could justify their treatment.

I'd never been more reluctant to board a plane in my life. If it wasn't for Aiden following behind me I probably would have turned and ran for the hills. Any talk of the hearing or anything werewolf related ceased as our company expanded to humans. It was funny, listening to their conversations. Most of them were leaving from visiting family at Thanksgiving, griping on about certain family members, or how their husbands hadn't spoken enough to their mothers.

It felt so normal. They were going home and I was going to a hearing with a bunch of werewolves. It never ceased to amaze me how we lived with humans undetected. We had to look like an odd traveling party.

"I feel like the plane is going to crash," said a woman behind me.

"Trust me, it won't." That was Jasmine, sitting in the opposite aisle. I suppose being in a plane full of witches was the safest flight these humans would ever have. I hardly took notice of the safety procedure that went on at the front of the aisle; instead I occupied myself with tracing Aiden's birthmark on his arm. I found it surprisingly calming.

"Feeling okay?" Aiden asked me quietly and I looked up at him with a sigh.

"I guess."

"I love you."

Managing a small smile I pecked his cheek. "I love you too."

∞

I had never wished for a plane crash more than when we began our descent. Aiden had told me when we crossed the South Dakota border and my nerves flew off the charts, so much so that I briefly caused the lights in the plane to flicker until my father stepped in and calmed me down.

I don't want to do this. I wanted to but I didn't. I wanted justice and I wanted Idaho punished but why did it have to be me? Why couldn't they just read my statement and leave me alone? I could think of more things I wanted to do than do this hearing. Shave off my skin was one, have my fingernails pulled out with pliers, scratch my nails across a chalkboard...there were many!

"My ears are blocked," Grace said loudly. "I hate landing."

"Landing is awesome. I love that feeling you get in the pit of your stomach."

"You're sick," Grace said with a wrinkled nose at Jasmine.

We were in Rapid City and unfortunately, the council was located only a forty minute drive away in Deadwood. I wish I could faint or something right now, anything to get me out of the situation I was in.

"Breathe," Aiden said to me. He took my hand and brought it to his lips. "I'm right behind you all the time, okay?" I tried to nod but it probably just looked like my neck was spasming. I stood up and grabbed my carry on and slowly began to filter out of the plane with everyone else.

"I can smell Idaho," Grace announced. "It's about an hour old."

A warmth shot up my arm as my father took a hold of my hand. "Breathe, your energy is running too high and your eyes are starting to change color." He leant in to my ear and whispered, "Humans might freak out a little bit. No one here will let them touch you, they'll die trying."

"I don't know if I can do it," I squeaked out.

"Evelyn. Remember how you felt when you wrote your statement?" The Luna said gently beside me. "All those memories, even things you thought you had forgotten. It could happen all over again to an innocent victim, because Idaho have no remorse and are obviously unable to differentiate between right and wrong. Don't you wish someone had stopped them for you?" I nodded, feeling my eyes well up. "You could be saving somebody else's life here today."

Taking a deep breath I didn't release the death grip I had on Aiden's arm, or my father's hand, but I managed to nod. "W-we aren't staying near them?"

"No, we are in the opposite accommodation building to them. We made that very clear that outside of the trial room they were to not make any contact with us." We began to move through the airport and I followed in a foggy haze, too caught up in my own mind to pay any attention to my surroundings.

I'd be facing the Alpha family of Idaho soon, my family and my attackers. I never thought I'd be doing this. A few months ago I was living under the impression that I'd soon be turned loose and I could live a life away from them and never have to think about them or see them again. Now I was in this world forever, where their name would pop up and I'll be forever known as the Luna who took them to trial for abuse.

It wasn't going to be how the humans did it. Our statements would be read, we would be questioned by one of the High Council members and they would then deliberate about the course of action they would take. I only just found this out, and I'd been sitting here for weeks terrified of some stranger trying to crack my story to prove Idaho were in the right and did no such thing.

I guess when it's a trial among wolves - creatures that can smell when you're telling a lie - there was no need for constant questioning like that. They'd have the truth in a heartbeat. I just wondered why Idaho hadn't pleaded guilty so that we didn't have to go through all this. It astounded me that they possibly had some sort of sick story to justify their actions.

I found myself in a van, whipping away from the airport all too quickly for my tastes. Couldn't they drive a little under the speed limit? It stressed me out that Idaho was already there. What would happen when they all saw me? They'd smell our arrival. They'd probably see it. The High Council compound wasn't large, but it was surrounded by very dense forest. I knew I wouldn't be alone at any time, but I still didn't like it.

"I never thought I'd go to South Dakota. It's like werewolf headquarters." Jasmine was snapping photos on her phone and I was glad at least someone was enjoying themselves.

Feeling a tap on my shoulder I found Christian. We didn't talk much; out of all the siblings he'd never texted me once I'd left Ohio. He seemed like the quiet type - which is why I was surprised that he had approached me. He leant in, glancing around the bus. "Don't let your fear stop you from getting the justice you deserve," he whispered. "You're not alone here."

"T-thanks," I said back quietly. He went back to looking at his phone so I faced forward, closing my eyes as I leant against Aiden's shoulder. Part of me had the terrible thought that I should have just let Aiden tear Idaho down, and then I wouldn't have to do the trial. I dismissed the selfish thought as soon as it entered my mind. I wouldn't let my own fears put innocent people in danger of death.

We drove right through Deadwood before we reached a more secluded section of town that was gated. There was a guard at the gate and after producing ID we drove through and my stomach turned at all the vehicles in the parking lot outside what I assumed to be the council building. We were directed to where we would be staying and as we pulled up outside the two-story building I hesitantly looked across the street to where Idaho would be staying and was relieved when I couldn't see anyone. A lot of people wandered the streets and I had to remind myself this place was also a pack, not just the council.

"I think we will have a big audience," the Alpha commented. "I remember when I was a boy and I came here for the trial of Alpha Newman. He was the Alpha who murdered his children after his mate died and then slaughtered his pack - there was barely any room to sit."

"I can't imagine why that would draw a crowd," Gabriel commented dryly.

Everyone got out of the van and the van behind us piled out as well. The air was cold and I wrapped my jacket around me tighter.

"Oregon pack...and company?" A tall man in a suit looked over my family confused. I guess he found it strange he couldn't scent them, but it wouldn't take him long to realize they were witches.

"Our correct name is Ohio Witch Coven, but company works well. I'm here to support my daughter Evelyn through this trial. Are you showing us to our rooms? Or are we going to stand outside on this sidewalk until we're needed at the council building?" I looked at my father in surprise. I realized he'd be seeing mom today for the first time in who knows how long. I'd forgotten the tension he may be feeling, too caught up in my own worries.

"Of course. If you'll all follow me." The man turned around and promptly led us into the building. A few people loitered in the halls but it was mostly empty. Taking a pile of keys off the front counter he handed them out. "The council requests that Alpha Greg James, Luna Claudia James, Alpha Aiden James and Evelyn Lilith Wright all be present in two hours in building one, room A. The rest of you are to find yourselves in building one, room C. Your side is on the right, Idaho is on the left. South Dakota pack members have reserved seats in the balcony. Any visiting pack Alpha's will also find themselves in the balcony seating."

Balcony? How big was this trial room?

"How many visiting Alpha's are attending this trial?" the Luna asked.

"Alpha Hudson of Alaska is in attendance with his Beta. Alpha Glenn from Washington has attended with his Gamma. Alpha York of Montana has attended also accompanied by his Beta and Alpha Richards of Indiana, accompanied by his Beta and Luna." My breath sucked in at the mention of Indiana, the pack my mother had once belonged to. So many Alpha's all in the same room. After the man saw to it that he was no longer required he left and we all stood in the foyer.

"So Idaho has two of its allied packs here, Montana and Indiana. Special invitation I'm sure." The Alpha looked displeased. "Why is Alpha Hudson here?"

"Apparently he has business to deal with in Wyoming," one of the guards supplied. "He's basically passing through."

"What would he possibly have to do with Wyoming?" The Luna asked with a frown. "They're three thousand miles apart from each other."

"I don't make it my job to question what other Alpha's do with their time and resources. It is nice to have an ally here though." The Alpha took the Luna's hand. "I suggest we all settle in before we have to go to the council building. Maxwell and Stevens, you two are on the front door. No one besides Oregon or Alaska come in here." They both nodded seriously and I watched as the Alpha put a guard to everyone's room door.

We could stand here and talk some more, really let time drag on, I suggested inwardly. Sadly everyone began to disperse, trying to find their rooms. I followed Aiden upstairs and he found our room.

It looked like a boring motel room really. Plain blue bedding and two set of drawers with a mirror. A bathroom was what the only other door led to. Aiden placed our shared bag on the bed with a sigh, unzipping it and going through it.

I was relieved to just be alone in a room. I could stay here forever and not have to face the impending doom that waited for me at the High Council building. I sat down on the edge of the bed and rested my head in my hands. Just be courageous. You can do it. You can't but you can. I felt Aiden prop down in front of me and I peeked through my hands at him.

"Where are we going to go to College?" He asked me with a light smile on his face. His question kind of stunned me at first; it was so out of the blue and so off topic, but it kind of helped and I realized he was trying to help take my mind of the situation.

"Somewhere super sunny and close to the beach," I murmured. That would be amazing.

"What's your major?"

"Art. It's not like I need to worry about my career," I said with a grin. Being the Luna would be all the job I'd need.

"I wonder where we'll be in the next two years," Aiden wondered aloud. "Do you ever play that game?"

"What game?" I asked tiredly.

"Where you try and picture your life in five or ten years."

I sighed and leant my forehead against his. "I never pictured my life for more than a week. I've only just started thinking about my future. I never thought I'd really have one."

"It's going to be great," he said with a grin as he pushed me down onto the bed, lying beside me. "We're going to travel a bit. We'll have to anyway. We have pack friends in packs across Europe.

"Really?" I asked in surprise.

"Yeah. You know first point of call is though, after all this is?"

"What?"

"Teaching you to drive." I thinned my lips at the idea, who knows how I'd handle that task. I could just imagine it with me totaling someone's car.

"We'll see."

The room was quiet for a while and I found myself calming to a point where I could almost fall asleep. The lack of sleep over the past few days must have been catching up with me. I could feel Aiden toying with the bracelet on my wrist - the one he had gifted me with - and it was quite relaxing.

"Do you ever think about a wedding?" He asked quietly and I flicked my eyes open and stared at the ceiling as I tried to take that in.

"A human kind or a werewolf kind?" I asked nervously.

"Werewolf obviously, the human kind wouldn't make much sense." He scratched under his ear and I saw his neck was going a little red. "I just thought…I mean I know a lot of wolves don't do it…but maybe we could have a small ceremony." I found myself blinking at him stupidly, not really sure what to say. "We don't have to," he said quickly, his face now red.

"No," I blurted out. He gave me a look and I bit my lip. "I mean, I've never really thought about it, really I've only just gotten used to the idea you're actually my mate." Thinking of it now though, a nice quiet ceremony with the pack members. "It's a good idea."

"Really?" He asked with a shy smile and just with that smile I found myself falling in love with him all over again.

"Yes. Actually it sounds perfect."

He was silent for a moment before he smirked at me. "I get to buy you a ring then."

"No!" I groaned out, "What did I say about buying me more things?"

"What did I say about getting used to it?" He laughed. "I'm going to buy you nice things all the time Evelyn. You're going to love them, but you'll pretend you don't want me buying them for you. Which is nice, I love that you don't feel like you need them - but I need to give you them. So you'll accept them, because you know it will make me happy and in turn you'll be happy."

I just shook my head at him, running my finger over his lower lip. "Then I have to buy you something."

He caught my hand and sat up slightly. "You are enough."

"Aiden!" I laughed at his corny remark.

"I'm serious."

Shaking my head I got up. "We better change; I don't think I should meet the High Council in my jeans."

"Probably a good idea," Aiden mumbled as he looked down at his ripped jeans and his sweater that housed a stain from eating on the plane.

Rifling through our bag I pulled out the outfit Grace had put together for me. It was a simple blue dress with quarter length sleeves. Taking with me my ensemble I went to the bathroom to have a quick shower. I was going to present myself with confidence. I had to. I wasn't the Evelyn they knew anymore and I never would be. I was so much more than that frail tortured individual.

I dried off quickly and got dressed, noting with distaste that my pantyhose had a small runner in them. The dress was modest, the collar ending at my collarbone and the hem ending at my knees. I'd prefer to keep as much of myself covered with Jonah in my presence. I let my hair hang down my back so I could use it as a veil if needed.

Avoiding the water on the floor I opened the door, eyeing the black pumps near my bag with a glare. Aiden was buttoning up his shirt and I tore my eyes from his exposed chest and went over to put the pumps on, already regretting letting Grace plan my outfit.

Heels will make you confident and taller.

Aiden came behind me and wrapped his arms around my waist. "Can you do me a favor once we're actually in a room with all of them?"

"Yes?" I said curiously.

"Don't lose contact with me. If you're not touching me I don't know if I'll be able to stop myself from killing Jonah." He turned me to face him and his face was earnest. "I'm saying this in all seriousness, it's not macho talk. I want him dead."

With wide eyes I nodded, running my hand down his cheek. "I promise."

Someone knocked on the door and I heard the Luna tell us it was time to leave. I found my hands bunching up into little fists on Aiden's chest and he took them both in his hands, kissing them. "You'll be fine. I'm with you the whole time."

"Okay," I whispered, mainly to myself. Picking up my black cardigan I put it on, remembering the chill outside. Taking Aiden's hand I led us from the room and into the hallway, following the voices downstairs and into the foyer where everyone stood, changed and looking less like weary travelers.

No words were really shared. We made our way back out to the van and all piled in to drive down the road to the council. I'm glad we didn't have to walk; these shoes probably wouldn't have let me. When we arrived my mouth went dry at the amount of people walking into the building. Was it really that important to watch?

We all climbed out and stood outside building one. A director was waiting by the door for us and I realized I wouldn't see the rest of our party until I entered the hearing room. It was a mixture of hugs and comforting words before I was shuffled along by the Luna toward the director who was waiting for us.

"Follow me please," he said pleasantly. "We're going to be meeting with the High Council before the hearing. Then it will begin." He looked at me and asked, "How are you feeling?" I could hardly conjure a sentence but I'm sure the look on my face said it all. We stopped outside a door and my heart thumped. "For what it's worth, I'm on your side. I read all the reports, yours actually sounds like the truth."

"Th-thanks," I said shakily. My stomach felt like it was going to heave up and empty its limited contents onto the floor. I was terrified I was going to puke on this nice man's shoes.

"Just go through this door. The council members are waiting for you." Opening it the Alpha walked in first followed by the Luna, myself and then Aiden. The room was sparsely decorated. There were four sofas, facing each other and a couple of plants and a gray rug. That was all. Seated on the four chairs were four men and one woman, all dressed in black robes and white collars. They looked like something you'd see in a Hollywood drama movie.

"Alpha Greg James," a large man stood up, his cheeks red. It felt awful of me to say it in my own mind but never in my life had I seen a werewolf...his size before. He must never shift.

"High Alpha Sinclair," Alpha James bowed his head, and we all followed suit. The power that radiated off these men and the woman was intimidating. "I must say I'd hoped we'd meet again under better circumstances than this."

"As did I."

"You know High Alpha Forbes; she's just recently joined us after the death of High Alpha Emerson. She's proved herself to be outstanding in this position." High Alpha Sinclair looked proud of the pale woman. Her lips were thin and she wore a firm expression, but there was a strange look in her eye when she glanced at me. "High Alpha Sloan," he gestured to an aging man. His wispy gray hair looking like it would need combing before he took to the panel. "High Alpha Conrad and High Alpha Radcliff." Both men regarded me openly and I wondered if this was who they imagined from reading the statement.

"A pleasure to meet you all," Alpha James said sincerely. "My Luna, Claudia, my son Aiden and his mate Evelyn. The reason we are here today."

"Yes." High Alpha Sinclair looked at me. "I know this must all be quite daunting. Just remember to breathe before answering a question. We have had an interesting confession from your mother. Which now means she will also be being questioned on her role in your treatment in Idaho. I've been told your real father is here today?"

Swallowing the lump in my throat I croaked out, "Yes Sir."

"He may or may not be called as well. There is a lot to your story that wasn't reported on their side. They chose today to tell us. For that I'm not happy with. I appreciate you all going through the proper avenues of solving this matter. I know it must have been hard to resist the urge to go straight into an attack," High Alpha Sinclair looked over at Aiden whose eyes were tight.

"It was Evelyn's compassion that spared them," he said simply. "If I had my way, we wouldn't be here right now and Idaho would no longer exist."

"I see." High Alpha Sinclair gave me a small smile before rubbing his hands together. "You will enter through that door just there," he gestured to the wooden door. "And take a seat at the table opposite Idaho. There is to be no talking to each other, no shouting. That room is silent at all times. We will follow after shortly. May you only speak truth, and we can solve this problem once and for all."

"Thank you," Alpha James bowed and we began the walk toward the door. I felt like I could hear my footsteps in my ears. I could hear the blood rushing frantically in my veins and my heartbeat got faster. Aiden's hand found its way to the small of my back and he pressed a kiss into the back of my head while Alpha James stopped to open the door.

Taking a breath I resolved myself to be strong. To feel strong. They couldn't hurt me anymore. As the light from the hearing room hit us, my step nearly faltered but I walked on, knowing that after this, Idaho would never be able to hurt me or anyone else again. If that didn't give me the courage, then what else would?

I'm not sure if I could name all the emotions that ran through me as I sat down at the seat Aiden held out for me. I hadn't even looked across at Idaho yet but I could feel their eyes burning holes into my face. Aiden sat beside me and rested his hand on my thigh and I hastily placed mine on top, holding it tightly.

I looked around the room to try and occupy my eyes from drifting over toward Idaho. The room was massive. It was all white marble flooring and I wondered how they kept it clean from shoe scuffs. The walls and the panel were all yellow marble, with a huge wolf head carved out on the center. The panel was two levels higher than us and I looked at the stand in front of them, wondering if that's where anyone being questioned would be sitting.

To my left were Grace and some of our guards along with my father and my siblings. I noticed the giant Alpha from Alaska sitting behind them, his eyes shut. His Beta looked around the room with interest and at the people seated next to him and behind him. Looking over the aisle I noticed many faces from Idaho, all staring at me with contempt. The pews on their side of the room were almost full and I wondered why so many came.

With no one else to really assess my eyes reluctantly wandered over to the table across from us. Fiona sat on the end, shooting me dark looks, her eyes near amber. She hadn't changed a bit. Lucinda, the Luna, sat beside her daughter, pouring herself a glass of water. My breath sucked in at the sight of my mother, sitting beside Michael with Jada and Laurance. Jada's eyes held rage like no other. Laurance however seemed to look smug, not looking in my direction but looking at the book in his hand. I tightened my hold on Aiden's hand when my eyes locked with Jonah's.

He gave me one of those cruel smirks he used to always give me when he was going to do something awful. It sent chills down my spine and I found my body angling more toward Aiden. Jonah didn't miss it and his grin widened. Aiden's hand tensed underneath mine and I remembered my promise. Looking up at him I noticed his eyes were fully amber. Gently I raised my hand and pressed it to his cheek and he looked down at me instantly.

"Stay with me," I mouthed at him, raising his hand and placing a kiss to it before letting it back down to my thigh. Taking a measured breath he nodded and I gave his hand a squeeze before looking back over to Idaho. Next to Jonah was Alpha Hess, and did he looked pissed. He gave me a look so cold that if he had any kind of magical powers he probably could have killed me.

I knew Heather and Zac were somewhere in the Idaho crowd but I couldn't bring myself to do anymore looking.

"All rise for the High Alpha's," a voice said from somewhere in the room. I got to my feet and noticed I was a bit shaky. Aiden's hand stayed in mine. "High Alpha Sinclair, High Alpha Forbes, High Alpha Sloan, High Alpha Conrad and High Alpha Radcliff."

As they walked in and took their seats I trembled. It was all happening now.

Chapter Twenty-Seven

"Please be seated," High Alpha Sinclair said. I noticed the room echoed enough you didn't even need a microphone. Not that werewolves would need one anyway. The room sat simultaneously and our ears were met with groans from chairs and shuffling of feet and bodies. "May I say again the rules of this hearing room are: No speaking unless being spoken to. No cursing or any kind of abusive language. We are here today to address the matter of Evelyn Lilith Wright vs The Idaho Pack in regards to the reports of her mistreatment and abuse during her seventeen years of residing there."

"There is no way of lying here today. Even if you are good at it we have a Reader assisting us with this case." I raised my brows as High Alpha Forbes gestured to a small dark woman in the corner of the room. I hadn't even noticed her. A Reader - well their name says it all - they read everything, body language, and your emotions. She would be able to tell in a split second if someone was lying. "We will first be calling Evelyn Lilith Wright of the Oregon Pack to the stand."

My eyes darted to Aiden's; I hadn't thought I'd be called up so early. Aiden gave me a small nod and I licked my dry lips, scraping my chair backward across the floor, cringing as the sound filled the room. I could feel my legs shaking as I walked toward the stand, avoiding all eye contact with Idaho. I climbed up the four steps and sat in the chair, feeling anxious as I got a full frontal view of the room before me. Turning my head I looked over at Aiden and I watched as he rubbed the mark I had given him. When I felt vibrations on my own I sighed in relief.

"Here is a copy of your statement," a young boy told me, handing me the ten page document. Placing it in front of me I looked toward the podium where each High Alpha was opening their copies. I took a breath and prepared myself. They read out every section of the statement, questioning me on the events once more and I had to go over the details out loud.

"...I'm in the school bathroom. Jonah, Zachary and Heather came in. They shoved me into the bathroom wall and slammed my head into the sink. They then pulled out a silver knife. Heather held me against the wall, pressing my head into the tiles. Jonah pulled down my pants and told me that because I was a half-blood we were going to tattoo my hip with an H. Taking my hand in his he forced me to cut myself with the knife, yelling at me or kicking me if I made any sound or movements. They laughed while I cried and screamed in pain. Once the wound was inflicted they left me on the floor."

High Alpha Forbes walked across the marble floor, her face as blank as a sheet of unused paper. She looked toward Idaho while talking to the rest of the room. "Supplied photo of said injury can be seen on the projector." The room was a mixture of murmurs and growls - the growls mostly from Aiden. I didn't look at the photo; I knew what it looked like after all. "Evelyn, you say that Jonah Hess, Heather Cooper and Zachary Keenan held you to a wall, tore your pants from your body, and carved with a silver knife a letter into your flesh?"

"Y-yes," I said, near fainting under her intense stare. The High Alpha looked over at the Reader who nodded her head slowly, as she had been whenever I'd been questioned. The court once again erupted in growl, causing High Alpha Sinclair to smash his wooden mallet on the bench.

"Moving on," High Alpha Forbes said loudly as the room quietened down.

"...Jonah Hess banned me from eating for one week. He said if I ate anything he would know and his punishment would be worse than I could imagine. I fainted in gym and the nurse gave me a biscuit. Jonah caught me the next day and beat me out the back of the school parking lot. Jonah banned me from eating often."

"I believe in your statement when you arrived in Oregon you weighed how much?" High Alpha Forbes asked me.

"I weighed eighty-eight pounds."

"What is your weight now?"

"One hundred and ten pounds," I uttered.

"I'd say you haven't been barred from eating am I right?" High Alpha Forbes asked me calmly. I shook my head at her. If anything the Luna tried forcing more food down my throat every day. "I've also got here Luna Claudia of Oregon's statement. It says in her own words: **'I was surprised and dismayed to see such a frail, withdrawn girl surrounded by a pack I once thought to be kind and decent. Evelyn has grown with us, but she had to be nurtured during her earlier time with us. I believe only recently we are starting to see the girl she really is.'** So, just for the Reader to affirm, Jonah Hess of Idaho ordered for you to starve yourself for a week?"

My eyes found themselves at their table and I near buckled under the glares and looks of ferociousness that came from them. Looking back at High Alpha Forbes I curled my hands into fists on my lap. "Yes he did."

It went on and on and on. When I was finally allowed off the stand I was sure that Idaho was ready to murder me and everyone was ready to murder Idaho.

"This hearing is adjourned until tomorrow morning at nine o'clock." High Alpha Forbes was the first to leave the room, followed by the rest of them. Everybody rose as they left before we departed through our own door, Idaho doing the same on the opposite side.

Once entering the door we were directed to, Aiden pulled me into his arms and I fell into them. I inhaled his scent, calming myself with it as I tried to regain my composure. That had been the longest two hours of my life.

"You did so well Evelyn," the Luna said behind me, taking me from Aiden and wrapping me in a hug. "Idaho doesn't have a leg to stand on." The door opened and Grace ran in along with my family who all took it in turns of passing me around and telling me how great I had done. Truthfully I just wanted Aiden.

"They were squirming!" Grace exclaimed. "I literally saw Alpha Hess squirm."

"I want to see Maria up there," my father murmured. "To try and explain why she let her child live in that environment."

"I would just like for it to be over," I whispered to myself. Feeling Aiden's arm go around my shoulder I closed my eyes and the room stopped its babbling. "She didn't read my whole statement. She left out the more…personal items."

"I believe she'd be saving those items for both Jonah and Zachary. They won't be able to lie. The Reader will pick it up. They've probably done it this way as well, to really show people how filthy Idaho is." The Alpha put his hand on my shoulder. "I'd much rather they ask him those questions, then ask you. It'd be better you were beside Aiden through this one."

True, I thought. Aiden would probably try and kill Jonah.

"At least we can get some food, wind down a little bit and then have an early night." The Luna said happily. "I believe all our meals are supplied."

"In that case I vote we had back to our hotel because I'm starving!" Grace took my hand as everyone began filtering out. "Really Evie, you did well." She kissed my cheek and then rushed off to where Sienna and Jasmine were walking.

Aiden and I followed, two guards at our flank which made me feel a little safer. I was not going to feel comfortable until we were back in Oregon, especially after putting Idaho on the chopping block in front of their allies and the High Alpha's. When the Reader detected no lies, the mood in the room shifted drastically. I could only imagine their reactions when they hear what Jonah did and how they'll feel when he couldn't deny it.

Arriving back at the hotel we were directed to another room where a table was set and piled high with food. I barely had an appetite but I made myself eat something, Aiden would pester me until I did.

The chatter over the dining table fell silent as Alpha Hudson and Beta Roan of Alaska entered. Beta Roan looked calm and relaxed, even shooting Sienna a wink. The Alpha looked as he always did, stern.

"Alpha Hudson," Alpha James acknowledged.

Alpha Hudson nodded at Alpha James before he looked to me. I think I shrunk five sizes when his steady gaze landed on me. Shaking his head he looked to Aiden. "If you ever wish to wipe Idaho out, I will help." With that he turned and left, leaving most of the table stunned while my father nodded with a grin.

"I like that one. Straight to the point."

"The scary thing is, he isn't joking," Grace murmured. "I suppose it's always a Plan B."

"No. Once this is done, it's done." Getting up from the table I left the room, heading upstairs where I could just go to my bed and ignore what was happening around me. It was bad enough we had to be here, any prolonged speech about Idaho was enough for me.

Entering the room I kicked off my shoes and turned on the lamp before throwing myself onto the bed. I just wanted to sleep, sleep this all away. I dreaded to think about what would be said on the stand tomorrow. I still couldn't understand why Idaho refused to acknowledge what they had done. There was no way they'd be able to lie. Did they really feel so justified in their treatment toward me that they simply believed I deserved what I got from them?

Rolling onto my side I stared out the open curtains, looking at all the different buildings in the compound and staring at each place with lights on. I knew not many lived within the compound but I still noticed people shuffling about through windows. I'd never given much thought to South Dakota. Well I'd never given much thought to werewolf packs in general as I had intended to live my life as far from them as possible. It struck me as odd how five Alpha's could live together peacefully the way they did without challenging the other. I wonder who chose South Dakota to be the 'in-charge' pack. Was it all self-elected or was their an actual process behind it? I found myself seriously lacking in pack knowledge and history.

I let my eyes drift close, sighing heavily as my body relaxed into the bed beneath me. I was going to sleep. Escape my mind for a while and allow myself to forget the problems I faced right now and what I would have to face tomorrow.

"Ev-ah-len of Oregon!" A cruel voice hissed into the marble room. "You are charging the Idaho Pack with mistreatment, are you not?" I shivered, the room felt icy cold and I found myself wearing tattered rags that barely clothed me. "Answer your High Alpha when he speaks to you!" Something lashed across my back and I cried out in pain, slumping forward on the marble countertop of the stand.

"Y-yes," I whispered, my lip quivering.

"You believe you did not deserve your treatment?" The voice asked in a child-like voice. "A half-breed didn't deserve their punishment?" I could hardly answer as the voice launched into its speech. "Where does our history as a race go - when a half-blooded werewolf can bring purebloods to a trial? This is why she needs to be eradicated. This is why we did what we did."

"What?" I gasped out.

Another lash.

"This is what happens to anyone who protects a half-blood!" Her voice shouted angrily, and it echoed through my ears and sent a tremble down my spine at its cold harshness. A light suddenly lit up an array of seated bodies before me and I screamed at the sight.

They'd all been executed, throats slashed in one clean cut. Horror rose through me as I saw my father and my family. How did I tell Stella that her husband had been killed? Then I saw my new family, the Alpha...the Luna...Grace. I cried out in pain when my eyes reached Aiden's lifeless body.

"No!"

"And this is what happens to half-bloods who try and shake up the system!" Cold hands latched around my throat and I clawed at them in fear as I felt my air supply tightening. I felt my eyes bulging, my vocal chords bruising. Looking up Jonah stood above me, a sinister evil expression on his face as he took my life with his own hands.

"Ah!" I cried as I sat up, my hands going to my throat.

"Evelyn?" Aiden was sitting beside me, his eyes scanning me for any injury. "You've been shouting in your sleep." Ignoring his words I threw my arms around his neck, hoping to shake the terrible nightmare from my mind. Aiden wasn't dead, neither were my family. It was just a dream and I was safe. I didn't know when I'd started crying, I only realized it when Aiden's shirt became wet beneath my cheek and I had to sniffle so I didn't put tear-boogers on him. "Hey Evelyn..." his voice was concerned but he didn't pull away which was a relief because I needed this closeness right now. I needed to know that he was here and I wasn't alone, that he wasn't going anywhere.

"I want to go home," I cried out, taking in a breath of air as I tried to calm myself.

"I know. So do I. Just one more day and we're out of here, it will all be over. This time tomorrow night it's going to be finished." He pulled back and I wiped my nose, looking up at him. "You have no idea how proud I am of you, how you handled yourself today up there, with them all looking at you. So many times I wanted to get up and kill all of them." He wiped my tears away and cupped my chin; I could feel it wobble in his hand. "Please stop crying," his voice was desperate and I knew it hurt him as well.

Closing my eyes I calmed myself down, before I looked back at Aiden. "I never want to do anything like this again."

"You'll never have to," he promised me, taking me in his arms and holding me until I fell asleep.

∞

"Heather Cooper you have come up a lot in the statement provided by Evelyn Wright. You've been accused of numerous attacks on her during her time in Idaho. What do you have to say about that?" High Alpha Forbes once again held my statement in her hands and I watched Heather up on the stand, looking perfectly groomed. She stared down toward me before looking back to the High Alpha. She didn't say a word. "Let me see if this will help jog your memory."

"...'I was sitting in my Math class, not really looking at anything when Heather came over, with her two friends. Her wolf was close to the surface and I wasn't sure what I had done. She grabbed my hair and yanked my head backward, shouting at me. She thought I had been looking at her new mate, Jonah. I would never willingly look at *him'*." The High Alpha emphasized the '*him*' before going on. "**She slammed my head down onto the desk, five times. I was near unconscious when she finally stopped. One of the girls raked their claws over my scalp. I have a scar at the edge of my forehead that runs into my hairline.'** Said scar may be seen on the projector." The image came up and I looked away, shaking my head.

"She was looking at my mate," Heather said out loud, her tone a terrible high pitched shout. "My new mate. Everyone in the pack knew she wanted Jonah." I made a face of disgust and I heard Grace snort loudly. "She acts all innocent, but no one knows what she's really like."

"So you don't deny using excessive force on someone whose strength does not match yours? You don't deny repeatedly bashing Evelyn Lilith Wrights head into the desk for presumably looking at your mate in a way you did not like?"

"No I don't," she said firmly.

"Do you deny being a part of the attack in the toilet where you helped restrain Evelyn Wright so Jonah Hess could cut her with the knife?" The High Alpha asked.

"No, I don't."

The High Alpha looked up from her papers a genuine frown on her face. "Miss Cooper you seem very nonchalant, considering your pack, the pack you're the future Luna of, is under scrutiny in such a way."

"I believe this whole thing is a waste of time," she said airily, inspecting her fingernails.

"How so?"

"No matter how this whole thing ends, Evelyn Wright deserved the treatment she got. She's a half-breed, she's nothing special and I cannot believe so many resources are being wasted on a trial over *her*. She's not one of us, she isn't a wolf, and we shouldn't even be here today. I'd do it all again."

The room housed a chorus of gasps and looks of disbelief were shared between people.

The High Alpha stared at her for a moment. "I see...how do you feel about the allegations she made in her statement that your mate and future pack Alpha, sexually assaulted her on numerous occasions?"

Heather's face turned red, not with embarrassment, but fury. "Excuse me?"

"...'**As I dressed for gym in the change room Jonah Hess, Zachary Keenan and Ben Maxwell entered the room. They proceeded to remove my clothing and force me to touch them. They touched me, roughly grabbing at my breasts. This was my punishment for talking back to Zachary Keenan.**'" High Alpha Forbes looked at Heather with raised brows while Aiden snarled so viciously beside me I thought he'd shift. High Alpha Forbes looked over to me, and gestured to the Reader. "Evelyn did Jonah Hess, Zachary Keenan and Ben Maxwell sexually assault you when you were readying for gym?"

"Yes," I whispered.

"What was that?"

Tightening my grip on Aiden's hand I looked at her. "Yes, they did," I said loudly.

High Alpha Forbes looked to the Reader who pursed her lips and nodded. The High Alpha then turned back to Heather. "Your mate sexually abused a girl. Are you comfortable with that?" Heather's face was blank as she absorbed the information and I almost felt bad for her. The High Alpha flicked back through some pages before nodding. "...'**I was getting myself ready for the gathering in Oregon. I was walking through the hallway when Jonah Hess stopped me. Removing my towel he proceeded to look at my bare body, not letting me leave until he was satisfied he no longer felt anything.**' I assume when Evelyn refers to Jonah no longer feeling anything, I believe you mean sexual attraction to your body?" She looked over at me and I nodded slowly.

"This is all lies," Heather hissed out.

"Are you telling me that our Reader is not sensing the truth and the lies?" The High Alpha asked Heather.

"I - I - This..."

"…'Jackie Morris held me down by my arms as Heather Cooper cut my hair from my head. This was punishment because she thought I wanted her mate…' tell me something Heather, are you threatened by Miss Wright?"

"No!" She spat out, staring at me with all the loathing she could muster.

"You seem to believe she wants your mate. Almost all the times you have attacked her, it was because you thought she wanted Jonah. Or maybe you feared Jonah wanted her more than you. How much energy must he have put into a woman that wasn't his mate? Did you feel neglected? Did you fear that maybe Jonah enjoyed Evelyn more than you?"

"Shut up!" Heather screeched.

"…'Heather Cooper broke my ribs because I looked in her direction.' For a future Luna you show some very violent qualities. Are you going to break everyone's ribs that look in your direction? Or just the people you think are beneath you?"

"I wish I killed you!" Heather shouted across the room at me.

Aiden stood up, his face red with anger as his eyes glowed amber. He slammed his fist down on the tabletop, snarling I quickly stood up, gripping his arm. "Aiden!"

"Order!" High Alpha Sinclair commanded as he slammed his own countertop.

I managed to get Aiden to sit but his breaths were uneven and he was trembling, like he was ready to shift.

"Heather Cooper you may leave the stand and this room. Benson, please escort her out." High Alpha Forbes folded her arms as Heather was taken by a burly looking man. Jonah growled as Heather was manhandled but one look from High Alpha Sinclair shut him up. "I'll now hand over to High Alpha Sloan. We now call Jonah Hess of Idaho to the stand."

The way he walked, all confident up to the stand had me bristling. He was just called a sexual abuser in front of an entire room full of wolves and he had the nerve to slide a slick grin my way. It made my skin crawl.

High Alpha Forbes took her seat and High Alpha Sloan made his way down to the floor, carrying with him his bundle of papers. He moved slower than Forbes but even for his age, he still looked like someone you didn't want to mess with. He stood in the center of the room, his thumb on his lip and he silently stared at Jonah, not even blinking.

Jonah looked around awkwardly, losing some of his cocky façade.

"Jonah Hess," his voice sounded gravelly, like any voice you'd expect to come out of a man his age. "Future Alpha of Idaho, a modest pack. You do well for yourselves?"

Jonah preened. "We do, sir."

"You have a good number of allies."

"Yes sir."

"Interesting." He moved over toward the podium. "How long do you feel Idaho will last once all this gets out? Word spreads. The future Alpha sexually abused a pack member. Beat a pack member on a number of occasions, tortured said pack member. Then continues to behave like he's done absolutely nothing wrong."

Jonah's face dropped slightly and his cheeks went red. "It's all lies."

"Oh really?" High Alpha Sloan raised his gray bushy brows. "I believe our Reader confirmed that she was telling the truth."

Jonah scoffed. "Evelyn is a good liar, just like her whore of a mother."

The room went silent; you could hear a pin drop as eyes darted from my mother, Jonah and High Alpha Sloan. "I believe you are referring to the elaborate lie Maria Wright told to cover up Evelyn Wright's conception."

"We all know Evelyn's mom slept around with a witch. We all know now that Evelyn seems to have some sort of power, according to what Maria said when she came back from visiting. What's to say Evelyn isn't using magic right now, and feeding the Reader energy to believe her?"

The High Alpha looked at the Reader who was frowning ferociously at Jonah. "My boy, if that is your only defense in the allegations against you, I hope you are ready to lose all your titles." Jonah's face paled. The High Alpha flipped open a booklet and began reading. "...'**Jonah Hess came to me in the library. He kissed me roughly and bit my lip, causing it to bleed. He grabbed me by the throat and told me he would kill me if I ever spoke about how he touched me.**'" He looked at Jonah and then looked over to me. "Evelyn, did Jonah threaten to kill you if you spoke of his actions?"

"Yes," I uttered. I looked over at the Idaho table to my mother, who wore a pained expression. Her eyes were stricken and she clutched the arms of chair. Luna Lucinda looked horrified as well, staring at her son like she didn't know who he was anymore.

The High Alpha looked to the Reader who nodded. "The thing about a Reader - and why any kind of supernatural being uses them - is because they are so pure, nothing can thwart them. Nothing can touch them. You can't lie to a Reader. If you could, this case would go nowhere. A lot of this statement is her word against all of yours. If we didn't have the Reader a lot of your offenses would be wiped off the table." Jonah glowered at the High Alpha. "The fact is the Reader senses truth in everything Evelyn has said. This means, your pack is in a whole lot of trouble."

"Disgusting pig!" Someone shouted from the audience.

"Silence!" High Alpha Sinclair ordered.

"Hide your women!" Another voice shouted.

"String him up by his testicles!"

"SILENCE!" The room went quiet as High Alpha Sinclair's voice boomed across the space.

"Jonah Hess you may leave the stand." High Alpha Sloan waved his hand in dismissal and I watched as the once confident walk, turned into an awkward shuffle back to his seat. "I would like to call Maria Wright of Idaho to the stand."

Aiden had been sitting tensely beside me the whole time, his jaw locking and unlocking. I ran my fingers up and down his arm, to soothe him and to help stop my mind from going into overdrive as my mother took to the stand.

"Maria Wright, the woman who started all of this." High Alpha Sloan put his hands behind his back. "You had sexual relations with a man who was not your mate."

"I did," she said quietly, her voice cracking. I looked over at Michael who was staring down at the table. His shoulders were tensed and I wondered how angry he had been when he first heard.

"You are aware in some packs there is a death penalty for such acts?"

"I am."

"But your old pack does not house that penalty."

"No." Her voice was strong as she looked down at High Alpha Sloan.

"It begs the question then, as to why you lied to your pack and mate that you were raped by a human and then kept the child in an environment you knew it would not be accepted." High Alpha Sloan walked to the center of the room. "Why did you lie?" My mother said nothing and High Alpha Sloan opened his booklet. "…'**My mother would show concern when I came home with any injuries. She would spend a bit more extra time with me, buy me something. I never told her all the things that happened to me, just the things I couldn't hide. I blamed her for a while, for not getting me out of there.**'" High Alpha Sloan walked over to the stand and firmly asked, "My question Maria is why you kept a half-blooded wolf in a pack that clearly despised her? Why you saw her come home with injuries and did nothing?"

"I was scared!" She said earnestly.

"Scared of what?"

"I didn't want to lose her. Evelyn…she…when I found out I was pregnant it was the best moment of my life. I loved her father, deeply. Having Evelyn allowed me to have a piece of him. I could never be with him, I couldn't stay with him. He was betrothed and I had a mate out there."

"You don't get best of both worlds Maria. You tried, but it ended up hurting the one person who was most important to you. The fact is you had a child outside of your relationship with your mate. Evelyn's life was ruined the moment she was conceived. Why not leave her with the father?"

"T-they wouldn't have allowed it!" She protested. "And how was I supposed to secretly carry and give birth without my pack knowing and the handing her off?"

"I believe if the situation had been explained your pack would have allowed you to carry to term before sending Evelyn away to her father." High Alpha Sloan raised his hand as my mother opened her mouth. "I have spoken to your previous pack, Maria. They confirmed my thoughts. Why did you keep Evelyn in a place where she was abused daily? Why did you not contact her father sooner?"

"She's my daughter," she whispered tearfully. "I couldn't lose her. She - she was my one link back to a life I could have had. A life where I chose who I was to be with. I had a choice."

"You regret finding your mate?" High Alpha Sloan asked, his eyebrows raised. I looked over at Michael and I felt sorry for him. Pain was etched on his features, and I almost thought I saw tears in his eyes.

"Never!" Mom whispered vehemently. "I love Michael with all my heart."

"You speak of your bond as a hindrance."

"It's not!" She near shouted.

"Maria I'm putting it down to the fact that your own selfish actions allowed your child to be emotionally and physically abused for the majority of her upbringing. In my eyes you are just as bad as the rest of her attackers. You enabled it. All so you could hold onto a scrap of your old life." High Alpha Sloan shook his head. "You're dismissed."

Mom gaped at him, before tucking her hair behind her ears and leaving the stand, walking solemnly back to her chair. I watched as Michael edged away from her when she sat.

"I now call Zachary Keenan of Idaho to the stand."

∞

My eyes were drooping by the time High Alpha Sloan had gone through Zachary and then Jackie Morris and a few other people I had mentioned in the report. None of them seemed to care to be there or showed any remorse, which didn't surprise me.

When Alpha Hess was called to the stand the room began murmuring and some colorful words were thrown out.

"Silence!" High Alpha Sinclair warned.

By this stage of the hearing, High Alpha Sloan had taken his seat and High Alpha Radcliff now questioned Alpha Hess. High Alpha Radcliff was a middle aged man. His skin was quite tan and he had a black moustache that kind of made him look like a Frenchman in my opinion. His brown eyes were hard as he regarded Alpha Hess and I wondered what he thought about all of this.

"Alpha Justin Hess of Idaho. I'm sure what you have heard here from the last few days has been quite new to your ears? I'd hope it is."

"There are a lot of things I was not aware of."

"There are things you were aware of however?" High Alpha Redcliff leafed through the statement in his hands and I squirmed a little in my seat. Alpha Hess looked over at me briefly before looking back at the High Alpha. "…'**Alpha Hess was aware of the fight in the pit against Heather. He came by to watch.**' You went to watch a weak pack member be beaten by a she wolf?"

"That's a lie."

High Alpha Redcliff raised his brows and turned to the Reader. She looked at Alpha Hess for a moment before shaking her head. "He's lying."

"Your son wasn't stupid enough to lie in front of the Reader. You're an Alpha and older. Why would you start lying now? Let me assure you, Alpha Hess of Idaho, the rest of this hearing is a formality. You and your pack are in a lot of trouble. The Reader has identified enough truth in Evelyn's statement to practically end your families reign as Alpha."

Alpha Hess spluttered, his eyes turning into slits as he looked over to me. I trembled as fear leaked into my body and my heart beat erratically. Aiden growled beside me and I quickly took hold of his hand and calmed him down, which in turn seemed to calm me.

"We have here all the doctor reports from Evelyn's visits to the pack clinic. The doctor in question is now no longer a part of your pack, requesting membership here if he handed over documents. He feared he would lose his life. Lose his life for telling the truth." High Alpha Radcliff shook his head before looking through the papers. "**…'Broken left leg, dislocated shoulder, broken nose, two black eyes, split lip, injuries causing scarring, evidence of depression, significant weight loss…'** we could be here for hours, sadly. This list of injuries goes on for about five pages."

Alpha Hess said nothing, but he looked like his teeth were clenched and I knew the doctor had made the right choice by asking for asylum here.

"There's interesting allegations against the way you run your pack in this statement. Evelyn was under the impression that once she reached eighteen she'd be either disposed of or turned loose." High Alpha Radcliff looked up from the statement toward Alpha Hess.

"We had discussed her leaving the Pack and living a human life. She wanted that."

"I can imagine in her case, to get herself out of Idaho and your pack would have been welcomed. I doubt the children who lost their parents felt that way though."

Alpha Hess seemed to pale and I watched as he swallowed thickly. "I beg your pardon?"

"**…'Any children that became orphaned in the Idaho Pack would be turned out. All pack links and scents would be taken from them so they were untraceable.'**"

The room's volume levels of hushed whispers exploded into shouts of rage and disgust. I yelped when someone threw what looked like their shoes straight at the Alpha's head. It was a mini victory when one actually struck the side of his face.

"Enough!" High Alpha Sinclair shouted.

"He should be hung!"

"Take away his titles!"

"Burn Idaho to the ground!" That came from Grace, her voice was unmistakable. It scared me at how many people cheered and agreed with her.

"I will empty this room if there is no order!" High Alpha Sinclair threatened. It took another minute but the noise decreased and High Alpha Radcliff looked towards me.

"Evelyn Wright, this is a massive allegation. I must ask aloud, for the benefit of the Reader: Did Alpha Hess of Idaho turn out orphaned children?" He looked toward the reader and my eyes went to Alpha Hess' who looked so murderous, so ready to strangle me that I nearly told a lie.

Aiden took my hands in his as I shook and I looked at him. He nodded at me, kissing my cheek and the shaking stopped. "It's okay."

Taking a breath I nodded and looked back at High Alpha Radcliffe. "Yes, he did."

"Children!"

"What!"

Looking around the room it was in a massive uproar and this time High Alpha Sinclair didn't try to stop the noise. He looked down the podium to Alpha Hess in disappointment and the scowl on his face did not look promising for the outcome of Idaho. Looking over to the Idaho table I noted they stared down at their hands and I knew they knew that they were finished.

"Perfect," Aiden murmured triumphantly under his breath. "You did it Evelyn!"

"They will get everything they deserve!" The Luna hissed, her lips tightly drawn as her eyes glowed amber.

High Alpha Radcliff growled in disgust. "We will be back in one hour with our verdict. Idaho is to be put under guard and not be permitted from leaving this room." He practically had to shout over the crowd and all the High Alpha's left the room. The crowd had to be escorted out and we made to leave as well.

"This isn't over Oregon. You have made a big mistake."

Alpha James snarled. "You are in no position to be throwing around threats, *Hess*." Alpha Hess growled at Alpha James for not using his full title. "I wouldn't threaten us. You'd have no allies to back you up by the looks of it. Or a pack, depending on the conclusion the High Alpha's come to. I wonder who they'll put in your stead as the new Alpha family."

Alpha Hess laughed but there was no humor in his tone. He looked right at me and hissed, "You should have stayed quiet. What happens now is all on you. Remember that."

"Don't speak to my mate, you disgusting, worthless *mutt*!" Aiden pulled me behind him before turning to face Alpha Hess with a murderous growl, his claws elongating from his hands. "So help me, I will end you right here."

"Aiden!" Alpha James grabbed his son's arm. "Leave it."

Aiden pulled me from the room then, growling like his wolf was trying to tear through his body. I was left with an ominous feeling, as the Alpha's threat washed over me, and I regretted ever coming here.

∞

"What we have heard here over the last two days has both been disturbing and horrific in some cases. Idaho has been accused of allowing sexual abuse, victimizing pack members, forcing orphan children to leave the pack and allowing their more powerful members to do as they please with no judgment or question." High Alpha Sinclair shook his head, pacing the floor as everyone listened on eagerly to what he was to pass down. "As a pack Idaho always held a favorable reputation. It worries us that so much abuse has occurred and nothing was said by any members. This leads us to believe all pack members are just as guilty as their leaders."

High Alpha Sloan spoke up then. "We believe that the current Idaho leadership is unfit to run the pack any longer. Both Alpha and Beta families are to be stood down from their positions in the Idaho pack." They all looked horrified, and members of Idaho who had come to watch looked at each other in shock, before crying out in anger.

"You can't do that!"

"Long live the Alpha Hess family!"

"This can't stand!"

"Silence!" High Alpha Sinclair snarled angrily. The room went deathly quiet but low growls could be heard among the attending Idaho wolves.

"Alpha Hess you have received a sentence of thirty years in our maximum prison, for abuse of your power as an Alpha and allowing such vile atrocities to occur under your watch."

"What!" Luna Lucinda screeched, but she was ignored. She looked stricken, like she was so confused as to why her mate was being put in a cell.

"Jonah Hess, Zachary Keenan you have both received fifteen years for physical and sexual abuse on Evelyn Lilith Wright of Oregon. Heather Cooper and Jackie Morris, you have both received eight and a half years for your involvement in Evelyn Lilith Wright's abuse." The room was in frantic murmurs as High Alpha Sinclair stared down the table of Idaho. Heather was a blubbering mess and Jonah had one arm around her, but he too looked ready to cry.

"You have two weeks to guide your pack until we find your replacement. Take that time to clear your houses and say your goodbyes." High Alpha Sinclair looked to the audience. "As a male wolf with a mate of my own, I understand how Aiden of Oregon would feel. He expressed his want to go straight in and tear Idaho down, but decided to go through the correct channels. This whole situation could have ended in a very messy bloodbath. We need to be reminded that all pack members, regardless of blood or gender, are living beings, with feelings and emotions. I hope that this hearing was an eye opener for those who have attended." He looked toward me, "I hope you are able to find peace, Evelyn and forget the atrocious attacks that you had to endure."

"They should get life in prison!" Someone called from the audience. "How can the poor girl just forget what happened to her? They'll walk free eventually but she will always be haunted by what happened to her!"

The room was alive with people agreeing loudly, shouting in favor of the speaker. Aiden nodded enthusiastically, especially when someone called out for the death penalty.

High Alpha Sinclair looked over at me with a solemn expression and I nodded at him. He was doing everything he could, and this had gone on long enough. No one needed to die over it. He closed his eyes and put his hands together.

"This case is dismissed."

Chapter Twenty-Eight

"THAT'S BETTER THAN I expected!" Alpha James said victoriously when we were back at our accommodation. "I wasn't expecting those sentences. All titles lost and jail time. The council actually came through."

"I couldn't be happier with the outcome!" Aiden declared with a big smile on his face. "They got more than what I thought they would and their name is forever tarnished. I can live with that!"

"I'm just glad it's over." Alpha Hess' threats were ringing in my mind but no one else seemed to pay any mind to it at all. It left me wondering if it all really was over, I felt nervous and sick and I felt I needed a really good night's sleep.

"Our flight leaves in three hours. We should get moving."

"We'll part ways at the airport, sadly." My father wrapped me in a warm embrace. "I'll be down in a week to celebrate an early Christmas with you."

"We'll all be there!" Sienna announced. "Mom will be dying to see you, my phone practically buzzed through the whole trial."

"Make sure you fill her in then," I said quietly.

"She basically has the whole gist of what happened. She's so happy for you!"

Alpha James had to go and say goodbye to the High Alpha's before we left, as well as the other Alpha's who attended. I wondered with a change of leadership if Idaho would retain its allies, or would they be too put off after everything they had heard today? Regardless that it was no longer the same Alpha family.

Michael, Mom, Luna Lucinda, Jada and Laurance hadn't been given any sentencing. Would they be turned out of Idaho or just given Omega ranks? It couldn't work; Michael's Beta side would want to take over. My mind was running with so many thoughts, mostly focusing on; what now?

"Let's go," Aiden murmured into my ear as he took my bag from me. Everyone began filtering out of the room and I nodded slowly at him. "I love you, you know?" He cupped my cheek and smiled softly. "You've done so well."

"Thanks for staying with me," I said softly. Leaning down he kissed my lips and I sighed, finally relaxing after days of stress. It felt good to just be wrapped up in his arms and feel safe, and having the knowledge that Idaho could never hurt me again helped a lot.

"Hey lovebirds, the van is here!" Grace called from the doorway.

Aiden let me go and I looked over at Grace who wriggled her eyebrows before leaving us. "Come on," he sighed, taking my hand.

I squinted as we came outside to the bright light and I was relieved not to see Idaho preparing their leave. I climbed in first, before Aiden followed after me and when he sat down I leant my head against his shoulder, finally feeling the first bit of relief in days.

But there was a niggling in the back of my mind that this wasn't over.

Saying goodbye at the airport to my family had been sad, but I knew they'd be back in a week or so, so I didn't let myself get too hung up about it. I gave each of them a hug and told Aliyah to message or call me if she needed to talk. My father held me for a long amount of time, telling me over and over how proud he was of me.

"I couldn't be more proud to have you as my daughter," he murmured.

"Thank you dad, that really means a lot." I gave him a shaky smile, willing the tears not to come, but thankfully he pulled me in for that very long hug.

By the time we were back in Oregon and pulling into the pack compound I felt so emotionally drained that I could probably sleep for a year. Too bad we had school tomorrow then. Life would go back to how it was, only this time my relationship with Aiden could get off to a proper start, there was nothing hanging over our heads anymore.

Everyone knew we were coming back today though, so the streets were bustling, people waving and cheering. I'd assume they'd been told the outcome of the trial.

"We should have a pack dinner tomorrow," the Luna announced. "A nice big celebration dinner! Aiden, you and Evelyn could also use it as your formal coming out party!"

"Ooh! Yes!" Grace agreed enthusiastically.

I looked at Aiden, feeling a bubble of excitement for the first time in a while. A coming out dinner? "That sounds good."

"I see great things happening from this point on," the Luna said optimistically. "Very great things."

"Christmas is literally like twenty-six days away!" Grace announced as we pulled up to the house.

"Oh Christmas, I don't even want to think about it."

Hannah and Lucy had been sitting on the front step but jumped up in excitement waving aggressively. I laughed at them and Aiden chuckled beside me. I felt relieved as I looked at the house; I was safely back in Oregon.

I had barely gotten out of the car when Hannah grabbed my arm and pulled me into her. "I'm so happy to see you! I have so much to tell you!"

"Congrats on the outcome Evie!" Lucy wrapped her arms around Hannah and me. "They won't know what's hit them in those jails."

"Grace!" We all turned around to see Trey running up the driveway. He looked well groomed - in fact since sort of being with Grace he dressed a lot nicer. I watched as her eyes briefly lit up before she put on her neutral expression.

"Hello Trey," she said simply.

"Nah. None of that bullshit, I haven't seen you in four days. You can go back to the cold shoulder after this." Grabbing her face in his hands he kissed her so passionately I had to look away. There was some throat clearing before he finally let her go and I looked to see a somewhat dazed expression on her face, accompanied by a pink tinge to her cheeks.

"As much as I love an outdoor gathering, I would prefer to go inside," the Alpha announced from behind us all. Everyone scurried to the side, letting him through along with the Luna.

"So you did Idaho in?" Trey asked with a grin, bumping my shoulder. "Wish I'd seen it."

"Should have seen their faces when the found out they had jail time." Aiden shook his head, looking amused. "But they actually tried to lie, like full on deny it."

"What?" Lucy demanded.

"They had a Reader there. There was no way out." Grace came out of her daze, grinning at Lucy. "They were toast!"

"Well I bet you're happy," Hannah said, beaming at me. "And here's why I'm happy." She cleared her throat and Lucy rolled her eyes. "Katherine has found her mate!" Everyone blinked at her, not sure why this news would make Hannah happy. I had a feeling though. "He has no titles and when she graduates she's going to live with him in Utah."

"Awesome!" Grace cheered. "Good things come in threes."

I was pretty happy; I just kept it on the inside. It bothered me that Katherine had contact with Jonah, now she wouldn't be living here much longer; it was comforting to know that my old life was fully disconnected.

"You're so quiet Evelyn!" Lucy exclaimed.

"I'm tired." I was exhausted; I really just wanted to curl up under my own sheets and sleep. I hadn't heard from my mother and I doubt I would. I'd probably caused a lot of problems for her now, not to mention she'd be finding a new place to relocate to. How would that go for her? Where would she end up? My stomach twisted anxiously. "I might take a nap."

"Okay, we'll catch up later!" Lucy promised. I gave a quick nod and headed inside, hearing Aiden's heavy steps behind me. I wanted nothing more than to just lay with him and sleep the last few days off. I went to his room, because his bed was comfier than mine and bigger.

"Are you okay?" Aiden murmured as he climbed into the bed after shutting the blinds. "You've been quiet since the sentence was given."

"I don't know," I shrugged. "I just…I'm not sure how I feel about it all. I guess - I guess I'm relieved…" I bit my lip and frowned, "I'm worried about what Alpha Hess said."

Aiden sighed behind me and hugged me tighter for a moment. "Don't worry about it. It was words from a pissed off wolf who just lost his titles and his home, not to mention really, the rest of his life."

"Yeah…I guess, but-"

"No buts." Aiden rolled me over to face him. "Come on Evelyn. No more worrying." He tucked a strand of hair behind my ear and grinned. "I mean, Idaho…all of that…it's all over. It's time to be happy. To live." He was right; I was getting way too hung up about all of his. Nodding my head quickly I smiled and put my hand on his cheek, taking his lips in mine.

Pulling back I nodded at him. "Okay."

"Alright?"

"Yes. You're right. It's time to live; I don't even want to hear their name anymore. I just want to be me, I want to be us and I want to enjoy the rest of my senior year. I want to enjoy our time together without having my mind clouded with all of that drama." I looked at him seriously, taking in the smile on his face and loving the way it reached his eyes. "I love you, I really do."

His eyes went a little amber before they flickered back to his brown, though the ring around his iris still flared slightly. "I love you too Evelyn."

I laughed and pushed his chest, feeling giddy from his words.

"Good."

∞

"It's cold out there!" Grace groaned as she came inside.

"Really?" I asked her in disbelief. "You're a full blooded werewolf and you're cold? How am I supposed to survive?"

"You won't. You're literally going to die once you step foot outside. Believe me."

Her words made me add another sweater under my black coat before I picked up my bag and wandered into Aiden's room. He was only just pulling himself out of bed, he looked beyond tired. "Please tell me it's like a snow day or something."

"Sadly no. It's just raining."

"I need more sleep," he face planted back on the bed and I felt bad for him. He hadn't finished his patrol until three in the morning.

"Maybe your dad could give you a break?" I suggested as I rifled through his draws for something for him to wear. "I mean you're in your senior year, you can't just ghost through it on four hours sleep every day."

"Yeah, but I'm learning the ropes. It's more than just running the border; I have to know the stuff he teaches me out there." He came up behind me and groggily rested his head on my shoulder.

I turned around and handed him some jeans, a shirt and black pull over cardigan. "You look exhausted Aiden, a week or two off wouldn't kill you. I feel bad."

"Why?" He asked with a frown.

"It's just…since my being here I'm sure I've created you enough drama on top of what you're already doing. Plus going to Ohio and South Dakota…I doubt your life's been easy these past few months." I looked down at my hands, hating having to say all this out loud.

"These past few months have been the best of my life Evelyn." I looked up and he smiled down at me. "I would do it all over again in a heartbeat." Kissing my forehead he left the room, probably to shower. I was left feeling all giddy and I nearly skipped downstairs. I stopped myself though; I didn't need Grace and her comments on that.

"Is he showering? We are going to be late," Grace muttered.

"Why don't you get Trey to give you a lift," I suggested lightly, trying to hold back my grin at the look she sent me. "I'm sure he'd jump at the opportunity."

"Cute, Evie."

"Girls, still here?" The Luna walked in and put on some coffee before turning to face us, also wearing a tired expression. Was I the only one sleeping around here? "You better hurry, you'll be late."

"King Aiden is having a shower," Grace told her. "We await the ride in his green chariot."

"Don't pick on your brother Grace; he had a very big night last night."

"Speaking of big nights, my mind link was *buzzing* for a decent three hours I'd say. What the heck was that? Clearly there was a private but not so private conversation going on…" Grace trailed off and I didn't catch what her mom said in reply because Aiden walked in the room, looking wide awake.

"Ready to go?" He asked a little too brightly.

I frowned but got my things all the same. "Yeah. Grace is dying to get to school." I looked over at Grace whose eyes were a little wide, and glazed over. I realized she and her mom were talking in mind link and I felt like I was intruding suddenly.

"Yep," Grace said suddenly. "Super excited for school and stuff, okay let's go."

In an instant I had been shuffled outside and I let out a gasp at the cold air that bit my skin. "Whoa!" I cried out. Racing to Aiden's truck I climbed in, switching on the heat as soon as he started the truck. "It's cold!"

Aiden's truck had only just gotten warm by the time we reached school and I was reluctant to get out and leave. Thankfully my next best option at staying warm was just sticking to Aiden, so I followed him to our usual gathering point, only the benches were wet and no one could sit down.

I nearly choked on air when I saw Trey kiss Grace - given it was a peck - but I nearly fell over when she smiled at him.

Clearly things were developing there.

"Don't you just love this weather," Hannah announced as she danced up to us. "Mm, it smells so good!" She was only wearing jeans and a sweater and I looked at her like she was crazy. "Evelyn, we're witches. We can warm ourselves up."

I looked at her blankly, not really registering her words. "Huh?"

She laughed and held out her hand. "Take my hand, I'll show you."

"It works. She warmed me up." Josh looked relaxed next to his tensely cold friends. Giving it a go I handed my hand to Hannah and I marveled at the instant heat radiating from her palm.

It traveled through my hands, up my arms, my neck, my face - everywhere, you get the picture. Suddenly I felt like it was too hot in my coat. When she gave me my hand back it tingled slightly but I felt comfortably warm. "Wow."

"It's pretty cool hey?"

The bell rang before I could ask her how to do it so I settled for taking Aiden's hand, hoping to share some warmth with him. I wanted him to feel as warm as I did, so his cheeks would go slightly red from the heat.

"Oh, yep. She did it," Aiden laughed.

"Really?" I asked in excitement, looking back at my hands in wonder.

Aiden rubbed his hands together happily. "Well I don't feel like I'm about to lose function in my arms anymore."

"Well that's unfair, why can't you do that stuff?" Grace shouted at Trey.

He looked at her in confusion. "I'm a werewolf?"

"Has the bell gone?" Lucy asked, running up to us, her eyes slightly red. It looked as if she had been crying and I looked over to Hannah who was frowning.

"Just then," Grace murmured. "Are you okay?"

"Yeah I-"

"It's always you seven. The bell has gone! Inside!" It was the grumpy old teacher as always. Right now I was more interested in why Lucy had been crying.

"It's alright, it doesn't matter." She gave me a quick look before giving Grace the same stare the Luna had. Something was definitely going on. We had to rush inside though and through all the classes I had with the girls, no one gave off any signs that anything major was wrong. I decided I'd break Hannah in art, if anyone would tell me something it'd be her.

So by the last period of the day I was well and truly fed up of the fake conversations and subject changing. The moment we sat down I turned to Hannah.

"Spill," I ordered. "What's going on and why is everyone acting so funky?"

"What do you mean?" She asked lamely. Her words were weak and I think even she knew she was going to tell me what I wanted to know. Giving her a look she sighed and ran her hand through her hair. "There have been like…a whole heap of rogue attacks lately."

"What?" I asked in shock.

"Since the trial…we've had heaps of rogue attacks. Nothing huge. Well until last night. The Alpha managed to catch fifteen out of a group of twenty, they're…" she lowered her voice, "they're in the jails being questioned."

I felt like I'd been punched in the stomach, Aiden hadn't said anything. It explained why he was so tired though. "Why was Lucy crying then?" I managed to say.

"Geoff was hurt last night, on a patrol. He's fine now, he healed. She was just worried."

I frowned and racked my brain. "Why didn't Aiden say anything - in fact, why didn't anyone say anything?"

"Everyone just felt you didn't need the drama. You've literally just come down from the trial. Everyone was a little worried about you. Plus your family is going to be here in like three days for your early Christmas thing. They just didn't want to worry you." Hannah waved her hands around like it was nothing. "It's nothing serious. We get rogues all the time, everyone does."

"In such large numbers though?" I asked nervously, not even listening to the teacher up the front of the room.

She made a face and sort of squinted. "Well…"

That did not make me feel good at all.

When I found Aiden leaning up against his truck so casually, I was angry. He should have told me, and he was acting like I still didn't know. This could be a serious thing and all that was running through my mind right now was Alpha Hess' threats on the stand. What if this was some sort of lead up. It was a little aggravating that Grace had gotten a lift home with Trey; I'd like to get her opinion on all of this as well.

As I got closer Aiden's expression changed and he looked at me knowingly. "I knew Hannah wouldn't be able to keep a secret."

"I'm not sure why it had to be a secret in the first place," I muttered, walking around him and hopping in the truck. It bothered me that everyone thought I was so mentally fragile that I couldn't handle hearing the news of a rogue attack. I'd taken out rogues by myself, I could handle hearing they'd been attacking us!

Aiden got in beside me, but didn't start the truck. Instead he faced me, his expression honest. "I didn't tell you for this reason; I can see the wheels turning in your head already."

"Are they turning correctly?" I asked him with raised eyebrows. "Are they connected to Idaho?"

He sighed and hung his head tiredly. "Some of them were paid by Idaho to scout the borders and return back with whatever information they had on how we patrolled. Some were along for the ride. We caught the majority."

"But some returned back."

"Yes. We've contacted the High Council and they said they would handle things on the Idaho end. Evelyn, look at me." I looked up and he must have seen the panic in my expression. "They can't do anything, they're rogues. Our borders are strong. It took only eight of our men to round up fifteen of them. That's a good thing. No one is getting through." He took my hand and brought it to his mouth. "Please don't worry about all this. Your family is coming up, enjoy it. Please don't let yourself get lost in all of this."

I nodded, trying to shake the weight from my shoulders. "Okay. Alright."

"Good," he sighed in relief. "Now onto something more important…" He looked nervous now, his neck was a little red and he rubbed the back of his head - his giveaway move. "I uh, was wondering if you'd uh…I was going to cook for you tonight. Mom and dad are going out and Grace has something on with Trey…"

I bit back my smile at his nervous rambling. Did he really expect me to say no? "That sounds great."

"Oh. Cool, okay." He nodded his head and I looked out the window. He was so confident, a lot of the time. Whenever he asked to do something with me it was as if he was genuinely terrified I was going to tell him no. He drove home with a smile on his face and I made sure to kiss his cheek before I got out of the truck and quickly ran up to Grace's room so she could help me pick something to wear.

∞

"Trust me, I wanted to tell you." Grace finished curling my hair, twisting it in places where it didn't sit right. "I was told not to. You worried everyone a little bit after the Idaho trial. You went too quiet."

"I know. I worry more when people keep things from me though," I gave her a look and she nodded.

"I know. Mom was being super obvious in the kitchen this morning. Woman has no tact." Standing me up she clapped her hands together. "Very nice, I am so good. I envy your cheekbones!"

I looked pretty. She had put me in a stretch cotton cream dress she owned that ended above my knees. It had a black satin belt around the middle that was tied in a delicate bow at the back. A little over dressed for dinner at home but it was still sort of a date. Even though I wasn't leaving the house she still stuffed me into tight and painful black tights before curling my hair and sweeping it over to one side.

"Thank you, I can't do this stuff."

"Well we're going to teach you step by step. I have to go to Trey's before my phone explodes. I'll see you later. Have a good night," she grinned at me and kissed my cheek before picking up her coat and bag and leaving the room.

Aiden's parents had left earlier and he'd been down in the kitchen for a while getting dinner sorted. Making my way downstairs my mouth watered at the smells coming from the kitchen, I didn't know Aiden knew how to cook but clearly he did.

Walking past the formal dining room my heart skipped a beat. He'd really set it up nicely. A white linen cloth had been draped over the table; and a couple of candles were surrounded by red rose petals. I walked into the kitchen with a big smile on my face, spying Aiden by the oven. He was dressed in nice black jeans and a blue button down, the cuffs and collar black. At least I had assumed right in the dressing up department.

"What's on the menu?" I asked lightly and he turned around, his eyes going up and down my body, taking it in.

"You look beautiful," he murmured after a moment. I wanted to tell him he looked beautiful too, but I don't think you can call guys beautiful right? "We're having Mexican."

"Very nice."

He laughed nervously. "Don't get too excited. It might be awful."

"I'm sure it will be fine." I walked into his open arms and took in his scent; this had to be my favorite place in the whole world. I was disappointed when the oven dinged and dinner was ready. I was hungry but I also didn't want to leave Aiden's arms.

He served up our plates and I fainted internally at the serving size he gave me before I followed him to the dining room. He even went as far as pulling my chair out for me. I poured us both a glass of water and inhaled the aromas of dinner with my mouth watering.

He watched me with worry as I lifted it to my mouth and I laughed. "You need to stop looking like you're about to poison me." I began chewing and decided it was amazing. I hadn't had Mexican in a long time, and I can't really remember what my mom's tasted like, but I decided Aiden's was the best I'd ever had. "It's great!"

"Really?" He asked nervously, picking up his own fork.

"Really, it's so nice. I can't lie, remember?"

"You could if you tried hard enough," he laughed.

We talked lightly over dinner, mainly about Aiden taking over as Alpha. He was worried that his father wanted him to take it over sooner rather than later, given all the duties he'd been doing had been upped on a larger scale. I hoped that didn't happen. I wanted to experience a decent amount of College with Aiden before taking over the pack. The idea worried me that Aiden and I would be in charge of such a large group of people. I'd never even owned a goldfish.

"How are you doing with your Grandma's journal?" Aiden asked as we cleared the table.

I laughed and grimaced. "I haven't read it. My father's going to kill me. He just needs to mark all the magic stuff; I do not need to read about my grandmother's *personal* life."

"So your siblings weren't overreacting then?"

"Absolutely not," I laughed, just thinking about the stuff written in that journal had me going red. Setting the plates on the countertop I turned to face Aiden, who was staring at me with an unreadable expression. I bit my lip and toyed with the hem of my dress nervously. "What?"

He came over to me, shaking his head. "Every time I look at you, I'm stunned by the fact that you're actually mine."

"Wow," I found myself saying. Way to make a girl go all warm and fuzzy.

"That's exactly what I think when I look at you." My heart was getting all fluttery and I could feel my cheeks going red. The way Aiden kissed me tonight was different from all the other times we'd ever kissed. There seemed to be a new kind of energy, an energy that had only just hit us. His hands were firm on my lower back and his lips were warm and persistent that had my brain going foggy as I tried to absorb all the sensations that ran through me.

His lips left mine and I jolted slightly when they connected with my neck, running down from my ear and to where his mark was, biting over it. My breath caught in my throat, I felt like my heart was beating in my ears as I let my head fall back, enjoying the feel of his lips worshiping the column of my neck.

Our lips found each other again and the way he kissed me, so softly...so tenderly. I had never felt more loved than I had right here in this moment in the kitchen. Pulling back I stared into his eyes, hoping to see what I was looking for.

"I want to mate," I said breathlessly.

His eyes widened slightly as he ran his thumb across my swollen lips. "Are you sure? We can wait, I can wait..."

"I'm sure," I assured him. I had never felt more certain of anything in my life. I wanted to be his in every way possible. "Make love to me Aiden."

I must have thrown him; I don't think he'd really been expecting it. It didn't take long though, after I had placed a reassuring kiss to his lips that his brain seemed to kick into action. We were quick to get up to his room, but things slowed from there.

The only light in the room was the lamp in the corner which was pretty dim. I was happy for that. The idea of Aiden seeing me fully exposed was a little nerve-wracking. Being in your most vulnerable state - it was normal to be nervous right?

He was gentle the whole time. He didn't tug or rip at my clothes; in fact he really seemed to take his time, as if he was savoring the moment. Soon it was just skin against skin. Warm flesh, and excited breaths, mingling in the quiet room.

Later on that night, lying atop his chest as he slept peacefully beneath me I knew, I would never forget this night.

Chapter Twenty-Nine

STANDING UNDER THE SHOWER THE next morning I decided I definitely felt different. It was a big step we had taken last night and I was glad I had. It had been amazing, it was easy to slip back into those memories and relive it all over again. I was a little unsure about going downstairs though; Aiden's scent would be more prominent now than ever before.

I could only imagine Grace's comments; hopefully people would have some tact and just not say anything. Even the idea of going to school was making me nervous.

"Evelyn! Come on!" Grace bashed on the bathroom door and I hurriedly shut off the shower, pulling the towel off the screen door and drying off. Wrapping it around me tightly I pulled open the door to see a grinning Grace with her toothbrush. "Thank you."

I gave her a shy smile and hurried off to my bedroom and she let out loud laughter after me. Closing the door I realized I hadn't slept in here for a while. There were however clothes everywhere, which helped with finding something to wear. It was still too cold for anything but jeans and sweaters so I put one of them on, picking up my favorite black coat. I left my hair in the bun I'd put it in before my shower, deciding it looked decent enough.

I made my way downstairs when I noted Aiden's room was empty. I noticed all the doors to the guest rooms were open so I assumed the Luna was getting the rooms ready for when my family arrived in two days.

"Oh Evelyn good, here have some breakfast. I've made bacon and eggs!" The Luna smiled at me, making no indication that she knew what occurred last night, even though she did know. I appreciated it. I was a little disappointed not to see

Aiden in the kitchen but I sat down and accepted my plate. "I bet you're looking forward to seeing your father again."

I smiled at her, relaxing. "I really am, this is my first Christmas with him, even if it's not really Christmas. I'll take what I can get."

"It's very exciting!" She smiled at me but it faltered and I knew she was going to bring up last night. "Um, Evelyn?" I looked at her, not trusting my voice. "Today will be a little different for you…uh…the other wolves will be able to smell your scent change." She cleared her throat and rearranged the folded tea towels on the benchtop. "Don't get too weirded out by all the looks, it's just, with you and Aiden having officially mated, your spot in this pack is pretty much cemented. You're the future Luna."

I could feel my neck getting hot and my ears burnt a little, I nodded though. "Uh okay."

"Okay good!" She seemed relieved. "Aiden is just in with his father, he's had breakfast already."

"Okay."

"Evelyn?" She asked again hesitantly and I felt embarrassment rising just by the tone in her voice. I squinted up at her, wishing my hair was down so I could hide behind it. "Um, I know you kids are smart, uh, I was just wondering…you used protection?"

"Oh…yeah, definitely." I did not need any more drama in my life, thank you very much.

"Okay good, well, inquisition over then." She laughed awkwardly before slowly gliding out of the kitchen. I dropped my head on the bench.

The Luna was right about the looks people gave me in school. So many people smiled in my direction, some even bowed their heads. By the time I made it to training in the afternoon I was feeling slightly overwhelmed and a little exposed.

Hannah laughed at my discomfort all day, but she did give me a comforting pat on the back as we briskly walked to the training compound. "It sucks hey? Everyone knowing?"

"It's awful."

"They'll get over it, trust me. It took about a week for them to not care anymore when Josh and I mated. Give yours about two weeks and you'll be fine. People are just excited that the pack is secure now. Wait until Grace mates, she won't be laughing then."

Grace rolled her eyes, flicking her hair. "That's not going to happen for a very long time. He still needs to prove himself."

"What are you going to do next? Get him to roll over and play dead?" Lucy sounded frustrated and I raised my brows in surprise.

"No, but he-"

"Grace, we all know what an idiot he was. The fact is he stopped being an idiot the moment he realized what you were to him. Give the guy a break, there's only so much he can take before he might just give up." Lucy walked off to set herself up and I looked at Grace who seemed to be lost in thought.

A hand clapped down on my shoulder and I turned to see Sharon, beaming at me. "Good job Evelyn, I'm happy for you and Aiden." She had been the only one beside the Luna to outright congratulate me, everyone else had just stared. "Hope you didn't use all your energy because today is going to be killer."

Cue being mortified. "Uh n-no, I uh…" My stammered words were met with her laughter before she went to the front of the room, shouting for everyone to get together. "Oh my God," I murmured under my breath as I waited for my cheeks to cool.

"Two weeks sweetheart," Hannah reminded me.

"Kill me," I whined.

By the time we were finished with training my muscles ached and I was wiped. Hannah however still wanted to practice more magic, though I doubted I even had the energy for it. I trudged after her sourly though, knowing it was important and she was the only one in the pack remotely capable of teaching me new things.

"It's important to keep using it, you need to make it like, muscle memory. You still doubt yourself at times and you need to know that you can do it. Which you can, you've proved it. So just keep doing things. Just play around with it."

"I never know what to do," I protested, folding my arms. "I feel like if I don't have to use it, then I shouldn't."

Hannah made a face. "But what if you have to use it and you spend too much time thinking about if you can actually do what you want to do, but if you had trained you wouldn't have had to have thought about what you had to do?"

"Huh?"

"Practice is important!" She said sternly.

"Okay!" I raised my hands in defense and closed my eyes. What could I do? Anything apparently, but that was such a broad word, anything. Could I really do anything? I wasn't allowed to bring things back to life anymore, so clearly that wasn't anything. What else could impact my health? What would make me stretch myself too far?

I settled on warming myself as Hannah had done the other morning. It seemed like a small enough task to start myself off with. I started with my toes, imagining they were warm and toasty and then that heat, rolling its way up my legs, my thighs and to my stomach - it was an instant that my whole body felt like I was sitting beside a fire with a warm cup of cocoa.

Opening my eyes I beamed at Hannah who laughed. "Your eyes aren't even yellow, they're orange. Are you warm enough?"

"Any warmer and I'd be taking off clothes."

"Save that for Aiden," she joked.

I made a face and even stomped my foot. "Hannah!"

"Okay I'm sorry, I promise. I'm on your side." Hannah closed her eyes and began murmuring something under her breath. The wind picked up around us and she flashed her eyes open as leaves and twigs got caught in our hair.

"Was that really necessary?" I shouted over the roaring sounds. "Seriously you're going to create a tornado." The moment I pictured stillness in the air the wind stopped immediately and Hannah pouted at me.

"Killjoy." We both laughed although she broke off suddenly, her eyes growing wide. "We aren't alone," she told me, hurrying to my side. My blood ran cold in my veins and I felt my spine straighten. She smelt the air, her eyes glowing amber. "There's a rogue, maybe two...three?" She craned her neck and I noticed she was trying to hear. They had to be a far way off, but I realized the way she picked up the wind must have carried their scents closer. It felt like I was experiencing déjà vu.

"Link the others," I told her hurriedly, feeling my stomach clench. *"This isn't over..."* Alpha Hess' words rang in my paranoid mind and I whimpered in the back of my throat.

"They're here. Be ready," she warned me, her eyes wide. "You can handle yourself."

They looked hideous, worse than the ones in the forest that time. I could smell them and that was saying something. They smelt like a mixture of a dead animal and clothing that had been left in the washer for too long. Their fur was matted, caked with dry blood and dirt. My stomach turned at their aggressive stance, watching as their impressive canines came on full display as they snarled.

"You are in pack territory, rogues!" Hannah hissed at them, her claws slowly coming out. "I suggest you leave."

They looked at each other, like two girls were going to stop them. I had to remind myself to stay calm, that I was stronger. I had to give them the opportunity to leave first; I wasn't just going to hurt them.

"Thank the Goddess," Hannah whispered under her breath. The rogues began backing off and I realized why, as five wolves rushed past us. I fell into Hannah when one of their flanks knocked me, and she hurriedly steadied me.

It was mess, the rogues fought instantly and I spotted Aiden's wolf, roughly tugging on a rogues neck as it yelped and snarled, twisting this way and that trying to free itself. They weren't killing them, just injuring them enough so they couldn't escape.

It was horrific to watch, claws slashing flesh and bits of fur flying everywhere. The snarls would be imprinted in my mind forever, along with the vicious looks on their faces. The rogues gave up eventually, they were greatly outnumbered and when they were forced to shift I kept my eyes on Aiden as he shifted.

He checked on me straight away and the moment a rogue wolf whistled Aiden had walked over and planted his fist in his face. "I will kill you, if you want," Aiden threatened. "There's still two more of your filth here that we can question."

My hands had started shaking, probably from the shock of seeing such a confrontation. Another group of wolves came back to escort us back to the house and Aiden gave me a kiss on the forehead before taking the rogues in a different direction.

"Are you okay?" Hannah asked beside me, taking my hand.

"Y-yeah...I wasn't expecting that to h-happen."

"Neither was I. Thank the Goddess Aiden was running a patrol."

"Hannah?" I asked her quickly, my panic starting to go past simmering. She looked at me in concern. "This is another rogue attack. There's been too many. What if this is all because of what I did to Idaho?"

"Don't freak yourself out, Evelyn." The wolves walking beside us shared glances, and Hannah went on. "Oregon is stronger than you think."

"They managed to slip past patrolling wolves," I said, sweating slightly. If rogues could do that, couldn't Idaho? There'd be a lot of furious pack members over there, losing their Alpha family who they loved and respected. Maybe I was being silly, but I suddenly felt terrified that I'd put my new pack and home in grave danger.

∞

When my family arrived I was still worrying over the attacks, however there hadn't been any - or from what I'd heard there hadn't been any. After my freak out episode, I doubted the Alpha or Aiden wanted me knowing if anymore rogues had been caught on the border. I was however subjected to two guards if I left the house without Aiden, which was weird, so I didn't leave the house without Aiden.

Two of the packs fighters had gone to pick them up instead of Aiden and me, and secretly I panicked over that. If

Aiden and I couldn't even leave the compound to pick up my family then clearly something was wrong. I felt sick to my stomach; I just had a looming feeling that something awful was going to happen.

I was happy to see my father and I hugged him tightly, grateful he was here and I could talk to him some more about the magic. I was swept up by all my siblings who wanted to be shown around the pack properly, so I spent the day giving my family a guided tour - well Grace really guided it, I still didn't know my own way around too well.

We exchanged gifts and I was glad the Luna had taken me shopping; otherwise I would have shown up empty handed today. It was mostly just cute cliché things, none of us really knew each other that well, and we couldn't buy deep and meaningful gifts.

My father however did present me with the family crest; it was a brooch type piece of jewelry, the family name chiseled out in elegant cursive, and then the crest which was a diamond shaped shield that had two doves flying toward it.

"Thank you," I choked out, my eyes welling up.

Sienna was pleased with her leather-bound notebook I had given her; I'd gotten her name embossed on the front. I'd bought Jasmine a white gold necklace with an opal stone in the middle and she hugged me tightly. I got Gabriel, Phoenix and Christian a deodorant kit, which came with shampoos and sprays; because well, they were boys and what else do you get them?

"Are you trying to hint at something Evelyn?" Gabriel asked with a wink.

"Yeah, she is. You guys stink." Aliyah clipped them over the back of the head before unwrapping her present. It was an elegant white photo frame, fully carved out in intricate little patterns. She demanded we take a photo so she could put it inside.

I'd given Stella a lovely hat and scarf I had found and I gave my father a pack of cigars the Alpha had suggested I buy.

My gifts from the boys were a stuffed toy wolf that was nearly the size of me. They then superglued a wand to its paw and put a collar on its neck, engraving my name on it. I wasn't sure what to make of it, but it did score a few laughs. Sienna gave me a hand woven bracelet she'd made herself, Jasmine had gifted me with a diary and Aliyah gave me a tin of homemade toffee.

It was a relaxing day and I was glad the Luna was allowing me to take two days off school to spend it with my family. It almost felt like Christmas. We decorated the house together and put up the tree.

Grace made a gagging sound when Aiden kissed me under the mistletoe.

Later on that evening, my father and I were on the front porch, each holding a cup of cocoa and staring out into the street. He'd been marking the correct places in the diary and was instructing me sternly to read them. He questioned me about the rogue attacks when we were alone but I couldn't give him much information.

"I think they think I'm on the edge of a nervous breakdown," I laughed airily.

"Are you?" He asked me, his tone serious as he turned to face me on the porch.

"Maybe."

"You worried me after the trial. You didn't show much emotion."

I bit my lip and took another sip of my drink, trying to think of how to explain how I felt. Deep down I still wasn't too sure. "It was kind of numbing I guess, suddenly it was all over," I shrugged. "It just seemed like it was too easy."

He nodded. "I'm still somewhat concerned about that Alpha's threats, especially since you've told me about the increased rogue attacks."

"Everyone else thinks I'm overreacting."

"Maybe you are, they are closer to the situation. It bothers me though, that they didn't fill you in on it. Then again maybe you aren't overreacting and that's why they don't want to share the information with you." He looked at me seriously and told me, "This is why I want you to know how to use your magic, to its full extent without hurting yourself. You just always, always, have to be prepared for anything. In a life or death situation, there's no time to think if you can or can't do it, you just have to do it."

"That's basically what Hannah told me," I said quietly.

"You need to be careful Evelyn. You seem to be getting yourself into some dangerous situations. You haven't tried bringing anything back to life?" He frowned at me, daring me to say yes.

I shook my head and laughed. "No. I learnt the first time."

"Good. It's okay if you have two or more witches doing it, but just one? Insane." He set down our cups and I was surprised when he took my hands in his. "I'm only just starting to get to know my daughter, don't take yourself away from me, okay?"

I laughed and hugged him, feeling that little bit warmer like I did when I touched any of my family members. "I promise I'll work extra harder to keep myself alive."

"Good." He pulled back and cleared his throat and asked, "How is Aiden treating you?"

"Perfect like always," I smiled blissfully. "He's great."

"I like him, he's a good boy."

The front door swung open suddenly and I spilt my cocoa in fright as I looked at Aiden's wide eyed expression as he held my phone in his hands.

"Aiden?" I asked, his expression worrying. "Aiden what's wrong?"

He seemed speechless as he stared at the phone, the rest of our gathering coming up behind him all looking equally as stressed. "Your mother called," he bit out, his eyes beginning to glow amber and I watched as he crushed my phone in his hand. "Idaho is on their way with an army, angry pack members and rogues. They have one objective, they want you dead."

I felt like I'd been punched in the stomach. I wanted to throw up, I wanted to rewind back and pretend he'd never said that. "Oh my God," I breathed out in horror. "The High C-Council?"

"The pack turned on the guards watching the Alpha and Beta family. The High Council have been alerted and are on their way, but by the time they make it here I think it will be too late." The Alpha's expression was cold and violent. "There's only one way now, to solve Idaho once and for all."

"I'll get all the children and non-fighters to the bunker," the Luna said, her face stricken with fear.

"I'm fighting!" Grace growled. "I will make them wish they never stepped foot into the territory."

"Good. With the amount they're coming with we're going to need every available fighter we have." The Alpha looked at Cornelius, his expression solemn. "I am so sorry this is happening, while your family is here."

"Evelyn is my family. I'm glad I'm here. I too will join the fight, as will my family. Evelyn is this packs future Luna and she's our blood. This pack is our responsibility as well. Our magic should cut out half their numbers." His voice was strong and I saw no trace of fear in my father's eyes as he spoke to the Alpha.

"Evelyn you should help my mother," Aiden told me calmly, taking me in his arms.

"No I can help. I have powers too!" My voice was wobbly and I could hear the fear in it.

"I'm going to need help Evelyn. This is what the Luna's do; we look after the babies and the people who aren't fighting. It's our job to make sure they're safe. We have a very good fighting team and the added help of your family is going to throw Idaho off a little bit." The Luna smiled at me encouragingly. "It will be okay."

"We need to get moving. They're about fifteen minutes off according to Maria." The Alpha's eyes glazed over as did the Luna's and I watched as the streets suddenly started filling with pack members, women and children mostly.

"Aiden," I said softly, gripping his hands in mine, never feeling this terrified before in my life.

"It'll be okay, I promise." He took my face in his hands and hurriedly kissed my lips as his father and my family began moving out. "Stay with mom, okay?"

"Okay," I whispered weakly, not wanting to let go of his hands.

It was horrible, watching him walk away from me like that. I was terrified I was never going to see him again but suddenly the Luna pulled me into action, leading me toward the assembled group of women and children on the front lawn. I'd say there were about fifty kids under the age of thirteen, each individual or cluster accompanied by a mother. There were twenty older female wolves, who I knew wouldn't survive in a fight.

"Okay, everyone calmly follow me into the Alpha House and we will assemble in the bunker." It was a frantic amount of footsteps and I hung at the back to shut the front door. Panic was etched onto all their faces, some of the younger children didn't know what was happening but they still looked worried.

We were a tight fit in the basement and watched in surprise as the Luna pushed a cupboard away from the wall and began pushing numbers on a keypad. The door popped open and we were met with a creepy dark tunnel. A couple of the younger wolves pulled out their phones for torches while the Luna handed out actual torches.

"Everyone hold hands in single file. Evelyn come to the front, it's just a straight tunnel but at the end you have one right turn and you'll come to another door. Put in the numbers, two eight zero and four. Gather in that room. I'll stay at the back and lock this door."

My heart hammered in my chest as I came to the front and all eyes turned to me, all looking for guidance. The Luna gave me a small smile and I nodded, entering the tunnel and turning on my torch. It was cold and it felt damp down here, and all you could hear were our footsteps on the cement. I heard the door shut behind us and the tell-tale signs of digits being pressed into a keypad.

I was surprised when a small hand squeezed mine hard and I looked down to see a small blonde girl, biting her fist as we walked through the dark. My heart went out to her as I realized I was the reason so many people were in this situation right now.

Coming to the turn I shone my light on the keypad and keyed in the numbers the Luna had told me, briefly terrified that I had forgotten what they were. When the door popped open I breathed a small sigh of relief and walked in, stepping to the side and allowing everyone else to file in.

Looking around the room I noticed it was set up quite comfortably. There were couches and a play corner for the children, a fridge and a couple of cupboards that probably contained dry food and a tap with running water. Enough to keep people going for a while.

The Luna walked in behind me and sealed the door, rubbing my arm. "You did great Evelyn; you got our more vulnerable members to safety."

"Are they okay out there?" I asked her frantically, my eyes wide.

"So far everyone is okay. Idaho is about five minutes off. Their scents are in the air now." Her eyes were glazed over but she was still talking to me. I wish I was able to link with the pack; I could make sure Aiden was okay.

I began biting my fingernails, feeling claustrophobic in here as well as fearful that the one person who meant so much in my life was about to be ripped away by the group of people that caused me so much grief already.

I could help them, I could defend myself. I had done it before. I needed to be up there, out there helping, alongside my family and my mate. My father himself said I had more magical ability than my siblings.

"I want to be out there," I blurted out to the Luna as quietly as possible. Her eyes came back to normal color as she looked at me, shocked. "I can't stay down here; I need to be out there."

"Evelyn, it is too dangerous. They have one goal here today and that is killing you."

"They'll kill everyone to find me," I protested, my panic rising. "I can - I can kill them."

She shook her head and rubbed her face, taking my shoulders in her hands. "Evelyn, you can barely say out loud you can kill them. You couldn't hurt anyone."

I swallowed the lump in my throat and squared my shoulders. "I will kill anyone who tries to take my mate or my new life from me. I will defend this pack."

"Evelyn I can't let you go out there."

I liked the Luna I really did, but with each passing second Idaho came closer and closer and my panic rose higher and higher. I needed to be out there, with Aiden. I had to help them. Looking around the room at all the panicked faces and even at the Luna's worried face I knew I was making the situation worse.

"Okay," I told her softly, a new idea forming in my head. Going over to a lone seat I sat down and put my head in my hands, hoping to look distraught. Taking a breath I closed my eyes and imagined everyone in the room was happily asleep, that they wouldn't wake up until I woke them. I yawned myself which was met by other yawns and tired groans.

Lifting my head from my hands slowly I looked around guiltily. Everyone was out cold. The Luna was slumped against the door and I quickly went to her side, gently pushing her backwards onto the couch. "I'm sorry," I whispered.

Taking a breath I punched in the keys on the keypad and let myself out, making sure it was properly sealed. To further their protection, now that they were asleep, I sealed the door with my magic, making sure no one would be able to get through. It surprised me to see a shimmering orb over the door, kind of like a curtain. I got a nasty shock when I touched it and I yanked my hand back quickly, scowling.

At least it works, I thought grimly.

Creating a flame in my hand as a torch I bolted flat tack down the passage way, hating the sound my feet made on the concrete. I felt like any enemy out there right now would be able to hear me and I would be done for the moment I entered the basement.

I realized I had no idea what the pin was to get out so I pushed the door open with a bolt of light, surprising myself at just how well my magic seemed to be working. Maybe it was the adrenaline or my intense need to be out there to help

Aiden. I was only growing more confident in it; glad I was able to use my magic under pressure.

Sealing that door with another nasty spell and not touching it this time, I turned around and shut off the flame in my hand and began to become more careful. I had to be so careful now. My sense of smell was as good as a human. I kept my hands ready to strike, also remembering that I had to be careful not to accidently injure an Oregon member.

It would be easy to spot the Idaho wolves, I'd seen them all growing up from my window. Plus an Oregon wolf wouldn't try attack me so that was another thing that would let me know they were friend and not foe.

The house that had only an hour ago been warm and full of laughter now seemed cold and eerie, like it had been deserted for years. I half expected to see cobwebs and leaves blowing across the polished wooden floor.

My hands were shaking and my mind was all over the place as I crept over to the side window near the front door, checking to see if the streets were clear. I felt like I could feel all the blood rushing in my veins, every hair stood up on my neck and every quiver of every limb resounded through my body violently.

I had to keep to the shadows, and I was glad I was wearing that horrible black dress Grace had put me in. Finally kicking off the stupid black pumps I pulled down the sleeves off the dress and took a breath of air before slowly opening the front door and stepping onto the porch. This was it, I was going into all of this and I had to be ready.

A cluster of howling and snarls in the distance had me near jumping out of my skin and I dove off the porch and ran across the yard to a tree, staring up and down the street.

A strangled screech left my lips when a big arm wrapped itself around my throat. My mind went into overdrive as I struggled violently and the arm became tighter. I ordered myself to focus, to calm myself.

"Don't kill her," a voice ordered. "They want her alive."

"I want to kill her though!" the voice snarled viciously in my ear. "I'm sick of taking orders from those purebred puppies. This one is mine," his hand roughly grabbed my thigh and my stomach turned. "We could have some fun with her before we top her off, come on Billy."

I screamed in terror and raised my hand to the arm around my neck. A searing heat came out of my hands and the rogue dropped me, shouting and cursing in agony. The smell of cooked flesh hit my nostrils and I recoiled in horror and disgust as bits of his skin were stuck on my palm.

"Ah! Billy help!" He yelled in agony, and I watched as the flesh continued to melt off his arm while he writhed around in pain. The other man, *Billy,* took one look at me with an open mouth and then back down at his friend before shaking his head with wide eyes and sprinting away. Raising my hand I held it in his direction and narrowed my eyes on his skull. Melt the brain, I thought to myself. Dad said you could do it, do it. "Kill her Billy!"

Do it, a voice whispered in my head angelically.

"Ah!" Billy cried in agony, his sprint faltering as he stumbled to the floor, clutching his skull. I scared myself as I watched his nose started bleeding, and then blood came out of his eyes and ears. His face seemed to steam and I watched in fascination at the mess I was causing.

It was a little sick actually.

It was as if his head exploded, because with a steaming popping sound it was gone and I found myself bringing up the contents of stomach when my eyes hit the headless corps.

The other rogue was still shouting and crying in pain and as I stopped heaving I turned to face him, nearly vomiting again when I realized his skin was now melting off his whole body. He was beyond words and he was dying, slowly and painfully. I couldn't let him suffer like that. Closing my eyes I snapped his neck with my mind.

The area was suddenly silent but it smelt like death and my lip quivered as I tried not to cry. I had just brutally killed two men. Their flesh and blood was stuck to my clothing, and my mouth watered in the way it does before you puke.

I breathed in deeply through my nose, trying to calm myself as I heard howling and growls in the distance and I realized it was in the direction of the training compound. I took off at a sprint, each growl and snarl echoing through my ears. My feet just seemed to get lighter and I felt like I was flying, like I was one with the wind.

I felt a searing pain in my leg and I screamed in anguish as a wolf bit into my flesh. It pulled me to the ground like a ragdoll, ripping into my leg like it was a chew toy. I hit my head on the road, grazing my knees and elbows. All I could register was pain and I knew I had to try and do something before it took my whole leg off. I wouldn't be able to save it then. Twisting my wrist I snapped the wolf's neck and all the pressure on my leg was released as I hurriedly put my hands on it.

Heal, I chanted in my mind. I pictured the flesh all intact, no lost blood. The skin repaired itself but there was still slight pain, but I was able to stumble to my feet, shakily. I looked down at the once wolf, which turned out to be a young girl, her human form naked on the floor. She couldn't have been any older than thirteen and as I studied her closer I realized who she was.

Annie Simpson. Her usually pale skin was now incredibly pale as her life left her body and I put my hand over my mouth in horror as I stared down at the young girl. So young. Idaho would feel her death the moment the link died.

I had to keep going, I could think about all this later. The emotion could get the better of me later, I had to find Aiden and my pack and protect them.

It was carnage when I reached the training field. Wolves ripped into each other, going in for the kill each time. No one was messing around. There were lifeless bodies everywhere and my blood seemed to run cold as I recognized faces of Oregon and Idaho members.

I was terrified I'd see the faces of my family or…or Aiden.

"Take that you fury little shit!" I heard a voice scream and I whipped around to see Aliyah, twirling a blue orb in her hands, electricity seemed to be zapping out of it. "Let me light you up!" She hurled it into a cluster of wolves, which thankfully were not Oregon wolves. I wondered how she had been told -

how my family had been told to distinguish between the enemy and us.

I ran to her side, clamping my hand down on her arm. "Aliyah!"

"Evelyn! What in Morgana's name are you doing out here - what is that on you?" She wrinkled her nose and I watched as her electric ball of light seemed to zap the wolves until they cooked.

"It's flesh. Where's Aiden?" I asked her hurriedly.

"Somewhere in all of that. We've all been stationed on the outside, just stay here with me for now! Some of the wolves haven't even shifted."

"I know," I panted. "I've dealt with two that were in human form."

"They're faster in their human form. Jasmine's already been in a scuffle, Phoenix nearly got strangled to death!" Aliyah looked at me worriedly and I wondered how she was able to take her eyes off the wolves ripping into each other. "You seriously smell like death, we need to get up that tree I wasn't even supposed to come down!" Taking my hand she led me toward a thick tree and in one swing she bounced to the first, second and third branch, perching herself.

Here goes, I thought doubtfully. My climb up was less graceful and I got a number of splinters in my hands, landing with a heave on her branch. Shaking it off I looked out onto the field, it looked worse from up here.

"There's dad!" I shouted, pointing toward the outer field. My eyes widened as I watched him spread his arms out horizontally, light coming from both palms. Bringing his hands together he clapped and numerous wolves fell to the floor, either from the impact or the aftermath of air that rushed around them.

"I'm going down to help," I told Aliyah. "Stay up here, okay? Please don't go down again."

"Are you sure? Evelyn it's crazy in there!" She looked at me, terror finally entering her eyes. "Evelyn, seriously be careful."

"Just…just cover me okay?" Swallowing the nervous lump in my throat I gave her a quick hug before checking to see if the ground below was clear, before jumping my way down on each branch - much more graceful than I had the first time.

I had only been on the ground for a minute when a fury object knocked me over, its claws raking down my chest. I screamed in agony, and I could feel the blood soaking my clothes. I heard Aliyah's scream and I gripped the wolf's fur, allowing hot flame to come out of my hands. The wolf lit up quickly but I didn't take time to watch, or listen to its yelps of pain as it burnt alive. I went to work on healing the wounds on my chest but I could feel my energy seeping away. I needed to avoid getting injured, I couldn't keep healing myself.

The amount of rogues scared me, the group Idaho had brought seemed larger than the pack and I had trouble spotting a wolf that was actually one of us. A fury head nudged me from behind and I turned quickly my arms raised, ready to strike.

The wolf's eyes widened and I watched as its form shimmered, and Hannah appeared, naked and dirty. "Easy!"

"You scared me!"

She looked me over, "I'm not sure I want to know. Listen, a lot of the wolves are shifting. Their injuries are too heavy to handle in wolf form. We are getting hammered Evelyn; seriously, Idaho brought at least eighty rogues and their entire pack. The entire pack, children included."

"What?" I demanded, feeling sick.

"You can do something," she told me frantically.

"What can I do?"

"Make everyone human. Our wolves are hammered they can't cope with the numbers, at least in human form they have renewed energy, and Idaho and the rogues will all be human too. Our hand to hand combat is exceptional, better than sloppy rogues. I'd told Oregon to be ready for it, and by the way, Aiden is angry you're out here so be prepared for a speech later." Hannah grabbed me by the shoulders and looked at me firmly in the eye. "Just think it Evelyn and it will be done."

"Oh my God, okay. Okay." Looking out the crowd of wolves I saw humans appearing, struggling to fight the fury beasts. It took one thought, and it surprised me. Wolves fell to their faces stunned as they looked down at themselves, realizing they were human. Some even tried shifting, growling ferociously when they couldn't.

The Oregon wolves reacted quickly, having been ready for it. I finally spotted people I knew and I saw Lucy's golden hair, she looked quite angelic as she ran through the crowd, until she jumped on someone's back and snapped their neck.

"Come on, let's get in there! Remember everything Aiden and training taught you. I'm right behind you!" Hannah pushed me forward and with a leap of faith I ran, right into the warzone.

The air of the area was terrifying. You suddenly get close to so many auras, so much energy bouncing off different people and you absorb it, and it fuels you. Fear and anger were the most prominent as well as determination.

There were burning carcasses thanks to the strikes from my family, human forms with slashes and deep injuries, lifeless on the floor. But many fought on. If it had been any other situation it would have been funny to watch grown men fight each other naked.

My heart leapt into my throat and my stomach near fell out of place when Heather stepped into my path, her face contorted into a vicious look of hate, but also triumph. There were no words, she leapt instantly and I was ready, bracing my feet as I raised my hand to her airborne form, grabbing her by the throat. Well I imagined I was grabbing her by the throat, she hung in the air like an invisible noose was wrapped around her neck. I dragged her to the floor, slamming her into the dirt roughly, but suddenly a real hand grabbed me by the throat and lifted me up.

I looked into Jonah's cold, hateful eyes and suddenly it felt like it was just me and him in this clearing. Two people with a massive score to settle, but he had the upper hand. Because around him old fears would come floating back, old trauma and wounds that would make me freeze and lose all ability to protect myself.

Jonah had a mental hold over me so strong that it made me forget who I was.

"You make it too easy, *half-breed*." His foot connected with my stomach my back and my thigh, each kick so rough that had me arch in pain. "I know my father wanted you alive, but he really isn't Alpha anymore so his word means nothing." His hands went back to my throat, squeezing hard and I gasped for air, clawing at his hands like I was a weak, frail human, that I hadn't just melted someone's flesh off fifteen minutes ago when he did the same thing.

Suddenly a body impacted with Jonah's and I had air back in my lungs. I sat up frantically, my body shaking like a leaf. Aiden and Jonah threw hard punches and I winced every time Aiden got hit, noticing lacerations down his legs and arms, that were healing slowly but not fast enough for my liking.

"You think you can touch my mate!" Aiden growled loudly, launching himself at Jonah as they both fell to the floor, each one trying to get the upper hand. It was terrible to watch and I wanted to step in but Hannah held me back, suddenly reappearing though with a bloody nose and what looked to be a dislocated shoulder.

"Evelyn!" I spun around to see my father, running towards me. "Why are you here?"

I shook my head frantically and quickly turned back around, ignoring his question. Aiden's eyes were burning with rage as he strangled Jonah, the muscles in his arms were bulging and his eyes glowed such a violent amber, that I knew his wolf was in absolute control.

I screamed in horror when two men came up behind him, ripping him off Jonah and then it all happened so fast. So fast I didn't have any time to react. Jonah leapt up instantly as the two men held Aiden's arms out. With a rough tug they both pulled and I screeched in horror as his arms were dislocated, the pain mirroring in my own. Aiden's moan of anguish hit me hard and I fell to my knees, dizzy and at a loss for what I could do. My brain couldn't function. Jonah raked his claws down Aiden's chest and the wound seemed to blister instantly, like they had been laced in poison.

And then the worst thing that could ever happen occurred before my eyes. In one swift motion Jonah snapped Aiden's neck and he fell lifeless to the floor, his eyes open and unmoving.

My body seemed to grow cold and pain raced through my veins like fire. I felt lost, I felt like I was drowning, my heart was beating so fast and my words came out garbled and panicked. It was then as I stared with heartbreak at my dead mate that I realized it.

I was feeling the start of a half-life.

Chapter Thirty

AGONY RIPPED THROUGH ME AS I screamed at Aiden's lifeless body. Not Aiden, not Aiden. He's not dead, I chanted to myself. He's not dead! Oh my God, I can't breathe. I sucked in air, raking my fingers through the dirt beneath me as I crawled towards him, my body a wave of grief and pain.

Aiden.

"Aiden!" I cried, falling onto his chest, shaking his body. "Aiden! Wake up! Aiden!" I threw my head back and let out a sorrowful scream which seemed to silence the field. Howls of devastation washed through the pack as they felt his links falling away. No, it can't. My hands trembled as I ran them over his face, leaning my forehead against his and crying.

He's not dead, he's not dead.

"Aiden!" I heard the Alpha's voice, broken and tearful.

The field seemed to ignite then, the fighting resumed, more ferociously than before. I zoned out, focusing on the lifeless body of my mate, the only person I loved so deeply. My head was dizzy as I cried into his chest, my eyes lighting up when flashes of light were shot out from my family, keeping our area clear.

"My mate!" I cried out, screaming as a hot rage filled my body. This wasn't fair, it wasn't going to happen. I had come so far. Ignoring what my father had warned me I placed my hands over his heart, and closed my eyes, trying to hold back my agony as I concentrated on bringing him back. I knew I could possibly die, but I couldn't let him die.

"Evelyn, no!" My father shouted at me, grabbing my arms.

I shook him off with a flick of my wrist and he fell to the floor. "Don't! I don't have much time, he's getting colder."

"Evelyn you can't!"

"Not by myself. You can help me." I looked up at him, my heart in my throat. "P-please Dad, I can't lose him."

He looked resigned and I knew I would feel guilty later about asking him. For now I was feeling selfish and distraught, I was beyond reasoning with. I wanted my mate and I didn't care how I got him back. If I had the power then I would use it. He reluctantly dropped to his knees and placed his hands over mine and he took a deep breath.

Sienna, Jasmine, Aliyah and Stella came to stand behind us and a jolt of energy raced through my body as they placed their palms on us. "This should help you two a bit," Stella whispered to me, her eyes glistening. Phoenix and Gabriel stood in front of us, blasting anyone who so much as came in our direction.

"Time to focus Evelyn, we have to bring back two beings, not just one." I nodded at my father, determination crossing my features. I would bring Aiden back. It would happen; it had to happen, because without him, there was no life. I'd lived a half-life too long to live it again. "I'm going to focus on Aiden's wolf, you focus on Aiden himself."

"Okay, okay!"

My father was chanting and I didn't understand it, but if it helped I'd take it. Closing my eyes I ignored the sounds around me, focusing on the thud of my heart, which seemed to be going too fast. I had to calm down; I didn't want to shock Aiden any more than he would be when he came back.

I pictured his heart beating that beautiful rhythmic tune it had when I'd laid my head on his chest the other night. I pictured his skin hot with the blood running through his veins. I pictured the light in his eyes when he laughed, or the way they softened when he looked at me. The way he smiled, the way he frowned, and his nervous neck rubbing habit. I pictured the way his skin flushed with anger or embarrassment. I pictured his arms back in place and the lacerations on his chest were gone. Most importantly I pictured his neck in place, and not horrifically positioned and snapped. I pictured Aiden how I loved him, alive and well.

My body shuddered and my palms glowed white and opening my eyes I saw my father's palms glowing also. His chanting got louder and louder my imagination with Aiden ran wild. Every time I had seen him doing things him, I pictured him doing it again. The way he brushed his teeth, drove his truck, struggled with the clutch when it didn't work properly. The way he grit his teeth when he lifted weights, not wanting to give up.

The way he looked as he shifted into his wolf the first time.

All the energy flew out of me and I took my hands from his chest, falling back onto my legs as I sagged. My father fell backwards, his chest heaving as he clutched it and gasped for air. Jasmine cried out as she grit her teeth, throwing all her energy into him as Stella filled me, looking exhausted.

"Look out!" Sienna screamed and I turned to my head hazily, my eyes widening as Jonah's wolf ran toward us, and I realized people had shifted again. I guess the magic ripped off them when I put everything into Aiden.

He snarled viciously, he was so close no one had any time to react. Until a golden colored wolf threw itself in Jonah's path. They collided with a massive thud and snarls erupted from the two. Spotting white flecks on the golden wolf's back I realized who it was.

"Maria!" My father cried out beside me.

She fought well, she fought viciously. She ripped into Jonah like I had never seen before, but he ripped back just as violently. She hurt him enough though, enough to make him slower. It took my mind off Aiden on the floor for a split moment.

"We have to help her!" I shouted.

"No. This is hers," Stella told me. "Save your energy Evelyn."

Mom was a good fighter but Jonah was an Alpha and had been trained by his own father. My mother didn't stand a chance and I guess she knew that as well. With a yelp she fell to the floor with a thud and shifted instantly into human form. Jonah took off before he could be blasted by Gabriel or Phoenix and I rushed to my mother's side, inspecting her wounds,

"Evelyn," she wheezed out and I inspected her blistering wounds. They seemed to be fizzing actually, like someone had poured acid on her. "It's Wolfsbane Evelyn. You can't stop it."

"Mom," I croaked out, holding her head in my hands.

"Don't - don't bring me b-back, please sweetheart." Her eyes were wide as she grasped at my hands, gasping for breath. "Promise me you won't. M-Michael's dead, s-so is Jada and Laurance." Tears leaked out of her eyes and she winced in pain as the Wolfsbane entered her bloodstream. "I'm so sorry Evelyn."

"No, don't be." I lifted her slightly, hugging onto her.

"Please f-forgive me Evelyn." She ground out her words holding on tightly to my arm. "Please tell - tell me you forgive me."

"T-there's nothing to forgive," I wept.

She sighed, her body seemed to slump. "My Evelyn, I love you so much."

"I love you too," my voice was broken and husky with emotion. Her eyes rolled into the back of her head and I cried out. "Mom! Mom!" Shaking her I felt like I was having déjà vu with Aiden all over again. This battle wasn't ending, it needed to end. There was too much death; it made me sick to my core.

"Evelyn!" I turned my head, placing my mother's lifeless body to the floor, not even having time to grieve as Aiden pulled me into his arms. "Oh Goddess," he choked. "Oh Evelyn, I was so scared."

"Aiden!" Wrapping my arms tightly around his neck I clung to his body, a sobbing wreck. "It worked, you're here. It worked." I pulled back and looked at him, taking in his features. Cupping his cheek I leant up and pressed my lips to his roughly, trying to put as much of the love I felt for him into it as possible. Pulling back he cupped my cheek, running his hand down my arms.

"Thank Morgana," Sienna whispered tearfully.

"Thank you!" I cried to all of them.

"Ah!" We all heard the scream echo across the clearing and suddenly we realized we were in a bloody warzone. My head whipped toward the scream and I saw Lucy still in human form being chased by a huge wolf.

Alpha Hess.

Raising my hand in his direction I bound his feet and he tripped heavily, face planting into the floor. I was surprised when everyone turned back into human form and I watched as my father blinked open his eyes, before charging off into the fight again. As did Aiden, much to my horror and fear.

I had to end all this now. I couldn't bring Aiden back twice and I was losing a lot of energy.

It was more or less a case of walking through the field and snapping necks. All I had to do was flick my wrist and wolves would drop to the floor dead. I watched as Stella took on Alpha Hess, which was a sight to behold as she raised him up into the air and pulled at his limbs in different directions, tearing his body apart.

It rained Alpha guts all over us.

I wanted Jonah of all people, and he seemed to want me as he immediately ran in my direction, wrapping his hands around my throat and dragging me to the floor. He wasted no time in stabbing me in the leg with his extended claws. This time I didn't freeze however, it's funny how heavy fear can be replaced with so much hate. I guess when someone kills the person you love it would do that.

"I am going to make you wish you had never been born," I snarled into his face before spitting at him. Bringing my head back I smashed it into his. I felt no pain; I made sure of that, Jonah however would have a splitting headache. He made to jump at me but I raised my palm. He was my puppet, and I found in some sick way that I enjoyed it.

His claws were still out and my mind flashed back to the day in the bathroom when he used my own hand to carve that disgusting letter into my hip. I smirked viciously as I used my other hand to make his move, bringing his caws to his chest.

"No! Please Evelyn!" He cried out, true panic finally hitting his eyes. "I'm sorry!"

I laughed humorlessly. "No you're not, you had a chance to be sorry and you didn't take it. You killed my mate and did not care. I bet you didn't know I could bring him back to life. You underestimated me big time Jonah. You're only sorry now because you're going to die in the next minute or so."

"P-Please!" He begged.

"It doesn't feel nice does it? Being restrained by someone with the intent to hurt you, wondering when they might strike and what they're going to do. You're in the old Evelyn's shoes right now, tell me, are they comfortable?" I was surprised at how calm and level my voice was. Inside I was panicking, overrun by rage and hate, feelings I hadn't felt so heavily before. "Tell me, how does it feel to cut yourself? With no control?" Moving my hand I dragged his claws down his chest. He screamed in pain and I realized as the wound blistered and hissed that he'd laced his nails with Wolfsbane. Even better.

The clearing seemed to go silent, and suddenly I was a spectacle. No one stopped me either.

"Try this on for size!" I shouted in anger as I flooded him with every emotion he'd ever caused me. Shame, fear, hurt, agony, terror. He cried loudly, looking weak and pathetic. It was a sickening image; he looked like me when I lived in Idaho. "What about this?" I shouted, throwing at him stomach aches, cramps, vomiting from nerves, vomiting from his sickening touch.

"Do it quick Evelyn," Hannah whispered beside me suddenly. "You're not cruel. Don't fall to his level."

Her words broke through my haze of rage and I looked at the blubbering mess I held in the air, the huge wound down his chest, the tears down his face, and the smell of him soiling himself. Sighing, I concentrated on boiling his blood, watching as his face seemed to swell like a balloon. His eyes went bloodshot and I watched as little drops of blood fell out before it just seemed to gush from his nose and ears. In one swift motion with my hand, his body erupted into a bloody explosion.

I looked at the clearing around me, dead bodies littered everywhere and suddenly everything swayed, my feet gave out beneath me and I was pulled into a cold darkness.

∞

Blinking my eyes open I was met with my bedroom, only it was more clinical looking at the moment. There was a drip in my arm and I was surrounded by monitors and chords. My head throbbed when I lifted it and I dropped it back on the pillows.

"She's awake!" Someone yelled frantically. It hurt my ears and I winced in pain, listening as someone shushed whoever shouted.

Suddenly a hand was on my face and a light was being flashed into my eyes. I didn't recognize the person though they smiled down at me. "Welcome back, Evelyn."

"W-where's Aiden?" I croaked out, my throat dry as a bone. I lifted my head, ignoring the pain.

"Evelyn?" Aiden appeared in my line of vision, his hands holding one of mine. His eyes were bloodshot and he was still covered in blood and dirt.

"Aiden," I breathed out, my heart swelled with joy and I squeezed his hand. "You're alive."

"It seems so," he laughed quietly.

"Where is everyone?" I asked, panicking. "What happened?"

The doctor and Aiden shared a glance but the doctor spoke. "Evelyn, how much of the battle do you remember?" He pulled out a clipboard and I licked my dry lips as I thought back to the horrific scenes now permanently etched into my mind.

I focused on my best memory, frowning as tears welled into my eyes. "I remember Jonah killing my mother," I whispered as an ache tore through my chest. "She died in my arms, I felt her die." I was consumed in grief an Aiden gathered me in his arms, holding me. They all looked at me, as if I should remember something else.

The doctor frowned, "I suppose given the amount of energy you used last night, how much magic you used a bit of memory loss it to be expected. Evelyn," I looked up at him, sniffling. "You saved the pack last night, plain and simple. We could have had higher causalities than we do. I'll leave you two alone for a moment but I'm going to be in soon to check you over."

I nodded at him and watched as he left the room, hearing a cluster of voices outside. I looked back at Aiden and ran my hand down his cheek. "I was scared we couldn't bring you back," I whispered. "You didn't show any signs of it working."

"It worked, and as much as I want to be angry at you for putting yourself in that kind of danger, I can't be, because I know I would have done the same thing." He kissed me lightly and I felt peace consume me, even if it was brief.

Pulling back I asked the most important questions. "What happened to Jonah?"

Aiden poured me some water and handed me the plastic cup. "Frenzy seemed to come over you Evelyn, no one can explain it. Your eyes were white, not even amber anymore. All you had to do was look at someone and they dropped dead." Guilt consumed me at all the lives I had taken last night and I felt my lower lip tremble. "You killed Jonah alright. And if you can't remember then its best I don't tell you how, it'll only serve to upset you." Oh God, how had I done it? "Your only intent was to save the pack and you did. Idaho no longer exists, Evelyn."

"Really?" I whispered in surprise, pushing Jonah into the back of my mind for later thought.

"You did the right thing, sealing the tunnels. The magic fell off though when you brought me back to life and let me tell you, my mom loves you but right now she's furious." He laughed and shook his head. "It won't last of course. She knows how important you were out there."

"I killed people," I said out loud, putting my hand to my head. "People are dead and I killed them."

"It was you or them Evelyn. That's the only way you can think about it, to make it easier to handle." He took my hand in his again, stroking my cheek. "You got your justice. Evelyn I am so proud of you, you acted like a true Luna. You secured the children and the people who couldn't fight and then you joined your people on the field. The pack is in awe of you."

It all just hit me, all my emotions at once. It felt good to cry, I was crying in joy and sadness. Joy for the fact Idaho would never be a problem to me again but sadness for the amount of lives I had taken, sad it had to come so far.

How much hate consumed Jonah and his family that they were willing to kill so many just to get to me? How could anyone allow themselves to hate that much? How cold would they be on the inside? They had only served to end their own lives and I was still here, living and breathing.

If they had just let it go, gave up, gave up on putting all their energy into me...I'll never understand why they did what they did, why they felt they had rage war on our pack. They were lost at the trial; it's like madness just took over.

War is madness, it just scared me at how many people had followed such a deluded Alpha, it worried me that I'd have that power to influence pack members. I was scared I couldn't handle the job, what if I got them killed? They'd be my responsibility.

"The others really want to come in," Aiden murmured to me, stroking my arm.

"Oh yeah," I shook my head. "Let them in."

I wanted to see everyone, to see all my friends and family still living and breathing. I hadn't seen Grace at all during the battle and that scared me. The door flew open and everyone practically ran in. It was like relief in my heart when I saw my father and my sisters and brothers. Stella looked exhausted but she beamed at me.

Trey sauntered in, holding Grace's hand and she waved at me, running over to the bed. I was surprised to see the mark on her neck but I didn't comment. I guess it took a bloodthirsty battle for Grace to realize she loved Trey. Josh and Hannah stood back, but they both smiled down at me.

The Alpha and Luna came in, the Alpha looked proud but the Luna's face was tear stricken and drawn. It was an endless amount of hugs and questions. It was the best reuniting ever.

"...This wolf out of nowhere just jumped on Grace, and we all thought she was a goner, you should have heard her in the mind link, she was so angry. She literally clawed him to pieces," Lucy's eyes flashed as she retold stories of the bloodbath the night before.

"…Then I turned around and stabbed him in the neck…"

"…Punched me right in the nose and broke it…"

"…Thought I was going to die when two wolves started ripping into me, but then Sienna blinded them…"

"…Should have seen my face when Evelyn came onto the field, covered in somebody else' flesh. I nearly vomited," Aliyah slapped my leg and I shook my head, wrinkling my nose.

"I did vomit."

"People have not stopped talking about it. Evelyn you are truly a hero and word has been spreading like wildfire throughout all the packs. 'The Girl Who Can Make Heads Explode', is what I heard today," Josh shook his head. "Kids out in the street playing were pretending to use their minds and blow each other up."

"That's not good," I said, worried. I didn't need children to be acting out that kind of violence, it wasn't right.

"They think it is. You saved our lives Evelyn, the numbers that Idaho came in…and enlisting rogues," the Alpha shook his head. "The High Council is about an hour off arriving, to get a formal report on this whole battle. We ran out of body bags, but we couldn't dispose of them until the High Council checked it all off."

"So where are they all?" I asked hesitantly.

"You don't want to know," Sienna mumbled. "It's feral."

"Do you think you'll be able to talk to the High Council, Evelyn?" the Alpha asked, taking my hand.

I nodded. "Definitely."

Looking around the room I noticed my quiet father who sat watching me and guilt ran through me like waves. "Um, can I have a moment…with dad?" I asked the room and they all seemed to look at each other knowingly. They filtered out one by one and not long after it were just dad and I and I hung my head in shame. "I'm so sorry," I whispered, feeling the tears come again.

"Hush," he told me, kissing my forehead. "You were not yourself out there, that magic consumed you the moment you started melting people's heads off." I laughed tearfully and he looked at me, sighing. "You need to be so careful Evelyn. That wasn't my daughter I saw out there, with this power comes massive responsibility. You need to stay in control at all times. The doctor says you can't remember anything after your mother dying?"

I nodded at him and ran a hand down my face. "Everything else is just dark blankness."

"I'm glad for it. If you remembered what you did you probably would have a very hard time forgiving yourself, you gentle girl." He took my hand in his, a sad look on his face. "We need to bless that field at some stage, and you'll need to let the darkness out of you, because it's in there. You can't kill that many people and not have it in you."

I nodded at him, deciding that was why I felt so sick.

"You saved a lot of lives Evelyn, I am so proud of you. Don't be sorry for asking me to bring back your mate. I would do it for Stella in a heartbeat." He stepped away from the bed and said, "Once the High Council has been we will do it. It's going to hurt."

More pain, that sounded like a great idea.

"Evelyn?" He asked me, his tone suddenly quiet.

"Yes?"

He cleared his throat, scratching his scalp. "I was wondering - well I've been meaning to ask you for some time now…" He looked at me nervously before hurriedly saying, "I was wondering if maybe you'd like to be marked with the family crest."

My heart leapt into my throat at the idea. He wanted to officially mark me as his daughter? Tears welled up in my eyes as I shook my head in wonder. My life had taken such a turn. "Y-yes," I whispered. "I want to be marked."

He seemed relieved as he took my hand. "Brilliant, I've been put off asking for some time, I just wanted you to feel like you were a part of us. Because you are. You are very much an Ahasverus family member as any of us."

"Thank you," I whispered, sniffling.

"We'll do it after the cleansing," he told me.

Nodding my head I smiled up at him, only feeling slight dread over the idea of the pain the cleansing would bring.

∞

The report with The High Council was long and tedious. They wanted to know every detail from anyone who had been directly involved in the battle. I didn't stay in the room when they discussed Jonah's death, I decided I didn't want to hear about anything else I had done. Just repeating it to them for the report made me feel sick.

They were now also heavily questioning me on my magical abilities and I had a feeling they were scared I could be a massive threat. I guess when you have powers that can single handedly take down a pack you'd be worried. The Reader they had brought with them though, confirmed I was telling the truth when I said I'd only ever use it as defense. They seemed satisfied but I knew they would forever keep an eye on us.

They took all the rogues that had earlier been caught days before the attack with them as well, wanting to question them more thoroughly. I was happy to have them out of our jails and out of Oregon.

The pack was inundated with phone calls from other packs, but Alaska's was the funniest. It seemed I had slightly shaken the biggest and baddest Alpha. He pledged a lifetime of alliance with us as long as I never tried to kill him; this he had done on a private phone call and made me swear not to tell anyone.

I still haven't.

By the time all that was done with, it was late afternoon and I was feeling the strain in my body. Unfortunately my father thought it was a good time to go into the field for the blessing and the cleansing.

Aiden was against the whole thing, but with all my siblings and father convincing him of its importance we went back to the field. There were no bodies now, but death hung in the air and it chilled me to my core.

"We will be asking for Morgana's forgiveness. We may have killed our enemies but we took lives, we still killed even if it was to save ourselves. We need to be repentant." We stood in the center and the death felt heaviest here. Grass had been kicked up that it was now mostly just sand. My bare feet dug into it as we stood in a circle all taking hands. We all closed our eyes and my father began chanting, quietly under his breath.

My siblings also joined in but I had no idea what they were saying or what I was to say. Instead I just closed my eyes, feeling the energy of my family, feeling the cold energy in this field and knowing I had caused a lot of the death out here.

I was sorry for it, big time. If you can't be sorry for killing someone, no matter what evil they had done to you, what kind of person were you? Life is a gift, a borrowed energy that we needed to cherish and protect, not waste it on hating one another and killing each other.

I was glad I still had time to learn and grow, to know these things. Idaho died maybe knowing or not knowing, not caring either way. My body trembled as my father chanted louder and rain drops slowly began pouring on us, wind began rushing around us and I felt myself being splattered with mud.

I wished it hadn't come to this, I wish I hadn't had to hurt so many people and I had to live with it for the rest of my life. I was aware now, of the damage and death I could create and I knew I would have to be very vigilant.

"Morgana!" My father shouted in English, which surprised me, and I hoped it was for my benefit. "Forgive us for the death we caused, the pain and suffering. Forgive us for the power we used from you, our Mother, to kill so many. Hear our plea and rid us of the darkness that death brings, that all those wandering souls may find peace."

"Hear our plea!" They all cried.

Hanging my head I quietly murmured, "Hear my plea."

The ground shook and so did my body and I jolted as dark light came out from all of our chests, floating in the air above us like ash. I felt the rush through my body, I felt like my chest was being torn open, darkness just floated high up into the air, contorting itself and growing into a huge black ball before it began changing color, going to gray to cream to pure white, nearly blinding me.

It exploded suddenly, like a grenade. It came down in little white fragments, floating around us and the field. The rain stopped and so did the pain. The sun came out and shone down directly on us through the clouds and my father sighed in relief.

"We are forgiven."

The lightness that ran through my body made me feel like I could fly; it didn't hurt so much when my heart beat and my head no longer throbbed. I felt like I was full of energy and the death that was once felt heavily in this field a moment before, disappeared into nothingness.

Letting go of my family I ran back towards Aiden and threw myself into his arms, it was all over. I was free of Idaho and so was the werewolf world. Aiden picked me up in his arms and spun me around and I noticed the field began filling with pack members, all cheering and celebrating with each other.

It was a perfect moment.

∞

Things were starting to finally relax in Oregon now. The pack was still in mourning over those we had lost, and we had one big funeral. We lost thirty pack members. We had more orphaned children that I was helping the Luna place in families.

I'd held my own private funeral for my mother, the pack wouldn't want the enemy buried with their own and I understood that. It was Aiden, Grace, the Alpha, Luna and I standing alone under a tree just near the pack border as her coffin was slowly lowered into the hole.

My heart ached with the idea that she was gone forever, and I knew it was going to take some time to come down from. She had died protecting me, her final act. If it helped her find peace I could understand that, I just wish she hadn't died.

Saying goodbye to my father, Stella and my siblings was hard. I didn't want to let any of them go. The fight had brought us so close together now, I truly felt like I was one of them. They had backed me up so strongly, backed the pack with conviction and loyalty. My father helped me bring my mate back to life - so much love was given to me so freely by these people.

The family mark had hurt to make, but it now sat proudly on my right upper arm, the family crest permanently imprinted into my skin.

It warmed me every time I thought about it.

We all missed so much school I was terrified we would have to repeat the year. Some smooth words from the Alpha however had us all working like maniacs over the short Christmas break to catch up on what we had missed, which was good, all the added work made it hard to think about anything else, and people were finished talking about the battle. It was a time to leave those thoughts and memories for when I got really blue and would quietly reflect on all the terrible moments in my life.

Aiden and I found ourselves in a small clearing one afternoon. Well, not just any small clearing, it was the one we'd had our night time date in. The one I had first showed him I could do magic. Lying in his arms under a thick tree it scared me at how close I had come to losing him, that if I hadn't lost my mind maybe he wouldn't be here right now.

"I can hear your mind ticking away," he mumbled into my hair, pulling a leaf out of it. "What are you thinking about?"

"Everything," I told him. "My life this year…wow."

"I second that." He grinned at me and pulled me closer. "I wouldn't change anything."

I'd probably change some things, like killing a whole bunch of people, but I got what he meant. "How scary is it that we're going to graduate this year?" The New Year had rolled in so quickly I couldn't believe our final few months of our senior year were upon us.

"I'm excited. I can't wait to get out of here for a while."

"It's weird, when we come back, you'll be Alpha."

He laughed softly before cupping my cheek, the emotion in his eyes changing, warming. "You'll be my Luna."

I closed my eyes and smiled, enjoying how that sounded. "Say that again."

"My Luna." His lips met mine softly, kissing me like he'd never kissed me before, kissing me like he had all eternity. Having him in my arms in this moment I thought how lucky I was, that I was getting a second chance with him. I had never felt more at peace than I did in this moment, with my mate under our tree kissing each other so passionately I thought my heart might burst.

Aiden pulled back, his face soft as he stared down at me. "I love you, so much."

"I love you too," I whispered, my hand playing with the collar of his shirt. Nothing could touch Aiden and me, not when we had each other. We were a perfect pairing and I realized doubting the Moon Goddess had been stupid. Doubting Morgana about my magic was stupid as well. Aiden and I were a perfect fit; we complement each other in areas we lacked in. We were half of the other after all, and I had never felt more whole in my life.

END

Bethany Shay Porteous is a young romance writer from Australia. She developed a love for reading and writing at a very young age and began writing her own stories at age eleven. With the encouragement of friends and family she sat down to rewrite Wolfsbane and it is now her first published book.

Want More?

Visit www.BethanyShayPorteous.com to learn more about the author and keep up to date with all her published works!

Printed in Great Britain
by Amazon